THE Island Gardens OF Takau

A NOVEL

G.L. Kay

RiverWood Books
Ashland, Oregon

♻ Printed in Canada on 100%
postconsumer waste recycled paper
First edition: 2006

Cover art by Susie Gillatt, Terra Chroma, Inc.
Cover design by David Ruppe, Impact Publications
Interior design and author photo by Christy Collins

Library of Congress Cataloging-in-Publication Data

Kay, G. L., 1958-
The island gardens of Takau / by G.L. Kay.
p. cm.
ISBN 1-883991-67-6 (pbk.)
1. Women physicians—Fiction. 2. South Asia—Fiction. I. Title.
PS3611.A88I76 2006
813'.6—dc22
2006005173

For my family and friends, who will recognize the allegory.

Slippery silt darkens her green dress and mosquitos buzz in her reedy hair, but Ma'rhu sings and dances on her way to a lovers' tryst. Wise with whispers from mossy boulders, she murmers as she gathers gifts in her deep basket. Coppery leaves, flecks of mountain gold, lost feathers, and the ashes of the dead. All tokens of love, all equal, all carried to her lover, the Sea. If you listen carefully, say the Rizha, Ma'rhu will share her stories with you.

IMAGINE ME, PORCELAIN-SKINNED, leaning on the railing, watching the water where the ferry sliced the river. I always stood on the prow of boats, in the wind. I still do. The deck kicked beneath me on a wave and I looked up to study the ferry's twin sister as it passed mid-river. Held together with rotting sisal and rusting iron bands, these clumsy barges rolled through each other's wakes a dozen times a day, every day. The smoke from the sister's coughing steam engine hit me in the face. I grimaced and turned my head.

I had one foot up on the corroded railing. My eyes fell on the shoes I wore at graduation from medical school. They matched the sensible dress from a Sears catalog. And they suddenly looked ridiculous. I was by no stretch of self-flattery a beautiful young woman, but, with my hair bobbed and wearing a straw hat, I fancied myself

1

rather dashing and heroic, out on my exotic quest. In that moment, however, I saw myself through the eyes of the sullen bricklayers, street cleaners, maids, and sweatshop workers around me. I vowed to adopt the local women's flowing shifts and sturdy sandals immediately. Then I smiled and hugged my leather satchel, aware I had just taken another small but deliberate step into my imagined destiny.

I still have that satchel, strap broken now, long since retired from use. Sitting dusty on my bookshelf, it holds in its cracked cowhide the memories of fierce devotion to a worthy cause. I bought it in London, in March 1927, the day before I boarded a passenger liner to India. Surviving the slow train journey from Bombay to Calcutta, I booked a berth on a local freighter that took me up the coast beyond the British colonial grasp to the Takau delta. From the coastal capital, Da'rha Ghand, I took the country's only train — a rattling, whistle-stop ordeal — to the foothills of Takau's northern province. There, I opened a small clinic in the slums of Am'rha Bo.

The ferry heaved on the waves, then resumed its smooth, weary push to the eastern bank. The Ma'rhu hissed around me, steadfast in its mission to carry the northern mountains down to the delta, churning the silt along placidly or violently in drought or monsoon. Trees, tangles of debris, and bloated cow carcasses sailed serenely by. To the north, the river was quick and lively, but south of the city, it widened onto the plains until one bank was not visible from the other.

I studied the single exception to the muddy expanse; a set of islands, fortified, standing west of mid-river. The ferry passed downstream of a spartan but polished pier and a dark bridge that leapt to the larger upstream island. Silvery walls rose from the water's edge. The islands formed a virile exclamation point in the space I traversed between the thighs of the city.

A faint, blessed breeze kissed my cheek. With summer approaching in Takau, the ferry crossing was the only sanctuary from the brutal heat. So far, that relief was my only reward for making this trip nearly every afternoon. I left the slums each day to campaign for support from the wealthy guildmasters and clan patriarchs in their ornate halls across the river. The segregation was, of course, a convenient and lucrative arrangement for them, ingrained in the culture and undisturbed by Western influence or the politics of the day. I was not making any progress.

I STORMED THE COLD STONE BASTION of the textile guild. Ignoring the arched, thirty-foot ceilings designed to make visitors like myself feel small, I marched down the main hall. Uniformed attendants stared listlessly from the corners. Businessmen hurried into dark rooms and ponderous doors slammed behind them. Odd that the textile guild had no carpets or tapestries in their hall, I thought. Neither was there a directory, receptionist, or any ventilation. But no one came here uninvited. Few arrived unannounced. None lingered longer than necessary.

Tile-encrusted pillars and a stream of scurrying bureaucrats identified the guildmaster's office for me. I charged confidently through the door, only to be blocked immediately by a phalanx of alert and suspicious aides.

"Good afternoon," I said, in my practiced Rizhmadi. "I'm the American doctor from Am'rha Bo. I have an appointment ..."

"Step outside, please."

"But I have an appointment to see ..."

"Outside!"

Taller, of course, than most Rizha, I scanned the room. Across this antechamber, I saw the guildmaster in his office, ensconced in pillows, dictating to his fawning secretaries. I had, in fact, sent a letter requesting an appointment at this hour. And, like all my other requests, it went unanswered.

"I have an appointment regarding ..."

"No appointments today. Shall we call the guards?"

Mistakenly, I took a step back. The aides, accustomed to far more aggressive Takau businessmen, slid forward in unison and, with waving hands, brushed me into the hall. The door boomed shut.

I waited on the spot for an hour, my feet aching on the marble floor. A dozen times, the door opened and officials filed in or out. I studied how they breached the line of aides by wielding the names of powerful employers or flashing lucrative contracts to sign. Eventually, the guildmaster came out of his burrow. Then I pounced on him like a Chicago news reporter. His aides surrounded him. I introduced myself over their shoulders, waving my papers. I guess it confused him enough to make him hesitate in the doorway.

"It's the first modern medical clinic in Am'rha Bo," I hurriedly explained. "Desperately needed. In time it will be managed by the local people. You will help save lives ..."

People in the echoing hall stared at us. The guildmaster, brocade jiggling, looked at me, looked down the hall, and flicked his wrist in a signal to a barrel-chested oaf, his personal bodyguard.

"She is not to be seen near me again," he said. The guard stepped toward me. I suddenly felt fragile. It must have shown. The guard grinned with broken teeth, grabbed me by the arms, and shoved me into the wall.

I grew up in a rough neighborhood, so reacted without hesitation. I pinched a nerve in his elbow — a nice trick learned in anatomy class. His knees buckled. Bumping him off balance with my hip, I was past him before he splattered onto the floor. I rushed after the guildmaster, who was already lumbering down the hall, secretaries trailing.

"The clinic will help prevent disease from crossing the river," I continued, "and you could specify services for textile workers!"

I thought it was a clever angle. He didn't seem to hear it. Instead, he ducked into another office. His secretaries scuttled in behind him. The bodyguard leapt in front of me, blocking the threshold. Now he was not grinning. But the sentries in the hall stepped out from their posts, awake now and eager to see what would happen next. I stood my ground, terrified but determined. A woman my age in the 1920s could handle some hopped-up goof on the street, but I wasn't up for an actual fight. The bodyguard sized me up — and glanced with dismay at the smirking sentries, who started teasing and taunting him in Rizhmadi slang I had not yet learned. Then, with a sudden lurch, he simply slammed the door in my face.

Chuckling to themselves, the sentries shuffled back to their places. I stood without moving for a long minute, staring at the heavy door in front of me. Suddenly, I felt very tired.

NEAR THE BROAD PORTAL at the entrance to the guild hall, I slumped down on a stone bench and hugged my satchel, quite at a loss for what to do next. I could feel sweat trickling between my breasts. I had an impossible craving for beef and a baked potato because I had eaten only rice and curry for weeks. I was thinking I hadn't allowed myself a good cry since I was about fifteen years old, but I was close to breaking down now. My stipend from home barely covered my expenses, and my meager medical supplies were already depleted.

Then a man walked past, toward the portal, but stopped and turned. I looked up. He turned with a lightness, a lifted poise usually reserved for dancers. He wore a white suit, French cut. Leather shoes, also European. But he had the high cheek bones, brown skin, and glistening black hair of the native Rizha. He hesitated, then smiled.

"The city is hard on guests this time of year," he said, in American English.

I must look as wilted as I feel, I thought. It was the only time I can remember not having something to say.

"Are ... are you all right?"

"Oh. Yes. I'm fine, thank you. Really." I looked down the hall. "Hot, miserable, and feeling defeated, but otherwise fine." I managed a smile for him.

He ventured a step closer. "Excuse me? Is there something I can do for you?"

I rallied my wits somewhat. "Oh, forgive me. Honestly, yes, everything's jake. I mean no, there's nothing you need to do. I am here on business. And really should be going soon. Thank you."

Now I had him thoroughly perplexed.

"Business?"

He paused, and tipped his head slightly, as if studying me from a minutely different angle might help him understand. Somehow, catching that detail made me smile again. I slapped down my satchel on the stone, leaned back, and laughed at myself. He told me much later it was my laughter that attracted him. Women of his culture never laughed so openly and so easily as I guess I did in those early years.

He sat down. Again, like a dancer, or like a Shakespearean actor. Now I was paying attention. A banker's son, I figured. Raised wealthy. Educated in Europe and in the States. Younger than I first thought; just a few years older than me, at most. But he had such dark, eager eyes.

"Katherine," I offered, extending my hand.

"My friends call me Kai," he replied. His hand was strong, but he withdrew it quickly. "What manner of business, if you don't mind my asking?"

"A quest, more like it," I said, then told him, with increasing detail as he kept nodding, about the clinic and my determination to bring modern healthcare to the people in the slums. I told him about crossing the river every day and how I had planned my campaign, and how I had presented my case to all the patriarchs of the city and to the guildmasters, that today was my last, and I went through all the arguments and the strategy I had used to no avail, and I described the icy reception I had received everywhere, and I recounted the most recent scene with the bodyguard that left me sitting where I was just then.

When I paused to breathe, he said, "You realize, of course, the old guildmasters profit from Am'rha Bo's poverty? They have no incentive to help you."

"Profit?"

"Oh yes. Cheap labor. Opium dens. Servants." I stared at him. "Of course, they don't believe you are a doctor, either."

"I have documents."

"Paper. They see forged papers all the time. You can't be a doctor because you are a young American woman. And they take you for a flapper, or worse."

I must have looked like a fish, gasping soundlessly. He saw my indignation.

"I am sorry. But this is what these men were no doubt thinking."

"They did look embarrassed to be seen with me."

"False dignity. They knew others would assume you were a prostitute. Forgive me."

"No. Thank you. You are being honest with me. I didn't see it," I rambled. "I mean, why would a prostitute be asking for medical equipment? I had no idea."

"Think of it this way," he said brightly. "They won't forget you."

"That's not how I care to be remembered."

He waited while I digested this new information. But then I startled him by laughing again. Imagine me being mistaken for a vamp! I shook my head and took a deep breath. "Well, do you believe I am a doctor?"

"Of course." He didn't say why. "How long have you been here?"

"Three months next Friday."

"Do you speak Rizhmadi?" he asked, in Rizhmadi.

"I'm trying," I responded in his language. "I have a helper at my clinic."

He smiled at my accent. Switching back to English, Kai suggested I join him for a cup of tea.

"Thank you. But I have to catch the ferry. It's late."

"You live over there?"

"Of course."

"Oh," he said, with concern.

I stood up, knowing another ferry ran in several hours, but feeling too hot and battered to be myself. Kai invited me to meet him on the Court Plaza where the wealthy businessmen met for the guildhalls and government monument. We would discuss my project, he said. Ten in the morning, before the full heat of the day. I agreed, and we parted. I don't remember the river crossing that evening, except for the sunset glow across the water falling on the walled island.

NOTHING COULD HAVE PREPARED ME for my first days in Am'rha Bo. Rank upon rank of hovels climbed the slope from the river's edge to the crowns of the hills. Alleyways wound along the contours. Fetid gutters and crumbling walls defined the corridors. Naked children and mothers in rags huddled in crooked doorways. They always watched me walk by. They watched with unabashed and seemingly unquenchable curiosity, studying me as I passed, even after I had climbed the same worn stairs fifty times.

The people sculpted low tenements of mud and straw that eroded away when the rains came. Some tiled their walls with hammered paraffin tins and other trash. Many used tattered blankets as doors. But they all exploited the river reeds for myriad uses — from thatched roofs to floor mats — because it was readily available and free building material.

It was here the poor and illiterate Rizha survived without basic comforts. The slums were a bombardment of the senses, a centuries-old injustice, and a showcase for human suffering.

But Am'rha Bo was also a magnificent paradox. Wildflowers grew out of rooftops. A decaying wall strained to hold up a wooden gate carved with leaves and branches finer than those of the tree felled long ago to make it. No exposed beam or lintel went unadorned. The Rizha carved and painted forests of botanical forms or, just as often, wild-eyed comically ferocious beasts.

Muscular and sensual in the evening light, the long, tawny façades curved ever mysteriously down the alleys and out of view. These buildings wore the marks of uninterrupted occupation over countless generations; endlessly blessed and cursed and repaired. Bare feet and time can carve deep indentations in stone steps.

Though most streets were mere cobbled pathways snaking between walls, I never felt trapped or cramped, because every tight spot opened onto a tiny plaza or perhaps to an unsymmetrical and intriguing five-way intersection. I navigated by landmarks: here a doorway with a faded inlaid peacock; next, a collapsed communal well decorated with broken water jars; then, the once-wealthy neighbor's house with the single Gothic pillar by the door. The city was full of curiosities like that pillar.

Throughout the old city, occasional towers punctuated the low-slung buildings. It appeared to me as I routinely hurried past that only some potent magic with mud and stone held them up. A spiral spine of stone gave them a curious, uplifting twist. Each had a flat roof. Later, in the monsoon season, waterfalls fell in sheets from the eastern face of each one.

Homes were full of surprises, too. The family heirloom — a broad carpet of exquisite detail and craftsmanship — often graced a dirt floor. People who owned almost nothing displayed their set of gleaming brass bowls and platters. One family, crowded into a single room with a roof made of river flotsam, owned a massive, illuminated book with hand-lettered text. No matter that none of them could read.

Every family had an oil lamp. They always polished the lamps with pride and never allowed them to smoke or flicker. And every home, no matter how wretched, had a little shrine in a corner. Always, come to think of it, in the southern corner, in line with the river.

Storefronts opened onto the widest alleys. Here, it seemed to me, the Rizha achieved their highest art. Cumin and oregano and a hundred bright and pungent herbs and spices I never was able to identify sat in perfect piles, or spread in illusions of abundance, on shining brass trays. Glistening cherries mixed in perfect proportion with glowing kumquats. Precariously balanced pyramids of tangerines vied with unruly heaps of lemons. Roughly carved scoops plunged into swollen baskets of rice with thyme, rice with mixed spices, rice with diced roots, rice with carrot bits, and even, in small baskets, rice with saffron.

Most abundant and most refreshing, though, were the hanging bundles of mint. The whole city was awash in mint. Mint tea was, and is, the national drink of Takau. Mint tea was often the only beverage available in the cafés. It was proffered to guests upon entering a house and with every meal. Mint tea appeared at every occasion hinting of hospitality.

All poor Rizha had collections of chipped and mismatched teacups shaped like miniature tumblers. They unceremoniously stuffed tiny teapots with fresh mint, leaves and stems together, then filled them with water. They brought this brew to a quick boil, then added sugar — usually a generous mound of sugar — before the tea was poured into the humble cups that burned a newcomer's fingers.

Sweet mint tea, hot or left to cool, is wonderful. I learned I could mix all manner of bitter medicines into it and gain the cooperation of reluctant patients. But I must admit my secret reason to cross the Ma'rhu as often as possible was to sit down in a comparatively clean European-style café with a good cup of coffee.

My MEDICAL CLINIC, and the tiny room behind it where I slept, overlooked the river in the less-decrepit district. The hill was not so steep, the street was cobbled, and some of the buildings had tile roofs.

I fashioned the clinic from one long room. For decades, it had been full of spindles and looms for making the famous fabrics of Takau. The business fell victim to the international market, they told me, and the owner fell to tuberculosis, so the little factory stood empty and silent and the family thought a "hospital" was the best use for the space.

I worked with a paltry display of modern medicine those first months. I had my personal field kit made up of my favorite tools and potions stuffed in a black, soft-sided case. I had a small set of surgical tools, laboriously shepherded through customs. I had my treasured collection of reference books. And I had one suitcase of medicines, mostly tinctures in alcohol, compiled by my Cornell medical school advisors based on sketchy reports about the needs of my new post.

My medical gear was woefully outdated by Western standards even then, yet where I set up shop my equipment garnered wide-eyed respect and fear. It was, obviously, utterly inadequate for the needs of my patients.

With greasy smiles, the local government officials granted me a license to practice. I explained my modest goals, but they nevertheless expected shipments of expensive medical gear to arrive from the States. They expected to profit by it. I was given permission, and little else.

I did, however, have help.

"Where on earth did you find that desk?" I asked.

"Guild hall near the ferry. Office with no work. Better the desk work," explained Tor, the Rizha I hired my first week to help me collect some necessities and translate.

Tor never talked about himself. I knew he had learned English as a servant in the embassy. He spoke Rhizmadi slowly for me and never wasted a word. The way he handled a knife and his stiff demeanor around people of authority told me he had been a soldier. He stood aloof from his neighbors, a common conceit among men who had once held positions of perceived authority across the river.

I guess we made a comical pair. He was dark-skinned, even for the Rizha, and muscles rippled under his loose shirt. He wore his silky black hair long. I never could guess his age, though a dusting of gray at his temples and hard lines on his face hinted he was older than his body and straight posture admitted.

"Here's money to buy some kitchen supplies. We'll set up in the back corner," I said. Tor hesitated.

"What's the matter?"

"Too much."

"I can't guess what things cost here yet, Tor. You'll have to help me." I tried to catch his eye. "I trust you."

He nodded and took the money. In a few hours he returned, trailed by two young women laden with pots, bowls, all the accoutrements of a Rizha kitchen, and huge bags of rice.

"Stove coming," he announced, with satisfaction in his voice.

In the weeks that followed, Tor was ever at hand, accepting any challenging request I put to him. He lifted patients from the floor mats effortlessly. He never once complained about the filthy nursing duties he performed for me. In fact, without my asking, he became my orderly, my nurse, my janitor, and my cultural advisor.

One night, I sadly informed Tor he was released from my service because I had hired him to help me move in, but could not afford to pay him any longer. He nodded.

"I understand," he said.

The next morning, Tor arrived before sunrise as usual, ignored my complaints, and set to work. In his perpetual companionship, Tor distilled the loyalty of the passionate people who surrounded me.

AM'RHA SA PRESENTED AN ENTIRELY different face. The east bank spent two centuries putting on European façades, and now the so-called new city enjoyed its artificially cosmopolitan ambience. Of course, in the shadows beyond the post-Victorian gas lamps, clans still feuded. In the fine mansions, old women still taught children about a pantheon of deities and monsters. But on the main streets, phonographs blared from restaurants with linen tablecloths.

"Look! Lindbergh made it to Paris!" I exclaimed, snatching up the English-language paper. Downtown Am'rha Sa bustled around us.

"In thirty-three and a half hours," Kai nodded.

I laughed. "The exact time is important?"

"Numbers aren't important to a doctor?"

"Only success or failure."

Kai pointed at a café sporting an enormous poster of Greta Garbo on the wall. "How about this one? They have the best coffee."

"Oh dear! 'The American Café'? How awful to see Takau invaded," I said, pulling up a chair.

"Awful? That's a funny thing for you to say, since you are bringing us American science and medicine."

"I know. I have an odd prejudice, I suppose."

We adjusted ourselves at a table in the precious shade and paused to look out across the Court Plaza, a vast, neatly cobbled expanse with an enormous fountain in the center. The heavy air shimmered. Directly across from us, the weighty Council Hall wavered like a mirage.

"All European design," Kai said, with a sweep of his arm. "But Takau is still full of gods, goddesses, and demons."

"And wonderful stories!" I said eagerly.

He took the bait. "And all the stories come down the Ma'rhu, you know. My nurse used to say she found her stories in the wash water. Listen for them when you cross the river. The Ma'rhu carries them down to her lover, the Sea."

I laughed. "All of Takau is a love affair." Even as I said it, and meant to explain the metaphor, but didn't, I flushed with embarrassment, a most foreign sensation to me. Fortunately, the waiter arrived.

"Even in such hot weather?" Kai asked. I nodded gravely.

"Two coffees, American style," Kai ordered. "And brioche." He looked at me. "Or would you like to try their pie? They almost make it correctly."

"No, thank you."

Kai gave the waiter a little Rizha hand signal to say that would be all of our order.

"Of course, the most famous lover in Takau is the god Sybalo, who comes to find his consort in the crowded plaza that holds all the people in the world."

"Well, that certainly sounds like Takau so far."

"Sybalo always finds her in the crowd, even though she has a different face each time."

"Oh, I like that part."

"He takes her to the palace at the center of the world." Kai gave me a conspiratorial look. "Rizha love stories always have a secret palace in them."

"I can guess what happens next!" I said.

"Well, yes, of course! But, soon after they've been … together, they are betrayed."

"Naturally."

"The famous Takau demons rush upon them! There's a terrible fight."

"Such a·nightmare!"

"Yes! Then the palace always crashes down around them." Kai frowned. "I'm not telling this very well. I should …"

"It's wonderful. Please go on," I said.

"Sometimes the palace collapses into the Earth, sometimes it burns. Or it turns to dust. Or it sinks in a flood. Storytellers in Takau have a limitless arsenal of disasters to choose from."

I nodded knowingly.

"In time, she gives birth to the first in each Rizha clan lineage."

I stopped him with my hand up. "And Sybalo has to go on a long quest, right?"

Kai nodded. "Oh yes. He struggles through one magical realm after another."

"More story material."

"Exactly! But, as everyone knows, he eventually comes back to find her again."

The waiter returned with our coffee. He unloaded his tray with noticeable panache, adjusted the setting to his satisfaction, and gave the plate of pastry a slight turn for its best presentation.

"Where did you learn to do that?" I asked him, smiling with appreciation.

"Bordeaux, madam," the waiter replied.

"*C'est bon!*" I said. I didn't admit that was about the limit of my French vocabulary.

He bowed, very pleased, and backed away from our table. I looked at Kai and caught him studying me.

"But now, I very much want to hear your story," Kai said. "Please tell me more about the work you do and your goals ... or dreams, for Am'rha Bo."

I was distracted by his sincerity. And by his soft smile. Nonetheless, my purpose was paramount, and I gave him my whole presentation again. He listened. And he unnerved me terribly by looking me in the eyes the whole time.

He asked about the building I had rented. He asked what the clinic needed. He seemed amused by my plan to gain the support of the guilds. We lingered too long and I drank several cups of coffee without noticing.

Kai volunteered very little about himself. Only that he had an engineering degree from the States and had been back in Takau about two years. He knew Boston well, but was most fond of San Francisco. His family was one of the oldest clans in Takau. Though he never said so, he gave me clues to suspect he was the last of his line.

At the bottom of the third cup of coffee and the last crumb of passable apple pie that we had eventually ordered to share, he ran out of polite questions about my work, and I reluctantly hesitated to press him to reveal more about himself. He set down his fork and studied my empty cup.

"*Ma'rhu ta yalathé,*" he said.

"What does that mean?"

Kai hesitated. "I guess it translates, 'Ma'rhu keeps singing.' It's what we say in Takau when lovers or enemies are parting and there is nothing more to be said." The next moment, he put his hand to his mouth. He started to apologize.

"No," I smiled. "I like that very much."

"What I mean," he stumbled, "is we could ... I hope you would like to meet again," he quickly offered. "Perhaps at my Autumn House? To discuss your business." He pulled a calling card from his suit pocket. "Here's the address."

"That would be swell," I answered, with my thoughts stumbling but my heart racing ahead. "I'd be deeply honored," I said in Rizhmadi.

"Friday?"

"Of course. Good."

"I hear the monsoon may roll in from the coast by then," Kai offered.

"God, I hope so! This is horrid! I can hardly wait!"

"You've not known the monsoon yet. Both blessing and curse. Like everything in Takau."

"Any relief from this hellish heat will be a blessing!"

"It could arrive any day now. You will feel it coming."

"Not a moment too soon."

There was another pause. I made a little show of snapping the clasp on my satchel. "I really should ..."

"Of course," Kai said, jumping to his feet. He quickly stepped around the table and pulled my chair away just a fraction as I stood up. "Time got away from us, I'm afraid."

"My assistant calls it 'Takau time.' I'm learning to forget about clocks."

"Good! Takau is timeless, really. Especially on your side of the river."

"Speaking of time, I've got to catch the ferry. Clocks or not, if I miss my mid-day rounds, my patients will be in a panic!"

He escorted me down to the dock. As we approached the river, the European flavor of Am'rha Sa gradually fell away. Though the city threw up a smiling mask of storefronts and offices along the bank, and the avenue was accustomed to the Fords chugging by, nothing could erase the smells of riverfront rot or the obvious poverty of the rugged commuters lining up for the trip across the chocolate water.

Kai kept his arms crossed. He flinched at the dockside clatter around us. He warily eyed the street cleaners shuffling onto the ferry.

"Are you sure you will be safe?"

I touched his arm. "I've been treating their children, Kai. I live here now." Still, he was reluctant to leave me alone. The ferryman repeatedly asked him if he was coming aboard. "Thank you for the coffee. And for listening," I said finally.

"You follow this avenue north, to where it turns up the hill," he said, pointing along the riverfront.

"Friday afternoon."

The ferry pulled away. I laughed at the silver-screen romance of the scene.

"Ma'rhu ta yalathé!" I called out. He nodded and waved.

THE NEXT DAY, THREE CARTS OF LINENS, bandages, antiseptics, and a dozen metal cots with mattresses arrived at the clinic.

"Beginnings are delicate. Yours, Kai," the note read.

WE MADE PARTITIONS between the beds with whatever we could find. Looking from the kitchen to the front door, I had to laugh. With frayed blankets and stained sheets hanging in rows, the clinic was a mad cross between a used carpet display and a laundry room.

"Which one is Tlia?" I asked.

"Behind the blue blanket," answered Tor.

"Okay."

I quickly learned the Rizhmadi vocabulary to explain hygiene and sanitation. And, as I gained a little trust, I began learning about the culture, too, because the Rizha, even when gravely ill, love to tell stories.

Tlia, it turned out, became my best teacher. She was a slight woman, a mother of five and aunt to dozens. The first time she came to the clinic, she was convinced she was dying. Overnight, I was convinced she was suffering from nothing worse than food poisoning. Nevertheless, when she recovered, Tlia was sure I had performed a miracle. And, since she knew nearly everyone in the northern quarter of Am'rha Bo, she did more than anyone to promote the clinic. After Tlia began telling her neighbors about me, the clinic always had a waiting list.

At first, Tlia was nearly always on that list. She came in complaining of imaginary pains, but I didn't mind, because she was soon following me around the room, mothering everyone. Even better, she began telling me stories.

"I've got to be home tomorrow, dear, because it's naming day for my youngest and we have all her cousins coming over for a party. Naturally, that means all her aunts and uncles, too, and they'll stay into the night, or longer. Goodness! It's not even her first; that was two years ago already. But we like to have a party every year, especially for my youngest. The boys pretend to be too busy, but they like it, too. They give me hints, dear, you know."

"We only celebrate birthdays in my country. What is naming day?" I asked.

"No, no, dear, we have birthdays, too. But on birthdays, the child just brings a gift to the mother. Of course, I get gifts year-round that way! But you don't have naming day? What do you do at the child's first turning?"

I learned that when the parents decided a child was ready, usually at about eight or nine years old, they held a turning ceremony to honor the child's emerging self. The child got a new name and an elaborate party followed. The next big event for the youth was a coming-of-age ceremony at adolescence. Birthdays were private little rituals when children thanked their mothers for bringing them into the world. It made sense to me.

Having again abandoned the ruse of being a patient, Tlia followed me with a tray of medicines. "Of course, it's the full moon, too. And my eldest has learned the hymns on the yala. I would just die if I missed hearing her! Oh, I shouldn't talk about dying, should I?"

"That's all right."

"I'm so sorry. I just get to chattering. No, no, give me those sheets. I'll make the beds. You've better things to do."

"Thank you, Tlia. You don't have to do that."

"Of course I do, dear. I don't know anything else but mothering. Let me do my job."

"That's not true. You know many things."

"But it's all mothering, dear."

"What do you do for the full moon?" I asked.

"Goodness, I forget how strange we must seem to you. You must come to my home for the turnings and hear my daughter play. We'll have you light the lamp on the solstice, too."

While I was listening to Tlia, I was examining a girl with frightened eyes.

"I've so much to learn," I said.

Tlia watched my hands as I felt the girl's abdomen. "And we have so much to learn from you, dear. That's how this works."

From Tlia's stories, it seemed to me the Rizha celebrated everything. They sang songs on the full moon and told stories during the dark night of the new moon. They marked the phases of each season. I laughed when Tlia said a change in the weather triggered a festival. She scowled at me — a serious reprimand. Festivals defined their lives. They commemorated family events, historical events, and a bewildering calendar of mythic events. I was enthralled.

"VISITOR," SAID TOR. Then he added, with perfect equanimity, "Trouble."

I peeked from behind the partition. A thin Rizha man in a drab brown uniform stood near the door, with two nervous subordinates behind him. All three carried long, slender batons.

"Here we go," I muttered to myself, and took a deep breath. "Who is he?"

"Tokmol," Tor said. "Like police. But trouble."

"Oh, the one who squeezes payments from all the vendors?"

That drew a rare smile from Tor. He was pleased, I think, to see I was beginning to understand Am'rha Bo.

I washed my hands slowly, watching the two men behind Tokmol fidget. They did not want to be this close to so many sick people. Tokmol, however, was calm. And he was watching me.

"Hello," I said cheerfully as I approached. "Would you like to come back to my office?" I asked, in my best Rizhmadi. I gestured toward my little desk by the kitchen. The deputies stiffened. Tokmol ignored my invitation.

"I have heard so much about the new Western clinic. Pleased to make your acquaintance," he said, with only the slightest hesitation in his handshake. To my surprise, he spoke crisp English. "Do you know who I am?"

"I believe I do," I replied, without, I hoped, too much venom in my voice. "What can we do for you today? Would you like a quick tour?"

"I can see what you have here," he said, nodding as he studied the room. "A good beginning, I am sure. When does the doctor arrive?"

"I am the doctor," I said simply. "I'm afraid I am all you get."

"I see." Tokmol squinted slightly, quickly weighing the implications. "The women will trust you," he concluded. "I assume you will be receiving more medical equipment?"

"Very little. The idea is to gain local support for the Am'rha Bo clinic as quickly as possible."

"An American notion, certainly. A difficult proposition in Takau," he frowned. "How long do you intend to stay?"

"As long as necessary."

He heard the conviction in my voice. Calculations flickered across his face. I straightened my posture, and he noticed that, too. This is no back-street thug, I thought. He catches every detail and reads consequences in everything.

"And no help?"

"I have wonderful help," I answered, tipping my head to indicate Tor, who was standing behind me. I waited. That was as far as Tokmol could carry a social conversation.

"I will need to see your license," he said, tucking his baton under his arm with the practiced snap of a British officer.

"Tor, would you bring my satchel, please?"

Tor allowed himself a disapproving glance at Tokmol, then nodded.

Tokmol was apparently quite at ease leaving people hanging in taut conversations. His deputies had settled on ignoring my patients. They gripped their batons and fixed their eyes on me.

"You have authority over the entire district?" I asked, to interrupt the silence.

"Originally just the Rhu'ta," Tokmol replied, referring to the neighborhoods from the ferry dock to the crowded hillsides above the clinic. "Now the Commissioner turns to me for matters concerning all of Am'rha Bo."

"You speak the Queen's English."

"Yes. I served in the British Indian Army. In the Punjab. Difficult service, but an excellent education."

Tor handed me the satchel and I pulled out the license earned at great bureaucratic expense in the capital. Tokmol rifled through the official certificates and letters, pausing to note the multiple blue stamps.

"Hmm. I shall need to take these to the clerk for verification."

"Then I will come with you."

"That will not be necessary. It could take some time."

"Oh, I don't mind," I lied. I knew if he took those documents, I'd never see them again.

"This is your license to practice, but you also need a permit to operate a clinic."

"Oh yes, of course. Here," I said, handing him another sheaf of richly initialed papers.

Tokmol studied the last page. "This permit is not complete," he declared.

"Everything is in order, I assure you."

His demeanor darkened. "This permit is not complete," he repeated firmly. "Of course, I cannot allow you to operate without a valid permit."

I made myself speak slowly. "What is it, in your opinion, that may be missing?" I asked carefully.

"This permit specifies a clinic. It says nothing about a ward with beds for long-term patients. That is another matter entirely."

"Every clinic has beds. Sick people need beds."

He was not accustomed to indignant defiance. "A ward with beds requires additional certification and inspections."

"Oh, inspections? Here's the schedule," I answered, almost relishing the game. I dug through the satchel and produced another document, listing dates in Rizhmadi with their English equivalents scribbled in my handwriting. He glanced at the letterhead, then abruptly handed the whole stack of documents back to me.

"Very well," he said.

I had won the first round.

"But a word of advice to a newcomer." He scanned the room again. "Paper offers scant protection in Takau. I don't think you understand how we conduct business here."

"I learn quickly."

He studied my face and nodded. "Then just one more thing, doctor." He took his baton in hand and paused. "I keep the peace here.

You heal the sick. Please remember this is not your America, and the political customs are very different."

"Yes."

"Pleasure to meet you."

"Thank you."

Tokmol flicked the tip of his baton. At this signal, his deputies retreated with thinly veiled relief. Tokmol surveyed the room once more, backed to the door, turned slowly on his heel, and disappeared.

I took another deep breath, allowed myself a grim smile, and turned back to the hall. Everyone was watching me. I looked at Tor. He simply nodded. I returned to the kitchen.

"What did that parasite want from you?" hissed Tlia, furiously dicing vegetables.

"Blood," I laughed.

EVERY EVENING I WALKED down the hill to the river, where I could buy dinner from the street vendors and catch a whiff of breeze from off the water. The riverside was a riot of life and rot. Sea birds blown far off course sparred overhead for snatched scraps of garbage. Sagging warehouses with tin roofs and split plank faces embraced the ferry dock on both sides. Heavy chains draped their doors. Symbolic tokens, surely, I mused, since any child could have torn those doors off their corroded hinges. Rats paraded in broad daylight around the crates and boxes as if their whiskered inspections were a necessary part of the regular commerce. Certainly the commerce was lively. Handcarts piled high with carpets crashed into wagons loaded with spice barrels. Merchants closed deals in pitched debates held from boat to boat. Barge captains enjoyed shoving matches with dark-eyed traders from the foothills who reached ominously for their daggers but never, as far as I could tell, actually drew them. All down the bank, the wealth of Am'rha Sa moved amid the squalor of Am'rha Bo. Even the beggars who lined the gutters were caught up in the entrepreneurial spirit. They were so taken with bartering amongst themselves for rags of varied quality, they often forgot to solicit spare change from the passing merchants and me.

A stone retaining wall buttressed the high water line. The wall sprouted vicious rusty iron straps and bolts left from buildings eroded away decades ago. I was the only one to notice such things; no one thought to reduce the public hazard. Upstream several hundred yards, the wall slumped into a bed of gravel, soon to be drowned in monsoon muck. Above that, the stones had been carried off for shanty foundations by earlier generations. For a mile in both directions, sheds and warehouses crowded the bank. They were built close enough together that one often supported its slowly collapsing neighbor. All the commerce of the region piled up in these rickety halls awaiting transport down the river. For now, they stood far back from the waterline, looking precarious on spindly, naked legs. Garbage, putrid beyond bearing in the relentless heat, piled up beneath them. The monsoon would flush it all away. It might take the warehouses, as well, people joked. Everything waited on the rain.

When its owners abandoned a warehouse because it had decayed beyond repair or the floor had sagged below the high water mark, the building filled instead with toddlers picking at splinters and grandmothers balancing altar tables on the crooked floor. I spent time among the families holed up in a long row of these disintegrating shelters. Friends in Rhu'mora, the district south of the ferry landing, laughed nervously over horror stories about entire families drowning when pylons gave way in the night, bringing a warehouse down like a castle of playing cards into the swollen Ma'rhu.

From a stall on the open square directly in front of the ferry landing, I bought a puffed pastry filled with diced vegetables and rice. If I were careful, it wouldn't fall apart when I bit into it. The vender watching me smiled broadly when I hit the red pepper. I laughed with him, tears in my eyes.

I accepted a piece of sugared flat bread from him and stepped back to take in the scene. Passengers poured off the ferry behind me and scattered into the marketplace. This was the bustling heart of the district. It was always crowded after the fierce sun had set. It was always full of cursing and laughing and stench and perfume.

Buildings from a bygone era of prosperity framed the plaza around me. To my left and right, storefronts turned into businesses slowly crumbled, worn thin and shabby by standing so long amid the tide of poverty that pressed down on the riverbank. The ashen-faced clerks who worked in these counting houses kept the windows shuttered.

On the other hand, the stately building facing the water stood battered but resolute. I knew from the first that this hall retained the mark of pride from the old Takau clans, and not just in a vague sentimental way. Gargoyles leered down at me over a broad veranda lined with fluted columns. A rounded stairway of stained marble poured into the square like the train of a wedding dress. Sculpted bronze plates armored the double front doors, and dusty gold boats floated in the richly carved waves rolling around the balcony. The windows along the second floor were gray the way only windows that have not been washed for decades can be, but they were glass windows, and none were broken. It was a warehouse today, but had once been a finely apportioned guild hall. I was a long time coming to appreciate the mix of disdain and deference the Rizha held for the wealth and power glorified in their history. I came from a country too young to have a history, they said. How odd to live where everything had to be new and time ran always in one direction.

I asked a crusty old man standing behind his shiny mound of limes and lemons about the building.

"Old river guild hall," he said. "They moved to Am'rha Sa thirty years ago. What a waste of space. Except we move the market up there when the rain comes."

"The guild lets you set up shop on the veranda?"

"The Rhu'pasham doesn't give a damn about us," he scoffed. "And, of course, the police come around for their take. They don't get crap out of me though."

"You have a choice spot right here," I said, handing him some coins for the bag of fruit I had collected. I knew I was paying too much, but I liked him, in spite of himself. His fingers rubbed the coins eagerly.

"Of course! I always get a corner stall. You don't buy what you don't see. Those lazy kids down there don't know the market," he sneered, pointing at a respectable couple sitting primly behind their perfect display of fruit a few stalls down. "Look at them, next to a damn incense seller. Bah! Stink up the place with smoke. Can't smell the citrus."

It was soon apparent he had a disparaging opinion of everyone and everything. Syrka knew everyone's business better than they did, and told them so, gleefully, with an acid tongue and most generous scorn. I don't know why in all my days in Takau I remained above Syrka's otherwise universal reproach. Perhaps I was too foreign to fall within target range of his heavily armed opinions, or perhaps I was just his best customer. I showed genuine appreciation for his produce, shipped from the coast, though he swore it came by mysterious channels from China. I bartered halfheartedly and lingered to let him regale me with complaints, his most valued stock in trade. He was my best source of reliable, albeit biased, local news.

NOT LONG AFTER I SETTLED IN AM'RHA BO, I was at Syrka's fruit stand with Tor when a wispy nine-year-old girl tugged on my sleeve. She nearly ran away when I bent over to hear her little voice, but her mission was clear: Someone in her house was gravely ill and needed a doctor. I scooped up my field bag, reassured the girl with a smile, and followed her along the quay.

There was an old woman in the house. She watched us enter without a change in her dour expression. Her presence distressed Tor. He bowed to her and spoke to her softly in formal Rizhmadi. He spoke quickly, even stuttering slightly. She sat on a cushion near the family altar. I thought she was just an elderly family member tucked in a corner. I ignored her, turning at once to the patient, who was curled in a fetal position on a mat near the back wall.

This house was large enough to have a rough wooden screen in the center, making two rooms. The floor was set with flagstones. That made it one of the finest houses in the neighborhood.

Tor interviewed the family for me. Yes, the sick woman was the little girl's mother. She had been struggling for breath for several days. She could hardly eat. Her responses to my questions were slow. Though it was difficult to judge by her haggard face in the dim light, I guessed she was about twenty-five years old. And she was dying.

The crone barked a command. Everyone jumped to get her a cup of heavily sugared mint tea. Still I paid no attention to her, intent on the little girl's mother.

"We've got to get her to the clinic," I told Tor, knowing how little I could do against advanced pneumonia.

"Magra will say no," Tor declared.

"So who the hell is Magra?"

Tor looked mortified. He motioned toward the door.

"No," I said, turning back to the young woman, who had fallen into a wretched fit of coughing.

Tor, who never once had touched me, grabbed my arm.

"You need to understand," he whispered violently.

Outside, I demanded an explanation.

"Magra is the old-ways healer," Tor said. "Magra is very strong. She knows who keeps life, and who dies. We should leave this one to Magra."

"You're afraid of her? Tor's afraid of an old witch?" I was immediately sorry I said it. He stepped back and looked away. "I'm sorry, Tor. Please, I'm sorry. You are right. I need to understand."

"Magra knows death here," he said.

In horror, I realized Tor might leave me over this. I would never see him again.

"Tor, please, I'm sorry! Help me understand. Let's talk to the family. We need to take this woman to the clinic so I can watch her closely." Tor studied the ruins of a house down the street. "Okay. I will talk to Magra first. To see what she wants. Would that be right?"

Tor looked at me. "Respect Magra. All the city knows Magra."

I squared my shoulders and went back inside. I turned to Magra. All eyes were on me. Tor slipped in behind me and herded the family into the other room. I approached her slowly. With one arthritic finger, she motioned for me to sit beside her on the floor. Yankee pride welled up in me; I was not ready to kneel like a disciple at her feet. I set down my field bag and squatted beside it with my elbows on my knees. With another twitch of her hand she called me closer.

Now, even in the dim light, I could see why this woman was feared. A thousand wrinkles accented the chiseled features of her face, framing her deeply set eyes. Her thin lips were taut and would not smile. Age only magnified her obdurate assumption of sovereignty.

I frowned and met her gaze. She raised one thin eyebrow, but just slightly. Then she leaned forward. When she spoke, it was almost a whisper, so only I could hear. And she delivered what would be the first of many surprises to me.

"She's dying," Magra declared.

I nodded. It's not a universal gesture. "Yes," I added.

"Can your medicine help this one?"

"Maybe. It is very late."

"Yes," she said, nodding.

I smiled.

"She's a young one. I had hope for her." I struggled to understand Magra's slurred dialect. But I certainly understood she was confiding in me like a colleague meeting in a hospital corridor.

"There are a few things I can do for her. She would have a better chance in my clinic."

Magra scowled. But I caught a twinkle in her eye. Right then I knew I needed this old bird's help and had nothing to fear from her. She poked me stiffly in the shoulder. "Next time, ask before you come."

"Oh, I am sorry," I said. "Honestly, I didn't know. I just followed the little girl here. I ..."

She shook a fierce finger at me. "Always know where you are going," she snapped.

I bristled, ready as always to fortify my medical authority. But Magra saw it on my face. "Another time," she hissed. And I took a deep breath, rescuing the moment.

I clutched my field bag. Magra sat back on her cushion. "More tea," she commanded in her full, raspy voice.

I stood and stepped away respectfully. Struggling to wipe the smile off my face, I turned to the back room. "Magra needs more tea," I said severely. "Tor, can you arrange to have our patient carried to the clinic tonight?"

Tor bowed, hiding his startled expression as best he could. "Right away, no trouble," he said softly, avoiding my eyes.

The patient's sister, clearly the head of the household, looked at me, then looked at Magra.

"My instruction," Magra said. "Take her tonight."

The little girl, trembling, served Magra a fresh cup of tea. I whispered an assurance to the young woman on the mat, getting her permission to take her to the clinic, as well. She was too weak to ask questions. As I turned to leave, I stopped, of course, to face Magra. She gave me a hard scowl and tipped her head toward the door. This would not be an easy alliance.

Yet, when I walked into the hot night, a surging sense of energy and confidence coursed through my veins. Thrilled and terrified, I shuddered at the feeling and clung to it at the same time. My heart was pounding, but I felt like singing. I had earned a place here. My work had begun in earnest. They needed me. I walked home through the dark alleys, briefly immune to the stale air and heavy shadows. And I fought against sleep, because I did not want to let go of the magic.

3

*I saw five women, the first just past childhood and the last a crone
with Magra's eyes. Each wore a different color. They danced barefoot in a slow circle around the old well encrusted with broken water
jars. I heard the clear, stately chords of a yala playing somewhere
behind me. And a flute. The flute joined in lightly above us, then
settled into a proud but gentle melody.*

*Lightless corners revealed themselves with solid edges, and the
world rose out of shadow into familiar forms. The ground under
my bare feet felt cool and sandy. The sparkling air kissed my skin. I
smelled oranges. I took a deep, eager breath like a child again.*

*The women danced hand in hand. They knew I was with them.
We smiled. Flowers grew out of the broken jars. Then I heard the
wet, hopeful sound of a fountain coming to life. The women raised
their arms. The old well filled to the brim. Happy trickles escaped
through the cracks in the stones. The well overflowed with luminous
turquoise water around my feet. Gradually, the women and the song
receded. The soft waves lapped around my ankles over white sand,
while sea birds called overhead and the surf whispered contentment
along the open beach. I looked out to sea. Then I woke up.*

WHEN YOU LEARN a new word, suddenly you see it everywhere. Magra was like that. After my first encounter with the harsh old woman, she seemed to arrive ahead of me everywhere I went on my medical rounds.

"Tor! She's here again," I muttered. "With her smelly potions and grumbling. We don't have time for this."

We stood on a plank leading to a sagging houseboat. Inside, two children were listless and pale.

Tor gave me a hard look. "Magra says nothing against you."

"Well, no. Not that I've heard," I admitted. "She just growls at me whenever I show up."

"One word from Magra — no one calls us."

"For crying out loud!" I fumed in English. Tor stared at me. I took a deep breath. "Listen," I said, switching back to Rizhmadi. "My medicine works. Magra's … incantations … just make people feel better for a while."

"Isn't that the same?" he asked.

"Real medicine cures people!"

"Sometimes."

"They call for me as a last resort, usually when it's too late! How can I convince them I've got real medicine that saves lives? I've got to get her out of my way." I folded my arms and stared furiously at a rotting barrel beside us that was breeding mosquitoes.

"Truth drinks mint tea," he declared.

"You'll have to explain that one, Tor."

He shifted his weight on the creaking plank. We stepped toward the doorway. "Your people share stories. They talk over their tea. They are all saying Magra knows the words, but you are very clever. They need you both."

"They need what works."

"They need you both," Tor repeated as we went inside.

THE DAY BEFORE I was to meet with Kai at his Autumn House, Tokmol showed up at the clinic door again. He kept his baton tucked under his arm. By way of greeting, he handed me a stamped document. Then he waited, watching me expectantly. It was written in formal Rizhmadi legal jargon.

"What is this?" I asked, not meaning to say it out loud.

"An eviction notice," he answered. "You have three days to close this clinic."

I'm sure my face turned red. "Why?"

Tokmol iced his words. "Failure to comply with Am'rha Bo health regulations. The notice is quite clear."

"Health regulations?" I laughed. "What health regulations?"

"I am surprised that you would admit such ignorance of our laws," he said theatrically. "I will not allow a foreigner to put innocent people at risk."

"Risk? Our clinic is the only place on this side of the river people can go for modern medicine, and you know it!"

"You could start an epidemic here. I shan't allow it." He turned, as if to leave.

"Now wait a minute," I said, torn between rage and fear.

Tokmol paused and slowly turned back to me.

"Yes?"

"What am I supposed to do?" I asked cautiously.

"You can try to comply with the regulations, though I doubt you can have a new sanitation system installed within three days. Or you can get out and go home where you belong."

I stared at him. Then he leaned forward, with a patronizing air familiar to every street vendor in the district, and lowered his voice.

"Or, of course, you could pay a modest processing fee, and I would see to it the proper waivers are filed." He indicated his modest figure, equal to about a year's rent.

Four children who had kept me up all night with their wailing fell anxiously silent behind me. In the street, a young woman with a sick toddler in tow stopped at the sight of the officers. She slipped away.

"I'm sorry," I said, waving the notice. "I don't read Rizhmadi well. You will have to give me some time with this."

"Of course," Tokmol said, tapping his baton in his hand. "The notice gives you three days. But I suggest you don't delay." He reinforced his threat with a glare, spun about, and was gone.

THE MONSOON ARRIVED THAT EVENING. Understand, the monsoon is not like a mere thunderstorm sweeping in to cool a summer's afternoon. Preceded by a torturous crescendo of heat lasting many drought-stricken weeks, the monsoon does not in any normal sense just begin; it arrives in cataclysmic glory, crashing across the landscape. First, the air crackles. Puffs of dust lift off the deserted plazas without warning or apparent wind, as if the Earth itself jumps to greet the approaching deluge. The sky abandons its monotonous blue as the clouds rush in too quickly for the human mind to accept without the aid of mythology. Everything that is not the monsoon stops. And the Rizha, desperate with anticipation, all come out to greet it.

Reluctantly, I had been working with Magra. We were in great demand because the onset of the monsoon is an auspicious time for healing. Everyone seemed distracted and edgy. I blamed it on the unbearable breeze-starved heat.

Magra dropped her herb pouch. She reached into her seemingly bottomless bag and brandished a small bowl. The Rizha clan around me caught their breath and rushed to gather bowls of their own. Someone handed me a chipped but respectable little soup bowl. We hurried outside.

Standing in the middle of the street, Magra lifted her bowl in both hands and saluted the cardinal compass points. Everyone mirrored her tribute. A curious whistle echoed down the lane, passed on by the locals streaming out of their hovels. At the very moment Magra turned back to the south and cocked herself slightly to the east to be perfectly aligned with the sudden gust, a downpour such as I had never experienced or imagined possible pounded exuberantly down on us all.

Magra caught the first of the rain in her bowl and drank. Everyone howled in delight, then followed her lead. And the rain hit the street with such ferocity it looked as if we were standing knee-deep in ocean foam.

Every person in Am'rha Bo — and all the gaunt and mangy alley dogs, too — danced in the flood. We staggered about, drunk on rain water.

"How did you know the exact moment?" I shouted to Magra over the roar.

"Paagh. You didn't feel it? You will. You will."

I was content to wander about, laughing with the children in the moist, cool air. A celebration wild with relief and promise rocked the city all night.

THE NOVELTY OF SOLID WALLS of rain knocking me back into doorways wore off rather quickly though, I must admit. As I left for my appointment with Kai that Friday afternoon, the street from the clinic to the quay had become a shallow stream from gutter to gutter. Rushing water broke around my ankles. Rain hissed on the river around the barge in a spattering haze, obscuring the banks and leaving me feeling we were drifting endlessly downstream. My little black umbrella was useless.

When the barge finally smacked against the dock — it had never actually wavered from its accustomed course — I stepped on the planks and promptly slipped, sending an old woman's basket skittering off the dock into the murky water. She cursed me in two dialects. No one helped me to my feet. When I asked her what had been in the basket and tried to slip her some money, she spat on me and tramped off the dock into the crowd. Others laughed. I didn't know if they were laughing at the old woman or at my attempt to set things right.

I felt my bruised hip, tested my wrist to be sure I hadn't sprained it when I fell, then hugged my satchel to my chest and marched doggedly into upper Am'rha Sa.

Rain sounds different when falling among fine buildings. On the avenue running gracefully up from the river and overlooking the business district, long rows of estates stood immune to the torrent. Channeled through the mouths of little gargoyles into a system of gutters, the water cascaded clear of the balconies laced with white grillwork. Water skipped past the framed windows and the tightly-clipped vines fanning up the walls. It spilled bubbling into iron grills, where it disappeared under the street. Up here, the sewer system swallowed water as quickly as the monsoon could deliver it.

Most of these estates crowded forward onto the street, eager to show off. If one façade had ornate grillwork across every window, the next had grillwork hung like iron icicles along the eaves, as well. Each mansion was painted in pastels popular at the time, giving the entire avenue the look of a monstrous box of confectionery.

I trudged past a long row of these three-storied petit fours. I stopped to catch my breath in front of one property that was distinct from the rest. A severe wrought iron fence was softened by a twelve-foot hedge of camellias growing through it. Pink blossoms ribbed with white sparkled across the living green wall.

Through the gate, a passerby could glimpse an old building, graceful in white, set far back from the avenue. Water glistened on the polished wooden beams and lilted down the heavy chains hung from the gutters at each corner. The water gathered in shallow pools at the foot of the low building and flowed over little staccato falls in channels on either side of the entry, vanishing under a pair of chest-high urns that exploded with irises. Magnolias lined the carriage entry.

Captivated, I stepped up to the gate for a better view. My umbrella tapped the iron. Out of nowhere, a woman in a black uniform sharply trimmed in gold braid appeared at the gate and swung it soundlessly open for me. Startled, I stepped back. Then I saw the address number. This was Kai's Autumn House.

With an almost imperceptible bow, the woman turned and led me to the front door. The gate closed behind us. Under the balcony, I paused to adjust my dress now clinging mercilessly to my skin. I made a feeble attempt to brush the mud off my leg where I had fallen. Embarrassed, I wanted to run screaming from the scene. But the broad front door opened. An elderly, empeccibly poised servant stepped aside. He bowed and offered to take my umbrella. Shaking water off my satchel, I stepped over the threshold onto a glassy marble floor where I was confronted by the most exquisite Takau carpet I had ever seen.

Kai appeared. He was dressed in the country's traditional billowy trousers and long, open-collared shirt. The light, crisp fabric rustled slightly as he moved.

"Glad you made it! Do come in. What's the expression? Make yourself at home? Ah, well, I don't suppose this looks much like home to you." He laughed nervously. I smiled, sidestepping the carpet with my muddy shoes.

Autumn House bewitched its visitors. Broad features can be recalled only through the frosted lens of memory, while random details stand out. That afternoon, the cool air hinted of gardenias. Azure tile glinted in unexpected corners. Furnishings were sparse, antique, polished, and expensive beyond guessing. A bowl, finely painted with lilies, set on a simple ebony stand. A circle of soft light from a window fell on it.

"A towel for the lady," Kai whispered, and the doorman dashed around the corner. "Welcome to the monsoon season," Kai said.

I took off my shoes. Leading me through the foyer, he invited me into a sitting room. A common feature of upper-class homes in

Takau, this was where outside business transactions were conducted and the proper place for a man to receive a lady.

The downpour had dampened my determination and focus. Inside my satchel, the ink had smeared on my license from the government. I recall being more concerned about leaving a water stain beneath me on the leather chair than I was about enlisting Kai's financial support. I sat on the towel. I fumbled with the cup and saucer when the coffee was served.

He asked what had led me to Takau. Or, more accurately, he asked how it was that Takau had been blessed with my presence. His verbal panache made me laugh, and then we both began to relax.

"When I was eight years old, I told my father I wanted to be a doctor. Not a nurse, but a doctor. Unheard of at the time. Quite impossible. But I remember my father looked me in the eye and said I could be whatever I wanted to be."

"You have brought your family great honor."

"Hardly. Americans don't know much about honor, anyway," I shrugged. "No one knew what to do with me. I broke all the rules, but I was a good student. I played baseball with the boys. I argued with the school principal. Nothing like a normal girl."

"In Takau, everything is prescribed, especially if you are very rich or very poor."

"Oh, you always have to fight dead traditions. In America, too. I was one of only three women in my medical school."

The rain made Autumn House rumble slightly. The pitch rose as a cloudburst sent torrents cascading off the tiled roof, then subsided. Autumn House had a fullness about it like a deep, still lake. I wondered how many servants kept the treasures dusted. I wondered what secrets the back rooms held. I caught myself wondering what sort of bed someone like Kai slept on.

"My father worked himself to death. American men often do that," I said. "We lost almost everything to the medical bills. So, it was all my mother could do to keep a roof over our heads. My sisters stayed home to help. My brother became a cop — it suits him well. I was the eldest, and most stubborn. I clawed my way through college," I grinned. Kai nodded appreciatively.

"Medical training taught me to stand my ground," I continued. I was young and still took pride in my defiance. "I told everyone that we should take Western medicine to places that needed it most. I guess it convinced my classmates and professors once and for all that I was hopelessly eccentric or downright mad."

"To make a difference in your world, rather than to merely protect yourself. Always seen as madness by most, I think," Kai said.

"I found one professor who understood. He had studied in Paris and worked in India. He became my mentor. He taught me how to teach myself, and slipped me books on tropical disease." I paused to reflect. Kai sat very still, attentive but not anxious. I laughed lightly, partly from my warm memories of a teacher who set me on my way to save the world, and partly from noticing how well this gentleman, enduring my sermons at that moment, could wait and listen. "I think he knew he was dying, and hurried to pass along his experience to me."

For me — and, evidently, for Kai — this was explanation enough as to why I was in Takau. Our conversation turned to local customs. He deftly avoided revealing much about himself. Of course, this stoked my curiosity and left me to fill in details with guesses. The truth exceeded my imagination.

"You're not married?" I asked as it occurred to me.

Kai blinked at my blunt question, momentarily startled by my total lack of Rizha etiquette, I think. He recovered immediately. "There was an arrangement, of course. She did not see her fifteenth birthday. Scarlet fever or something."

"I'm sorry."

"I had only met her once, when we were twelve." He paused and glanced around the room as if the walls were listening. "I am forever grateful I never had to … ingratiate myself to her clan," he said with a sheepish grin. I gave him a motherly frown and we both laughed.

"After that, I was conveniently out of the country at school."

"A regular Joe Brooks, no doubt," I teased.

He answered with his unreadable smile. He was the original tall, dark, and handsome, I thought. All the Western girls must have swooned in private, though they could never bring him home to their parents. But they never got to see Autumn House.

"And you?" he asked. "Your turn."

I had all my clever retorts. A whole collection from college. All of them deflected attention off my heart. No hint of loneliness. All sassy. They all fell flat for the moment.

"Fellas my age all seemed like boys to me," I answered honestly. "I was caught up in my studies. I wasn't after a white picket fence and a baby carriage anyway. Do you know what I mean?"

I didn't like to tell anyone about the boy I had dated for five years just because my family was comfortable with him. And how many times I had refused to marry him because he had no dreams. But, I also could not admit even to myself how lonely I was in Takau, with no one safe and familiar to hold me when I felt overwhelmed.

"You would be what we call a dragon in a bird cage," Kai said. "You would never fit into the traditional life. I am the same."

We took a quiet moment to feel our friendship deepen. Then in good time, and after some extraordinary cinnamon cakes, we began discussing my efforts across the river. Soon I struck on the subject of extortion.

"His name is Tokmol, and he forces all the half-starved merchants in Am'rha Bo to pay up or lose their stalls or get clapped in chains, or worse! Now he's playing the same game with me."

"Business as usual in Takau," Kai said. "You could offer him half, and some alcohol."

"Absolutely not!"

Kai raised his eyebrows and blinked back my vehemence. "Well," he ventured, more slowly, "Tokmol is only covering expenses on orders from the Commissioner, who has always neglected Am'rha Bo in his police budget. You might pay a small installment. That would give us time to see about getting Tokmol's instructions … modified."

"Out of the question. Even if I had that much money, which I don't, I would never succumb to his threats. Think of how much medicine that money could buy!"

Kai nodded. He was already growing accustomed to my hard-headed stance on every issue.

"Then what are you going to do?" he asked.

"I don't know."

Kai nodded again. I looked glum.

"So, Tokmol reports to the Commissioner over here in Am'rha Sa," I continued with a new breath, thinking out loud. "They tell me the Commissioner works for the City Council."

"Something like that," Kai said.

"I'll go straight to this Council. Expose his dirty little racket. Or at least get him off my back."

"Ay! Please don't try that!" Kai cried. He clasped his hands together in mock supplication. "Seriously, that would be disastrous. The Council is made up of all those fat old men you failed to impress before. I can guarantee you there is only one member of the Council who wouldn't laugh you right out of the chamber."

I frowned. "Who?"

"Me."

I sat back. My damp dress stuck to my shoulder blades again. Kai deflected my unspoken questions with a soft wave of his hand.

"Listen. Give me a day to see what I can do. My clan has never been dishonored by bribes or blood payments either. I swear it." The room seemed to amplify his conviction. "Of course, I haven't shown up for the Council meetings very often, either. But I grew up under their feet. And my family has a considerable stock of favors to be returned to us."

"I can imagine," I breathed.

"No, probably not. Takau politics goes back over two thousand years. I inherited quite a mess. But may I inquire on your behalf?"

"I trust you."

For that, I received one of his probing momentary glances and a smile. Then our conversation turned abruptly to the festivals held after the monsoon and the difficulties a Western mind must have taking in the dizzying Rizha world view. I burned my lip on the second cup of coffee.

"But at least it's all based on the cycle of seasons," I said.

"Seasons of the year, and seasons of life, yes. Though sometimes even we get confused by the crowds of minor deities that have been added over the centuries."

"I love the little rituals, like always telling stories on the dark of the moon, and celebrating a child's naming day."

Kai leaned forward. "People still keep those old ways over there?"

"Oh, yes," I said excitedly. "In just about every household I've visited. Maybe the poor in the slums know the culture better than the filthy rich of Am'rha Sa." My words clattered on the polished teak floor. "I'm sorry ... you know I didn't mean ... "

Kai laughed. "It's true, no doubt! I must come see for myself."

Without warning, two stern businessmen appeared in the doorway, escorted by Kai's doorman.

"I'm afraid other business calls me away," he said, standing slowly. "The time got away from us again, didn't it?"

He escorted me past the two new guests, who stepped stiffly aside. They had an icy avarice in their eyes. They will surely have a hard time of it, trying to strike a deal with Kai, I thought. He tipped his head to them then returned his attention wholly to me. At the door, I pulled on my muddy shoes.

"I will contact the Commissioner for you, I promise," he said softly. "And," he added, hesitating, "I do think it important that I visit your clinic. So I will understand better, don't you think? May I?"

"I would love it if you would! But it's … it's not the kind of place you're used to."

"I know," he smiled. "But you will be there to protect me."

I struggled to read his enigmatic expression. There was no trace of sarcasm in his voice, and I couldn't translate the glimmer in his eye.

"Do come visit. Soon," I said. I touched his hand.

"Thank you. And perhaps someday," he whispered, pointing over his shoulder, "we will even convince men like this to help us." He shrugged again. It was a foreign gesture to him, but he was trying to the last to make me feel comfortable.

Then I was standing on the avenue, looking down the long row of pastel boxes. He said "to help *us*," I thought. The rain was steady, but seemed lighter.

Rain is a capricious old witch named Ashka'rhuna. When rain falls, it is Ashka'rhuna who has let down her long gray hair. At first, say the Rizha, she croons over the fields and hillsides because she likes little flowers. But she can't see very well, and she forgets what she is doing. So it keeps raining.

Even though Rizha children are admonished to save seeds and plant all the flowers they can to make Ashka'rhuna happy, still there are never enough little flowers, or children, and they don't last forever. So compulsive old Ashka'rhuna combs her hair harder and harder. Soon she forgets about the flowers. Then she madly combs her hair for days and weeks without end.

"TOR, WE'VE GOT TO DO SOMETHING about this," I said. "Now."

The wall at the back of the kitchen was swelling and seeping. At first, a puddle spread from under the stove. But now, deep into the season, the water flowed across the kitchen and into a crack in the floor.

The main room of the clinic stood out from the slope behind us and its walls were made of stone, so it was secure, except for the five bucket-filling leaks in the roof. But my little bedroom was behind the kitchen. Water poured down the wall and pooled on the uneven floor, more than an inch deep in the corner. It was like trying to sleep in a grotto. It was unbearable.

Tor splashed into the kitchen. "Rain comes five, six weeks more," he said.

I groaned. "Either this wall is going to cave in, or we're going to drown in here!"

Tor nodded. It wasn't much of a joke. In Am'rha Bo, people died in mud slides every year. Tlia came in with a stack of dirty bowls.

"Getting worse, isn't it?" she said, sweeping the floor with her soggy sandal.

"Have you seen my bedroom? Look at this!" I cried, pulling the curtain aside.

"That's why Rizha sleep on raised beds if they can, dear."

"Another day and my bed will float out the door."

"In my brother's house, he has a little trough that runs along the wall and collects the water. It all goes through a little hole and out to the street. Of course, sometimes the street floods, so it all comes back in. And I've told him that's how the rats keep getting in, but he doesn't listen to me."

"Another reason to sleep on raised beds," I shuddered. At the time, I hadn't yet experienced the horrid spring cockroach infestations.

"In Am'rha Sa, no problem," noted Tor.

"The old clans, they know how to work the water," Tlia declared. "In the big houses, water runs up the walls if they want it to."

"Tlia has never seen Am'rha Sa," Tor said with indignation.

"That's what they say, dear."

"Well, they do have plumbing and gutters," I said. "By the way, my friend Kai is coming to visit the clinic. Maybe he'll have an idea."

"The rich one?" Tlia teased. "Crossing the river? He must like you very much, dear!"

"He's not like the others. You'll see. I think he will help. And yes, he is rich. You wouldn't believe it."

"Rich is trouble," said Tor.

Tlia hefted a heavy sack of rice with practiced ease. "Next time you cross the river, you could stop and ask the Kyornin," she said, still smiling.

"What's the Kyornin?"

"On the islands, middle of Ma'rhu," Tor answered. "Old."

"Oldest clan in Am'rha Sa," said Tlia. "They built the new city. And they can make the river do anything they want out on their island."

Tor growled.

"And you can't say I don't know what I'm talking about," Tlia scolded him, "because my aunt was a chamber maid there for thirty-five years. She told us about the bedrooms as big as guild halls, and about the kitchens that could feed half of Takau. She told us the old clan patriarch, the old Kyornin, never left his room, except to sit on the balcony overlooking the gardens. She said the river comes right up through the ground and shoots all over like it's dancing. And it runs through the flower beds backwards, upstream."

Tor grunted and retreated down the aisle of curtains.

"Just because he hasn't seen it," Tlia scoffed. "But flowers grow out there in every color you can think of, year-round." Tlia stoked the burner for the stove. "It's true. My aunt, she didn't make things up for fun. Not like me, dear."

I laughed.

"She said the flowers grow as big as trees. And the trees are so fat you can hide five people behind one."

"Uh huh."

"Some people say the Kyornin died and now there's no one out there but ghosts. But you can still see the black boat coming and going from Am'rha Sa."

"So you think I should ask the ferry pilot to drop me off on the way over? I'll just go up to the gate and ask if they can help with a flooding kitchen."

"I think you should, dear," Tlia laughed. "You're so pretty they'd fall in love with you on the spot and offer to build you a palace."

The rain had been pounding down steadily for hours. Water burst through the roof in yet another spot. Tor rushed over to move a bed — with the patient still in it — out of the way.

"Maybe they would just let us borrow their boat," I sighed.

KAI DID COME TO VISIT. He came alone, except for a swarm of local children who followed him up from the river. They trailed at his heels, solemnly whispering among themselves. They pretended to hold umbrellas like the one Kai carried, and they scattered into doorways and behind stalls if he turned his head.

He wore simple Rizhmadi clothes, but they were well tailored and made of finer cloth than was generally seen on the back streets of Am'rha Bo. So he had gathered a train of curious, less-than-polite spectators by the time he reached the clinic.

"I guess they don't see many businessmen," I said, scowling at my neighbors.

Kai smiled. "I bet they followed you, too, when you first arrived."

"Still do. Well, welcome to the Am'rha Bo Rhu'ta District Medical Clinic," I announced grandly. I felt an awkward wave of pride and embarrassment.

"It's much bigger than I thought. You have room for more beds." He pointed to one small empty corner. I watched his face; again, he was being gracious, not sarcastic.

"It used to be a textile factory. Of course, there's not much privacy."

Kai studied a bucket that was about to spill over with rain water. "Here's a common problem throughout Takau, I'm afraid."

"We have more than our share of that," I muttered. "Oh, Tor! Come here, please! I want you to meet our guest. Kai, this is Tor, my assistant. I'd be absolutely lost without him."

Tor seemed to stifle a salute. He settled for a crisp, stiff bow. Kai smiled, and bowed a little deeper. This clearly flustered Tor.

"We are honored by your visit, sir," Tor said, in formal Rizhmadi.

"The doctor tells me you have been of inestimable service to her. I am pleased to meet you."

Tor glanced at me, hoping to be rescued.

"Would you please dump that bucket up front, Tor? It's about to overflow again. Thank you." Tor nearly ran out the door with the sloshing bucket. "We've got some real water problems in the back. Actually, I was hoping you might have some ideas about it."

"I see what you mean! This is no good."

"No. And my bedroom is a swamp."

"You sleep in here?"

Now I felt nothing but embarrassment, thinking back on Autumn House.

"This is no good," he repeated. He took a breath. He turned and studied the dripping kitchen wall, measuring with his eyes. "Don't mind me. You go about your work, doctor."

With that, he walked outside. Before I could find my stethoscope, I heard scraping and thumping sounds outside along the back wall. A few minutes later, Kai reappeared at the front door, spattered with mud. He stopped in the doorway, dripping.

"I believe that's what umbrellas are for," I said.

He smiled. "Do you think Tor would know some reputable men who need work?"

"How many hundreds do you want? Of course."

"Five or six would do the job in a few days. We'll need some construction materials, too."

"Tor? We need your help."

Tor stood at attention, mop in hand.

"The hillside behind the kitchen has slumped against the building. The pressure against the wall is serious. That back room could collapse any minute. But we can excavate back there, build a retaining wall, and backfill with gravel. That should do it."

Kai counted off a list on his fingers. Tor nodded, repeating, "Six men with spades, pick, wood to hold back mud, brick and stone for the wall, and gravel enough. One hour?"

"Excellent," said Kai, counting out a generous handful of cash. "Take my umbrella if you like."

Tor accepted the umbrella; quite a status symbol in these streets. He bowed again and left. I turned to find Kai a dry towel, but my rich guest followed Tor outside. I heard more bumping and scraping, precariously overhead now. I was afraid he would fall through the roof. When I next saw him, he looked like a typically tattered, mud-stained peasant.

"I think we can fix these leaks, too," Kai said, pointing at the dribbling ceiling. Everyone, including the patients in their beds, stared at him. None of us had seen a wealthy man happily caked with mud before. He looked down at himself, then flashed his enigmatic smile.

"A cup of tea?"

Despite steady torrential rain, Kai spent most of the next two days behind the clinic with his construction crew. I was sure he was not accustomed to hard labor, but he masked his stiff muscles under his habitual grace of movement and smiled through the mud comically streaked across his face.

Each night, he refused dinner and politely excused himself. He slipped quickly down the hill toward the river alone. The curious children didn't, or couldn't, follow him anymore. Pushing through the crowd along the quay with him one day, I had experienced his uncanny ability to evaporate around a corner. Though I studied how he sidled into shadows and poured around knots of people, I could not begin to imitate how he did it. There was no slinking to it. In fact, it was the seamless ease of movement that led my eye away from him, I think. I swear I once saw a cat watch in admiration as he passed. Something in the way he slipped through doorways left the startling impression he had simply walked through the wall, instead. So when he tipped his head in farewell at the end of the day, he seemed to vanish, and no one recalled seeing him leave.

In contrast, I was a constant source of amusement to my patients and neighbors as I stumbled over their culture with my odd American ways. But they knew I was always sincere in my interest in their lives and my desire to understand, so they readily forgave my social gaffes and scrambled syntax. And they accepted Kai's visits as merely another curious aspect of my mystifying presence.

TOKMOL RETURNED, ON SCHEDULE. This time he had five deputies behind him. Felt he needed reinforcements, I thought with amusement. They scanned the street while my neighbors quietly disappeared.

"Good morning, Tokmol. Everything is calm in the district, I trust?"

"Yes, thank you, doctor. There was an altercation on the waterfront last night, but my officers prevented any serious injuries. And your practice? The local people are accepting you?"

Tokmol had the gracious manner of a veteran military officer when it suited his purposes. And that striking cordiality put me off balance. I reminded myself why he was here.

"It's been wonderful. People are coming to learn what Western medicine might do for them," I said.

"Good, good." He stepped inside and dropped the pretense. "Now, regarding the little matter of documentation?"

"Oh, yes," I said nonchalantly. "One moment."

I strolled back to my little desk and pulled an envelope from my satchel. He expected a payment. I was looking forward to reading the dismay on his face. With a touch of ceremony, I handed him a letter embossed with the seal of the Am'rha Sa Council.

Tokmol squinted slightly, but instead of revealing his surprise, his face went blank, betrayed only by a slight pursing of the lips. I watched him intently; even his breathing remained steady.

"It is signed by the Commissioner," I gloated. "Acknowledgment of receipt, all requirements in order, from the Council Administrator. Health regulations and all," I added.

The tiny wrinkles around his eyes deepened. I wondered how much he was reading between these lines.

"I see. Very well. This should settle the matter for the time being," he said, without rancor or threatening tone.

"Good."

He offered me a tight, momentary smile. "Evidently you have found an influential friend in the short time you have been here. My regards."

"Thank you."

Then his tone darkened. "But this is, nevertheless, a dangerous station for you. I cannot guarantee your safety here, you understand? And with my limited budget, I cannot give too much special attention to foreign guests."

"I understand. And the U.S. Cavalry won't be riding to my rescue," I said with a grin. Tokmol squinted again, as if this were an actual contingency he should have considered. Grace under fire, yes. But a sense of humor, no.

"Tokmol, I relieve children of the symptoms of scurvy, and I treat cuts to prevent infection. I offer some comfort. In return, my neighbors watch out for me. I am well cared for."

"Yes, I see that. But choose your alliances carefully, doctor. I am sure you do not wish to inadvertently assist those who would bring more suffering on the city." He handed the letter back to me. "This is not your America. And not everyone around you shares your noble ideals." He made his customary about-face. "Good day, doctor."

I stood a moment, puzzling over his parting words. The Rizha, despite their blunt, childlike pronouncements, often spoke to me in riddles. Perhaps he could not help mixing veiled threats into his well-intentioned advice. But an infant began wailing behind me, so I left the matter at the door.

AS THE SOGGY WEEKS PASSED, I became a familiar customer to Syrka and the rest of the riverside merchants. In the dry season, they crowded their stalls up close to the ferry dock, but with the onset of the monsoon, they moved their displays under the protective cover of the old river guild hall veranda. Almost every day, I climbed the slick marble stairs to escape the rain and meet new friends. I elbowed my way among the shoppers, who were all squabbling happily with the vendors. I asked why it was that the whole market was never pushed right off the veranda onto the cobblestone plaza behind them.

"It happens," Syrka laughed. "But it won't happen to me!" He showed me how his fruit stand was lashed to a guild hall colonnade. "Fools lose their tables. I say they deserve it."

Syrka had a new angle on his business. He had, God only knows where, acquired a chipped porcelain juicer and a pair of glass tumblers. For a premium price, he offered orange juice.

"What happens if you have more than two customers at once?" I asked.

"They wait their turn! Not even I can carry on three arguments at the same time."

So that was the key to Syrka's success: A customer who drank a glass of juice also purchased the latest news and a debate.

He had launched into a verbal attack on bureaucrats in general when I moved on through the market. Out from under the shelter of the old guild hall, everything was drenched. Handcart wheels spattered my calves with mud. Strangers pressed against me as we ducked into doorways during cloudbursts. The Ma'rhu muscled high against the banks. It tickled the underbellies of the old warehouses.

I watched the swollen river warily. It swirled just shy of flooding the riverbank now. The seething current made the ferry crossing treacherous. But a moldy assortment of private boats swarmed around the dock like flies and slipped across the eddies along the shore. I saw a line of agile children run, laughing, from the ferry pier across the water to a half-sunken riverboat by leaping and skittering over the bobbing tangle of rowboats, rafts, and skiffs. The people dance over their hardships here, I thought. The children's trick was to keep moving. A good lesson.

Kai crossed the river once a week, sometimes more. He supervised small engineering projects: He made a washed-out road on a steep hillside passable again, and he shored up a crumbling wall that threatened a crowded alley. He took tea with the local merchants to hear their hopes and frustrations. And he visited the clinic. He never lingered, though, because I always seemed preoccupied with my patients. Tlia scolded me for not making a fuss over him the moment he arrived.

"Oh, he doesn't expect to be treated like a prince," I groused. I deliberately focused on my patients when Kai was in the room. I told myself he would be impressed by my bedside manner.

"The gentleman doesn't want to talk to the back of your pretty head, dear," Tlia warned.

In truth, I hated to admit I got terribly nervous on the days I thought he might drop by. I didn't go to the market for fear of missing him. I made Tor mop the floor twice. I fumbled with tinctures and forgot what I had just read in my reference book. I glanced at the door a thousand times an hour.

I must have gone pale when I suddenly realized the rain would not drive Kai away, but my feigned cold shoulder might. Tlia knew she had made her point and her eyes laughed as she walked away with a pile of linens in her arms. And on his next visit, I dropped what I was doing and insisted that Kai join me on the wobbly chairs of the only café in Am'rha Bo.

It was a stiff hike up the cobbled road from the dock and uphill from the clinic. The Café Royale commanded an open view from its covered balcony. This lofty and protected enclave was, by tacit law, reserved for the wealthiest local merchants, the rare visitor, and, by dubious extension, me. The café was built of gray stone, a bulwark against the sea of frail slum shanties spread before it. Generous floor space downstairs included a real kitchen. I led Kai up the narrow spiral stairs inside.

There was no menu, since the café only offered the usual vegetable curries, deep-fried dumplings filled with meat of questionable origin, stale anise cookies, and, of course, mint tea. Kai was gracious about it. We drank our tea and watched through the rain as the yellow light from oil lamps flickered out of doorways below.

"This area must have been an open plaza once," Kai observed. We looked down on the dense tangle of stalls and sagging shacks where families crowded against the deluge. It was hard to imagine any open space for miles around.

"How can you tell?"

"It's the only flat expanse in the old city. And look how all the alleys seem to meet here. I think this place was once the hub of Am'rha Bo."

"Still is. I come past here on my way to any other point in the city, except to the river."

"And the avenue down to the guild hall on the river is the straight-est road."

"And the widest."

Kai sipped his tea. "Come to think of it, have you noticed this area never floods? All the alleys drain from here."

"Hmm, okay. But what about the hillside above us?"

"It drains around this point, too. Through that old culvert with the stone bridges to the north, and down the gully between here and your clinic to the south. Easy."

"Hard to imagine this an open plaza."

"An open plaza, full of stalls on market day. Then the stalls were left in place. Then they were reinforced for the monsoons. Then people set up housekeeping and moved in."

I enjoyed the certainty in Kai's voice. "How is it you know so much about engineering?"

"Harvard, class of '25. And a family tradition," he said. Kai stared out over the rooftops and added, slowly, "I'll show you some-time, if you like."

There. I was finally going to learn this man's secrets. As we sat there, I recognized — with a girlish shock — that he had won my heart and I was quite helpless to catch myself.

"I would like that very much," I purred. I think the silky tone of my voice frightened him.

Nevertheless, three days later, Kai appeared in my doorway just before dusk. I ducked into my dim — but dry — bedroom and hurriedly straightened myself up. I rifled through my meager collection of scarves and bracelets to find my one little bottle of perfume.

"We'll have to sneak out like gangsters," Kai said. He pretended to wrap an overcoat around himself. I laughed and pulled my travel-weathered blue cloche low over my eyes.

"Hmm. You look more like a movie star. Don't you have a shawl, like the local women wear?"

"Ooh, a disguise! Just a minute." Tlia had given me just such a shawl, long and dark. I draped it over my head in the manner Tlia had taught me. Of course, I still towered over all the Rizha in the street.

Everyone was outside, enjoying a rare break in the clouds. We followed the avenue down toward the ferry. But at the river guild house, Kai touched my arm.

"This way," he whispered.

I followed him through the evening crowd. He moved quickly, with his head lowered. He turned with a fierce look of disapproval when I greeted a woman I knew. He led me along the market road, upriver to where the bustle on the street gradually dissolved. We stopped beside a warehouse. It leaned wearily into the riverbank.

"Do you see anyone following us?"

"You're serious?"

Kai glared at me.

"I don't think so," I answered soberly, studying the street. "No. Not even the children." The only person in sight was a wizened little man picking through a pile of fetid garbage.

"This way," Kai said again.

We slid along the old gray building. I thought I saw someone or something move between dark crevices ahead. I couldn't tell if Kai had seen it or not, but he hurried forward. Upstream of the warehouse lay a creaking pier.

"Watch your step."

I hardly needed the warning. One false move would have landed me neck deep in muck and flotsam. The glassy eye of a dead river bird glinted up at me.

"I hate to make them wait here," said Kai.

"Make who wait?"

"Please hurry."

I stepped gingerly on the boards. The next moment, I stifled a scream as a dark figure stepped out of the shadows right beside me.

PLEASE," SAID KAI, TAKING MY ARM.

In an instinctive fighting stance, I faced the man in black who had stepped onto the dock. I shot a quick glance at Kai. I saw immediately that not only was he unconcerned, he had no idea why I was wide-eyed with fear.

"Katherine, please," he said gently. "You know we don't want people to see us here."

Questions stuck in my throat. I forced myself to take a breath and looked again at the man blocking my escape to the street. He was a small, middle-aged fellow in a pressed and perfect black uniform with gold braid on the cuffs and collars, just like I had seen at Autumn House. He had a startled look on his face. He was wondering why this tall American woman seemed about to knock him into the river sludge.

I turned around. Moored to the crooked pilings of the pier, a sleek black boat waited. Its uniformed crew stood at attention. The deck ran low to the water line but the ornate prow formed a tall silhouette of a tree. The last evening light glittered on the water.

"Oh," I said, with my hand over my mouth. Slowly understanding, I nodded. "Oh, yes."

Kai offered his hand as I stepped on board. I climbed among the six oarsmen. The crew studied me furtively but would not meet my curious gaze. A woman at the rudder bowed discreetly.

With a nod from Kai, they set about the ship without a word. Like a whisper, the boat pulled away from the dock. Oars dipped, and the craft pulled quickly away from shore. I clutched a rail near the prow and strained with all my senses as we slipped into the Ma'rhu's grasp.

At first, the black boat ignored the current. We angled upstream into the open water. Dusk had stolen the color now; the Ma'rhu retained a silver sheen, broken only by the sharp, dark outline of the islands.

My hand moved from the brass to the lacquered teak. I felt the current quicken. I stared at the islands. Kai stood beside me.

"Kyornin," I said.

"Yes."

"I've heard stories."

Kai chuckled softly. "No doubt."

We swept toward the massive walls at the outermost edge of the main island. It looked like a playful god had dropped a medieval castle in the water, then left it to be worn glassy-smooth by the river. Within the ramparts, a line of cedars and canopies of elm and maple towered like cathedral rooftops over a city skyline.

The woman at the helm steered toward the warning beacon at the upstream tip of the island. Now the boat strained hard against the swell to pull around to the eastern, deep river side of the island. As the water heaved us toward the ominous walls, we seemed certain to slam into the jagged rocks lit by the beacon. I looked anxiously from the beacon to Kai, but he wasn't paying the slightest attention to the boat's course. His deep-set eyes were watching the fading light over Am'rha Sa. But he noticed my concern and turned slightly, a subtle shift of weight I had at first thought expressed an inherent timidity but learned to read as a watchful, wordless question. I heard the river lapping at the bouldered feet of the beacon tower where the island split the river. I held my breath. Then the boat caught the surge of the deep current and slid lightly past the rocks. The oars lifted from the water, leaving the boat to glide effortlessly along the island's eastern edge on the river's broad back.

Kai smiled. "They like to cut it close for guests," he quipped. I laughed a little too loudly, more relieved he had broken the tense silence than that we hadn't broken to pieces on the rocks. He leaned closer.

"I'm glad you've come," he said. "I want ..." he stopped and gestured nervously at the looming walls slipping past. "If you ..." he tried again, then looked pained. He forced another smile. "The dahlias are blooming," he concluded earnestly, as if that explained everything.

The deck rolled gently under us as I put my hand on his and leaned in, almost kissing his cheek.

"I want to share your ... secrets," I whispered. I'm seducing this poor man, I thought, and the smile that crossed my face completely unnerved him. He took a deep breath. He pretended to steady himself as the boat rocked on the swell. Finally, he pointed toward the island.

"The Great Hall starts about there. You can tell because of that red maple." He sounded suddenly like a tour guide, and I giggled. He tried to ignore me. "The house was built in the *Roh Ta* Dynasty. They say there's no finer tile work in the world. And the beams are nearly a meter thick."

The wall dropped away from us suddenly as we swirled into the eddy at the downstream tip of the island.

"There's the gate," Kai said, with pride.

The last trace of azure left the sky and the island only a silhouette. But I could see that a stout bridge crossed from the towers and gate to a simple dock on the second island.

"The moon will be out early tonight, and nearly full. A good night to see the gardens."

In reply, I stroked his arm. And smiled again. What has gotten into me, I wondered? I decided not to fight it.

With a sudden flurry of action from the crew, the boat swept up beside the dock along the tiny droplet of island at the downstream tip of the palace grounds.

This island, carpeted with tall grasses and crowned with willows, was little more than a rocky extension of the main island, but it made a perfect mooring. Kai took my hand again as we disembarked. I released my grasp slowly enough to make a point.

The bridge crossed from the dock to a graveled walkway that swept gracefully to the front gate of the palace. The bridge was almost as wide as it was long, and, like the boat, was lacquered black. Jasmine wrapped around the low railings as tightly as the sleeves of a lamb-swool sweater. The river breeze carried the perfume to us.

As we walked across the bridge, a servant ran ahead. She returned with a lantern. The gate — large enough for a locomotive to pass through — opened without a squeak as we approached.

"Oh!" I exclaimed as we crossed the threshold. Instead of a marble dome or anything with a roof at all, we were greeted by an open corridor flanked with cedars. The arched entries to the palace buildings stood beyond the trees and across a lawn on either side.

Shadowy servants lit lanterns. Each new flicker revealed more of this fantasy. A shallow stream set in gold-flecked salmon stone carved a line down the center of this cathedral, running out from black obscurity to end in a pool in front of us. The water sang a soft invitation and welcome.

"Over here, the private quarters and guest rooms. To the right, our Great Hall, and kitchens, and ... well, let me show you."

I followed Kai under the trees to our right and across the grassy strip that seemed to be sprouting statues. He threw open the arched doors to the Great Hall.

Again, I could only manage a breathless, "Oh!"

The Great Hall of Clan Kyornin was so spacious that it swallowed our lantern light and the echoes of our footsteps. To my right, I could make out the hint of dragons and armies smoking and charging across heavy tapestries. Down the center of the room ran a double colonnade of pillars that mirrored the cedars outside. On my left, a row of arches framed windows that opened to the gardens beyond.

"Hundreds of people could pour right out onto the terrace," I said in a hushed voice.

"Can you hear them?" Kai asked. "Clan Kyornin used to hold state banquets here. The clans and guilds marched in great processions before they sat down to eat. They say one banquet lasted five days and only ended when there was a duel between two clan lords right here in the hall."

We walked the length of the cavernous space, padding softly from one long Takau carpet to the next. The carpets floated on a shimmering ocean of inlaid tile. Our whispers got lost among the massive beams overhead.

At the far end of the hall, Kai led me up five broad steps into a salon where he described European costume balls held a century before. A singing sheet of water poured out of the wall. The water ran under the floor and emerged in a reflecting pool outside, Kai explained. The pool led to a view overlooking a privet and yew labyrinth. It was too dark now to see across the maze.

"Mmm," I said. "More secrets."

"Oh, there's a trick to it."

"I bet you played in there as a child."

"The nurses were always afraid to go inside. So I camped out with a stock of cinnamon cakes by the little fountain in the center."

"Show me sometime."

"You might not find your way out."

"I'm lost already," I said, taking his hand again.

Strolling back along the terrace outside the Great Hall, we returned to the cathedral of cedars. With the front gate securely locked on our left, we stepped across the rivulet and crossed the lawn, paying no heed to the terrible Takau dragon that had landed there and turned to stone.

We briefly toured the private quarters of the west wing. Unlike Kai's dark and opulent Autumn House, this palace, though much larger, was light and crisp. Most of the rooms opened outward to the gardens. Many simply had tall arches and brocade curtains for walls. In time, I would come to know them well.

But on this first visit, we returned to the cedar cathedral and followed the channel at our feet upstream, crossing a footbridge to a raised courtyard jutting into a sea of greenery. Airy double colonnades of marble formed a circle of windows around this courtyard. To one side, the private rooms gazed darkly back. Across the way, the Great Hall glowed in lantern light. Behind us lay the inviting entry from the gate and before and below us spread gardens like I had never dreamed possible.

The moon came out, nearly full, as promised. Then I could see the wellspring of the rivulet we had followed was a fountain in the center of this courtyard. Eight streams flowed to the compass points through shallow troughs in the caramel and salmon stone. Each stream took its private course through the landscape. One spit from a demon's mouth, another lilted down polished steps. Some vanished and reappeared as showers over fountains, some rested still and lily-clad in long pools until they dashed over glistening edges and crashed around the resident stone monsters. All eventually merged with other waters and swirled down playful channels into the moonlight and out of sight from the courtyard where I stood, mesmerized.

Servants brought dinner to us at a table on a terrace that floated beyond the edge of the colonnade, cantilevered over a pool. The fountains provided the background music. I remember lamb, and saffron rice, and fresh greens, and even little wedges of Italian cheese. Fresh mint tea, of course. And I remember we rarely spoke.

After dinner, we wandered into the landscape. We paused with suspense at a glossy blue gazebo draped with silk. I peaked inside. It was rich with cushions and pillows. Where the azure fabric pulled back around the pillars, gardenias bloomed by moonlight. Kai watched me.

Suddenly I was floating. I was sure. I had never known it like this. I drifted down the path with every tingling nerve aware of Kai close behind me. Lighter still, I began to run. Laughing past another gazebo resting in the embrace of a triangle of willows, I bounded off some steps and down a long lane with jets of water arcing on either side. I came up short before a graceful pavilion surrounded by a shallow pool and shimmering with silver. Kai was at my heels. He embraced me from behind and I hugged his arms to me so he could not let go.

For a long moment, neither of us dared move. Then he led me across the narrow stone slabs set like stepping stones over the pool. We poured through a pearl-beaded curtain. The pillars around us now were polished spirals of speckled marble banded with sterling. We kicked off our shoes to sink our toes into the carpet. The air was cool on my skin, with a scent of roses. From deep in the garden I heard a songbird call, just once, followed by a silence that gently relaxed into the sound of fountains in the dark.

I threw myself into a heap of pillows like a child discovering a feather bed. Kai knelt beside me. He stroked my hair. With delight, I realized he was trembling. There was no hesitation left in me. I bared my breasts to the moon glow.

6

LIKE ANYWHERE ELSE IN THE WORLD, the calls usually came in the middle of the night.

"Magra gives permission," said the family guide sent to lead me through the dark alleys. I slipped on my sandals and followed, arriving with my water kettles, clean towels, and my field bag. Several men sat outside the house in the rain, joking nervously among themselves.

Inside, I bowed to Magra. I introduced myself to the women attending the birth and set to work.

"The *makli panjira* can wait," I instructed, requiring their traditional new-mother's soup be set aside so the hearth could be dedicated to boiling water in my kettles. My primary objective was to achieve some primitive level of asepsis. Of course, these people had no notion of germ theory, but they comfortably accepted ceremonial purification of water for the occasion.

I felt the tension in the room ease as soon as I presented the attending women a block of the particular incense reserved for births. Magra nodded. They went back to their incessant chanting.

"How long?"

"Since midday," reported a grandmother.

The young woman gave a prodigious groan and bit down on the cloth she clutched — a ritual item customarily passed from mother to daughter. This one was clean, I noted with relief.

A quick examination assured me of a normal birth, and that the work would soon be done.

"How many children before?" I asked.

"Just two."

"She's doing fine," I observed.

No other procedure in medicine provides such satisfying results. After nine months of discomfort, the patient is suddenly better. And the doctor, who in most cases provides no more than reassurance, gets part of the credit. I wonder how many hundreds of births I attended in the dark hovels of Am'rha Bo. I saved the lives of a few mothers, too. Of course, many of the children never saw their third or fourth birthdays. But once I had shared the *makli panjira* with the women, I was forever part of their families.

More often, I was called to the bedside of a fading life by a family's vague hope that Western science might be worth a try, after Rizha medicine had failed. Usually, my instructions had to be brief and severe.

"Keep the children out of the house. Burn that heap of clothes. And," I added with sad finality, "call for Magra."

In time, the strict old witch and I shared authority in the eyes of the people for officially declaring a death. But Magra knew the right words to say. I could only hope to restrict the spread of disease. I encouraged the relatives to immediately call the coroners: a grim caste of unthanked public servants who collected corpses and presided over the endless cremations conducted on the high stony hill overlooking the city.

WE LET EVERYONE ASSUME KAI was a civil engineer assigned to Am'rha Bo by the government. A simple ruse and barely half a lie. My neighbors always watched us come and go, of course, but it surprised no one that the American doctor and the educated young man who spoke English would often be seen together at the café.

Kai could hide his noble identity but not his elegant boat. So he always crossed back to Am'rha Sa on the regular ferry. I left later, on the last run, then lingered in the gas-lit shops of the eastern bank. We kept the Kyornin's boat upriver on a well-guarded dock among the gaudy regatta barges of other wealthy clans. I joined Kai there or met him discreetly at Autumn House. We slipped out after dark and between rains.

In those first months, I never saw the garden in the unforgiving daylight. Our path was marked by white azaleas set aglow by the full moon that reclined in the pools and danced in waterfalls. For me, the garden is cast forever in the cooling shimmer of lunar silver.

There was a long walkway in the shadow of the guest wing that was so lush with ferns and palms, cycads and orchids, I naturally called it "the jungle." I had never known the tangles of a real jungle or of real love, I mused—and immediately laughed at my own melodramatic thoughts. Kai gave me that funny sidelong glance and smiled.

"I love to hear you laugh," he said.

"And I love to make you smile."

Night after night, we escaped together to the garden. The servants anticipated our needs, then vanished. The tea was always hot and sweet. For a time, the burdens of the day were balanced by our abiding delight.

MAGRA APPEARED AT MY DOOR.

"Come," she ordered.

I hesitated, but recognized that declining was not an option. I set down my stethoscope and followed the spry old woman into the long shadows of a late afternoon. We climbed directly to the funeral hill.

"It's Ma'norin, who died yesterday," Magra rasped, breathing hard from the climb. I nodded. Ma'norin had been the matriarch of a large family. I had done what I could to make her comfortable at the end of a long battle against tuberculosis. The only real defense against the disease at that time was the local custom of cremation.

"But why do you need me now?"

"Need you?" Magra scowled. "You are family. You are *shen'te*."

"Just helping with a birth or death, that kind of thing, makes me *shen'te?*"

"Caring makes you *shen'te*. You understand their lives."

"By that account, you must be family to everyone in Am'rha Bo."

Magra shot me a nearly toothless grin.

"Paagh!" she snorted. "Yes. Yes, I think so. Paagh!"

We walked behind the last crumbling hovels that had been pushed toward the crown of the hill.

"Looks like a volcano up here," I muttered.

Along the crest, cremation fires burned steadily, belching acrid smoke. Soot coated the coroners' wagons, the hill's exposed rocky ribs, and the young man with a patch over one eye who trudged past us. The place felt powerfully foreign to me. And, I didn't know what role I was expected to play. My mouth was dry.

"You know, I laughed when I first heard the Rizhmadi name for this place meant 'Death's Door.' That sounds funny in English. But now it seems right."

Magra ignored me and marched straight toward Ma'norin's clan. Here at the gates of Hell, Ma'norin's kin and loved ones gathered. And to my nearly panicked dismay, they all looked like children waiting in line for a carnival. They hovered eagerly around several large baskets on the ground.

In Takau, light blue is death's color. Westerners have a hard time with that.

"Black is heavy, and full," Tlia once tried to explain to me. "But death makes you lighter, and clear. Don't you think so, dear?"

So Ma'norin's clan, despite their soot-stained feet, all wore skirts or vests or at least scarves of robin-egg blue.

From one basket, a woman I recognized after a moment as Ma'norin's sister handed out strips of golden yellow cloth to each of the gathered family and friends. She presented Magra with one of these ribbons. She offered me another.

"Ma'norin's favorite color, since she was a little girl," the sister smiled.

"She'll be watching for it, no doubt!" said a very round woman who was holding the basket for the sister.

"She'll laugh at how much we have for her," said an old man with wiry hands who was trying to tie one of the strips into a headband. It looked cheerful with the pastel-blue tunic that hung on his gaunt frame.

"She won't get lost for a minute. We'll make sure of that!" said the sister, with undisguised mirth. Magra tied her ribbon around her left wrist, so I did the same.

Next, two sturdy men I took to be Ma'norin's sons bent over the second basket. It was large, even by Takau standards, and Takau is a country held together by cane and river reed. A child could have hidden inside, with room for her toys. It was bottle-shaped, with a hat-like lid. Its frame was adorned with sky-blue satin bows. Despite leather handles and reinforcements, it sagged from heavy use. The funeral basket was apparently community property, and under Magra's administration. The sons set it down at her feet.

"She's ready to go," Magra declared, and lifted off the lid.

Now, I had been in Takau long enough to expect surprises out of that basket. I anticipated lustrous masks with bug-eyed demon faces. Or armfuls of flowers. Crazy hats with feathers wouldn't have startled me. But at Magra's signal, the deceased woman's sons began distributing what seemed the most unlikely assortment of objects possible.

Tambourines. Rattles. A hoop drum. A whistle that must have escaped from Mardi Gras. Three wooden flutes. And they handed me a cowbell.

I wasn't entirely mistaken. There was a bug-eyed demon mask. One of the sons put it on and charged his aunt with a terrible howl. She blew the whistle in his face.

They had flowers, too. The round woman stepped forward with yet another basket, and it was brim full of marigold blossoms.

A young woman from the clan appeared with a yala on a shoulder strap. Magra nodded, everyone waved their yellow ribbons, and Ma'norin's sister raised a small glazed urn over her head. All of Ma'norin's friends and family shouted and banged and rattled and whistled their greetings to her.

I shuffled to one side, a foreigner again, terrified of offending the family by some ignorant word or act. As a doctor trained to stave off dying but not taught at all about how to help people face death, I did not care to spend any more time than I had to at Death's Door. I was relieved when the gathered clan started down the road toward the river.

The road skirted the city to the north, following a deep ravine. There were no houses along this road. Everyone knew the ravine was crowded with ghosts. Travelers took a long detour around the ravine and behind the hill.

Thousands of upright poles lined the road. Some at the head of the ravine held the tattered remnants of family crests. These gave way to rank upon rank of slender sentries tied with strips of cotton in a rainbow of favorite colors, raised to guide the spirits to the river and left to fade where they fluttered.

We made a handsome racket with our instruments. It looked like a small-town Easter parade. And we tied our ribbons to the poles along the way. Magra brought up the rear of our procession, waving her arm with the yellow ribbon on her wrist like she was signaling someone to follow. And that, of course, is exactly what she was doing.

"Daughters and sons!" shouted Ma'norin's sister. Each grown child called out his and her name in a clear voice.

"Grandchildren!" someone else cried. A dozen young people called out their names, right down to the little boy struggling to carry a tambourine in his pudgy hands and keep up.

"Ma'norin in the flood of '21!" an old man bellowed. "Remember her shoveling mud out of her kitchen!"

"Ma'norin helped with the birth of half the children in Am'rha Bo!" shouted Magra in her raspy voice. Everyone whooped and pounded the drums and affirmed that it was the truth.

With a litany of memories, we escorted Ma'norin down the long ravine to the old pier. Frail and sagging like a fallen tree soon to be swept away with the current, the pier jutted into the river from a rocky shore. We waited briefly at the end of the road for another family to finish their ceremony over the water. Stepping with added caution as the pier swayed under our weight, we gathered shoulder to shoulder on the last gray planks. For a moment, I studied the water glittering between the cracks, blurred by my tears. Magra and Ma'norin's sister offered a brief prayer and raised the funeral urn to the sky again.

"Ma'norin! Welcome home!" Magra cried, and tipped the ashes into the water.

LOVERS REACH A POINT WHERE they can walk silently together for a long time and be utterly at ease. But I was nowhere near that place in those days. I chattered away about my hopes and concerns. Kai listened well. No man has ever endured my enthusiasm better. I turned out to be a woman who needed a man to listen well, even when other needs faded.

But in those hot tropic nights, I splashed barefoot through the fountains with my skirt hiked up. Kai greeted my barrages of water with arms outstretched. I slid my hands over his skin as we stood in the deep shadows of the terrace, engulfed in a chorus of cascading water.

The private quarters of the palace opened over the gardens to the essential river-cooled breeze. I neglected to close doors. I watched mosaics in the ceiling by candlelight through Kai's thick hair. I was impatient with tangled sheets.

On nights too sultry for touching, we sprawled on linen pillows in the blue pavilion and discussed the state of the world. I find intelligence erotic. His muscular ideas entwined in my eager dreams gave me visceral thrills as potent as our impassioned tangling of arms and legs. Our wordplay made me tingle on steamy nights. Kai tired of words, though, answering instead with his fingertips on my leg, and kisses on my neck.

One morning I awoke with pollen sprinkled like gold glitter on my skin from flowers cascading down the pavilion arches. I clutched Kai's body and I clawed the pillows. Growling, I engulfed him, drew him into me, took his breath away. The garden welcomed my body's ecstasy like it accepted the rain. I collapsed, joyfully spent, and turned to inhale the pungent musk of dewy flowerbeds. I wasn't naked; I was dressed in leaf shadows.

I SPENT LONG HOURS CRISSCROSSING the district with Magra. We could as well have gone door to door, since it was a rare home that didn't shelter some grim ailment. But we followed a complex formula, divorced from my notion of medical triage, by which Magra calculated the order in which we saw patients.

I trailed the old woman, offering the magic of Western medicine with my shiny stethoscope. In those days, even in the West, medicine was more art than science, with the great victory of antibiotics still years away. And I had to admit Magra's concoctions — custom brewed and carefully administered — brought better results than most of my meager pharmaceuticals. After all, the Latin names, so impressive to American patients, were no more exotic, and therefore no more powerful, than my notes scribbled in English. But Magra's familiar, foul-smelling roots convincingly reeked of potency.

"There is little we can do here," I said quietly, with my hand resting on the forehead of a small girl.

"I know," Magra said. "But our strongest medicine comes when we walk out the door."

I offered the child a herb bundle to clutch. Magra gave the girl's mother elaborate instructions for brewing a tea, though it was mostly ginger. Then we gathered our trinkets and left.

"What do you mean?" I asked.

"Maybe I have horns and claws," Magra said. Her eyes twinkled at me. "They think I am Yasol'rhishá's mother. Death walking in."

"They think the longer we linger, the worse the circumstance."

"Yes. So when we leave, they know the child will not die; not just yet. And hope is powerful medicine."

I meditated on this twist of the doctor's role as we marched in silence to the next house.

WE WALKED AT DUSK BESIDE A WALL of ivy near the reflecting pool. I had just asked Kai to tell me about how it was to grow up in such a magical playground. Then he disappeared. Literally. One moment he was half a step behind me, and then he was gone.

I took a slow breath. A slight settling of ivy leaves gave him away. I stretched my arm into the vines and found, in this one spot, there was no wall behind them. I shook my head, parted the veil, and stepped into the maze.

Flawlessly sheared yew, cropped at eight feet overhead, framed a gravel path. I turned right. Kai whistled behind me. Before I followed him to the left, I made a mark in the gravel with my foot.

The maze divided, then divided again. The woody yew was interspersed with glossy privet, but nowhere could I have pushed through or crawled under the living walls. Two blind turns in, I came to a door. The rough-hewn wood was weathered and reinforced with wrought iron. Irresistibly, I had to try the latch. With a handsome click, the door opened. But for my curiosity I was rewarded with a brick wall nicely laced with spider webs.

I made another mark in the gravel and plunged forward. I heard Kai through the foliage.

"This isn't fair!" I called. No answer.

Right, right, left, I counted. Here was another identical door. I hesitated before trying the latch. This one opened to another narrow lane. I left the door ajar after I passed through and turned toward what instinct told me should be the center of the maze. I stepped softly, hoping to catch Kai spying on me around each corner.

Some long, sneaky minutes later I reached yet another door. But there was an arc in the gravel that showed the door was recently opened. I studied the spot more carefully and concluded this was the same doorway I had been through before. Kai must have shut it behind me.

"Kai! That's enough! It's getting dark!"

"That door leads into a blind corner!" Kai called from what seemed to be several hedge-rows away. "Everybody falls for it!"

"Help me? Please?"

"Now, from that doorway, turn to your right, take the first left, then stay to your right!"

"Left, then one right?"

"To your right, then left and stay to the right!"

I took a few steps. "The first left?" I cried.

"Right!" Kai laughed.

I followed his voice and after a few turns the maze suddenly opened onto a grassy circle with a small fountain in the middle. Kai lounged against its blue-tiled side. He stood up when I appeared.

"Congratulations, love! You made it to the heart."

I folded my arms and pouted. I refused his embrace. "You shouldn't tease me like that."

"I was never far away."

"I know."

"And now we are safe. They say no evil spirits can find their way in here. And this circle is dedicated to the god Sybalo and his lover."

Kai took off his shirt. I turned my head away. He kissed my neck. I took a step. His fingertips caressed my shoulders. I closed my eyes and unfolded my arms. He wrapped himself around me from behind. I leaned into him, eagerly relenting. His hands slid over my body. I turned, and my dress fell away. In a quick flurry, we spread our clothes on the lawn for a bed. His warm weight pressed me into the soft earth. We rolled and tangled together, sweating, laughing. I pulled him to me with all my strength.

We listened to the trickling fountain beside us for a long time, until our breathing became light and soft again. Finally, I sat up on one elbow and traced a line down his chest.

"Getting in here is one thing. Do you know how to get us out?"

Kai put his hands behind his head. "Like I said, there's a trick to it. I'll show you, I promise."

I put my head on his chest and snuggled close. I listened to his heartbeat and we dozed a while. But the dreaminess ended abruptly when a bug in the lawn bit me. I yelped and jumped up. Kai, chuckling, gathered up our clothes, taking care to shake them out.

"This way," he said. He led me across the lawn and around a corner.

"No more trick doors," I fretted as he reached for a latch.

"Oh, you will like this one."

The secret tunnel through the hedges was dark, but it ran in a straight line out of the maze, undetectable from the twisting corridors on either side of it. Through a gate hidden from the outside by a screen of purple clematis, we stepped into the rose garden. The evening was still young, and Kai filled it for me with delicious abundance.

ANOTHER MOONLIT NIGHT, I sauntered with Kai toward the upstream tip of the island, sharing a narrow path bordering a pond. Across the lilies and reeds, the water swirled near the palace wall. This pond knew about the powerful Ma'rhu current just outside; standing on the bank, I could see the deep green water slowly eddy clockwise, building tiny drifts of flower petals against the cattails. Nothing in the garden was stagnant or ever entirely still. It moved and therefore sparkled. I took it as inspiration. And I took Kai's arm.

"Have I told you today that I love you?"

"Lots of ways."

"Can I tell you again?"

Kai shuffled his feet and glanced away.

"I love you."

He kissed my forehead. "Mmm. Thank you." We had this exact conversation as often as I felt like it. I guess he was never sure how to respond.

"Oh, here's the old boathouse!" Kai said abruptly. "Let me show you something."

Willow branches dripped to the ground, hiding a rugged wooden structure that huddled low and close to the pond.

A single long, slender boat hung just out of the water, suspended from stout beams by chains. It was partially covered by a faded tarp, sagging and threadbare with age. Its exposed keel, lacquered black, promised speed and stealth.

"In more dangerous times, my ancestors felt they needed an emergency escape." Kai smiled, pleased at the colorful history. "If the island were ever overrun, the family could dash out here, drop this boat into the water, get across the pond, slip under the outer wall through a hidden portal, and make their escape into the middle of the river."

"Did they ever use it?"

"The boat is still here, just in case," Kai grinned. "Look, the pulley is still greased."

I opened a cabinet, expecting to see oars or empty, dusty shelves. "Oh, dear."

"Hmm. I should have those polished." Kai laughed, hefting a fierce-looking sword from a rack in the cabinet. "This is the style preferred by the Kyornin in the late seventeenth century. I'm told my grandfather wanted to replace these with pistols, but my grandmother scolded him and made him leave the boathouse unchanged, for luck."

"Guess she was right."

"Look at this! Heeya!" Kai posed with a lance, jabbing at the doorway. The weapon had been leaning casually against the open-framed wall for more than a hundred years.

"Can't you imagine? A loyal servant would have leapt into the boat and used this to shove off into the pond, then held back their pursuers with this end!" He twirled the rusty tip and struck up another fighting pose.

"What's the matter?" he asked.

"I don't like it."

"That was real life."

"I know. Too real. It's not funny."

Kai frowned like a petulant little boy. He carefully replaced the lance in its spot against the wall. I studied the way a water lily hovered outside the shadow of the hanging boat's prow.

Kai tried again, conspiratorially.

"Here is one of the Kyornin's deepest secrets," Kai whispered. "It's probably bad luck for me to tell you."

"Then don't tell me."

"Oh, c'mon, look. This is great! A real trap door … here."

Kai lifted a plank out of the coarse boathouse floor. "For generations, we kept a treasure chest in here. Gold and jewels enough to bribe our way to safety. Probably enough to mount an army."

"All I see is dirt. Who got your treasure?"

"Times change," he shrugged. "My grandfather used it to subsidize improvements to the city. A good investment. More useful than antique gold coins."

"Not very romantic."

"Oh, but it was. He could have spent it on extra houses and books that gather dust. But Clan Kyornin always gives gifts to the future." He kicked the trap door back into place. "Practical gifts, like building the sewer system in Am'rha Sa in the 1850s. That is what he did."

"A sewer system. Now, that *is* romantic," I teased.

"Something a doctor should appreciate," Kai said, sounding hurt. "I mean romance like the stories of your knights in shining armor."

"King Arthur with a pipe wrench. That's you, all right."

"Now wait. You could be treating sprained ankles in a safe little town in … in Ohio, but instead, you're here."

"Of course! Kai, we are both hopeless romantics, and have no choice! That's why we belong together."

I remember this conversation so well because I remember feeling so uneasy about it. We left the boathouse and strolled slowly through the rose garden.

"I guess the difference is that I always try to do what I can for people right here and now," I said.

Kai nodded. "But if you don't plan for a future, how do you get there?"

"You can never know if you'll get there anyway."

"You know, this conversation is upside down! You are from the West, where there is no past and everyone lives for the future. I am from Takau, where everything runs in circles and hangs on the past."

"But you are full of dreams." I kissed him.

He sighed. "Breathing life into dreams," he said quietly.

"What?"

"That's what my father used to say about working on these fountains."

"Mmm. I like that."

"Say, you want to see how they work? We've had some of them drained for cleaning this week, but we can turn them back on now. More secrets."

"Oh, yes!"

I followed him along the path under the willows and behind the terraced pools below the Great Hall. Without another word, he led me down a mossy flagstone walkway. We came abruptly to a deeply recessed, Gothic doorway. Rust from the sagging hinges streaked the door like faded blood stains.

"More trick doors," I noted.

"The Waterhouse," Kai declared, and turned the immoderate latch.

The door opened to a corridor that ran deep into the palace wall. Kai lit a small, softly glowing lantern and led me inside. The stone around us was damp and slick. I balanced by running a finger along the slippery wall.

We entered a chamber where complex shadows enfolded the light. The centuries had given it the feel of a natural cavern. But, like a hollow under a tree tangled with roots, the chamber was veined with water pipes. And a living sound filled the room; not quite hissing, but not a roar and rumble either: It was the sound of water surging under pressure.

The Ma'rhu powered a waterwheel hidden under the eastern wall. The perpetually moaning wheel replenished cisterns within the palace foundation. By the hydraulic magic of Kai's forefathers, the water celebrated its freedom in the fountains and pools after coursing down from the cisterns through the Waterhouse and out through the secret arteries of the garden.

I took a deep breath. The air smelled rich with life, slightly salty, hinting of fish but tempered with sunshine and a northern breeze. I could taste the river where it waited in the reeds and the flavor of the deep, roiling flood midstream, as if these qualities had been distilled into a fine, clear, sweet wine. And it intoxicated me.

"These old pipes, you can feel the pressure inside," said Kai. He spoke softly, yet his voice echoed around the chamber.

"Swell," I said, just to hear my own voice whisper back at me.

A ten-inch pipe ran waist high through the room. I laid my hand on the iron and felt it throbbing. Kai smiled.

"These two," he said, twisting twin valves overhead, "are the nymphs above the rose garden."

"And this?" I asked, daringly grabbing a large crank with both hands.

"Not so fast! That's the plume over the main pool." He pried my hands off the crank. When he touched me, I shivered. A sweet escape from the sleepy heat outside.

"First, we have to build up some pressure."

"Oh, of course."

Kai leaned his weight into a valve that complained loudly as he turned it. I watched the muscles flex in his arms and back.

"This one," he said with a grunt, "turns everything inward to the gardens. Gives us the power we need."

I took another deep breath.

"We call these 'ticklers,'" Kai explained, as he flicked down the levers on seven small pipes that wove their way between the main lines and into the wall. "So the stream at the front gate is starting to flow. And those goddesses tucked into the grotto are getting wet."

We paused to listen to the changing timbre of the pulsing water around us. I looked at Kai and ran my tongue across my moist lips. His eyes flashed back at me.

"Together," he said, nodding to an array of pipes that ran parallel to the floor. It made the staggered valves look like notes on a sheet of music. "These get all the demons up around the arbor and the jets around the pavilions."

"Oh, good!" I said, and my sultry voice echoed back to me. In a flurry of hands and laughter, we turned all the valves together.

"Now turn on the dragon," Kai said. "It's that gate valve there. Push it all the way."

He handed me a long handle and I fitted it into a socket. I gripped the handle, greased against rust, and leaned into it with all my weight until it stood erect and I felt the flood surge through the line. I let out a whoop. Kai threw back his head and laughed with me. Our voices merged in the dark and came back to tease us.

Slowly, I backed into a soft corner. Kai's hands whispered over my body. I put my cheek on his shoulder. His skin glistened. My trembling hands tore at our clothes. He pinned me to the wall and held me up as we made love, rocking, gasping, biting, clinging, merging.

LONG AFTER DARK ONE AUGUST NIGHT, Magra and I stood at the bedside of a skeletal old man whose digestive tract was failing him. His home was little more than a hole carved in a wall. All his earthly possessions fit in a bundle he used for a pillow.

"Why," I whispered, "are we using the same mixture for him as we used for the pregnant girl this afternoon?"

Then I started to laugh. Choking back waves of giggles, I didn't dare look up. I knew Magra was giving me her most disapproving scowl. This, of course, made me laugh harder. It was no use. This just happened sometimes. I thought of how funny it was that I was laughing, foolishly, here in this sad, cliffside cell, standing over an old man in embarrassed discomfort. I laughed harder.

"Out!" Magra hissed. "Outside!"

I nodded, but then I glanced up and met Magra's withering glare. I don't know why that set me off again.

Fortunately, laughter is terribly contagious. As I turned to escape, the old man grabbed my arm with startling forcefulness. A huge, nearly toothless grin lit his face. Our eyes met and we guffawed together.

He had no idea why we were laughing either, but he was Rizha, and poor, and he surely knew how precious laughter is. We held hands and chortled until tears poured down our cheeks.

Magra was not utterly immune. She crossed her arms and shook her head, trying to look stern, though she struggled against a smile. She stood immobile like a tree stump in the near dark. That idea, unfortunately, struck me as very funny.

Eventually, the old man's laughter decayed into hacking and gasping. Unable to speak, he motioned to me he would be all right. I staggered outside, gulping the night air to regain some control of myself.

Magra came out and waited beside me.

"They are herbs for the stomach," she muttered. "And in any case the only herbs we have left."

"Oh, I know. I know. Don't be angry, Magra." I wiped my eyes. "No harm done." I took a deep breath. "I guess I should go home."

Magra watched me with a look on her crinkled face somewhere between forgiveness and exasperation.

"Enough for tonight," she agreed.

"I will be in the clinic all morning," I said.

"But then we continue, here in Rhu'mora," Magra insisted. I nodded. I was slow to recognize that Magra constantly drove me to the limits of my stamina. In Magra I met the uncompromising ideal of service and devotion; though she may eventually save the world, she consumes your soul.

She evaporated into the dark street. And I walked smiling into the night.

FINALLY, THE RAIN STOPPED. The air was distinctly different. A wispy fog lilted over the riverbank and softened the hard edges of the scrapwood roofs and broken tiles. It got tangled in the few scraggly elms hiding between the rows of shacks, and it poured along the eroded streets. The fog eclipsed the gas lights of Am'rha Sa across the river, relieving the residents of the slums from the constant glittering reminder of their station in life.

That night, standing outside the clinic, I mentioned this insulating quality of the fog to Tor.

"The Rizha word for this fog says 'fog-dance,'" he answered. "We keep a style of song for this time. Played only when the fog-dance comes in."

"Oh, that's wonderful. I'd love to hear it."

Tor, as always, took my oblique request as a problem to be solved. He frowned for a moment, blinked, then nodded his head.

"I know who to ask. I will learn where they plan to dance tomorrow night," he declared.

With a solution in his mind, Tor said nothing more about it. We stood quietly for a few restful minutes, watching the fog-dance wrap around the crumbling neighborhood. A child's cry called us back to work inside.

The next night, Tor led me and Kai to a small plaza tucked against the hillside high above the river. We wound through a labyrinth of alleys to get there. I recognized the neighborhood. Nothing had changed here for centuries, and life still revolved around the drinking well.

"Not my place," Tor said, and left us. I didn't question him.

Kai was quiet and alert. I stood with him at the end of a narrow alley and peered through the fog.

Wrapped around the well, a tight knot of musicians played with abandon. Before us, a swarm of women swirled by. The strings of a yala seduced them and the flutes teased them with suggestive harmonies. Then the men pounded past, hard on the drum beat, laughing with the syncopation.

I glanced at Kai. He was intent on the drums' conversation. I tried to follow. Just as I thought I found the pattern with my primitive Western sense of rhythm, it flowed into something other, and more hypnotic. A phrase from the high singing drums rang out. A chorus of throaty midrange drums answered. Below these droned a deep heartbeat drum. It was not content to keep time, but happily jumped in with unexpected thunder. The yala, its voice unearthly and soulful, kept its poignant commentary, exuberant for a turn, then mournful, then lyrical again. The flutes rose and fell, vanished and re-entered in tight harmony as if their voices were chained together. All these rose above the chattering of the bead rattles gamely carried by the young children who mimicked the grown-ups in a tight orbit around the musicians.

I let go. I leapt in with the dark women as they swept near. I was barefoot with them. They welcomed me with knowing laughter. It felt like we were swimming inside the drums. My Rizha friends, completely free from puritan inhibitions, moved from the hips, swinging and thrusting. After a few moments, my foxtrot steps dissolved, then my culture fell away and I was not American, not Rizha, but purely woman, barefoot, dancing.

As the women flowed with the rhythm, the men stomped to the beat. Together we were the music in motion. We whistled and shouted fiercely if the men came near to touching, then surged in pursuit as they howled and pounded away.

The first turn around the plaza, I saw Kai still standing at the head of the alley. The next time around he was gone. I feared for a moment he must have left me. But the tempo rose and then there was nothing but dance.

I fell into the percussive embrace. The women moved their arms like snakes or swept them down as if caressing a man's chest. I heard hissing and little kissing sounds all around me. Then a defiant scream swept through us. Flying hair brushed my face.

On a cue I felt but didn't hear, the women lifted their arms and the men poured in among us. Now there was a single drum, fast and fierce, building an unbearable tension as we all held our ground.

Flutes called out, and the yala's harmonies tumbled through the crowd. All at once and not a moment too soon, the drums flew into a frenzy.

Spinning and weaving in pairs, in groups, in lines, and in circles, we poured around the plaza. We circled in chorus like a flock of birds dipping and weaving in the wind. I was caught up in the center. I clapped with the children. I whirled with the women. I stomped with the men. I smelled perfume and sweat. We flew around the plaza again.

Abruptly, Kai stood before me, drenched in sweat. It seemed he didn't recognize me. Trance-like and fluid, he was dancing with every woman on the plaza at once. Then our eyes met. He reached out his hand, nearly but not touching, and followed the contours of my swaying body. He danced backwards, pouring around others, keeping his gaze locked on me. We circled the plaza. His feet were everywhere with the racing drums. He was liquid. He was magnificent. Other dancers began to notice, and more, until Kai spun around the plaza in a space of his own, with all the dancers pulled along as if by gravity. I followed like a moon.

I don't know how long this went on. I remember at some point the musicians ran through three false endings, built to a fierce crescendo, and finally slammed to a precise and shocking silence. Most of the dancers staggered around aimlessly for several minutes. They whistled and laughed with that ineffable satisfaction only the wild communion of music affords. Everyone acknowledged Kai with respect, and raised their eyebrows at me, laughing about what an inspiration I was. I laughed, too.

There were line dances and circle dances. There were jugs of cool mint tea. There were oranges and herb cakes and a jar of horrible, potent liquor. There was much merriment at my expense when I took a sip and spat it out, gasping. Haughty young men boasted, earning taunts from their defiant women.

The two of us eventually left the plaza, hearing the music pick up again behind us. Without a word, we walked down to the river. Shrouded by the fog, the Kyornin's boat waited for us. The mist wrapped the garden in cool stillness. We tacitly chose the silver gazebo. Kai didn't wait to get all my clothes off before pulling me into the pillows. Beneath him, my body recalled the dance. Soon after our loving, still without a spoken word between us, he fell asleep in my arms.

7

As Takau turns to the dark of the year, Mortash'rhondí awakens. It is his shadow that shortens the days. When he awakens, he is hungry. He reaches into the heavens with his terrible claws and snatches stars, the traveling souls, out of the fabric of the sky. He drops them into his broad, black, shallow bowl. Perhaps you have seen it: Sometimes the bowl blocks the light from the moon.

Mortash'rhondí eats souls for breakfast. He greedily pops each soul into his snarling maw, grasping them one by one like grains of rice between his yellow claws. He savors each one. A dozen demons surround and forever pester him. They try to snatch choice morsels from his bowl. Mortash'rhondí slaps off their heads with a grunt. The demons flounder about until they grow new heads, then return, ever hungrier and more daring. The old heads, still snapping their teeth, roll around in the dark, often under children's beds.

As autumn descends, the Rizha love to tell macabre tales about Mortash'rhondí, the Eater of Souls. But sometimes Mortash'rhondí comes down and suddenly lifts the blanket of the Earth, looking for the dead. He rips the world with his claws. You hear his awful growling. Many stars fall in his bowl.

FOR SOME REASON, I didn't linger in the evening market. I didn't stop to discuss the freshness of the fruit with Syrka. I didn't pause under the old guild house arches to study the crafts on display from the foothills. That evening, I returned home directly, so I was standing in the kitchen when it hit.

An impossibly low rumble transfixed the whole world. I felt the vibration come up through the floor. The stove rattled. I took one step.

The floor heaved and dropped, then kicked again … and again. In a cloud of dust with pieces of the ceiling clattering to the floor around me, I crawled on hands and knees toward the door. I heard a grinding crash behind me.

Braced in the doorway, I watched the cobbled avenue ripple like water. Even the air shuddered. To my right, the single marble pillar at the doorway of the house next door snapped like a brittle stick. The balcony above it collapsed across the doorway. But I had only a moment to wonder who was trapped inside.

"Look out!" I cried, stupidly in English.

Two women, clutching babies to their chests, crouched in the middle of the street, fighting for balance. They saw me point at something behind them. Across the street, a stone façade swayed and shivered. Instinctively, the women lunged toward me. The neighboring building buckled, and the wall tumbled into the street behind them.

"Stop it! Stop!" I screamed at the Earth. The ground pitched and rolled. The thunder drowned my voice. A cloud of smoke and dust poured down the hill.

They say it lasted fifteen seconds. Every second stretched for a lifetime. Every second claimed lives. It was more than long enough to shatter the world we had known.

Then, stillness. The quake was followed by the most awful stillness. I held my breath. Smoke hovered. I looked into the eyes of a terrified little girl hugging a straw doll.

Nearby, a timber snapped. I coughed. A baby wailed. Up the street, a man screamed in anguish. I saw him dive into a pile of rubble, digging furiously. People began running in all directions.

I turned around. The clinic was still standing, though I could see the sky through a gaping hole in the roof. The two patients who had been inside had flown from their beds and gotten out ahead of me.

They were gone. Without thinking, I ran into the kitchen, where I had left my field bag.

I paused just a moment when I saw the back room, my bedroom. The collapsed roof buried the bed and my moldy books. I slung my satchel over my shoulder. As I gathered up what medicine vials and ether had not shattered on the floor, the first aftershock hit. A beam across the middle of the ceiling pulled loose. It swung down, smashed a bed, and splintered. I got the message. I grabbed my field bag and clamored back to the door through the choking dust.

"HOLD IT HERE. KEEP PRESSURE right here to stop the bleeding. You will be okay," I told the boy. About twelve years old, he had big, alert, brown eyes. Blood soaked through the rag he held to his temple. He tried to get up. "No, you've got to lie down. You'll get dizzy, and that's no fun." He would probably pass out, actually. And there was no one to watch him.

"You are very brave," I assured the next child. "How old are you? Eight? You are such a big boy for eight years." I tried to keep talking in a soothing voice — it didn't much matter what I said, or even if I lapsed into English — while I inspected wounds.

"I need to take a look at you, okay?"

I gently lifted the dirty blanket off the ashen-faced boy's legs. I swallowed hard.

"Such a brave boy," I repeated. His left foot sagged limply on the hard ground at a grotesque angle to his leg.

"Where are your parents?" I asked slowly.

The boy, quivering, stared at me. I asked again.

"He lives down there," said the older boy. He pointed down the hill — toward the fire.

AROUND ME, DEATH'S DOOR FILLED with a shocked swarm of people escaping to the only open ground. The toppled shanties of Am'rha Bo burned below us. The funeral pyres lay still and cold, but smoke and stench choked the night.

"Tor!"

"I knew to find you here."

"I'm so glad to see you! Are you all right?"

Tor didn't bother answering. He gently set down his end of a charred plank that he and a burly young man with soot-covered clothes had used as a stretcher to carry a woman up the hill. She had both arms wrapped in rags. In the faint oil-lamp light, I saw her face was red with blisters.

"The plaza, is it still burning?" I asked Tor.

"Stopped at the ravine. Still burning near the café."

"Hold that lamp closer for a moment, will you?"

I didn't need to look beyond her elbows under the rags. I reached for my field bag. "Are there many more like this?"

"We are going back now," Tor said.

"I'll stay in this area. So you can find me. Be careful."

The young man tucked the plank under his arm and disappeared with Tor into the night.

I SEIZED ON EVERY CRY in the shadows around me. I counted the hours by the smoke-shrouded moon. I fumbled with sooty bandages.

The rocky ground heaved. Everyone gasped. Some screamed. The aftershocks rolled under us again and again. The early ones hit nearly as hard as the first quake, but surprise retreats into fear. They came like painful memories to slap down our faltering courage. One knocked me to my hands and knees. Walls weakened by the first quake fell into the streets. Cracks at our feet widened. Already torn off their foundations, tenements toppled down ravines. New fires erupted. Charred skeletons of burnt buildings collapsed. I tried to smile some comfort into terrified eyes.

"HAVE YOU SEEN MY WIFE? A little woman, round as a barrel. A gray streak in her hair. High voice. Have you seen her?"

"No, I'm sorry. But it's dark up here. Have you checked with that group over there?"

"They're from the brass market; they don't know anyone. She should be up here. Where else would she be? I don't understand."

The rail-thin old man clutched a limp shawl against his chest. He shivered, though the night air was tepid and still.

"I don't understand," he rambled. "I need to tell her about the house."

"Maybe you should go wait near your house."

"She must be looking for that old cat again. Have you seen my wife?"

The old man wandered into the dark.

I SHOOK MY HEAD AND BLINKED BACK my heavy eyelids. I finished wrapping a young man's head and helped him lie back on the ground.

"Keep still," I told him, then looked up.

"I'm sorry, Tor. Say that again."

"That woman. The first one we carried."

"Oh, yeah. Is she still sleeping?"

"She stopped breathing."

I sat back on my heels. "We did what we could, Tor."

"Yes."

"You have saved many lives tonight."

He looked into the shadowy crowd around us. "Yes."

I slowly got to my feet. I wanted to hug him. I wanted to scream. More than anything, I wanted to sleep. Instead, I quickly surveyed the murky scene around me. "I think these lamps are almost dry. Could you … ?"

"No more oil. We could light a fire."

I tried to read his face in the shadows.

"A fire." I managed a smile. "You know, it will be morning soon. We could take a break. Just for a little while."

"Yes."

"WHAT ARE YOU DOING HERE?"

"Trying to help," said Kai, standing in the middle of the room with a baby in his arms. He studied me. "I'm glad to see you."

"Oh. Yeah." I stumbled toward the kitchen. We were in the Café Royale, the only building that seemed sturdy enough to be safe. I had converted it into an emergency ward.

"I heard you were up on the hill," Kai said.

Nodding absently, I spooned some cold rice into my mouth.

"How much sleep have you gotten in the last two days?" he asked.

"Oh, a couple of hours, I guess."

"Katherine, you can't help people if you kill yourself."

"I don't need any patronizing lectures from you right now."

I turned to Tor, who had followed me in. He carried a young burn victim. "Maybe this mat for her. We'll get that woman a place near the door," I said.

"Kath, that woman has been blinded. This is her baby. Tor, talk to the man on the end there; he's breathing better now. I'm sure he'll give up his mat for the girl."

Tor nodded, glanced at me, and carried his whimpering burden over to the bed near the door. I felt myself about to cry. I straightened my shoulders.

"I'm sorry, Kai. Guess I'm tired."

Kai smiled. "Listen. Tlia said she'd be back in an hour or so, after checking on her family. Their house was spared, she said. So we've got things covered here. Why don't you go back to the store room — it's empty — and get some sleep?"

I slumped against the doorway. "How's the island?"

"Everything is on the floor. A few cracks. Nothing," he said, holding the baby in one arm and offering me a blanket.

"Surprised you know about babies," I muttered.

"God, I don't," he smiled again. "Get some rest."

AM'RHA BO BECAME A CITY OF REFUGEES. People were afraid to sleep under a roof, so they camped in any open space. Around the edge of Death's Door, soft smoke from cooking fires climbed in segregated columns bordering the renewed funeral pyres. Families huddled in the tiny plazas at intersections along the hillside, though their rescued household possessions sat like market day before the swarms of newly homeless who passed by. Hundreds built crude shelters along the waterfront. But no one sat under the arches of the old guild hall. It stood remarkably unscathed; people said its carved boats helped the building roll with the waves. But why take the chance, they muttered, glancing over their shoulders at the rubble of collapsed buildings nearby.

The ground could not be trusted, so the water became refuge for many. The Ma'rhu always rippled and rolled, and in her constancy was comfort. So, if one family member owned or worked on a moored boat, the whole clan crowded onto the deck. A tangle of cargo barges lashed together became a little floating city, complete with markets, kitchens, altars, and a dispute tribunal. The barge captains extorted rent from all on board, thereby making good money without facing the risks of trade and travel along the river. For the displaced families on the river, living conditions were cramped, dirty, tedious, and edged with despair, but they never felt the aftershocks.

I continued to work among the clans scattered across the huge, devastated space in front of the Café Royale. All the stalls and shanties burned during that first hellish night. A few charred posts marked lines where alleys had run. My eye fell on a burnt corner of a carpet, a blackened brass plate, the stub of a table leg.

The first three days, we pulled bodies from the wreckage. I was the only one who kept a list of people reported missing. Looking for children and wives and husbands, people methodically worked their way down a row of shrouded corpses. Some horrors are best left undocumented here; they are written in lingering private nightmares.

Merchants and shopkeepers squatted in circles in the ashes. They rarely spoke among themselves. They made no effort to rebuild or assist others. They appeared to be waiting. It is a common affliction in lands of perpetual poverty and disaster. I, too, wished we could just hunker down together in silent circles until we all woke up again.

Children don't wait. They started games among the ruins. They went treasure hunting. With sooty hands and runny noses, they formed gangs and worked themselves into noisy excitement over childish concerns. Until the Earth shook again. Or until night fell, when they woke screaming from their dreams.

Small miracles bless every disaster. Two toddlers, presumed dead, returned — unscathed and well-fed by strangers — to their mother. Rescuers pulled a boy, thirsty but uninjured, from a mountain of rubble where he had been trapped under a stout table for days. A young man I knew rushed back from the foothills, only to find his home reduced to ruins. But his despair vanished in a heartbeat as his new bride greeted him in the street. A moment before the quake hit, she had gone to borrow an egg at the house next door, and their neighbor's house had not collapsed.

I treated the sick and injured among two rival clans that found comfort in familiarity. They forgot their feud when the quake became their common enemy. They acted as though they had just invented the concept of cooperation. To these old warring tribes, it was indeed a new idea.

Generosity steps forward in disaster, too. Clans freely shared perishable foods in the streets. A team of boisterous young men roamed through the neighborhoods, but they were not looting damaged shops and homes. Instead, they opened paths down shattered alleys and cleared rubble from doorways.

After about a week, survivors grew angry. Oh, they were angry with Tokmol, of course, for keeping residents out of areas where buildings or hillsides were likely to collapse. People, practiced at surviving with almost nothing, had to get by with even less. They were angry at God. At whichever manifestation of God was nearest at hand. They were angry at their homes for falling down, angry for being left behind by those who had been killed, and angry at the ground under their feet. The ground, without anger or compassion, kept rumbling. Aftershocks kept us all on edge and sleepless. We were all furious that Mortash'rhondí stole from us the basic right to walk on solid ground.

The fire after the quake razed everything on the flat ground in front of the café. It burned until it was frustrated by a ring of old stone buildings that now, stripped naked, betrayed their relation to the historic architecture of Am'rha Sa. Stately rows of arches, boarded over until burned bare, faced each other across the broad open space at my left and right as I stood in the café doorway. And directly across from me, multi-leveled tenements stepped down the slope on sturdy foundations toward the river. It was apparent now this had indeed been a grandly conceived plaza slowly overrun by the expediencies of poverty.

For weeks after the quake, though, it was for us a poorly managed disaster area. We worked without any aid from outside the slums. I could not understand why absolutely no assistance reached us. The explanation came while I interviewed a distraught, malnourished woman carried to me on a stretcher.

"What is she saying? I can't understand her dialect."

"Says her husband is across the Ma'rhu. Can't get back," Tor translated.

"Aren't the ferries running?"

"No," Tor said. "Am'rha Sa is afraid of looters."

I stared at him. "You mean we're completely cut off from the east bank? They think people over here are going to take the ferry across for an afternoon of looting?"

Tor gestured with empty hands. "Police along the bank. No boats allowed."

"They have all the food and medical supplies for the region."

"Yes."

"They probably don't have nearly as much damage or injury."

"Strong buildings. Little damage. Of course."

I slumped into a café chair. "It is too easy to cut us off from the rest of the country."

Tor nodded. "You know," I said, "if they don't open supply lines, there will be riots."

"Every few years, there is a revolt. Like the monsoon coming and going. I think it changes nothing."

"The army should bring us supplies," I fretted.

Tor considered this an absurd notion. "The army only brings supplies for the army."

"That should change," I declared.

Tor shook his head like he did during Tlia's stories. "Water flows downhill," he said, and left me alone to fume about injustice and the lack of canvas for making tents.

"KAI, THIS MAKES A DOZEN CASES. All near here."

"Same symptoms?"

"Dizziness, nausea, gross diarrhea. Textbook. Next come seizures, lethargy. Then the pulse fades, body temperature drops, and they'll turn blue. I don't want to see it. Usually fatal."

"A cure?" Kai asked.

"For cholera? No."

"How is it transmitted?"

I looked up from my notes. "You know, we need you here," I said.

Kai looked puzzled.

"Everyone has been blaming gods or guildmasters or one myth or another for the quake. For everything. But you ask a good, educated question," I smiled. "I love you."

"You're too tired again."

"You're right, I am. Well, it's in the water. Transmission of the *Vibrio cholerae* bacillus usually comes from polluted water."

"The district well … "

"By the latrines."

"That's thousands of people!"

"Right," I nodded.

"We've got to close it off. Without causing a riot."

"We'll explain it to the police."

"But we'll also have to find another water source," Kai scowled. "Any ideas?"

"That's down my line, I guess. I'll think of something."

"I'm sure you will," I said.

"What else can we do?"

"Wash our hands. With clean water."

"I mean ... "

"I know. I'm sorry. First, let's make some warning signs we can post at the well."

"Have to be in several dialects," Kai nodded.

"Most can't read. Is there a symbol we can use?"

"Ah, sure!" Kai drew a jagged shape with a crescent at the bottom and an angry eye at the top. "That's the sign of Mortash'rhondí. The skull and crossbones of Takau. Everyone will get the message. Find someone who can draw it better than that," he chuckled.

"That's perfect. Okay, there's no time to lose. I'll have Tor find some small boards and paint."

The door rattled. We froze. The walls shivered and the ground growled again as yet another aftershock rumbled around us. We waited to see if it would pass, or if we had to leap into a doorway for safety, or if it would be a big one, bringing yet more destruction. This one caused streams of dust to pour from the cracked roof overhead, then abruptly departed, leaving that breathless silence behind. I looked at Kai. He touched my shoulder. I sighed wearily, not quite capable of a smile.

"Got to keep moving," I said to myself.

POLICE OFFICERS PLOUGHED into the crowd, jabbing people with their batons.

"Back off now! Back off! Break it up!"

Tokmol followed behind them, like a shepherd directing his dogs. The crowd gave way and a space opened around the well as Tokmol stepped up to the low stone platform. He squinted momentarily at one of my signs, then tore it down.

I pushed forward.

"Are you crazy?" I cried. "Everyone has to know this well is contaminated! I have a dozen confirmed cases, all from this source!"

Tokmol turned to me with a stony expression betrayed by his smoldering eyes.

"So, you're behind this?"

"I identified a known vector for cholera, yes."

"You had no authority to post these signs."

"Oh, for … I'm a doctor. I save lives if I can."

"Look at this crowd. It could break into a mob any moment. Then how many lives will be lost?"

"If they're angry, it's over the way they've been treated by your men," I snapped.

Tokmol ignored me. Instead, he reached for the second sign. Kai stepped in front of him.

"We need to keep the signs posted," Kai said quietly.

"Who the hell are you?"

"You'd be surprised."

"Out of the way. Now!"

"No."

Tokmol drew himself back like a snake about to strike. He signaled his men with a flick of his wrist. One officer knocked me aside with a blow to my sternum. Another jumped Kai, threw him to the ground face first, and planted a knee in his back. Tokmol tore down the sign.

Behind us, shouts of protest shot through the crowd. But three of Tokmol's men carried rifles, and raised them now. The crowd shrank back, forming wary clusters hissing with muffled complaints. The officers gathered around us in a tight formation, like a school of fish that senses a shark nearby.

"Listen," I said.

"We've had a terrible disaster," Tokmol interrupted, returning to his most exasperating tone of voice. "We are both doing all we can for these people, I am sure. But you have to accept the need to keep dangerous crowds under control."

I watched Kai pull himself to his knees, visually examining him for injuries, while I tried to calculate my response to Tokmol's assault. Tokmol watched my expression.

"You will report to me with legitimate public health concerns before you take drastic actions again."

"You call posting a sign a drastic action?"

"You've created a dangerous situation."

I was taller than Tokmol by several inches when I stepped close to him.

"So I'm to wait weeks while people are dying because you have paperwork to fill out?"

Tokmol neither retreated nor flinched as I glowered down at him. But he watched the angry crowd. Another dozen men in khaki uniforms, armed, carved a path toward us.

"You are taking me for a petty dictator," Tokmol said. His affected British accent made my skin crawl. "I will gladly consider your recommendations and take appropriate, swift action. But I will keep control here."

"So quarantine this well."

"As soon as an alternate water source is identified."

Kai, standing again, spoke from over Tokmol's shoulder.

"Call in wagons with barrels of drinking water from Am'rha Sa."

Tokmol shook his head, but didn't turn toward Kai.

"Impossible."

"Why?" I demanded.

"For how many? And for how long? It's impossible. You should have thought of that before you posted your signs."

"I was thinking of protecting people."

"I will remind you once more this is not your America."

"That's for damn sure!"

"But it is my Am'rha Bo," said Kai. "And I will see to it that we have a source of fresh water here right away."

Now Tokmol turned. He studied Kai, noting his unbowed stance and his tailored shirt.

"From where?"

"We'll pipe it down from the Esh'rhu, where it flows under the northern highway about two miles from here. We'll run it along the road as far as we can, then cut along the hillside."

"When did you ...?" I stammered. Kai looked at me.

"Thought of it on our way up here," he shrugged.

"That will take some time," Tokmol said, memorizing Kai's face.

"That's why we'll need your help organizing some kind of water brigade, maybe from the Rhu'mora district. Even that would be better than trying to filter river water near the docks. And we will need to keep this well closed."

Rhu'mora, where Magra and I spent much of our time, was

downriver on the Ma'rhu bank where people dug into the cliffs for shelter. The area got its water from a gritty seep not far from the old river guild house.

"A reasonable solution," Tokmol nodded.

"And we need to keep track of how many people show the symptoms," I added. "And organize teams to educate the whole district about the disease, and … "

"We must work within our resources," Tokmol declared. "We can tell if more people suddenly are ill."

"How? By counting funeral pyres on the hill?"

Tokmol flared. "Sick people are your business."

"Of course, sick people don't start riots," I snapped. "And that's all you care about."

"That comes first here, yes," he said, more quietly. A large swarm of young men in the crowd was growing impatient with the stand-off. Suddenly, Tokmol spun about.

"We'll make the arrangements in the morning."

He signaled his men.

"What about the signs?" I asked.

"Only the Commissioner's office posts signs."

I started to protest again. Kai raised his hand to stop me. Tokmol marched away. I snarled at him. Kai stepped closer.

"Word is out now, Kath," he said, gingerly touching his bruised cheek. "No one will use the well after this."

"I hope you're right."

Tokmol and his men pushed out in teams like a slow explosion radiating out from where we stood. They broke up the knots of people who had been watching us. When Tokmol looked back over his shoulder and gave us a menacing jerk of his head, I took an angry step forward. Kai grabbed my arm. I relented.

"You're quite the diplomat," I said.

"That ground is hard. It hurts."

"Why didn't he recognize you?"

"Context. These clothes. And I haven't spoken before the Council very often," Kai whispered. "To his credit, Tokmol avoids those meetings, too!"

"But now he will check into it."

"Oh, yes, he'll check. He'll know."

It felt to me like another disaster about to happen, but Kai looked unconcerned. It was in any case a problem for which I had no answers, so I turned instinctively back to crises I could work on. "Can you really pipe water from up north?"

"A family tradition. We'll see."

There was still a circle of people near the well. They were watching the police push across the plaza. They were also watching us.

"Guess we had better get out of here."

"I'm glad you think so."

THE NEXT MORNING, when we climbed back up to the burnt plaza to negotiate with Tokmol again, we found new signs posted at the well, with neatly printed letters and Mortash'rhondí symbols.

"A thin victory, to be sure," I said, "but enough for me."

"Tremendous progress, considering," Kai nodded. "I think we'll see barrels of fresh water arrive from Rhu'mora today, too. He recognized the need for it."

"Why is it that everything has to be made harder than necessary?"

Kai smiled. "This is Takau! Someday, all this will make a good story."

"Well, I'm ready for the next chapter," I groaned. "Never mind 'someday.' People are suffering now."

"But suffering less because of us."

"Seems like everyone is fighting me, even after all this," I said, waving vaguely at the well.

"Everyone?" asked Kai with impatience slipping into his voice.

I stared blankly at the quarantine signs, letting him wait for an answer that didn't come.

"Ma'rhu ta yalathé," Kai said. We left together, but without another word.

8

A blur of people, crushed together, swarmed toward me. I ran hard, fighting for every stride. Hundreds of voices roared in my head. I ran into a blinding fog and the city faded away. But the crowd followed me. The fog glowed red. Spinning slowly like autumn leaves off a tree, sleeping faces fell away toward deep water far below me. I staggered from the feeling of a dizzy height. If I stopped, I'd be crushed. If I kept running, I'd fall into the void.

A small aftershock woke me. Sitting up, drenched in sweat, I couldn't remember what happened next. I rubbed my eyes. Shaking my head, I decided if dreams fade from consciousness so quickly, they cannot mean anything. Anyway, the first light of dawn framed the window.

WE STOOD IN A ROW UNDER the overhang of the Café Royale. Tor stoked the stove while I served scoops of rice. Tlia chopped onions. Kai arrived with a large crate of smelly cabbage-like vegetables.

"A little brown on the edges, but still good, mostly," he declared.

"That's great, dear," said Tlia. She set to work, dicing the cabbages with blazing speed. Kai laughed, unable to keep up with her.

A line of hungry people stretched across the bare, sooty plaza. I had heard rumors about a few clans struggling to survive without even one full meal a day, so I thought we could help tide them over. I underestimated the need. Now, from our makeshift field kitchen, I could not see the end of the line. Tokmol's men kept the ragged families in one long, lethargic column; necessary for crowd control, the police argued.

I shifted to a full pot of rice.

"Tlia was telling me stories about the Kyornin," I said.

"Oh?" said Kai. He gave me a furtive glance.

"Well it's all true, dear." Tlia never needed much prodding to tell stories. "Am'rha Bo was just a tiny fishing village. The River Guild controlled the river and its islands. But the Kyornin made a deal with the Council. If the Kyornin could stop the monsoon floods in Am'rha Sa, his clan would be granted the rights to the islands in the Ma'rhu as reward."

Tlia never paused between cabbages. The line of hungry people never got shorter. I shoveled rice and listened. Kai worked hard to keep up.

"The Kyornin built new roads with tunnels under them to catch the water. If you go over there you can see them, with little mouths in the street, can't you dear?"

"Not old enough," Tor frowned.

"That's right, Tlia," Kai complained. "The sewer system in Am'rha Sa is only about one hundred years old. I think the island gardens of the Kyornin are much older than that."

"Of course, dear! They've rebuilt Am'rha Sa many times since. That's why it is called the 'new city.' I'm talking about Takau in the old dynasties. The time poets sing about. Long before Europeans. You must know those stories from books, don't you dear?"

"A little. Most of my books are about building things," Kai said. I watched him. Kai was hiding his concern. After all, if Tlia suspected his identity, his secret would be out. Then, at the least, everyone would constantly fawn over him for favors, and his hard-won relationships in the Am'rha Bo community would get mired in formality. More seriously, any member of the Council — and certainly one with the mythic reputation of clan Kyornin — would be a prime target for kidnapping or murder by the increasingly hostile mountain clans. Kai could never safely set foot in Am'rha Bo again.

"What else did the Kyornin do?" I asked, to get her back to her tale.

"He made the good water flow uphill or wherever he wanted," Tlia declared. She brandished her knife, as if daring anyone to question her authority. Tor shook his head. Kai smiled. Again, I encouraged her to continue.

"So the Council gave the Kyornin the islands. They say the River Guild has never gotten over it. But that's when the Kyornin built the palace out there. Here you go, dear, but you need a little more oil in the pan before you fry this."

"Okay," Kai grinned.

"We'll throw it right in with the rice. They'll like that."

"Okay. But what about Am'rha Bo?"

Tlia didn't miss a beat, starting on another batch of cabbages.

"Well, people came from all over the country to work on the palace. They cut all the stones for the walls right here where we're standing. They say the Kyornin made this whole area flat so people could work through the monsoon."

"Then the people stayed on?" asked Kai.

"That's right, dear. Of course, the palace and all those gardens took lifetimes to build. So over the years the workers built their own houses and New Year's towers. And here we are." Tlia wiped her brow. "That's ready for the rice, dear. Just throw it in. This little girl will be the first lucky one."

"Interesting story," Kai muttered.

"All true, dear. People in Am'rha Sa forget the past. But over here, nothing changes, so the past is still with us."

After struggling with the stove, Tlia launched into other family histories. But I was intent on making a quick medical diagnosis of each person who held up a bowl for a meager portion of rice and vegetables.

Eventually, our rations ran out. The line of people with empty bowls dissipated without complaint. But just as we were packing up our mobile kitchen, another aftershock rolled under our feet. I watched the plaza ripple like a lake. Then the eerie silence returned. People turned to see how I would react, so I tried to stay very calm. I forced a smile back onto my face. We cheerfully carried our kitchen supplies inside the café building.

That evening, I bid Kai goodnight at the door.

"I hear the regular ferries are running again," I said.

"They've opened the Am'rha Sa docks. And on this side, it looks like families are moving off the barges. Things are settling back to normal."

"Can't go back," I said.

"Forward is fine," Kai answered. He gave me a concerned look that softened to a smile. "Hey," he said. "Come out with me to the garden tonight."

"I'm sorry, I can't. I have to be up early tomorrow."

He nodded. I kissed him. He slipped down to the river alone.

SEVERAL WEARY DAYS LATER, I ran into Kai on the northern edge of the plaza, where he was working with a survey crew. He drew me aside. It was a gentle day, with a breeze from the north, yet I felt heavy and anxious. Kai seemed pensive. I was afraid he was about to announce some new tragedy.

"Kath."

"Tell me."

"I checked the archives," he whispered. "In my library, and in the city. Tlia's story is true."

"Huh? Which story?" A visceral wave of relief flooded through me.

"This was the supply yard and staging area for everything built on the island. Statues carved, timbers shaped. All the blocks for the walls." He pointed across the expanse. "It makes sense. It never floods right here because my family engineered it so work could continue all year. And the Café Royale … it's made with the same masonry as the Great Hall."

"That's why it stood through the quake?"

"Of course it did!"

"That's great, but … "

"But Kath, I found the records." His voice changed. I looked into his eyes. I saw his delight. His voice was soft, but filled with a solemn pride.

"The Kyornin holds the rights to the entire Rhu'ta district."

"You own it?"

"No one 'owns' land in Takau. But the Kyornin holds the right to finance and manage construction and development."

I stared at him. The survey crew decided they could take a break. They sat in a circle, out of earshot, politely ignoring us.

"That means," Kai said, almost shaking now, "I can go to the

Council and get permission — maybe even help — to build a new plaza. New housing. The water system. Think what we can do for Am'rha Bo!"

"Do you think they'll care? Do you think any of them will support any work on this side of the river?"

"If there might be profit in it. If it ties up the Kyornin's funds so there is less competition. A new plaza — with a market — is better than an old slum. Especially if another House pays for it. They'll let us do it, Kath!"

I looked around, trying to transform the desolation around me with my imagination. "Cost a fortune," I said.

Kai lifted his hands. "This is what Clan Kyornin does!" I heard that deep pride again. "We'll get help. I have some people in mind. And don't you think we can find the manpower?"

"Everyone in Am'rha Bo," I nodded. I was beginning to see it. "And we can make it a place for ritual. A place they can call their own. Do you really think … ?"

"I know it," he said, with unassailable conviction.

"Kai, if people see you paying for all this … "

"I will just be the foreman. They know me here now. They will all think I'm working for the Kyornin. Or the government. I don't care. But if you can keep my secret … "

"Of course!"

"Then I can be here, all the time, with you. And build this," he said, waving his arm at his vision. I touched his shoulder and began to imagine carpet sellers and spice vendors around us.

"Together, Kath. Together we will transform all of Am'rha Bo!" And he laughed. "Now, I'll need your help right away. But it's a tough request."

"Anything."

"I want you to come with me to the Council meeting. Next Tuesday, at sundown. But you've got to promise me you will keep quiet."

"I don't know if I can do that," I admitted.

"Promise!"

"I'll try."

"Good." He stepped back. "I had better get back to our survey."

"Okay." I was still taking in the vision.

"Meet me tonight?" he asked.

"Yes. Of course. Yes, let's."

"Good." He gave me a short bow, like a wink with his whole body.

Gathering up his survey crew, Kai headed up the hill. I walked slowly back to the Café Royale. We were closing it as an emergency shelter that day so the owners could go back to serving their mint tea. Soon they will have new customers, I thought. Maybe they'll serve coffee. I touched the gray stone that now hinted it might be salmon-pink granite under several centuries of grime. And I studied the doorway, carved, I now realized, like the portal into the Kyornin's library. What a delicious secret!

I rode that night out to the gardens under a new moon. We stopped near the silver pavilion. Its shallow moat was drained, due to cracks from the quake. A small thing, and one more loss to accept. But now we had our work set before us. And we could always rest here, I thought. The garden would be our easy refuge.

ON THE APPOINTED EVENING, I took the ferry across the choppy Ma'rhu, marched past the faded Greta Garbo poster at the American Café, and climbed the stairs of the Council Hall. I thought I had wandered into a medieval pageant. I had never seen such a parade of jewel-bedecked old men. They took themselves very seriously in their great-grandfathers' costumes as they waited for the doors to open. Their medallions and broaches added weight and glitter to the heavy fabrics embroidered and veined with gold thread. The councilors, most of them bearing the crests and accoutrements of guildmasters as well, touched handkerchiefs to their sweating faces and hissed reminders and instructions to their fawning secretaries. One, the chairman of the Council, might have looked quite regal but for his habit of artlessly adjusting the bright sash around his capacious middle, each time causing such a jiggling of his whole person that he seemed to bounce across the room. Yet, he watched with alert and piercing eyes as people arrived. It was a highly developed skill in Takau to be ludicrous and shrewd at the same time.

Kai arrived, but his costume set him apart from all the peacocks on the stairs. His lightly ornamented robes were the color of new leaves edged with gold. Unlike the others, he was not wearing a turban-like hat or shoes stolen from a fairy-tale genie. And unlike the other secretaries, his aide was a young woman dressed in the simple black uniform I'd come to associate with proud, silent service.

A bell chimed, and everyone turned in unison to enter the Council Hall's cavernous lobby. The building was a jarring architectural hybrid, with a façade of monolithic gray blocks slapped on a gilt chamber decked in florid Takau splendor. I thought it a perfect reflection of the country; a stark Western face concerned with mundane burdens that concealed an inner world of dream and desire. Beyond the dull Doric columns that guarded the entry, a marble floor glittered like a map of the heavens. Inlay of polished stones veined doorways built for giants. Goddesses and demons studied us from perches over every archway. Carved greenery overran the high windows. Spirits darted between clouds on the vaulted ceiling. One imp pointed down at me, laughing.

As we shuffled with the procession into this opera set, Kai whispered, "Everyone will be painfully formal tonight, because we have the military visiting." He pointed to three grim-faced officers. Their uniforms dripped with medals and braids.

"Why are they here?"

"Trouble on the borders again. They are here to politely demand more blood and bone."

"Bright young men and tons of food that should be going to earthquake relief."

Kai nodded. "As old as Takau, I'm afraid."

He pointed to a guildmaster draped in burgundy and gold who was maneuvering over to the chairman. Adjusting his sash, the chairman jiggled forward to greet him.

"Who is that?"

"Tet'shri, the Rhu'pasham. The river guildmaster. He may be our best ally on the Council. I sent word to him through his aides. His response was 'interesting proposal.' That's a very good sign, very encouraging."

"But is he the kind of ally we need?"

Minor city officials puffed up with jewelry and self-importance surrounded us. The inner doors to the Council chamber had not yet opened. Kai drew me aside.

"Tet'shri wanted to build a series of locks to open the Ma'rhu to shipping barges," Kai said, as he carefully noted who was entering the hall. "He even approached me in private to get my opinion, knowing I had an engineering degree from the West. Unfortunately,

I confirmed for him what he had heard from others before; the effort would be terribly expensive, certain to bankrupt the Rhu'pash. And it would be obsolete before it recovered costs."

"I've heard he also has a small army of thugs to ensure he gets a take from everything that moves on the river," I added.

"Well, yes. A poorly kept secret. A traditional part of business in Takau. So of course he is looking to extend his influence on river trade in other ways. I think he will support the water project in order to open the road because the road is sure to increase ferry traffic."

"Ferry traffic he controls."

"Right."

"Well, whatever it takes."

The enormous doors of the Council chamber swung open, and the gathered peacocks strutted into the domed room.

"Good luck," I said, squeezing Kai's arm before he joined the councilors at the head of the procession.

Muscular, spiral columns partly embedded in the wall rose like a sacred grove around us and led my gaze from the mosaic of the marble floor to the dizzying frescoes arcing overhead. Hushed voices echoed off the pantheon of deities surrounding us. The humbled dignitaries ascended to their personal thrones across the rotunda while the rest of us poured into the ornate benches.

THE CEREMONIAL TRIVIALITIES DRAGGED ON. I nodded off during the chairman's speech. But I paid close attention while the designated spokesman for the army officers stood at parade rest in the center of the rotunda and painted a patriotic picture of what I knew to be petty border disputes. He delivered marching orders to the city fathers to supply the army with more conscripts and to open warehouses for military stockpiles, since this was the army's primary supply route to the north. The Council sat utterly motionless, their blank faces expressing an eloquent contempt and resignation.

"They'll fight for weeks behind closed doors to protect their assets," whispered a secretary beside me. "More paperwork for us."

The chairman responded with a long, vacuous soliloquy about the Council's unbroken record of dedication to the glory of Takau. Mundane matters of business followed; the Council's usual concerns about uptown property rights and delayed minor earthquake repairs. There was no escape from the chamber. Even the stoic military brass fidgeted in their seats.

Eventually, though, the Council recognized the Kyornin. Kai rose with his customary grace. I never found it within me to understand the depth of his family pride, but I saw how well it served him as he strode to the middle of the chamber that evening. His fine robes swirled with each step. From where I sat with the secretaries and functionaries, I saw Kai in profile as he struck his dancer's pose before the Council. His robe kept shimmering after he stopped walking.

"Mr. Chairman, council members, Mr. Commissioner, guests," he began, echoing their formal language. "Clan Kyornin respect-fully begs your indulgence and requests permission to address your honorable persons with a matter of great consequence to the fair city of Am'rha Boae'Sa and our sacred homeland Takau. I am the Kyornin. I hold the keys of Clan Kyornin in direct descendence from Kyornin A'rhu. Does anyone present question my right to speak at this auspicious gathering?"

Several members of the Council allowed themselves some au-dible, disgruntled muttering. Kai noted who they were, and waited. The chairman raised his hand to silence the chamber.

"There are some among us who recall with dismay Clan Kyor-nin's long absence from these proceedings," the chairman said.

Kai's father stopped attending the Council years before his death. Most of these old grouches remembered him, I figured.

"And those who remember a young Kyornin sitting restlessly in the front row among the secretaries," Tet'shri chuckled amiably. "Gentlemen, he grew to be a modern young man who brings honor to his clan, and he stands before us now. The Rhu'pasham suggests we afford him the Council's respect."

With the alliance between Tet'shri and the young Kyornin overtly established, surprising even Kai, no one on the Council said an-other word. The chairman signaled Kai to proceed.

"As you are no doubt aware," Kai said, "the situation in Am'rha Bo after the earthquake is grim."

Kai had told me he was sure these men had never in their lives been across the river.

"The subsequent fire ravaged the old city, causing a terrible loss of life and creating a serious housing shortage. The people of Am'rha

Bo are grateful to those of you who have generously supported the reconstruction effort."

I stifled a laugh. Of course, no one on the Council had offered so much as a ferry token in aid. They all nodded gravely and eyed one another. Kai continued without a pause.

"Now, Clan Kyornin proposes to exercise its established rights to the land that has over the years become the central plaza of the Rhu'ta District. Keeping the tradition of my clan, we shall undertake the development of the central plaza of Am'rha Bo to provide for the public good and greatly increase the prosperity of our beloved city."

At this, the councilors, in unison, sat back in their chairs.

"Commissioner?"

The Commissioner was a stone-faced, white-haired man resplendent in a white uniform, modern military in style but accented with antique ribbons and medals. He was in charge of both the management of the courts and the paramilitary forces in the region. The army officers sat with easy familiarity on either side of him, directly across the rotunda from me. He spoke with a gravelly voice expected from a talking statue.

"We are in possession of documents provided by the Kyornin and verified by the State confirming Clan Kyornin's historical claims to the land rights under discussion."

I caught myself imagining what would happen in America if the courts, with all the lawyers, became a branch of the military. I shuddered and made myself concentrate on understanding the Council's formal Rhizmadi jargon. Kai was very good at it.

"I know you share my concern for the public health threat posed by the lack of fresh water and concomitant need for adequate facilities, particularly in the Rhu'ta District," Kai continued. "Therefore, I request your approval, and some measure of financial support, for the construction of a new water supply line and access road to the district, and your permission to erect such new structures in the plaza under the Kyornin's land rights as necessary."

No doubt this was the most radical, ambitious proposal the Council had faced in years. Kai gave them a few moments to take it in.

"The advantages to our beloved Am'rha Boae'Sa — and to the Council — are clear," he added.

"Does the Kyornin recognize the expenses incurred by the city for such an undertaking would be staggering?" asked a wispy councilor, not allowing an answer. "The populace of Am'rha Bo should be expected to use their own resources. For a change."

It was immediately apparent that a number of councilors would, as they always had, unite to oppose any assistance to the slums.

"The city cannot be expected to build an elaborate water system over there, especially with the pressure on the Council for current military needs," added a greasy-looking councilor sitting in the back row.

"A water line beyond the Rhu'ta falls well outside your land rights," groused another.

"Certainly," Kai responded. "This is where Clan Kyornin requires the Council's assistance. The foresight of this Council will carry Takau into the future, with tremendous returns on a small investment. The new road will encourage trade with the northern province, and the water supply will save thousands of lives."

"We are not gods. We cannot prevent disease," scoffed the greasy councilor.

Kai bristled. "The river is no obstacle to disease. We are one city. Disease in Am'rha Bo crosses to Am'rha Sa. To your family."

With all his innate poise brought to bear, he stared down the councilor. I wanted to cheer. I bit my lip.

"Clan Syftarhó agrees it is inappropriate to squander Council resources based on alarmist claims," said a man who looked to me to be wearing a Takau carpet as a robe. This was the textile guildmaster I had chased down the hall long ago. "Commissioner, what is the actual public health situation over there?"

"My officers do not report any major public health concerns," the Commissioner predictably reported, turning stiffly to the row of uniforms behind him for confirmation. He nodded to one in the shadows.

It was Tokmol, who rose to address the hall.

"Naturally, we cooperate fully with the local medical professionals," Tokmol declared. "And we provide assistance above and beyond our jurisdictional obligations."

Involuntarily, I rose to my feet. Kai shot a vicious glance my way. I caught my breath and, red faced, sat down. Tokmol must have noticed me, but the Council, I hoped, had not.

"However, the earthquake did cause some ... disruptions," Tokmol continued. "Concerns about the water supply have been raised, your excellencies. The proposal for a new water supply for the district under discussion has some merit."

"The Commissioner's men have taken extraordinary measures to carry water by wagon across the district in order to avert an epidemic," Kai said with a flourish. "They should be commended, and provided with a permanent solution to the problem!"

I thought I saw Tokmol nod slightly to Kai. The Commissioner, however, looked startled, then angry.

"Colonel, I will expect a report this afternoon!" the Commissioner rasped at Tokmol.

"Of course, sir. It is the first item on our agenda. A polluted well in the Rhu'ta is hardly an unusual occurrence, sir. The situation called for a prompt response, so I made the arrangements. You will have a full report today, sir, of course."

"Polluted wells are common … over there?" asked Syftarhó.

Tokmol fought to keep his customary calm. He had not expected to come under attack from both the Commissioner and the Council.

"The population is growing, sir. Sanitation is less than adequate in some areas, yes."

I could have choked the whole Council with statistics. Did they need to see the ravines caked with raw sewage? What about the children down near the dock quarantined with dysentery? The cholera victims? I stared at my white knuckles.

The greasy councilor winced. "They get water from barrels?"

"A temporary measure," said Kai, taking the attention off Tokmol. "And up to us to remedy."

Tet'shri interrupted a minute of general grumbling.

"I believe the Council should consider the new road that accompanies the water supply line as the most important potential asset under discussion."

I noticed the army officers straighten and glance at one another. Tokmol took the opportunity to retreat, sitting back into the shadows against the wall.

"Can it even be done?" asked the wispy guildmaster. I disliked him intensely. He controlled the rice trade between Am'rha Sa and the capital.

"In the tradition of Clan Kyornin, I assure you we are quite capable of overcoming the engineering obstacles involved. I have design specifications here for your inspection. We would channel water from the Esh'rhu."

Kai's aide jumped up and presented maps and blueprints. The councilors fingered the pages with pursed lips and knowing expressions. Obviously, they understood very little of what they were studying.

"Along the hillside?" asked one.

"Yes. In concert with the access road. The road, as our rivermaster suggested earlier," Kai smiled, "would become a major artery to the northern province."

The army officers leaned across the Commissioner, pointing at Kai's map in front of them. They whispered a message that cascaded across the chamber. When it reached the chairman, he squinted, adjusted his sash, and addressed Kai.

"Does the Kyornin believe this proposed road could support modern military vehicles?"

"With technical assistance from the army, of course," said Kai. He stepped quickly across the room and pointed to landmarks on the map in the officers' hands. "Only one bridge, here at the edge of Am'rha Bo. And some engineering work here at the Esh'rhu. Grading, some fill here ... and here."

The officers nodded gravely. They pointed and whispered, with the Commissioner trapped between them and pressed against his chair.

I watched Kai, who watched the chairman. The chairman watched the Commissioner. And the Commissioner, after a hushed debate with the officers, looked at the chairman and nodded. The chairman rose, suppressed his jiggling, and turned everyone's attention back on Kai, who remained poised on the glassy floor of the rotunda.

"The Council finds the Kyornin's ambitious proposal to have significant and timely application to the economic, uh, hygienic, and strategic development of our beloved city and region." All the councilors nodded. "Assuming, of course, Clan Kyornin takes full, um, responsibility for property development above and beyond the basic, uh, hydraulics of the required infrastructure on the land under Kyornin jurisdiction," the chairman said, with his fellow councilors grunting their approval around him, "and assuming, in addition, the national military will graciously provide assistance with construction of the access road," he continued, acknowledging the smiling officers, "so as to ensure," he squinted, "compatibility with contemporary convoy requirements, then," he gasped, with his sash straining as he drew another breath to continue, "this Council wishes to certify our qualified support, within financial constraints to be negotiated," he noted, glancing to his peers for affirmation, "of the Kyornin's request, upon review of his design specifications, naturally, and pending, oh" he managed to add, waving his hand wearily, "completion of the necessary documentation and acquisition of, of … "

"Community resources," suggested Tet'shri.

"Yes," the chairman concluded. The councilors rose in unison and bowed. Kai, with no more than his enigmatic smile flickering across his face, bowed deeply in response and returned to his seat. I gasped a little too loudly as I began breathing again.

Finally, after more tedious archaic formalities, the chairman declared the meeting adjourned. Strategic clusters of politicians and aides coagulated around the rotunda. Tet'shri drew Kai aside for a moment. After a brief exchange, Kai nodded and clasped his hands together in a gesture of thanks.

I watched as a particularly weasel-eyed councilor imposed on Kai's conversation, followed by a prodigiously overweight companion. I slid closer to hear.

"We of Clan Tyrnin are pleased to see the Kyornin taking his rightful role of leadership again," the weasel oozed. "Your grandfathers would be proud."

Kai nodded, waiting.

"And we would certainly be interested in hearing more about development … opportunities … across the river."

"We see you have something more than fresh water for the slums in mind," smiled the fat one.

"New life for Am'rha Bo," Kai answered.

"And a vital link to the northern province," added Tet'shri, as if the road were already built.

"A trade route through the city! It's brilliant, Paku," said the weasel. "And new business for the Rhu'pash, too."

Tet'shri nodded. "Obviously."

The portly one grinned. "The boy … forgive me … the Kyornin

knows exactly what he is doing. It will open the north for us. And, of course," he winked, "put him in good graces with the government."

"Ah, this convoy route, it will take the damn army off our backs," the weasel blurted. "Yesss. I see now the skill that made clan Kyornin the greatest power in Takau!"

Tet'shri frowned in disgust and looked away. Coincidentally, he turned in my direction and our eyes met for a moment. He saw I had been listening. I took a sudden interest in the mosaic over the doorway. He discreetly turned his back to me.

"Please, gentlemen," Kai said, preserving his formal tone. "What I propose is for the good of the people."

"Oh, of course," smiled the weasel. "For the people. Well said, yes."

I WAS SO RELIEVED TO BE OUT of the Council Hall I wanted to dance. I was not alone. Aromas of curries and mint swirled in the perfect evening coolness to draw the entire population out to the great nocturnal waltz around the Court Plaza.

Free of the Council proprieties, Kai handed his satin outer robes to his aide, who vanished into the night with the robes and blueprints. We joined in the promenade as observers and participants. Gangs of swaggering young men practiced their comical mannerisms. Swarms of young women, dressed up for each other, pretended to not care about the swaggering young men. Families — whole clans, really — turned out together, with the patriarchs wearing the family colors and the children running dizzy orbits around the adults. Clucking to one another about the scandalous fashions of the day, old couples shuffled at their timeworn pace around the circle until they had to slip off down the side streets for their soup and bread.

I tried to let myself feel far away from the burdens of ruined buildings and lives. I tried not to scan people for medical symptoms. I tried to enjoy Kai's excitement about his victory with the Council. And in the coolness of the evening and the gaiety of the crowds around us, I gradually felt lighter. We ended our evening at the centerpiece of the plaza.

I remember Kai chasing me in a mad sprint, staggering from laughter, around the lip of the fountain.

Such a fountain! Every great city has one. Mythical beasts spit water in all directions at the feet of a towering, half-naked woman.

Breathlessly, Kai sat on the rump of a nearby stone lion. He put both hands together, prayer-like, as he always did when working out a serious thought. I stopped laughing, and waited.

"A fountain," he said, very quietly. I leaned forward. "But more like a stream, flowing in a circle." He looked up, not at me, but at his vision. "We could disguise the intake and outlet from the pipeline. The water would appear to flow endlessly around. We'd commission the seasons, and all the calendar deities, and have them dancing in the water."

"Where?"

"In the center of our new plaza. We'll build rows of new apartments on one side of the Café Royale. Set up an open market. And the fountain will flow in a circle there in the center."

I studied him. "You already know how it will look, don't you?"

Kai smiled brightly. "Every detail," he whispered.

I fell in love with Kai because of the look on his face when his imagination sparkled with a new idea. I guess the ideas eventually took on the appearance of burdens. But that night we could still dream bright visions for the future. We slipped down into the cool river air and out to our garden.

9

Not all of Ma'rhu's daughters are beautiful or kind. In the high country, dark-eyed Jha'gharoná weeps down the canyon walls. Her children are lost. She searches for them between the crags. She calls to them in all the secret places of the mountain. But they are lost. You can hear Jha'gharoná keening and crying behind the rain. Disconsolate, she flees from the laughter of human children and gathers herself into the hidden canyons. Finally, driven mad by grief, she rages down to her mother. Do not stand in her path.

AM'RHA BO, expansive in its boundless poverty, began accepting refugees from the north. Residents of tribal villages on the northernmost frontier lived with a border that slithered back and forth by government decrees so frequently they could not know from one day to the next if they had awakened in Takau or not. Finding themselves put upon by old enemies and their own government's soldiers alike, whole tribes migrated to Am'rha Bo to take up with relatives in the city until the savage border disputes faded, as they had in the past. This time, they forfeited their ancestral lands the day they left. Army barracks squatted where their shrines stood for generations.

When the matriarch of the Khoda, a clan living on the flank of Takau's most sacred mountain, responded to the increased government oppression by closing a trade route, the army moved against her with a vicious attack intended to intimidate all the mountain tribes. Swooping down on the clan during the Festival of the Trees, a holy day, the soldiers burned the Great Hall, igniting a wildfire that charred sixteen thousand acres of forest. During the raid, the matriarch's eldest son was killed along with most of the Khoda men and, the story was, an equal number of sword-wielding women.

Word travels quickly through the high passes. Rival clans invoked the name of the Khoda and suddenly discovered they could share meals and heartaches again. New fear and outrage swallowed old mistrust. As their children played together, the women shared herbs and secrets of survival. In countless smoky huts, the men compared knife blades and discussed dark plans. Spontaneously, these clans united under the name Khodataal.

The story reached Am'rha Bo on the same wings. The city, swollen with mountain refugees, smoldered and flared with new violence. Men hunted by the army found it easier to hide in the crowded alleys of the Rhu'ta District than in the rugged mountain canyons of their birth. So while Am'rha Sa courted the military budgets, the Ma'rhu became the new battle line to the north and Am'rha Bo became a city under siege.

Ironically, it was the army that first sent me into the northern province. In a remote valley, a flash flood swept away an entire village in the night. Military medical staff, I was told, could not be spared from a trouble spot on the border. Knowing I had good relations with the clans, the Commissioner's office recommended me to the army detachment, and left me little choice but to accompany a small load of supplies to the scene of the tragedy.

The village in normal times was only accessible by horseback, so certainly only pack horses could reach the victims now. I was not an experienced rider, and, of course, there were no Western saddles. Pride alone kept me on that animal because my guide was an insolent border-tribe outcast who had no patience for my inexperience. I rode into the high country trailing four pack mules and a fiend intent on my torture. Or so it seemed to me.

I ended the first day too sore to sleep. The second day, the green foothills quickly gave way to switchbacks up scree and over slick shelves of shale. I gave myself up for dead a hundred times, as I had to trust the horse not to slip and send us both glissading into the abyss a step away.

"Just sit still," said my guide, amused by my ashen face. "The horse does not want to die either. Don't throw her off balance. I'd hate to lose her." I held my breath and kept the reins in a death grip as the old beast stumbled across the loose rock.

The trail led into a gorge so narrow I only saw the noonday sun and spent the rest of the afternoon watching cold shadows slide over the cliffs. Late in the day, we dismounted in a small clearing with the thunder of a mountain stream filling the air. When my guide blindfolded my horse to get her across a swaying bridge, I suggested he might have to do the same for me. He thought I was hilariously funny, and, after leading all the animals across, he squatted on a rock to watch me stagger and lurch over the bridge alone. All I could hear was the roar of the frothing, hungry torrent under my feet. The mist from the white water swirled around me and soaked the creaking planks.

A few steps onto the bridge, I pulled my foot back and clutched the wobbly handrail to save myself. I had almost stepped on a small animal. I blinked and stared at it, sitting on its haunches, looking back at me. I stepped forward to convince myself this creature was just a diminutive gray squirrel. Was it injured, I guessed, or rabid? No, its bright eyes darted back and forth, watching my feet. Then it whisked to one splintered plank, and, with a deliberate hop, pounced on the next one. Forgetting the canyon under me, I took another step, and another, chasing the squirrel. It looked over its shoulder, waiting for me.

The Rizha tell of little guides, the *Nisché*, who lead spirits and lucky people through difficult or dark paths. They do it for fun. Children hope the mouse running across the kitchen floor is a *Nisché* who will lead them to treasure. You can tell if have met a *Nisché*, I'm told, if it looks you in the eye.

The bridge was sturdy enough, after all, for horses to cross, so the danger was my fear. Teased across by the little animal in front of me, I found myself standing on the rough stone steps on the far side.

"So, finally found your feet," said my guide, as he cinched the loads on the pack mules. Without a word, I got back on my horse, patted her neck, and motioned that I was ready to move on.

THE ISLAND GARDENS OF TAKAU

By THE AFTERNOON of the third day, we reached the site where the village had stood. Houses, granaries, council hall, paddocks — everything was gone. Only a swath of sucking black mud remained, thick and lifeless from one side of the little valley to the other. Trees stood inverted with their roots hanging in the air. A mile downstream, where the canyon turned sharply to the left, a pile of debris — all that had been the village — slumped against the cliff.

I stood where the stream, placid and innocent again, quietly carved a new course through the rubble and silt. I could feel where young mothers, awakened by a strange hissing sound approaching in the dark, had perhaps had time enough only to sit up and think of their children before the wall of water roiling with boulders, trees, and mud slammed into their huts.

I WORKED IN THE VALLEY for a week. Most of the survivors were those who had been out of the valley visiting relatives in neighboring villages. Lack of food and shelter had weakened everyone, while corpses in the mud threatened us all with disease.

The people accepted my services mutely, and with scant hints of gratitude. At first I thought their behavior was understandably due to shock and horror. I was a foreigner who had appeared uninvited after the gods swept their whole world into oblivion. Yet, as the grueling days progressed, I became painfully aware it was not shock and bewilderment I was facing, but seething resentment. And it was only during my last hour in the valley that I discovered why they replied to my every effort with sullen bitterness. The boy loading my pack horse said an army regiment had camped less than a mile from the village for a week prior to the flood. In that time, the soldiers had used a year's supply of the villagers' fuel wood and ruined an essential fishing hole. Then they abruptly struck camp and moved to higher ground. Their scouts, who had been hunting upstream for a small band of rebels, saw the threatening flash flood conditions in the side canyons and reported to the regiment commander. The commander, however, neglected to warn the village.

I stood by my horse, with my impatient guide waiting for me to mount. I glared at the drying mud, curled like shattered pottery around us, and I understood the army had sent me as their meager afterthought response to a tragedy they could have prevented.

By the time I was safely back on the plaza in Am'rha Bo, my

heart was locked into the lives of the Khodataal. No longer able to feign an impartial stand, I thought I understood their rage. I left a part of myself behind in those deep canyons.

"PAINT THE MARK HERE, on the forehead," Magra said. I leaned over, watching her gnarled hands. A boy of fourteen, reduced to skin and bones and fear, stared up at us. Magra traced a design with her finger dipped in ocher.

"This makes you stronger," she rasped at the boy, using the old dialect. He nodded, still wide-eyed with terror. No one expected him to survive. He had been shot in the belly with a military carbine. Massive trauma to the liver. Internal bleeding. Possible spinal damage.

"Always say that while you draw the mark," Magra said.

It was close to midnight. I had followed Magra since dawn, nursing, instructing, and absorbing her art. Many weeks had passed since my trip into the mountains. The monsoon of 1928 gnawed at the thatch roof overhead and eddied in the open doorway. It was nearly over, I thought with relief. The fog-dance music would come soon.

"Perhaps he can sleep now."

"Yes, sleep," Magra repeated. She closed her medicine pouch. We stood over the boy.

"More tomorrow," Magra said, then yawned. She tried to hide it from me.

"And the next," I agreed. "They keep coming out of the hills."

I threw a roll of gauze back into my field bag. The old woman put her hand on the wall. I gingerly adjusted the boy's head on the straw pillow. He stared up at me still. I touched the mark on his forehead and smiled at him. He tried to smile back, and closed his eyes. I saw life draining out of his young body and there was not a damn thing I could do about it. Sighing, I hugged my field bag.

"There are three wounded down by the dock," I said. "They came down the river hanging onto a tree."

"You go. You know all the words now. Take these," Magra added, handing me the last of our bandages.

"But they always expect you," I said.

Magra turned. She leaned heavily in the doorway as we left the room. "These wounded. They need your hands, not my herbs."

Why hadn't I noticed before? The deep shadows could not disguise the old woman's exhaustion.

"Dear, dear Magra! You go prepare for tomorrow," I said, offering her an excuse. "I'll go down to the dock, then quit for the night as soon as I can." I almost reached out to hold her up, but she pulled her shoulders back.

"Mint and that hot little brown pepper, if they have been in the river," she rasped. But she turned away from me without another terse command and shuffled painfully down the alley. I bit my lip in thought for a moment, then spun about and pushed myself on toward the riverbank.

WHEN THE RAIN STOPPED and the fog lay across the Ma'rhu, we tacitly surrendered, too. Magra retreated to her tiny hut to sit alone with the secret thoughts of a crone. I sat upstairs at the Café Royale with a bottomless cup of tea. I remember learning then that Amelia Earhart had crossed the Atlantic earlier that year. Kai brought me an English-language newspaper, and I read dispassionately about Herbert Hoover. I was vaguely aware of men and equipment moving across the plaza toward the hills. Tor sat with me, as reserved as ever and more at ease with just sitting. My thoughts raced in weary circles. Tor sat as if listening to his heartbeat, making no judgments about past or present. He was good company for me. And soon the next battle arrived, masquerading as great news.

"We've done it, Kath! The army finished the road. The water line is ready. Come see!"

Tor and I followed Kai out of the café.

"We only had one major problem," said Kai as we trudged up the hill. "The local construction crews wouldn't work on the bridge that spans the funeral road."

"Too many ghosts?"

"Exactly. To build the scaffold in the ravine I had to find a Bengali crew," Kai admitted. "They just put up their shrine to Shiva and went to work. I guess our dead didn't bother them. Then the Am'rha Bo crew was comfortable working on either side." He laughed. "I have a small army of wooden nature spirits on order to guard both sides of the bridge. They'll put the locals at ease."

"Speaking of armies ... "

"They were sure eager to open this route. They've built a camp in the foothills. More troops arrive every day." We pushed past a gang of old women haggling over onions. "Their convoys will have to run through the city, right through the new plaza, too. But we finished the road in record time!"

"And the pipeline runs beside it?"

"Right. It flows in an open channel most of the way from the Esh'rhu."

"That's two miles from here!"

"We ran it along the road as far as the Bishtafi ruins, then cut along the hillside. Leaks a lot. Needs work. But it gets the water here."

We reached the ravine as the sun set behind Death's Door, engulfing the new road in early shadows. The sturdy bridge framed with thick, rough-hewn timbers sailed cleanly over the ghosts at our feet. I walked out and leaned on the railing.

"The pipeline runs under here?" I asked.

"Yes. A length of iron pipe ordered from Chicago, actually," Kai grinned. "I told them it was for you, so it got here quickly."

Tor nodded approvingly. I laughed.

OBVIOUSLY, I AM NOT SUPERSTITIOUS. But it was hard not to fear October as it arrived with new threats of disaster. The anniversary of the earthquake was on my mind as I choked on the exhaust from an army truck as it pulled off the ferry ahead of us. Kai stood beside me. He was escorting me home after a fruitless meeting with the Council.

The monsoon was long past, so merchants stood at their prominent posts in the center of the dock yard, where everyone had to pass in front of their stalls. Disembarking ferry traffic had turned to the right for decades, maybe centuries. But this truck inched straight forward. I saw soldiers knock a woman and her table of leather bags and belts to the ground.

"Hey! Hey, stop!" I shouted, shoving other disembarking passengers aside.

The truck nosed its way like a bulldozer straight across the waterfront plaza toward the corner of the guild hall where the road started up the hill. I leapt in front of the soldiers.

"What the hell are you doing?"

I think Kai caught me before I hit the ground. I had never been thrown like a sack of rice before. I regained my footing, intent on jumping back into the fight. Kai grabbed my arm.

"Kath! Wait."

"But ... "

"Syrka," Kai pointed.

I looked up in time to see the defiant old man, still inside his fruit stand, facing the truck. Two soldiers grabbed him by the arms and pulled him aside. The truck lurched forward. They threw Syrka face first onto the cobblestones amid his splintered stall and an explosion of tangerines and lemons rolling off the truck's hood.

The commotion attracted a crowd like a train wreck. Children scrambled under the soldiers' legs, snatching fruit. I knew most of the little scavengers. So I called to them by name.

"A free orange if you bring me an armload!" I shouted. "Which of you can bring me the most?" In a moment I had all the little urchins working for me.

I reached Syrka, who sat up swearing. Rhizmadi is a terrifically colorful language for curses. And Syrka, even injured, employed the whole vocabulary. Kai recovered a few of Syrka's baskets. Rescued fruit tumbled in and around them as the children proudly dumped their collections. Behind us, the truck pushed through the market, perfumed by the fruit crushed in the treads of its tires.

"Damn you!" I said, with more conviction than eloquence, and hurled a lemon with my best baseball pitch at the back of the truck. Almost hit a soldier, too. But the truck carved its line of destruction from the dock to the guild hall, then roared up the road.

"No one's helping," I scowled.

"Or looting," Kai replied.

"Of course not!" It had not occurred to me they might.

"Ha!" Syrka spat. "Half my fruit is gone." He continued with a rich description of the unwholesome lineage of the crowd around us.

"Didn't they warn you?"

"That parasite came by yesterday, told us we were in the way."

"Tokmol?" I asked.

"That's the one. Told us to clear out. Not to be here today."

"So they warned you, but you didn't move?" asked Kai.

"Some didn't believe they would do it," Syrka scoffed. "That was stupid. I just didn't think they would come so soon."

"You wouldn't have moved anyway," I scolded. "Let me look at your forehead." I dabbed the blood off his brow.

"You're right. Damn!"

"Sorry. But that's going to keep bleeding unless we wrap it."

"Can we help you back to your home?" asked Kai.

"I slept in my stall."

"You must have family."

"A granddaughter. She won't let me in."

"The way you look right now," I said, "she'll have to. Is it far?"

"No, it's … " Syrka staggered when he tried to stand. I caught him. Only his ferocious grumpiness kept him from fainting. With absurd difficulty, we eventually delivered Syrka and his remaining baskets of fruit to his granddaughter, who was matron of a respectable household up the hill near the plaza. She in fact took him in with undisguised reluctance, and perhaps only because we were with him.

"Surprised he wasn't murdered years ago," she muttered.

Syrka, for his part, managed to complain about the bed she provided and groused that the plate of food she brought to him was already cold. So I knew he would recover quickly, if his relatives didn't throw him back in the street out of exasperation. But the waterfront would never recover its welcoming ambience or cheerful anarchy.

10

IN THE DAYS AFTER THE ARMY convoy crashed through the market, trucks and wagons coagulated along the riverbank, but they never paused on the climb between the guild hall and our new plaza. Lines of soldiers and creaking loads of supplies entered the plaza from the southeast corner between two arched buildings on the perimeter of the square. Their route ran around the plaza on its south side, turned directly in front of the Café Royale, then climbed sharply up the hill along the new pipeline road. The noise and exhaust often drove people into the side alleys.

In contrast, the syncopated music of construction also rang in the dusty air. Kai made his headquarters in the middle of a long row of half-finished apartment buildings. His plan was to house hundreds of families in the neighborhood surrounding the plaza, where they would all have access to fresh water and a modern sewage system. With a limitless supply of men and women willing to work, only the scarcity of building materials slowed him down.

Kai led me out to the center of the plaza between rough blocks of stone and heaps of sand and mortar. As usual, Tor was at my side. We threaded our way around stacks of clay pipe. I greeted a team of stone masons chiseling grotesque Takau demons. Growing out of a huge circular trough, the great fountain was taking shape.

"It reminds me of anatomy class," I said, "with all the veins running through it and all the guts strewn about."

Kai grimaced.

"Sorry. Doctors see things that way. I had no idea it would be this big!"

"Here's Ashka'rhuna, who brings the monsoon. We've left room here to plant flowers for her. Then water spirits," he pointed. "Then one of our little jokes — this section will always look like it's overflowing, or flooding."

I looked at him and laughed, recalling the clinic during the rain.

"They tell me we must have all twelve of these demons surrounding Mortash'rhondí. It's almost impossible to get the water pressure equal for twelve mouths, but I'll make it work."

"They'll look great. Very scary."

"The sculptors are doing a wonderful job. It seems to be in the Rizha blood."

"It looks like the whole fountain drains out here."

"Not quite. It's another trick. The volume of water draining through Mortash'rhondí's bowl equals the amount gushing around his claws here and here and here," he said, pointing to a tangle of pipes.

"Once you connect it, can you turn this thing off?"

"Oh, of course. All these lines can be diverted through a main behind the goddess so we can clean or repair the fountain. Or if it's too loud for the band playing around it."

"Your ancestors would be very proud."

Kai gazed into my eyes. "This is my way of sharing in your life, you know."

"It's bigger than you and me," I told him. "You are changing lives here."

Kai forced a smile. He glanced at Tor, who was mutely listening to everything we said. The rhythmic pounding of hammer and chisel on stone filled a sudden void between us. Lack of privacy protected me from intimate conversations. When I threw up that defense, Kai could not breach it. Abruptly, he pointed at the plumbing again.

"Now, these lines run to fountains that represent the New Year's fires."

"I've heard about that. On the spring equinox. Old tradition. Why did it stop?"

"Against the law," answered Tor. "Tower fires became a call to arms. Now they are forbidden."

"In my father's day, it was the big event of the year, something like American Christmas and New Year's Eve rolled together. But all for her," Kai said, pointing to a towering statue of a woman draped in billowing robes.

Her outstretched arms embraced the whole plaza and her huge hands reached out in blessing. A mason was still at work on her, carving intricate patterns into her nearly translucent stone robes.

"The water drains here at Yasol'rhishá's feet, but of course it will appear to flow between her legs and around the fountain again."

I studied the symbols taking shape. "So she's the fertility goddess."

Kai looked up at Yasol'rhishá's alluring face and frowned. "Yes, springtime. But death, too. The gentle kind. She wraps souls in her long robes. You'll see these designs he's carving here in most Takau carpets."

"Death and beauty," I nodded.

Kai gave me his sidelong glance. "The young people ask her to bring them good lovers. The seasons don't end."

"We should bring them back," I declared suddenly. "The tower fires. And the New Year celebration with them."

A barely perceptible grimace flickered across Tor's face. I only caught it because I knew him so well. I laughed.

"You won't have to do all the work, Tor. Many will want to help. It will be good for everyone, you'll see!"

"The fountain will be finished by then. We could make it a dedication of the new plaza," Kai suggested.

"Perfect. Tlia told me how they used to carry the goddess through the streets," I said.

"A beautiful young woman, sitting on a bed of flowers," Kai added.

"But there are children now who have never seen her," I complained. "It's like an American child never knowing Christmas!"

We threaded our way back out from the base of the fountain.

"I'd like to see a circle of trees out here," Kai continued. "But that may have to wait. The next thing to be done has to be a heavy cobblestone road across the plaza, running in front of the café. Carts coming down the new road are cutting ruts that will be impossible when the monsoon hits. And trucks, like that one," he added, pointing, "are much worse."

At that moment, a heavy army transport rattled through the arches onto the plaza. It maneuvered slowly through the construction site.

I watched it for a moment. "Tor?"

"Must be the one."

"I think so, too." I skirted a pile of sand and dashed along a line of bricks. I stepped in front of the truck as it rolled parallel to the café.

The driver leaned out his window. In the passenger seat, a heavy-browed soldier scowled at me while he fingered a rifle held between his legs. I wondered if he had ever blown a hole through the brim of his hat. But I smiled at the driver.

"This truck is carrying medical supplies, isn't it?"

"Yes, ma'am."

I noted they were both wearing crisp, new national army uniforms.

"Good," I smiled. "I'm the doctor here. I ordered a shipment weeks ago."

The driver retrieved a crumpled paper from the dashboard. "Sorry, ma'am, the manifest says I deliver all this to the Bishtafi camp."

"That would just be a wasted trip," I said. I tried to sound sympathetic and helpful. "These supplies are needed right here. You'd just have to come right back down the road."

"That may be, ma'am, but I'll be sent to the northern border if I don't follow this manifest."

"We'll send a message. I will sign for them."

"You are not authorized to sign for them."

"Look. You're carrying medical supplies for earthquake victims. I'm a doctor. Let me sign for them, and it will be my problem."

"Can't do that, ma'am."

"Let me see that," I said as I reached through the truck window and snatched the paper from the driver's hand.

He yelped and threw open the door as I walked quickly to the back of the truck, where Tor was waiting.

I studied the manifest. The inventory included specific British pharmaceuticals I had ordered, but far more than I had dared request.

"I could set up a whole laboratory with what's in this truck! Look at this!" I cried. The inventory was written in English, and the drugs were recorded in Latin, and in any case the list would mean nothing to Tor. He was watching the driver, who was trying to take back the paper.

"Lady, I need that back!"

"Ethyl alcohol! I could make enough ether for an army of surgeons with this!"

"Lady!"

Tor stepped in front of him.

"And typhoid vaccine! My God!"

The driver tried to push Tor out of the way. With fierce ease, Tor slammed him against the truck. Behind me, I heard the unmistakable sound of a rifle bolt sliding into place. Tor and I turned, slowly and carefully.

The heavy-browed soldier had his gun trained at Tor's chest. The driver regained his balance and, swaggering, snapped the manifest out of my hand. Then, with their best menacing glares, the two got back into the truck and threw it in gear. Gravel pelted our legs as the tires spun. They swerved wildly through the plaza and disappeared up the hill.

"Sorry," I said.

Tor's only response was to relax his shoulders slightly.

"Have you lost your mind?" Kai yelled, catching up to us.

"Kai, there goes our vaccine."

"But Kath … "

"Everything goes through Am'rha Bo, but we're left with nothing," I said.

All of Kai's stone masons moved in behind him, hammers in hand. A dozen roofers came down from their ladders among the new market stalls and joined them, watching.

"Tokmol," Tor whispered, pointing to the gate of an alleyway with a jerk of his head.

"That didn't take long," I sighed, watching Tokmol and his usual assistants step out of the shadows.

"Back to work," Kai commanded. "Back to it, everybody."

"Your hard work is our answer to them," I added. "And we have to get the plaza ready in time for the big New Year's celebration."

The workers' eyes lit up. They waited to hear more, to hear if I truly meant what I was hinting.

"Yes. The procession of Yasol'rhisha," said Kai. "There's not much time! Let's go!"

The workers nodded and looked at each other. Whispering excitedly among themselves, they hustled back to their jobs.

"Guess I just started something, didn't I?"

"I wonder if you know," Kai answered. Then he stepped forward to intercept the five uniformed men. "Good day, Tokmol. You approve of our work?"

"The construction work, you mean? Excellent craftsmanship, yes. You are keeping these people employed. Indeed, I approve of that, sir."

Tokmol tucked his baton under his arm as he approached us, scanning the plaza. His men stood ten paces off.

"I am concerned, of course, that it may create a focal point for uncomfortable situations."

"Of course," I growled. Tokmol ignored me.

"Tell me, for instance, what was that little scene about just now? With the military supply vehicle?"

Kai glanced my way, wondering, no doubt, what snippy comment I would make to heighten the animosity that vibrated almost visibly in the air around me.

"The doctor, as I understand it," Kai said softly, "is concerned about medical equipment ordered some time ago for her practice. I believe she was seeking information about its delayed delivery. That was all. Right, doctor?"

"Right," I told Kai, since Tokmol was pretending I wasn't there. "I'm sure Tokmol is aware of the dangerous lack of basic medical supplies in his district."

"And concerned, quite so," Tokmol said. He didn't like it when I mimicked his intimidation techniques, so he addressed me directly. "But, unfortunately, military medical equipment will never be diverted for civilian needs. And these army personnel, they don't know anything beyond their immediate orders." He spoke with a conspiratorial tone, as though we were fellow police officers. "You understand, these days I must take special interest in such matters, because I have been specifically charged with ensuring the military transports move unimpeded through the district. Difficult enough, you can imagine, with the crowded route up the hill."

"And mounting tensions, it seems," Kai said. "I hope everyone can avoid … overreactions."

Tokmol stepped closer and lowered his voice. "Which brings me to my next, more pressing, question, sir. That is, if you could help me understand your long-term intentions here, I believe I may be of considerable assistance to you."

Kai glanced at me and leaned forward. "What kind of assistance do you believe I need?"

I could barely hear Tokmol over the renewed hammering of the stone masons. "If you please, sir, the personal safety of council members is, of course, a high priority for the Commissioner. But the reality of Am'rha Bo dictates that I will be hard pressed to guarantee your safety, should your identity be revealed over here."

"Do you intend to reveal my identity?"

"Certainly not! You misunderstand my intentions entirely." Tokmol looked around, then frowned. "Let me be candid, for once, sir. Despite a reputation for petty despotism that I seem to hold among the local citizenry — yes, of course I am aware of it, and it serves a purpose of sorts — my duty and honest intention is to maintain order and, as much as possible, peace." He allowed himself a tired little laugh. "And it falls to me to assist the army, as I've said. Beyond that, I have further responsibilities to serve the special needs of the Council. So, what I am respectfully suggesting, sir, is that you please consider the depth of your personal involvement with these people."

"They believe I am an engineer hired by Clan Kyornin to build this plaza. They think no one ever sees the Kyornin himself. But they see me here improving their lives. And I hope to draw other great clans into my little conspiracy, too."

"Other clans are vultures, begging your pardon, sir."

Kai nodded. "But their gain often improves life for all Takau over time."

Tokmol pursed his lips. "I thought at first your idealism was just a clever charade."

"I am following the tradition of my clan. We build gifts to the future."

Tokmol considered this. "I applaud your intentions. But the future is a most ungrateful recipient of gifts."

Kai smiled. "Not looking for gratitude or honor."

"No. I see that. Not likely you will get any, either. I don't."

"Other rewards, I hope."

Tokmol caught himself. "I am pressed with the burdens of the present, sir. We must use what we're given today. You understand?"

"Yes, Tokmol. And I don't expect or wish that you take special precautions to protect me. There is no need."

"Very well," he said. "Then let me add only that you must appreciate that I cannot divide my loyalties, sir." He turned back to me. "Please, doctor. Be careful what you set in motion. The Takau gods often require a heart sacrifice."

With that, Tokmol saluted, spun about, swept up his men, and was gone. We were quiet a moment.

"Did you understand all that?" I finally asked.

"I think so," Kai said. "I hope so." His voice trailed off.

THE ISLAND GARDEN remained our sanctuary. There, camellias bloomed. Rosy-pink blossoms reminded me of blown-glass ornaments against the soothing, glossy foliage. And shattered petals carpeted the mossy path like new snow. I smiled to myself.

"What is it?" Kai asked.

"I had forgotten. It's Christmastime."

Kai nodded. "High holy days in your culture. Do you miss it?"

"My family wasn't religious. Not in that way, at least. But when I was a little girl, we always had a Christmas tree and exchanged presents and all that. You must have seen Christmas at Harvard?"

"Oh, yes. I enjoyed the decorations and singing and the mood of it. Very nice. Showed the best of your culture, I think. I especially like the story."

"Which story?"

"About the baby in the desert. How every new baby brings hope to the world."

I smiled at his interpretation. Thoughts of Christmas, and the breeze sliding down from the north, made the night soft and restful.

Many say December is the best time to be in Takau. The weather is temperate, with a tingle on cool skin in the shade. It is a flower-painted time, with a palette of tropical blossoms competing for an award for extravagance. The winners are chosen by little girls, who make crowns and necklaces with them.

Also, there is usually enough food for everyone in December. Perhaps that is why the Rizha traditionally hold their coming-of-age ceremonies and weddings at that time. The hosts know that all their guests can be fed with honorable generosity, even if the entire clan has accepted the invitation and even if they all stay for three days. And the guests, for their part, can bring baskets brimming with fruits and nuts and those funny little wedding pastries.

Tlia's household was like that. Her house had grown over the years into a substantial compound, with rooms added around a dirt courtyard. Doorways were crooked, privacy was scarce, and water had to be hauled in buckets from a well down the street, but an iron gate guaranteed safety and pots of geraniums added perennial color.

Tlia presided over perpetual special occasions and clan gatherings from her place at the kitchen counter. From her tiled, altar-like command post, the food, advice, and stories poured freely into the courtyard. Twin ovens smoked behind her. Herbs and braids of garlic festooned the ceiling. A great bundle of fresh mint hung by her left shoulder. As quickly as the bundle was stripped for tea, a new fistful hung in its place.

I felt more at home in Tlia's house than I ever could in Kai's ornate chambers. I laughed with tears streaming down my cheeks while chopping onions. Tlia and her sisters laughed at my lopsided attempts to make the traditional rice cakes. In the evenings, we in the kitchen called out jokes to the men, who sat in the courtyard playing with the children. Of course, I came running when any of them fell ill. And I lit the oil lamp on the solstice and heard the old tales.

"Takau has a Father Christmas, too," Kai declared suddenly.

I stopped and looked at him with exaggerated disbelief.

"We do! Fa'rhouzi is a skinny little man, who dresses all in red, by the way, and brings gifts to the children. His skin is blue and he is so skinny he can slip through the cracks of a closed door."

"Much easier than coming down chimneys," I admitted.

"Fa'rhouzi appears at New Year's."

"In the spring?"

"Right. And he loves to play tricks on the grownups."

"With the children's innocent assistance, no doubt."

"Exactly."

We laughed together. Hand in hand, we walked near the Great Hall under an ancient monarch of a maple tree that kept its ancestors' ways and shed its leaves on schedule, despite the tropical warmth. This night the branches were full of stars.

"We had a maple where I grew up," I said. "So big it shaded the whole back yard. Small yard, anyway. And my father built a playhouse for me there. I immediately turned the playhouse into a hospital for all my dolls. Haven't changed, I guess."

We paused to look over a balcony at a line of descending fountains sparkling by lantern light. "I can't imagine what it was like growing up in a place like this!"

"Lonely," said Kai. "I felt like I was always waiting. And there was all the burden of the clan heritage. Of course, my father put high expectations on me, too."

"Tell me about your father. The stories make him out to be a recluse who became something of a madman, staring down from that balcony over there," I said, pointing across the landscape toward the end of the private quarters. I only knew the elder Kyornin from legends heard at the tables of the very poor. Suddenly, he was Kai's father, and I winced at the indiscretion of my words.

"It was that one," Kai answered, pointing, without rancor in his voice. "The balcony off the dragon salon." He leaned against a marble column, remembering. "He wasn't mad. Just broken, I think. You may have heard that Takau made an attempt at democracy back in about 1904. My whole family was involved. My aunt was the parliamentary representative for the region, and, as I understand it now, a leading candidate for president."

"I can see how that would be possible here," I smiled.

"Oh, yes. Rizha women would take office — if we had a democracy. But, the country was not ready, and factions were at war. My aunt, and her husband, her brother — my Uncle Kai — and my three cousins were murdered on a campaign trip to Da'rha Ghand."

"Oh!" I gasped. "Oh, I am so sorry! How unbearable!"

Kai offered a wan smile. "Such is politics in Takau. Idealism has few friends."

We watched quietly as a pair of ducks waddled casually toward the pond. Kai continued his story. "My mother died when I was very young. My other aunts followed your calling to help the sick, but they fell to the influenza epidemic. So, Clan Kyornin was reduced to my father and one young, unruly son. He used to call me to his side and point down here with a steady hand to tell me which fountain or waterfall should be turned higher or lower."

"Were you close?"

Kai shook his head. "I was young. I thought I had better things to do." He continued down the path. I took his hand and folded his fingers between mine. He paused to study the pitch and timbre of a rivulet pouring around a stone snake. "Now, sometimes I feel the water is the most important thing in the world. The fountains are a gift and a promise."

"I guess they require constant care."

"Like any promise."

Christmas indeed, I thought. Time of reflection and remembrance. I sighed. Kai glanced at me. He gave me a soft starlit smile, then returned to his own thoughts. We passed the boathouse. I let go of his hand. He drifted to the edge of the pond. I stood behind him, restfully empty for a moment.

"I've slowly come to understand my father suffered from the Kyornin family curse," Kai said to the water.

Burdens poured back into the emptiness; I made myself listen carefully. "What curse?"

"He felt good fortune should be shared."

"Terrible idea," I said.

"He spent twenty years bringing what seemed valuable from Europe to Takau. You can see it in Am'rha Sa. He tried to open the country to the modern world. The Council choked him at every breath. The government nibbled away at every feast he offered."

"And, after all that, the Council berated him for not continuing to finance their luxury," I surmised.

Kai's silhouette remained still. "We call it 'giving diamonds to rotten fish.' They don't appreciate it and they make a stink anyway."

My laughter broke the spell. Kai was eager to lighten the mood, too. So we hurried from the pond together and cut across the rose garden. We crossed the lawn and threw open the double doors of the private quarters. The first room on the left was the Kyornin's library. It was a favorite, familiar hall. I pulled Kai inside.

Handsome books with cracked leather bindings greeted us. The room had the proper sharp, hardwood hush about it. Bookshelves lined the long walls, loaded to the ceiling. One of those old rolling ladders helped us reach odd anthologies that waited, sagging, far out of reach. The room always satisfied my senses with a pleasant, austere, and patient dustiness.

The secrets of Clan Kyornin's engineering success crowded these shelves. Collections that spoke of free-ranging curiosity begged for browsing. I found titles in English, French, Italian, and Rizha. Fat tomes with middle German script anchored the bottom shelves. No matter they would never be read again. In contrast, there was a wall devoted to frayed and worn encyclopedias of horticulture.

It was not just the books that made this room so restfully distracting. There were cabinets for maps and prints, with wide, narrow drawers and shiny brass hardware. There were careful stacks of parchments and scrolls, their papers brittle with time. There was even a bin of sheet music from the turn of the century.

I surveyed the room again in the soft light. Three places to sit and get cozy with a book or a lover. First, in a corner defined by a Takau carpet in azure blues and burgundy reds, two overstuffed leather chairs befitting a baronial English manor invited us to retire in their strong arms. Dark, lacquered wood and French porcelain completed the effect, with only a stone hearth missing. I liked the velvety, cool leather and the squeak of these chairs. They were just right for curling up with Charles Dickens. One good choice for a Christmas night.

In the center of the hall, a low, muscular table stood ready for laying out maps and folios. Polished mahogany trimmed with ebony, this was a table fit for illuminated manuscripts and illustrations of great cities. Kai once showed me a map of the Ma'rhu. It ran the length of the table and charted every shoal and sandbar. A note in the legend hinted the map had been completed in 1875. This night, illustrations and schematic drawings of fountains covered the table.

But I chose the back corner of the hall, which set it apart from any musty library in Europe or America and revealed the true love of its owners. A large, softly carpeted circle seduced a reader across a threshold to enter an inner sanctuary for literature. The world outside the pillow-strewn circle fell away and left the reader happily immersed and alone with the written world. Here was a library built by people who read until they fell asleep, wanting to be assured of waking up in a sea of stories.

Kai's eldest servant, Pao, brought a tray with mint tea and chocolates. The lean old man winked at me and slipped out of the room. We pulled a few books, then threw ourselves into the cushions. Our eyelids grew heavy. We made love and fell asleep with Shakespeare's sonnets open beside us.

11

On the vernal equinox, New Year's Day in Takau, the Rizha build bonfires atop towers scattered throughout the land. The round stone towers spiral above the rooftops and the smoke spirals to the heavens. The perfumed fires attract fair Yasol'rhishá, who arrives to bless the season. The crops rise out of the soil to hear Yasol'rhishá's beautiful song. She calls the woodland animals together. Birds decorate their nests to welcome her. And it is her blood that flows from a woman. She drives young men mad.

She is also Death's beautiful sister. Those who have suffered from long illness or unjust hardship find comfort in her embrace. Yasol'rhishá gathers weary souls into the soft folds of her skirt.

When the flowers are taken from the altars and the departed are at ease, the Rizha start the new year. Yasol'rhishá stays to offer her good luck and blessings for as long as the fires burn and the celebration continues. So the Rizha stoke the fires and dance for three days and nights.

I TOOK A ROOM IN THE STOUT BUILDING that stood in the southeast corner of the plaza, where the road turned down the hill. It was a corner room with narrow windows on two sides. If I leaned out my north window, I could see what was going on around the

126

fountain. And out my morning window, Am'rha Bo tumbled down the hill to the river, so I could see over the rooftops to the shimmering water, over the walls of the island with its billowing greenery of trees within, and across to the sharp lines of Am'rha Sa beyond. A life-saving breeze often wafted through the high room, carrying with it complex aromas up from the bazaar or, at times, the reedy scent of the river. I laid out my altar, rolled out a sleeping mat, and called it home.

I crossed the plaza and met Kai early one morning to celebrate a minor miracle. The Café Royale had begun to sell freshly ground coffee, bistro style.

"I recognize the fellow they have behind the counter," I said. "He used to work at the American Café across the river."

"Makes you feel at home?"

"Feels like Paris!" I laughed. We pulled new chairs up to one of the iron café tables set out on the plaza. We ordered our drinks and listened to the familiar muffled noise of the bazaar coming to life with the first light. A sleepy-eyed waiter brought two steaming cups.

"So," I ventured. "How did it go last night?"

"Very well," Kai nodded. He sipped his coffee.

"A medical supply law?"

"Oh, of course not, Kath. I hope you never thought the Council would actually support such a thing."

I set my cup carefully into its saucer and studied it.

"Kath, it was a great victory for us that they even let me talk about it! They listened to all our arguments. They heard our concerns. It was Tet'shri, of the river guild, who made the chairman quiet the hall so I could raise every point you and I had discussed. Then Tet'shri proposed a motion to enter officially on the books that the Kyornin had raised these concerns for Am'rha Bo. The Council approved it. Don't frown, Kath. It went far better than I had expected."

"A good first step, I guess. But how long will it take?"

"Try to think in Takau time," Kai smiled kindly.

"Then their grandchildren might do something about it."

"Kath."

"Oh, I'm sorry. You are right, of course. That's a great first step. And I know it was politically expensive for you to take it to the Council. I'm proud of you."

Kai sat back. "There is more," he said. "The Council had been so responsive, I decided to ask about New Year's."

"You did? What did they say?"

"They remembered the New Years' bonfires to call the goddess. It got them thinking of their childhood days. The chairman himself reminded us how everyone used to come out to watch the fires light in succession across the river until it looked like a glowing snake slithering over the hills. His words!"

"The towers would look like that from a distance, one lit after another ... so they remembered?"

"The Commissioner's men were upset at the idea of allowing the tower fires to burn again, but the Council was so enjoying their boyhood memories, the Commissioner did not dare argue."

"They'll let us do it?"

"I proposed the Council repeal the ban on tower fires for the purpose of the New Year's festival. The Council approved it!"

"Kai, you are magic!"

Visions of a full-blown festival to light up all Am'rha Bo filled my head. "If we can light the towers, then we will have the parades, and the music, and the food!"

"Mmm. Honey sticks," Kai grinned. "Children all over the plaza, dripping with honey."

"Mothers will call for your head on a post," I laughed. I savored a swallow of quite decent coffee. "Oh, this will bring the city back to life, Kai!"

"The festival, or the French roast?"

"Both!"

I WAS AFRAID MAGRA would be angry because I was taking time off from our housecalls. I carefully explained that I needed more time to organize the festival. Then I braced myself for her reproach.

"Yasol'rhishá must wear a wreath of rosemary and lilies," she said. I blinked. "And she always travels to the right. People forget that her right shoulder is the dawn."

"You don't mind if ... "

"Now, if you can't find someone who remembers the exact order of the song cycles, I know a graybeard who sang them all and never lost track. He'll know the cycle, even if his mind has lost the words."

"You're not concerned about … "

"You'll be short of lilies this year," Magra mused. "Use daffodils. The goddess won't mind. And the old ones insisted on good incense for the towers, but that is a terrible waste. She will know who's calling. Use the tired stuff. Save the best incense for the altars."

So Magra doubled my workload of preparations for the festival with an overwhelming list of ritual details. She made me interview a dozen elders who had held responsibility for some part of the celebration in decades past. Each recalled with excruciating precision the steps they said must be taken.

"Magra," I finally complained. "It's too much! These people used to work all year to prepare these things! We can't possibly do all of it in a few weeks!"

Magra scowled like a teacher scolding an inattentive child. "Of course not. You choose the essential pieces. You choose what you believe will touch our hearts. Paagh! Keeping exact traditions is for grandmothers with indigestion. The festival is for the children. You use what will bring it to life."

Again and again she made it clear that she indeed meant for me to make the choices.

"Magra, we have time to make the garlands around the plaza or the streamers for the towers, but not both. Which should we do?"

Magra just pursed her lips and watched me think.

"Okay. More people see the garlands, and the greenery sets the mood. Maybe the clans will decorate the towers for us."

Magra agreed. She would have agreed had I chosen to drape the towers in pink sail cloth.

"KATH! THEY'RE COMING! They passed a resolution last night making the festival an official event, and they argued over which of them will make speeches!"

"Over here? On the plaza?"

"We'll build a stage for them on the east side, overlooking the fountain. They'll review the parades and take credit for our work," Kai laughed.

"They will see what the Kyornin has done, you mean. They will finally see the real Am'rha Bo!"

"Security will be tight, of course. I hope it doesn't frighten people."

"Everyone will be celebrating," I said. "The whole Council, you think? Will they really come?"

"Fear of stepping outside versus a chance to show off their robes and jewelry. They will come, I think."

"And the Commissioner?"

Kai nodded. "He will have to escort them. He will want to look like he's in charge of things, I suppose."

I laughed, too. "He'll get up with his starched white uniform and be very impressive, I'm sure. Wielding the authority vested in him by the power of all those shiny medals!"

"They'll upstage all your decorations, I'm afraid."

"I'll get more drummers. To drown out the speeches."

"Good idea!"

I took a deep breath, thinking about how important it could be for us to have the guildmasters finally cross the river. They would see our beautiful plaza. They would see all the people in the midst of a great festival. Soon it will be one city, united by commerce, I thought.

"Oh, Kai. You are terrific."

He stroked my cheek. "You are making it all possible," he responded. After a pause, he added, "But don't forget to get some rest now."

"I'll make it." I smiled with good-humored resignation. "There is always something, of course. We found out this morning that the fourth tower is in such a sorry state that no one dares climb the steps. It almost wobbles."

Kai frowned. "This is no good," he declared. "I will send a crew…"

"There's so little time! You can't take your men away from the plaza. You need … "

"I'll send a crew. We'll shore it up from the inside. Fix the stairs. Don't worry!"

"I shouldn't have mentioned it. But thank you."

"The bonfires are important. Everyone is talking about the race between the towers! It would never do to skip one. I just hope it doesn't get out of hand."

"I know what you mean. All my volunteers will be watching."

"You've heard the rumors?" Kai asked.

"About the Khodataal? Of course I've heard. Wild threats, I

think. What can they do, really? The whole city will be out greeting the goddess."

"They want to make it too difficult and too expensive for the government to keep control over the northern province. They think that makes Am'rha Bo their battleground. This could be their chance to strike."

"But if they disrupt a festival, that only makes them outcasts in the city. More enemies. Can't they see that? It makes no sense."

"I don't know, Kath. People forget what their fight is about."

"You would think after generations of clan rivalry ... "

"Fighting is all they know."

"Then our festival is one way to educate them," I declared. "They will see we can celebrate together."

"Let's hope so."

AS THE FOUNTAIN neared completion, Kai had to throw up a makeshift fence around it so the excited crowds would let him work. The motley canvas wall had the effect of a circus tent, arousing everyone's curiosity. To heighten the suspense, mysterious gurgling noises erupted from inside. Sounds like ocean waves roared for a minute then fell silent. Sudden jets of water burst overhead, only to drop back out of sight. Children swarmed around the fence, peaking through gaps in the canvas and shrieking with excitement with each splashing hiss. I wondered if Kai knew he was raising the anticipation across the plaza to a frenzied pitch.

I called to him through the canvas. When he came out, soaked and dripping, people backed away from us. They watched his face.

"What's going on?" he whispered to me. "Why do they look so worried?"

"They want to know your work is going well," I answered. "That's all."

Kai lifted his pipe wrench and smiled. Everyone laughed and whistled with relief.

"So, how is it going, really?" I asked quietly.

"Three demons to go," Kai answered. "Still working on the water pressure. How are your festival preparations?"

"The wood has been delivered to all the towers by now. The clans have their assignments, though for a while I thought the feuding would lead to all-out war. There are two clans who both claim the ancestral honor of carrying the flame from one tower to the next."

"How did you work that one out?"

"They'll trade off, carrying and escorting the torch. But I'm not sure what will happen at the thirteenth tower! Such a mess."

Kai laughed. "And the parade?"

"The flowers come in tomorrow. Mountains of them. It took a week to choose the girl who will be Yasol'rhishá; they finally picked a stunning young woman from Rhu'mora."

"That's great! Oh, we got the fourth tower reinforced for you. We can rebuild it next year."

"Yes, I heard. That's wonderful! Thank you. But what about all this? You're sure the fountain will be ready?"

"Of course. Almost done," Kai said. "You and I need to spend some time preparing the dedication."

"Me?"

"Yes! It won't have life in it without you!"

I took a deep breath. I forced down a wave of panic as I looked blindly at the crowd on the plaza. Not another burden, I thought. Please. I do not know if Kai could read my face.

"I'm tired," I said, as if that sufficed. "But if we pull this off, Am'rha Bo will never be the same."

The sound of water overflowing onto flagstones caught our attention.

"No doubt of that," Kai answered lightly as he disappeared back into his circus tent.

"Yes. No doubt," I whispered.

ONLY TOR KNEW how tired I was, and never in all our time together did he criticize me or question my judgment.

"I don't think anyone has thought of building the platform to carry Yasol'rhishá," I worried. "It's almost too late! And we need a team to carry it."

"You assigned a clan to build the platform two weeks ago," Tor reminded me. "It is sitting behind the Rhu'pash hall. And the carpet apprentices … "

"… agreed to take turns as bearers. I remember now. Sorry. But the lamp-lighting ceremony … "

"Starts tomorrow at dawn. You are invited."

"Oh. Right," I yawned. "I think I'll just show up at the first tower. I can't do everything, after all."

"You organize. You inspire. You heal. That is everything."

"Thank you, dear Tor. And you always stand in to take my punishment."

"But they wanted you to approve the goddess costume this morning, remember?"

"Oh. Right. We'd better get over there. The ladies will be in a panic!"

"The dog sleeps by the door, or he sleeps by your bed."

I shook my head. "What does that mean?"

Tor hated it when he had to use extra words to explain something. He struggled with a translation. "Either it gets done, or it doesn't. Maybe it doesn't matter."

I laughed. It felt so good to laugh. With the sun setting, I hurried off to see to all the last-minute details.

WHEN THE TIME for the dedication of the fountain arrived, people packed the plaza. And when the canvas fence came down with great fanfare, a religious hush fell over the crowd. At the center of attention, there stood Kai across from me on the lip of the watercourse. The fountain was full and still. I swayed on the edge at Ashka'rhuna's feet and squinted in the afternoon sun. Kai called upon the cardinal compass points and invoked a long lyrical list of deities. Nervously, I recited a water prayer. The chanted response rumbled from the gathered throng. I repeated the last line. The crowd chanted again, louder. I looked at Kai. Once more, he signaled. I recited the line in a big voice. Again came the chant, followed by the warbling Takau whistle. The Rizha had such a natural flair for ritual, everyone knew how this should go. Kai raised his arm. It felt like the plaza itself held its breath. He dropped his arm to signal some unseen assistant, who cranked the main valve. The fountain sprang to life with a sparkling eruption and cascade.

No one in Am'rha Bo had ever seen anything like it. A monsoon flood exploded behind me and surged through the seasons. All twelve demons spat angrily. Fountains shot overhead in a line, mimicking the bonfires planned for that night. And the water swirled under the goddess with a fine mist that dampened her flowing robe.

The illusion of water rushing in a perpetual circle was stunning. The fountain was clearly a work of magic and miracle, and the people immediately took it as their own.

AT DUSK, I waited at the base of the first tower. We stood outside Rhu'mora, at the southern edge of Am'rha Bo, in a sloping tangle of shanties. People waited, glancing up between laughter among neighbors at the tapered silhouette against the purple sky. Children tripped over my feet. Tlia shouted stories in my ear, but I stopped listening.

An honored clan matriarch arrived with the flickering oil lamp that had been the object of a full day of ritual. Lit from the equinox sun, the tiny flame caused the packed congregation to part in awe. The tower door creaked open and the matriarch stepped in. She took a painfully long time to climb the steep spiraling stairs inside. I secretly suspected the lamp had gone out and someone had scrambled in the dark to re-light it. No matter. All eyes were looking heavenward when she appeared atop the tower, flanked now by costumed fire tenders. She held out the glowing lamp for us to see.

The matriarch waited for my signal. I had tried to evade this responsibility, but I had been credited by all with bringing back the fires. Tlia winked at me. I raised my arms. Then everyone in the jammed street raised their arms and shouted. With a pop and crackle, the bonfire overhead burst into life. With it, I felt the people's sense of unity and pride rekindled.

Some old men had been overly zealous with the scented oil, causing the fire tenders to jump back and almost topple over the ledge. Even if they had, their fall would have been checked by the cheering crowd around the base of the tower. The flames illuminated the excited, upturned faces around me.

The next moment we began racing up the alley in pursuit of the torch bearer pelting toward the second tower. Banners waved from every window. Children stared in happy terror from their fathers' shoulders. I ran at the head of the charge to the next three towers. I felt tossed and tumbled by a wave at high tide. But instead of sea foam, I had smoke and streamers in my eyes.

I stepped aside, breathless, into the doorway of the dark ruin of my old clinic to let the wave of people roll by toward the ninth tower. I imagined how this fiery prayer looked to the spectators across the river as it swept through the old city, upstream and uphill. I hoped the old guildmasters were watching.

We lit all thirteen towers. We celebrated before glowing altars set out in the streets. Kai came to my side. We sang and paraded and threw presents to children. Then everyone swarmed into the Rhu'ta plaza.

I leaned over as honey dripped from the long tube of crispy pastry shell. I licked my fingers. Kai laughed, and powdered sugar blew all over his face.

"Now this is a great tradition," he declared.

"Mmm," I replied.

The cool night air was hazy with the aromas of cinnamon and mint. Around us, excited faces glowed by lantern light. Everyone was dressed in their finest clothes, while the poorest, wearing the only rags they owned, pranced about happily with the bright ribbons we gave out for bows and arm bands. Even Kai, who never drew attention to himself with rich attire, had to brush the sugar off his green silk shirt. And I enjoyed the way the long Rizhmadi dress Kai had given me for the occasion swirled around my legs.

A string of firecrackers went off almost under our feet. Fa'rhouzi, the clownish Takau Santa, appeared before us. Dressed in red from his slippers to his cap, his hands and face were bright blue. A swarm of children followed close on his heels. Some little ones tried to cling to his legs. Fa'rhouzi spotted me, pranced close, and bowed deeply. He was played by a weaver's apprentice I had chosen for his mirthful smile and comic demeanor. He handed me a piece of candy, then bowed again. But when he lifted his head, he hit me in the face with a handful of confetti. The children, delirious with laughter, chased him on through the crowd.

Next, a band of drummers blasted a path with a deafening roll of thunder. People scrambled to pull toddlers aside as the band shuffled through the sea of people.

"I hear there was some trouble at the thirteenth tower, like you predicted," Kai shouted over the cheerful noise.

"Oh, some of the young men got rough," I said. "Clan rivalries, you know. But by then, everyone was out of breath!"

"No trouble from the hill tribes?"

"None at all!"

"It looked great from across the river."

"You were out on the island?"

"At Autumn House, saying goodbye. Hey, those were great fireworks!"

"That was our big surprise at the last tower. I wanted everyone to remember this night for a long time!"

"They will!"

I could smell the sweat of a dance troupe as they wedged their way past us in pursuit of the drummers. They carved through the crowd with howls and whistles. Kai's words slowly sunk in. "What do you mean, 'saying goodbye?'"

"Goodbye to Autumn House." He studied my face. "You didn't know? Just as well. I sold it to finance the construction here. The river guild bought it."

My jaw dropped. "You sold it? Autumn House?" I grabbed his sleeve. "How could you … I mean, why would you do that? I never thought … I assumed you had so much … "

Kai waved off my complaints. "Limits to everything. But Clan Kyornin holds the rights here," he said, sweeping his arm across the packed plaza. "It is a glorious investment for us! As soon as I found out we could build here, I knew what had to be done. And now we have all this in common, Kath!"

He was proud and happy. I rushed to recover. "Your great-great grandfather would love that fountain," I said carefully. Maybe Kai didn't hear me through the din of the crowd.

"Love? Yes, it is all done for love!"

I flashed him a smile and took his arm. We allowed ourselves to be swept along by the slow current swirling around the plaza. Taller than most in the crowd, I could greet acquaintances, wend our way around families drifting in tight formation, and still keep an eye on the event over confetti-sprinkled heads. Blinking back tears from a passing cloud stinging with grilled onion, I saw the platform carrying Yasol'rhishá. She waved to the bystanders from her bed of flowers as she floated around the plaza on the shoulders of several dozen young men. I noted they were moving clockwise, as instructed.

"We're missing the speeches from the Council!" I shouted to Kai. "What a shame!"

He laughed again and we ferried our way across the current toward the stage, careful to keep an inconspicuous distance for Kai. About a third of the Council had dared to come. They sat on a stage set with tall-backed chairs facing the fountain. Of course, they all assumed the Kyornin would be their host on stage with them. But the gross impropriety of the young man's absence was forgotten as the spectacular platform of the goddess passed by. The councilors rose to their feet in unison. With jewels sparkling in the bright lantern light, they certainly added to the festive scene. They dripped with even more satin and brocade than usual. They wore velvet hats with feathers that bobbed when they turned their heads. They pointed and clapped like children on a field trip.

Tokmol's officers stood nearly shoulder to shoulder with their backs to the stage and batons poised, watching the crowd. As long as these sentries stood still, no one paid them any attention except to avoid getting pushed within arm's reach by jostling neighbors.

The aged Commissioner, in full dress uniform, stepped forward. He apparently intended to address the crowd, despite the happy cacophony roaring at his feet. In his chalky white uniform, he looked fine and craggy for the occasion. He rooted himself at the front of the stage and surveyed his audience, who, for the most part, was still intent on following the goddess around the plaza or dancing with friends.

Adding to the festive noise, Kai's fountain gushed, sprayed, and sparkled behind us. Standing on tiptoe, I could see it had become a stage for a tight knot of young people. They were distinctive in their modern, if rumpled, Western-style dress.

"Great to see teenagers getting involved in the traditional culture!" I said.

Kai shook his head. "Looks more like trouble."

We shouldered our way closer, trying to hear over the splashing water and the orbiting drum troupe. The youths had a growing audience, causing the parading throng to eddy around them. I pointed to an angry young woman who seemed to have taken command.

"Can you hear what she's saying?"

Kai nodded. "She said she hopes the rich bastards on the Council can see how little we have to celebrate over here."

"Oh."

The young woman stood on the lip of the fountain. Water cascaded around Mortash'rhondí behind her. She wore a pair of men's baggy trousers and a white tuxedo shirt. She raised her voice and pointed at the stage.

"What have you fat old farts in the Council done for us since the earthquake?" she cried. "What have you toads ever done? Hell, just use us and spit us out! I see your faces. You know it's true!"

Those who had been swept along with the parade shuffled to a halt around us. By chance there was a pause in the drumming and everyone heard what the young woman said.

"She's got guts," I said.

"She's in trouble," Kai replied, pointing across the fountain. A line of policemen crossed in front of a band of startled musicians and hurried toward us.

"Maybe we should get them out of their damn walled gardens!" the woman cried. "Maybe … "

"Look out!" I yelled. My voice cut above the noise. She looked over her shoulder.

The crowd was too thick to make way for the officers. They carved a path straight at us by force. The police moved with precision. Batons flashed to the left and right. Unable to escape, people threw up their hands to ward off the blows. A wave of people crashed over and into the fountain.

Then we heard three sharp pops. Gunshots. The electrified air filled with screams. I looked back at the stage. The Commissioner snapped to attention. With a furious, indignant expression, he looked in the direction from which the shots had been fired, right in front of us. He raised his right arm to issue a command. Then he shuddered. Red stains spread across his bleached uniform. He toppled like a statue off a pedestal.

I saw a thin man in a mountain tunic wave a pistol. He fired a shot barely over our heads.

If one person in a crowd screams, everyone else turns to see what the trouble might be. But if ten people scream and start to run, the whole crowd responds instinctively. People sweep up children in their arms and run from the danger. They do not wait to see what the danger is. But in a moment, the surge of the crowd itself becomes the peril.

The press of bodies tore me away from Kai, caught up in the flood, and swept me across the plaza. Fighting for balance, I found myself pushed against Yasol'rhishá's platform. The boys carrying it stumbled. The platform tipped. On my knees, I caught Yasol'rhishá as she slid down in an avalanche of flowers. The poor girl was tangled in her ceremonial robes. We helped each other stand for fear of getting trampled.

I looked into her terror-stricken eyes as she tried to pull away from me, caught in the tide of panic. I hugged her fiercely, with my head down and my feet rooted in the wreckage of the platform. A sudden surge from our left threw us to the ground. Tokmol's men passed by, guarding the Council members huddled inside their tight formation. With batons flailing, they beat a slow escape across the plaza.

The next moment, I heard the stage collapse. It crumpled under the weight of too many people clambering up to escape the crush. Lanterns hung around the stage fell to the ground with it. Now people climbed frantically over those in front of them to evade the splash of flaming oil.

I regained my footing and stood my ground, blinded by smoke and deafened by screams. The wave crashed against the edges of the plaza. There were too few exits and they were narrow and jammed. The wave of wild-eyed people, mostly ignorant of what had set them in motion, splashed back around the fountain. I stood there, holding the sobbing young woman with a garland of a goddess askew on her brow. I stood there while the wave crashed over us twice more as the people rushed for the escape routes. I stood there until the plaza had quieted to pools of shocked and horrified survivors standing still around me. When I finally loosened my grip, my young Yasol'rhishá staggered off into the darkness without a word.

Ribbons and honeysticks and all the symbols of my festival lay lifeless on the flagstones. A few lanterns flickered around the perimeter, lonely now in the empty darkness. The garlands hung limp on the walls, bereft of purpose.

I forced my feet to move. I shuffled past a rack of wreaths and necklaces scattered and trampled. I absently picked up a woman's shawl, paused beside a child's sandal. The only steady sound was the fountain in the center, out there by itself, splashing through its illusion of an endless circle, with angry demons still spitting and a goddess still folding the blessed dead into her soft robes. I walked away.

Many had been crushed to death in doorways and alleyways. Someone had to organize an effort to tend the injured. The police were gone. I immediately set to work and kept myself occupied through the night. Café Royale, looking blasted by a hurricane, was again my first-aid station. I dispatched a team of men across the plaza to find those who needed help. Tor soon appeared, and I sent him to get my field bag and our stock of bandages and splints. Through the long, late hours, we worked our way methodically back and forth across the café full of victims.

When Kai found me, I was intently examining a woman in her forties who was panting against the pain in her swollen arm.

"Are you hurt?" I asked him.

"No."

"Did you get off the plaza? Where have you been?"

"I've been looking for you."

I looked the woman in the eye. "Your arm is broken here, and here. Not your elbow, though. That's good. And lucky." She nodded and gritted her teeth. "I can set the bones. We should do it right away."

She smiled bravely. "I understand," she said. "Please do it."

I brushed the streak of gray hair back behind her ear and nodded my sympathy. She was obviously no stranger to pain. I rummaged through a basket of crude splints.

"Kai, you should have known I'd be here helping the injured."

"You were swept away from me. I couldn't find you anywhere near the fountain. No one had seen you. I was worried sick, Kath! I've been looking among the dead."

"I couldn't find you either. All I could do was get to work here."

"I'm glad you're safe."

I looked up for a moment. "Thank you, Kai. We'll talk later, I promise." I knew I had several broken legs waiting for my attention too. "I've got to stay here for a while yet tonight."

"I'm not asking you to leave. I just said I've been worried for you."

"Bite down on this," I told the woman. "This will be a lot quicker than childbirth." She laughed knowingly. "Here we go, sister," I said with a deep breath. She never made a sound, and the radius and ulna aligned nicely.

Kai helped tie the splint. "I can get you plaster for casts in the morning."

"Great. We'll need it."

"Looks like you have things under control here," he said. "I'm glad you're safe," he repeated.

I moved on to the next victim. Kai left. I didn't dare pause to think about the night. Near dawn, I crossed the plaza to get back to my apartment. Later in my life, I crossed other battlefields. But no field of deliberate violence has ever matched the ashen desolation of that long walk.

12

WE SCRUBBED BLOOD stains off the fountain. We swept up all signs of the incident and hauled away the wilted garlands. Where people are poor, tragedy soaks into the ground and becomes a firm footing for mothers carrying children on their hips.

I crossed the plaza each morning and stopped at the fountain, where self-appointed caretakers kept the drinking water clean. Kai gave them steel buckets and straw hats. For a small fee, they filled water jugs and liberally dispensed news and gossip. Children played an endless game of tag against these caretakers, who, despite long switches and vehement curses, fought in vain to keep the quick youths from splashing in the pools during the noonday heat.

Old women silently jostled for places in the scant shade offered by the new trees Kai planted in a circle around the fountain. The matrons sat there all day, moving with the shade like sundials, watching for their neighbors and clucking about the strangers coming and going. They watched the businessmen who met at the fountain with elaborate ceremony and strutted away officiously for tea. And they policed the flower beds around the trees.

Elsewhere, Kai's flower beds soon would have been trampled by the crowds that swarmed across the plaza on market day. But this was Takau, and the greenery and color was sacred to the Rizha.

People did not step in the narrow beds. Instead, they pulled cobbles to make more room for flowers. The beds were part of the fountain, which had, from the moment of its dedication, become a shrine. Devotees planted marigolds and chrysanthemums like Catholics light altar candles. They ensured the beds glowed with waves of new flowers. The devout first hung garlands of flowers around Yasol'rhishá's neck during the festival, then guaranteed the statue never went flowerless the rest of the year.

I foolishly feared people would cut down Kai's new trees for kindling because of the desperate shortage of cooking fuel. Instead, the revered trees nearly died from care and over-watering. Tree keepers saw to it that well-intentioned fountain visitors did not drown the frail saplings or overload them with fetishes and prayer bundles.

The plaza grew famous. Young acrobat troops from mountain villages, costumed storytellers visiting from the coast, and even white-haired sadhus from India attracted circles of curious people. Across the plaza throughout the day and late into the night, these ephemeral audiences gathered and dissipated like the first fat drops of rain on hot pavement.

Partly by design and partly of necessity — but primarily driven by ingrained custom — Kai's neat rows of market stalls quickly matured into a thriving bazaar. The construction was modern, but the complex tapestry of trade and tradition that spilled into the aisles was as old as the patterns in a well-worn Takau carpet. Lanes about two horse carts wide divided long parallel double rows of stalls. Reed baskets of all shapes cramped the intersections. Leather sandals and plucked chickens hung side by side. Freshly dyed shirts hung by their sleeves overhead like banners, and the hammered brass that crowded the walls reflected the bright colors.

Market day arrived with great fanfare each week. Carts poured in from the north country, laden with everything from produce to pigs. Local vendors stuffed their stalls to bursting. Women sold potpourri and hashish. Honest boys offered to carry loads; others picked pockets.

Syrka, half buried by a mountain of oranges at his new post in the bustling heart of the bazaar, was as caustic as ever, obviously delighted beyond measure at having so many new and wonderful things to complain about. As I approached, he broke off an amiable argument with the silver-bearded carpet seller next door.

"Syrka," I chided him, "you are an old dog barking at the wind."

"The brass vendors will ruin everything, you'll see," he declared, handing me a magnificent orange exploding with fragrance. He refused my coins.

"Please, Syrka, give away your treasures like this and you will soon be sitting at your granddaughter's door again."

He folded his arms indignantly. "If I cannot please the ladies with my favors, you can dump my ashes in the Ma'rhu right now."

I inhaled the citrus perfume. The old vendor crinkled his face in pleasure as he watched my blissful expression.

Three precocious girls came down the aisle, weaving from stall to stall and singing. Each shopkeeper waved kindly at them. A young man with an armload of bracelets frowned and ducked behind Syrka's stall to disappear down a side alley.

The girls recognized me and rushed up to tug on my skirt, remembering too late to bow, and giggling, and showing me their loose teeth. Rizhmadi children have their own dialect of sorts, full of unfiltered humor and word magic.

"Sing, little ladies!" I said. "Tell everyone your story."

These inseparable friends held hands and repeated their performance:

> Old tiger is prowling
> Little birds fly into the trees
> The quick mice are laughing
> Old tiger prowling, sore paws!

"Run ahead, now. Hurry!" I said.

The girls danced down the row with shoppers stepping out of their way. A moment later, Tokmol and his officers came around the corner. No one was surprised.

I tipped my head to the carpet seller. He lounged comfortably on a sagging pile of his inventory and did not move, except for a slight wave of his chubby hand in his lap. I stepped into his open stall and took a special interest in a fine antique rug hung on a pipe near the back.

Tokmol stopped at Syrka's table and hefted an orange. I watched through the fringes of the hanging carpets. Syrka quoted him a high price. Tokmol set the fruit back precisely in its place.

"You are a lucky one, sir, to have a corner stall here."

"I've always had a corner stall," Syrka answered flatly.

"Oh yes, I recall. Near the ferry dock." Tokmol surveyed the aisle. His men took up sentry positions facing both directions. "You might have heeded my advice there. Unfortunate scene."

Syrka's eloquence with muttered expletives had not abated. I bit my lip.

"I tried to warn you, sir. More than the army did."

"All the same to me."

"I suppose," said Tokmol, dismissing Syrka's insolence. He leaned forward. "So, grampa, what's behind these rumors of a new association between the brass bangers and fruit vendors? Are you going to start selling candlesticks?"

Syrka pulled at his scruffy beard. "The merchant guild. Everyone in the Rhu'ta bazaar has signed on. We watch for trouble among ourselves. They were glad to have me join because I've been watching trouble for eighty years! I'm sure they will call you if you're needed," he added with exquisite scorn.

"And who organized this … guild?"

"The engineer. I know you can't touch him. He works for the Kyornin," Syrka said. I cringed.

Tokmol's voice remained steady. "Careful now. Calling a group of peasant shopkeepers a 'guild' does not give them any legal authority."

Syrka laughed. And Syrka had the most derisive laugh I have ever heard, honed with decades of practice.

"The merchant guild will be a demon that eats Am'rha Sa. It will eat you, too, if you're not careful!"

"Very poetic," Tokmol sneered. "Now listen. I won't be here to watch over things personally anymore."

"We'll miss you, of course."

"I strongly suggest you do not let your sharp tongue turn my deputies into new enemies."

"I am an old man who makes enemies every day because it is my eyes that are sharp, and I have nothing to lose but a pile of fruit!" Syrka said gleefully.

Tokmol forced himself to speak slowly. "Please remind your friends that my deputies are the only police authority in the district. You will all find it best to keep it that way, believe me."

It was abundantly clear to Tokmol his warnings and admonitions were going unheeded at this fruit stand. He signaled his men, who closed in around him. Tight-jawed and restless, they squinted at everyone who looked up at them.

"Best you keep to yourself, old man," Tokmol growled, as a parting shot. He marched off at a brisk clip with his officers pulled in his wake.

I fluttered out between the carpets.

"Why did you tell him all that?" I cried.

"Ah, if he learns it from the old fruit seller, maybe he won't crack down on the guild officers, who are young shopkeepers with families and much to lose. Besides, he looked so pissy when I told him, it was well worth it! But you missed the show. You were hiding in those old rags, like a bug in the bark of a tree," he cackled.

"Rags!" exclaimed the carpet seller. "What do you know, over there with your rotting fruit?"

"Excuse me, gentlemen," I said. I left the two old men deep in another vitriolic argument and rushed out of the bazaar.

I knew where Kai was working. I hurried to warn him. And I found him at the bottom of a hole that was going to hold a septic tank. He waved when he saw me and handed a blueprint to his foreman. I waited anxiously as he climbed the ladder.

"So," I said. "Tokmol knows about the guild."

"Good," Kai answered lightly.

"That's not a man who likes surprises."

"Shouldn't be a surprise."

"It's a direct assault on his authority. Aren't you concerned about what he might do?"

Kai regarded me thoughtfully. "Tokmol seems a burden, but he may prove to be an ally in the end."

I looked away and sighed.

"I endorsed him in Council for his new position," Kai said.

"You what? How could you?"

"He knows Am'rha Bo. He knows us. We will need him."

"He's a thief and a butcher."

"You have passed judgment. And you never change your mind about anything. What can I say?"

"Show me some evidence. Give me reasons to change my mind."

"You stop seeing reasons to change."

My stomach tied in a knot. "That is not true … and it's a hurtful thing to say!"

I stared at him. Kai did not apologize. He looked down at the septic tank hole.

"It's my job to read people," I continued coolly. "I have to make quick decisions all the time. When I'm wrong, people die. So … " I stopped. I looked away again. "And I don't have to defend myself."

"No. You don't."

"He will be here any minute."

"Who?"

"Tokmol! He just found out."

"I will deal with him. Did I tell you I found the laws governing new guilds?"

"Really? It's written down somewhere?"

"I found the latest version of the statute. Almost three hundred years old, but still in effect. Turns out I had an original draft in the library."

"Well, that should help."

"I think so."

"Guess he shouldn't see me here."

"Does it matter anymore? Up to you."

"I'll go then."

"Okay."

Neither of us moved.

"Kai, this guild idea. It's fantastic. I just worry."

"I know. Try not to add me to your list of worries, Kath. I'm the exception in your life, remember?"

I looked down the street, expecting to see Tokmol march around the corner. Kai tried hard to sound cheerful again.

"Hey, in fact this subversive new guild is meeting tomorrow night! We have dozens of new members. It should be quite a party! Chaos, rather," he smiled. "I'd like you to attend as my guest of honor!"

"If I can get away."

"We start late. They are all merchants, after all."

"That old building, across the plaza?"

"Right. After moonrise, as they measure things over here. Will you come?"

"I'll meet you there. It's great, Kai. Really."

Kai nodded. I looked away. I could not find room for any exceptions in my life. I felt alone again; a familiar, empty feeling. I swallowed hard and forced it out of my heart. The only way I knew to counter my uneasiness was to throw my love at it.

"Maybe after the meeting," I suggested, tipping my head toward the Ma'rhu. Kai leaned forward and kissed me. Then he suddenly straightened his shoulders. I saw how he distributed his weight like a fighter. His lips tightened into that bemused smile he wore only for politics. I took a small step back, ran my fingers through my hair, and turned.

Tokmol had just rounded the corner. We watched him approach. His men took up guard positions around the construction site.

"Hello, Commissioner," Kai said with a bow. "Congratulations on your new position. I am sorry for the circumstance, but glad the Council has shown their confidence in you."

Tokmol returned the bow. He tipped his head to me, as well. He pointed at the gaping hole at our feet.

"Septic tank," Kai answered. "Number three of a series for this edge of the district."

"Ah," Tokmol said. "I guess this confirms it. You truly are not in this for the money."

Kai laughed freely and I stared in disbelief and covered a startled smile with my hand. It was the only time I heard Tokmol try to crack a joke.

Kai pointed at the hole. "We both deal with the same kind of thing much of the time, don't we?"

At first Tokmol frowned, missing the point. Then we discovered he had a boyish, dimpled grin when something struck him as funny. But it was a trait he thought he could ill afford to reveal. It was a moment of grace for us all, but then he pulled himself back into his perpetual formality. He cleared his throat.

"Sir, this guild idea. You should have come to me first."

"You were busy. You had your orders to crack down on the district after the New Year's tragedy. Everyone understands that. A new guild is surely the least of your worries."

"I need to work with facts now, not rumors. This idea, it could be construed as seditious. Could be a cover. I didn't know who was behind it."

"I thought you'd be pleased. We intend to regulate trade and prevent trouble in the markets. Take some of the load off your men, I hope."

"If you work with us! Sir, multiple claims of authority, taken together, leave no one in command. The situation over here is so fragile now."

"You are in a difficult position, we know. Did you catch the assassin?"

"We know his clan. We have rounded up some of his accomplices. We've at least frightened many of his sympathizers back into the hills."

"Yes, you've frightened everyone," I said.

"Doctor, if the army takes jurisdiction over Am'rha Bo away from me, you will have better reason to complain. I am required to demonstrate clear control of the city … and cooperate fully with the military. Believe me, I've been moderate."

Kai nodded. "Yes, by Takau standards, you have," he said, as a jab to me, I suppose. "But this is where the merchant guild comes in. It could be a strong stabilizing force, especially in this district."

"You are still too far out ahead of us here, sir. Thin legal ground. You've not brought this to the Council."

"The law is on the books. I'll have a copy sent to your office. A guild can be formed for the purpose of regulating a specific trade or market. Once established, a new guild then lobbies for a seat on the Council and may enter into contracts with the government."

"Hmm. In this case, they already have a seat on the Council."

"In effect, yes."

I watched Tokmol take in every shred of information, including words, gestures, and Kai's tone of voice. He would make a very good commissioner, I thought, if his heart were in the right place.

"I need allies," Tokmol admitted, including me with a turn of his head. "But as Commissioner, my situation has become far more political, of course." He checked around us for possible eavesdroppers and considered Kai with a calculating gaze. "It occurs to me, sir, with a viable, active guild behind it, Clan Kyornin could gain a stronger voice in the chamber."

"One of my objectives, Tokmol, certainly."

"Ah. What are your objectives, if I may ask, sir?"

"We are working on a new banner. I suggested the motto 'Peace and Prosperity.' That is what all the merchants want, after all."

"Noble ideals again, sir. What are your objectives?"

Kai smiled, bowed his head slightly, glanced at me, then looked Tokmol in the eye. "I need a counterbalance to the river guild's monopoly, a base from which to negotiate international trade, and economic stability to quench Takau's endless political upheaval. For a start."

I blinked back my surprise. "Kai! We … you have never talked about it in those terms before." I folded my arms and shook my head a little. "Your vision for all this … it's grown!"

"Every idea that takes on a life of its own, grows," Kai said softly. "If it is strong enough, it keeps growing, even without us."

Tokmol considered Kai's list. He pursed his lips. His eyes wandered to check the position and demeanor of his guards, who stood watchful but relaxed because the construction site was nearly deserted except for the foreman and three shirtless workers with shovels in the pit below us.

"This guild. It is firmly under your control, sir?"

"It is democratic, so it's been rather chaotic so far. But yes, they still listen to my advice, usually."

That was an unsatisfactory answer to the new Commissioner.

"Solidify your authority. Then we can finesse the details, as the Council chairman likes to say."

"You will allow us to meet without interference?"

Tokmol tucked his baton under his arm in his customary way. "Within the confines of the law, yes. For now."

"Thank you. Thank you very much," Kai repeated with a slight bow, to acknowledge a formal agreement. Tokmol tipped his head.

"But we will be watching," Tokmol had to add. "Be careful with whom you align yourselves." He glanced at me again. "Is that clear?"

"Yes, of course," Kai answered for us both.

Tokmol considered the septic tank hole again.

"Politics," he sniffed, and that impish grin flashed momentarily across his face. He spun about, snapped a one-word command to his officers, and marched back the way he had come. We watched him go.

"Big plans," I said.

"Dreams," Kai shrugged.

His crew below us had hit a rock too big to dig around. They shouted a complaint up at us.

"And there you have it," Kai chuckled.

I finished the thought for him. "Something always gets in the way of a good idea."

He kissed me again and swung himself onto the ladder. I headed off to meet Magra for our afternoon rounds.

THE FRESHLY PAINTED FACE of the building seemed to be smiling at the plaza. Kai had torn this old but sturdy structure down to bare walls and beams and rebuilt it with a new floor plan. Piles of plaster-dusted rubble lay to either side of the front door, hemmed in by precarious stacks of planks and bricks and tile, the common landscape of Am'rha Bo since the quake. But a thrum and a glow inside betrayed a dangerous liveliness at hand.

"This will be a proper guild hall some day," Kai said, "but right now it's a bit hollow, I'm afraid!"

Kai opened the door for me. The hall was clearly a work in progress. Walls rough-framed between pillars defined rooms not yet closed off, and a cement floor waited for new tile. A checkerboard of scars ran across the ceiling; a fossil record of how the building had been subdivided into a honeycomb of lightless chambers before Kai put his hand to it. An arsenal of sledge hammers and shovels stood at ease beside a fleet of wheel barrows in a corner. The room had nothing to soften the thunder of fifty animated debates already raging as we entered.

I guess I had expected a low-budget version of a Council meeting. Costumes and protocol and speeches. I was mistaken. This gathering was far more typical of Am'rha Bo. Packed with people I recognized from market day and the neighborhoods, the room roared with exuberant arguments.

A flurry of nods and gestures and bows honored our appearance, but, after a moment, everyone turned back to their cheerful arguments, each person shouting to be heard above the din. Because it was loud and exciting and probably illegal, the shop owners and street vendors loved it.

Extraordinary in its democratic composition, the assembly packed into this room defied common social conventions. Street hawkers in their best gray and tattered rags discussed new tariffs with a riverbank wholesaler. Two women who did their business from baskets on their hips bantered with an uptown lady who operated three cavernous fabric stores. Syrka barked at a tranquil Asian with a ledger book in hand. Maybe he really does get some of his fruit from China, I mused.

Kai, fluid as ever when moving through tight spaces, led me into the fray. Everyone acknowledged us with a quick bow as we passed.

"You certainly have gotten the word out, judging by the size of this crowd!"

"Customs run deep. The way these people do business won't change overnight," said Kai. He had to shout into my ear. "But the guilds have been with us for centuries, too. Everyone knows how the guilds work. So it was an easy sell." We slid between knots of shopkeepers happily swearing and gesturing at each other. "Oh, here!" Kai called out. "Kath, here is someone I want you to meet!"

He introduced me to a boy of about sixteen standing in the middle of the melee, looking dazed. He was as thin as the simple wooden flute he held in his hand. But he was very happy.

"This is Jemal. Family from Dhaka. He sells these beautiful flutes down along the waterfront. I've sponsored him as a new member of the guild. And he just closed an excellent deal."

"She say she sell all flutes I make!" the boy exclaimed in broken Rizhmadi. "She take them south!"

"I introduced him to a woman who commissions woodworkers all over town to carve demon heads for a big market in the capital," Kai explained. "She sends a shipment of Am'rha Bo crafts down the river every month."

"I get my whole family make flutes. We get rich!"

"They'll have steady work. And Jemal will meet master carvers."

"That's wonderful! Congratulations, Jemal!"

The boy stood there beaming, flute in hand. I think he already saw himself dressed in silk. We moved on across the room.

"But this is crazy in here!" I shouted. "How can you get them all to talk about one thing, much less agree on anything?"

"Oh, some things have to be done on Takau time. I make a suggestion to certain people. The debate filters through the bazaar for a week or two. Sometimes I hardly recognize the idea when it gets back to me. But I learn what the members are ready to accept."

"Then you push it a little further?"

"Exactly."

"Just like medicine."

Kai laughed. "Yes. They have to believe in it before it will work. Then they are ready to consider the next new thing."

"And they have to think it was all their idea."

"Yes! Which reminds me, the guild has an important job for you."

"For me? What can I do? I'm no shopkeeper."

"Some of the people running food stands have joined the guild, too. You could get them together. Teach them that a clean stall sells more food and makes more money. Get them to agree on better sanitation standards. That would be a start, wouldn't it?"

"Kai, that would be great!" My thoughts raced ahead. "Regular classes. Some kind of certification program. The guild could hire inspectors! We could ... "

Kai waved his hand. "On Takau time, remember!"

"Here he is! Here he is!" cried a lanky merchant from out of the crowd. "Kai'ajhi! They will swallow the plaza!"

"Set up right next to the fountain!" complained another. "People trip over them, sprawled out there!"

"In the aisles!" said a third vendor. I knew him; he was always squawking from behind his piles of cheap trinkets. I remember he sold New York Statue of Liberty souvenirs. "They're setting up in the shade at our feet!" he fumed.

Kai threw up his hands. "Wait. Now slow down. You mean the day vendors around the plaza?"

"Three evictions this week already," said the first merchant. "All turned violent."

"They'll ruin us. Wreck the market for everyone," added the trinket-seller.

"I thought the guild had established rules for that," Kai said.

"Sellers outside covered booths must pack up at dusk," declared the tall merchant. He smacked the palm of his hand for emphasis. As an authority figure, he needed some practice.

"No sales inside the circle of trees," quoted the second merchant.

"They are reserving choice spots among themselves," said the trinket-seller. "Sleeping on their blankets overnight!"

"Ah," said Kai. "Then perhaps you could set up a registry. Have them come to the guild to reserve a place the next day."

"Limit the number of reservations … " nodded the lanky leader.

"Keep one booth in the market where they come to sign up. New list every day … " added the second man.

"Then we control the space again."

"Just like the state army. And the puppet guilds that feed it," said a low, resonant voice beside me. We turned. The new speaker had dark, leathery skin and smoldering eyes. He was stout and barrel chested. He wore a fine tunic in browns and rust. I noticed his mountain boots. Instinct suggested weapons were concealed under the folds of his robes.

"You assume the right to force people out," he said. He studied Kai. "Why do you make the laws?"

The merchants sidled closer together. Even I resisted an urge to step back. Kai, better trained in politics, responded slowly. He offered a fraction of a bow.

"Those who live here are making the laws together, sir. A common good."

"No good for those who have been coming out of the foothills on market day for generations. You cannot live without them here. Now you treat them like criminals."

"We've built a plaza for everybody," Kai said. The merchants agreed too enthusiastically, looking like a comic chorus line.

"No. You built a road for the army. And built one water supply for most of the district. Easily controlled. You deny it?"

"We've not met," Kai said, as a question.

"But I know you," he said. "And your kind."

Kai folded his arms. "I think not. And I think you choose not to see my true purpose here."

I folded my arms, too. "This is Tash'anghani, clan chieftain from the foothills above Bishtafi," I said. "I've treated a number of his people for gunshot wounds."

Tash'anghani glanced my way. "The American doctor. She is generous with her arts. And the engineer is generous with his science. I am asking to what purpose? For the clans of the Rizha? Or for the animals in uniform? Who pays you?"

"I get my reward," Kai answered.

"Yes, you will," Tash'anghani growled.

"Hey, we're not interested in your threats," I said. Kai was always so damn polite about these things. And I always pulled courage out of indignation. "Where were your people after the earthquake? They weren't here helping Am'rha Bo. Have you tried to negotiate with the government? No, you send your children out with antique swords. And now you're talking to the one man who can do more for the northern province than anyone in Takau, and you make these ugly accusations! My Rizha assistant likes to say, 'Easy assumptions are cold snakes. They bite you when the sun comes out.' You should be thinking of what's best for your people."

Tash'anghani laughed at me. It was a short, bitter sneer of a laugh.

"Americans. Telling the world how to live."

Kai touched my arm. "And they have much to offer. Tash'anghani, you are not here to express your gratitude, and we won't ache without it. You were not invited here, either. What do you want?"

"The enemy of my enemy is my friend," Tash'anghani said. "I am looking for ... friends."

"Then you must look elsewhere. We have no enemies."

Tash'anghani laughed again. "If you think so, then everyone — both sides, everyone — will use you. A pity."

A serpentine man slipped through the crowd to Tash'anghani's side. The man wore a similar mountain tunic. He had a dark scar that ran from his left eye to his sharp jaw. He made no attempt to conceal a long dagger with a well-worn sheath at his hip. He whispered urgently in his clansman's ear. Tash'anghani nodded, then frowned at us.

The front door burst open and cries of alarm cut off all debate. Merchants fell back, tripping and cursing. Soldiers with rifles at the ready carved a line into the hall.

"Nobody move!" shouted an army commander. "Step away from the door! Against the wall, everybody!"

THE SOLDIERS CLEARED the middle of the guild hall. Their commander marched into the gap. Tokmol walked in behind him.

Kai stepped forward. "Tokmol! You and I had an agreement! You'll see the statute: A guild has the right to convene!"

"You and I, yes. Permission to meet, yes. But you — all of you — are under arrest for harboring a rebel fugitive."

"What?"

"The army tracked him here."

The soldiers brandished their guns in our faces. The merchants maneuvered to hide behind one another. The big room smelled of sweat and fear as the soldiers shoved carpet sellers and brass craftsmen aside, searching among us.

The commander grabbed Jemal at random, pulled him into the middle of the room, and put a shiny revolver to his head. The poor boy still clutched his crude little flute. His knees buckled. The commander held him up by the arm.

"Where's the fugitive?" he shouted. "We know he's here. Turn him in and nobody gets hurt." He jabbed Jemal's temple with the barrel of his pistol.

General confusion followed. Few knew who he was talking about. I turned to the trinket seller.

156

"Where'd he go?"

"B-b-back door." He pointed behind us.

"Kai, there's a back door?"

"Of course."

I took a deep breath. I stepped out beside Kai, keeping my eyes on Jemal.

"Commander," I said, in a less than steady voice. "Too late. He was here uninvited. We didn't know. But he got out the back door."

Tokmol reacted first. He shot past me toward the back of the building. The commander signaled for some of his men to follow. We heard a brief clattering. Tokmol returned a moment later.

"Snapped the lock," Tokmol calmly reported. "Someone outside took down your sentry."

The commander cursed. He dropped Jemal on the floor. Without another word to us, he turned his back and strode out the front door. Tokmol shook his head at Kai, then followed the commander. The soldiers, guns still leveled at us, backed out behind them.

I knelt beside Jemal. He was ashen, but unharmed. I looked up at Kai. We shared a glance laden with pain, shaken resolve, and a breath of relief. The merchants stared, frozen, at the door. They slowly turned their heads to look at us, alone in the middle of the room. Kai looked around at them and managed a smile.

"You see, the guild has nothing to fear! The law is clear." His audience was not so easily convinced. "They were only hunting down a criminal, don't you see? If they intended to frighten us … think! Would we all still be standing here?" The merchants muttered and straightened their shoulders. "Look, the army is not interested in commerce. Unless you sell guns, I suppose." He got a nervous laugh from the room. "But don't forget — we are dangerous," Kai continued in a serious tone. "Dangerous because we are united. Not united against anyone, certainly not against the government." Everyone nodded, because everyone knew his words would be repeated in the streets and in the Commissioner's office. "But we are united to bring prosperity to Takau, beginning right here, beginning in our Am'rha Bo, at home." He scanned the room and let his words sink in. Then he smiled again and glanced at me with his mischievous grin. "So, we have work to do tonight. Someone has proposed a registry booth for day merchants on the plaza. What do you think?"

The room exploded with opinions and abruptly returned to happy chaos. The meeting continued for hours while Kai and a few savvy leaders guided the debates toward something like consensus. I gingerly helped the food vendors form a committee. When the meeting adjourned, most of the merchants left the hall with a sense of accomplishment and a mood of defiance.

Kai walked me to my little apartment. I felt the tension in my shoulders ease in his long, soft hug. But we did not go out to the island that night as planned. With reluctant acceptance of my exhaustion, he left me and slipped into the dark street alone. I stood very still for a time at my window, trying to catch the sound and scent of the river below.

TYPICALLY, THE NEXT MORNING showed no sign of unrest. I walked out at dawn to find half the plaza carpeted. The Takau rug sellers convened on regular goddess feast days to sell and trade patterns and drink tea. Then even some of the upper-class residents of Am'rha Sa crossed the river to catch the bargains and get a taste of the exotic excitement in our bazaar.

The air filled with the musical sounds of bartering over blankets and chance meetings of friends among the crowds. A trio of girls with angelic voices and a badly tuned yala made a fortune in coins from smiling visitors. A circle of drummers met under a low stone arch at the far corner of the plaza and played their ever-shifting rhythms until the soft May breeze quit for the day and the sun reached them in their echoing grotto. And always in the background wafted the splashing song of the fountain, where the water ran through the seasons around and around in a miraculous circle.

Magra and I traversed the plaza countless times a day as we went about our housecalls. Kai set up a new office for me where precious medicines could be safely stored and I might do a few things with Western efficiency. I saw some patients there and occasionally rested my feet. But most of the time, I practiced my humble arts from my field bag and kept notes in my battered satchel.

I knew all of Magra's herbs, and I knew which ones worked in fact and which ones worked merely because we said they did. I knew how to tell fables of foolish neighbors as the best way to convey healthy behavior. I knew which prayers to recite and when to leave a house so as to impart a shred of hope.

It was a time of substantial accomplishment but ceaseless effort. The Kyornin, his identity still a secret beneath simple clothes and small lies about our "financial benefactor," invited me to a full calendar of ground breakings and ribbon cuttings. He worked on his ambitious projects, never retreating to his comfortable past. He built apartments near the square with communal storerooms below and terraces and balconies for style. New tenants took pride in the sanitary conditions inside the complex; a concern not often seen in Am'rha Bo. Magra and I rarely needed to visit these buildings.

I helped where I could, and mastered the language, and ingested the culture. There was always more that had to be done. And along the way, we lost track of time. Perhaps that is the first symptom.

And there was more trouble: a political poison spread through the northern province, and I watched helplessly as it infected Am'rha Bo. The army, thinking itself the antidote, hastened the disease in countless ways.

As the army tightened its martial grip on the province, the clans answered with defiance. Skirmishes erupted between government troops and the Khodataal in the foothills. Ambitious generals cried constantly for reinforcements. Reputations were made and promising military careers were built out there.

Inevitably, where military posts sprang up, traditional villages disintegrated. In gentle mountain passes where soldiers set up blockades and conducted rude searches, trade caravans evaporated. The caravans preferred to struggle through dangerous alternate routes over rocky ridges. Small clans that lived at the base of the old trails depended on the caravans for trade. Without the caravan traffic, traditional villages had to be abandoned. Deserted villages became havens for the Khodataal. Now the army had something to attack. Soon, no village was safe. The army burned any meager cluster of huts where Tash'anghani's clansmen got food. With nothing left to lose, the villagers joined the Khodataal or came out of the mountains to Am'rha Bo. Or both.

In the city, we heard the stories. Soldiers caught a shepherd with a regulation-issue pistol. The regiment ate his sheep, then used the shepherd for target practice. The Khodataal hijacked a firewood cart as a cover for moving weapons. Now, every gray-haired woodcutter in the mountains feared for his life from soldiers and rebels alike. Soldiers on patrol caught five sisters foraging in a secluded canyon. They raped the girls. The army transferred the soldiers to another battalion for their safety.

Such gruesome stories worked their way into the chatter on the street during a season that was blessed with rare food surpluses. Also that year, an explosion of wildflowers brightened every crumbled hovel and refuse heap. Takau, my Rizha friends laughed, is where paradox was born. With a bouquet of larkspur as payment, I moved on to my next patient.

KAI PULLED ME AWAY from my work one afternoon, and we walked casually from the café into the shade and fragrances of the bazaar. It was a sparkling day with sharp edges and deep textures. The clear light made everything jump out in high contrast. We stood at the incense vendor's stall, trying to judge the subtle differences and grades with our noses, while the merchant, who thought he smelled a big sale, lectured eagerly on the merits of his expensive, imported product line.

A familiar group stepped from under an alley archway and approached us. I recognized their leader. Up close, I saw she was about twenty years old, and the eldest of the gang. She had beautiful, deep-set eyes and long, black hair tied in a rope-like braid. She folded her arms across her white tuxedo shirt. I liked her immediately. By way of greeting, she tipped her head, with only a faint, conspiratorial twitch.

"You always stand up to those uniformed bastards," she said. "We've seen it."

"Thanks," I answered.

Her hands went to her hips. Trim figure under that costume, I noted. "All that crap in the north. And shitloads of army supplies going to the border that our people need here. Who the hell do they think they are? Those things should stay in Am'rha Bo!"

"You're right. Nothing that crosses the river ever stays with us. It has to stop."

She shot a glance over her shoulder at her gang. They all nodded and struck delightfully exaggerated, defiant poses.

"My name's Kavita."

"Katherine," I smiled.

"We know who you are," she announced, wagging her finger at me. She pointed at Kai. "You, too." I caught my breath. "You're the engineer who did the fountain," Kavita declared. "And the new buildings."

I exhaled. There was an awkward pause. "New Year's, during the parade. Guess they didn't catch you," I offered.

Kavita grinned. "Not a chance."

"You must have known they would come for you," Kai said.

"Oh, shit, yeah. But we didn't have anything to do with that ... that shooting."

Kavita lowered her eyes. It might have just then occurred to her she was partly to blame for all those deaths and injuries. Her head snapped up and she looked fiercely from Kai to me.

"All those fat-assed sons of bitches across the river can go to hell," she said. "What are we going to do?"

"As long as the Ma'rhu splits the city, this side will suffer," Kai answered quietly. "We need to find some unbreakable link, some kind of bridge between the two."

"Why ... that's it," I said, catching my breath again. "That would do it."

"What?"

"A bridge. Open Am'rha Sa to everyone in Am'rha Bo. Everyone! Imagine! A constant stream of people — and food, machines, hardware, everything! Motor trucks, foot traffic, even vendors' carts!"

"I didn't mean a real bridge. I just ... "

"But we'll have to do it. A real bridge. You're the engineer. Don't you boys love to build bridges?"

"Now, Kath, you don't ... "

"It doesn't have to be the Brooklyn Bridge," I said, hunting for eye contact. "Two lanes. No railroad. Just trucks. And lots of people!"

"You have no idea how difficult ... "

The idea took hold. Kavita studied us.

"Kai, we have to do it. We'll build it with money from Am'rha Sa. The guilds can open trade across the border to the north."

"It would take more than that."

"Okay," Kavita said, joining me. "The government can move their damn army up the road from here if there's a bridge. Let them pay for it. But then it will connect the north to the capital, and us to the coast."

"The river does that."

"The river is slow," I countered. "The river can't be navigated by big ships just north of us. You know all that." Strategies sprang to my mind. "The politicians and the guildmasters have new automobiles and they need roads, not rivers! They'll do it! And they will open Am'rha Bo to the future at the same time."

"But the span … "

Kavita accidentally dropped her swaggering posture. "It would be the pride of Takau," she said in a hushed voice.

"But … "

I didn't even hear his technical concerns. The vision exploded full-grown before me. It seemed so necessary. It burst upon me as a certainty, an inevitability. From the moment of the idea's inception, it crashed on us like destiny.

Kai scowled. "It would take a number of enormous piers, and we'd have to anchor it mid-river, and … "

"Think of all the people a project that size will employ!" I gushed. "The job alone will breathe life back into Am'rha Bo!"

"You'd put the ferrymen out of business," Kai said.

"Oh, hell!" Kavita laughed. "All twelve of them? That's what they get for taking bribes to transport the rich and making us wait."

"A bridge means new jobs for hundreds. Thousands!" I added.

"It would take years."

"And not a moment too soon! Won't that be great for the laborers in Am'rha Bo who lost their livelihoods in the quake?"

"The engineering … "

"You can do it. I know you can. Your classmates will be envious."

About then, I became aware of a familiar tune, sung by little girls down the aisle: " … the quick mice are laughing. Old tiger prowling, sore paws!"

"Time to go," said a young man in a tattered army overcoat.

Kavita wagged her finger in Kai's face again before she left. "Don't let those rich bastards stop you," she said. "Tell them we'll kick their asses and burn their prissy palaces if they don't give us our rights!" Her gang ducked into the alley. "And build that bridge!" she called out to us, then disappeared.

I looked at Kai and chuckled. "Don't take it personally."

"I don't want to talk to him right now," Kai said, glancing about.

"Please, no," I agreed. We slipped around a stall heaped with mint before Tokmol and his men came within sight.

We retreated to a place nearby where a little grandmother who was all wrinkles served tea on a cracked balcony that happened to command a panoramic view of the river. We might have been her only customers, which was just as well, since she could barely walk. But it was always private. We rearranged her three mismatched chairs and a rickety wooden table. Every time I set down my tea tumbler, the table listed seriously toward the open vista.

"Kai, we have to do it," I repeated. "What do you think?"

"We should just bring her a new one."

"What?"

"A table."

"Kai, I meant about … "

"I know. It's too big. You'll have to give me some time."

We had by then grown comfortable with long pauses. The tea was fresh and sweet. "She might be offended," I noted.

Kai gave me his sidelong glance and a smile. "One moment you are talking like an American industrialist, and the next you are thinking like the Rizha!"

"I must be difficult."

"Yes. You are. But I love you."

I reached out to touch his hand. The table wobbled. We laughed softly.

THAT IS HOW THE IDEA was born and that is where we left it at the time. But a few weeks later — as the temperature rose and a dysentery outbreak spread, after soldiers gunned down four young men on the docks, after a clan from the high mountains numbering close to a hundred tried to camp beside the fountain but were driven up to Death's Door, and after I fell asleep at a table while attending a woman in labor across the room because I had not been home for three days — I crossed the mud-bloodied river and walked alone to Autumn House.

14

I STEPPED ONTO the familiar polished marble floor. The room had a sharper edge. The same lacquered panels and translucent tiles. The air still deeply cool, still a refreshing rescue from the ponderous pre-monsoon heat outside. But it tasted different from before: The air was too still, and felt locked up and musty. Autumn House had lost the light fragrances and easy clarity of Clan Kyornin.

I turned to greet my host. Tet'shri walked through a curtained archway with a welcoming smile and a brisk bow, as if he had been expecting me.

"Welcome, welcome, doctor! Oh yes, I know you. I know about your great service to our city. Takau is deeply in your debt. The Rhu'pasham is honored by your visit, truly. I am eager to hear what brings you to our door!"

He bowed again, then shook my hand. This guildmaster was a smooth host, by Eastern or Western standards.

"Since no one in this house is ill, I assume you are here on pleas-ant business!" he chuckled. "But please! This way, into the parlor. First, a cup of tea."

I was back in the parlor where I had described my clinic to Kai. New furniture, and each piece was singular and fine, but I frowned at the mismatched Victorian chairs. Trophies, I thought, not furniture. And nothing Rizha.

I scolded myself. Just odd to see someone else in a familiar house. Of course it is. But why would anyone put that ghastly rosewood cabinet in that corner? I smiled and took the seat Tet'shri gracefully offered.

I reviewed my speech as his servants arrived with silver trays of tea and sweets. It will modernize Takau, I'd tell him. He could help avoid violent unrest if he could balance a flow of supplies to the slums. Open the northern border for trade. Get military contracts. Big business opportunity.

"I've heard the monsoon will reach the coast in the next few days," said Tet'shri. "Right on schedule, I think, from a scientific point of view. But it never arrives early enough for us, does it?"

I agreed, but had a mouthful of cinnamon cake.

"You know, of course, that it was the Rhu'pasham who brought the monsoon? Oh yes, in the days of the first Rhu'pash, all of Takau dried up in a terrible drought. Lasted many years, with weather just like today. Too horrible to imagine, isn't it? The country was turning to dust, and something drastic had to be done."

Tet'shri sipped his tea and studied me as he told his story. His steady smile began to put me at ease.

"The people came to the great Rhu'pash, known for his mastery of the river, and begged him to do something, since he could speak to the waters. They say he walked right out onto the river and called upon Ma'rhu herself. Perhaps you've seen the picture in tapestry designs? That is my forefather. He called to Ma'rhu and stopped the river. It simply stopped flowing into the sea."

"But how would that end the drought?" I asked, playing along.

"Well, the great father god of the sea was distraught, of course. Spurned by his lover." Tet'shri smiled even more broadly. "Soon he churned himself into foam and piled up the clouds so he could ride them inland to find his mistress, Ma'rhu. She told him she would return to his arms only if he brought water back to the land. Eager to impress her with his passion, he sent the first monsoon. And every year he sends the rains again, to keep his lover happy."

"Oh, I see. And, naturally, the Rhu'pasham has been accorded mastery of the river ever since," I said, as though finishing his story.

"Yes!" Tet'shri beamed. "Not that I'd try to stop the Ma'rhu," he admitted playfully. "But my clan has held the rights to the river since history began here."

His claim had an edge of ferocity that sapped the lighthearted mood from the room. But I was used to savage clan pride in Takau.

"Yes, of course," I answered simply.

A servant poured me another cup of tea, then bowed and backed out of the room. Tet'shri sat back in his chair and regarded me with a more serious demeanor.

"But now," he said, "I do not think you came to hear old fairy tales. Americans always mean business. I like that. What do you have in mind, doctor?"

"Conditions in Am'rha Bo are … difficult," I began. "So many goods and services just can't be found. Raw materials, supplies, even food is sent to the north or gets shipped downriver, while little of it stays in Am'rha Bo, where so many are eager to work and contribute."

Tet'shri nodded. I was speaking in terms he could appreciate.

"As I am sure you are aware, there are great opportunities for trade in the northern province and across the border, but merchants can't get their goods safely across the river to Am'rha Sa and down to the capital, especially during the monsoon."

"Unfortunate trouble in the north right now," Tet'shri said. "And the dock yards are limited. But yes, good opportunities there. No one knows it better."

"And that is why I'm here," I said. "My concern is healthcare, of course. But without trade and support from the rest of Takau, my work is mostly wasted. We need to open Am'rha Bo to the world. And," I added carefully, "I think clever businessmen could find significant profit in it, too."

Tet'shri chuckled. "I see why America has become the greatest nation in the modern world, blessed with such women. Now, what exactly do you have in mind for the Rhu'pasham?"

I took a deep breath. "Some of us have talked about whether the time has come … to build a bridge across the Ma'rhu."

I was afraid just voicing the idea would get me summarily thrown out in the street. He might call the idea sacrilege, a plan to desecrate the sacred river. He would also see it as a threat to his business empire. But now I'd said it.

"A bridge!" Tet'shri replied brightly. "We have dreamed of building a bridge to the western bank for many, many years! And just recently, the army has looked into it, with their concerns about the northern border, you understand. I see you are a woman of vision, indeed."

I had laid out all my arguments in my mind, with economics and politics and science and patriotism and greed carefully worked into the formula, but now my pitch fell apart because the one circumstance I had not considered was that my idea was not new. Suddenly, I felt awkward and foreign again, recalling my early visits to the guild halls.

"I was afraid the Rhu'pash would oppose the idea because it would ruin the ferry traffic," I stumbled.

"The ferries?" he laughed, "They are nothing. A headache. An impediment to commerce." He grinned and raised his eyebrows at me. "Naturally, with a bridge, the guild would expect to levy a small toll to compensate us for maintenance."

"Of course. That's how these things go," I agreed, relieved.

"A bridge would open the northern province for trade, in one stroke," Tet'shri declared. "Good commodities at hand. Important resources. Link to the border. I don't need to tell you the government thinks about these things, too. And a bridge would bring Am'rha Bo and Am'rha Sa together at last." He studied me another moment. "That, of course, is your concern, am I correct? Ah, you know that where I see profits, you will see jobs. Better food. Houses. And medical care. Yes?"

I was speechless only for a moment. Then I recited the litany of symptoms resulting from the disease of segregation brought by the river. With my old enthusiasm, I spread before him my vision of tangible justice and budding prosperity for Am'rha Bo, or at least basic public services, I argued.

"Expensive dreams," he said, pursing his lips. "But you are a blessing to Takau." He sat forward and brushed some crumbs off his lap. "You think a bridge will change centuries of tradition? I don't know. But," he smiled and wagged his finger, "I know for certain there's a fortune to be made on the building of it."

"So I thought, with your position on the Council and your trade and government connections, if you would voice your support for the idea ... "

"You need far more than a voice of support!" Tet'shri laughed. "You need financing and contracts." He thought a moment. "You need control of both river banks for construction. Labor crews. Machinery. Mountains of steel. And you need political influence," he winked.

"But you believe it can be done?"

"The problem is," he continued slowly, "I know of only one Western-trained engineer in Takau capable of designing such a thing. I think you may know him, too — the Kyornin?"

He was watching me carefully. "I know him," I answered.

"A farsighted young man," said Tet'shri. "Wholly committed to raising Am'rha Bo out of the dust and filth. I hold him in high esteem."

"You've been supportive of his proposals to the Council," I said. "That is why I felt I could talk to you."

"Ah, yes! At Council. That is where I've seen you before! Of course." He paused. "Did the Kyornin send you here today?"

"No. He doesn't know I'm here." I did not want to reveal that Kai might know and care I was meeting privately with Tet'shri.

"Ah," Tet'shri repeated. "The young Kyornin gave me good advice some time ago regarding a wild scheme I had. Oh, it involved building a series of locks upriver to open the north to coastal commerce." He waved his hand. "Financially impractical, and the Kyornin explained why, in terms an old fool could understand. It would have ruined me."

"But it shows you are not afraid of ambitious construction projects."

"And that I know when to seek expert advice! I will come to you if I get sick. I suggest we go to the Kyornin to design a bridge. But our Ma'rhu is so wide here. I wonder if it is even possible."

"They can build caissons and sink pylons midstream," I said.

"Yes, yes. In a normal river that is so. But I wonder if any bridge can withstand the monsoon floods."

"The Kyornin can do it," I declared. I realized as the words came out that I had just made my relationship with Kai transparent. Tet'shri did not visibly react.

"He respects you," I quickly added. "I think he will agree to help us, if the request comes from the Rhu'pash."

Tet'shri stood and walked across the room. "There are, hmm,

political considerations, of course," he said in a low voice. "While I am very fond of the Kyornin, if you know the old-fashioned ways of Takau at all, well … " he paused. "Please understand, the river guild mustn't be seen to be in Clan Kyornin's debt."

"This would be strictly a business deal," I suggested quickly. "A partnership of sorts, right? And the Kyornin only wants what's best for Am'rha Bo."

Tet'shri turned back to face me. "Ah, that may be. You seem to know him well," he said, with a bit of question in his voice. I nodded faintly. He clasped his hands together. "Such a bridge would be the pride of Takau," he declared gravely. "If you could help win his support, this would be a great, great gift to the country. For generations to come."

I remember feeling all this bordered on melodramatic, but I dismissed it as the awkward sincerity of a shrewd businessman who had feigned sincerity too often. Nevertheless, I felt suddenly wary and wanted to stand on firmer ground.

"I suppose it will take months of planning. The big ones take years to build."

"And not a moment too soon! Won't it be great for the laborers in Am'rha Bo who lost their livelihoods in the quake?"

"That is just what I've been saying!"

"Of course! Well, you came here to win the support of the river guild. You have it. Indeed, you don't know how much this means to me."

He poured me more tea. I consciously steadied my trembling hand.

"So here is our business plan, doctor. If you will secure the Kyornin's support, I will co-sponsor the proposal in Council with him. He will be given all the credit, of course."

"The Kyornin is already thinking about the design. Naturally, he has doubts about the practicality of attempting such a massive project here in Takau. The first step is to convince him we have working partnerships. With the guilds, I suppose. And the government."

"I will make some quiet inquiries. I have certain … connections … in the capital. I can make suggestions to the brass, so to speak. And I can begin the arrangements for the construction site. Then I will discuss the details with the Kyornin personally."

"Tet'shri, from the moment the idea came up, I have been absolutely convinced the bridge can and must be built. With your help, we can do it."

"I feel it, too," he said. "An era of cooperation for the good of Takau. And prosperity," he smiled.

He led me graciously to the door. The sun was sinking behind Am'rha Bo. "This will be an exciting time!" he added with enthusiasm. "I am most pleased you came to me. Not a moment too soon."

"Thank you," was all I could manage. I felt a little queasy, but did not understand why. "Thank you," I repeated. Beaming, Tet'shri bade me good evening. In the first moments, we never know the magnitude of what we have set in motion.

ALLEYS BECAME FLASH FLOOD CORRIDORS. Houses collapsed in the night, and malarial mosquitos bred in stagnant corners. The constant deluge of another monsoon season became routine. I shouted medical advice over the thunder of rain on tin roofs. I diagnosed a bed-ridden woman while water dripped down my back from a leak overhead. When the doctoring was done, we stood in doorways telling stories, ignoring the water that eddied around our ankles.

Yet the limitless ingenuity of the people prevailed. They diverted runoff by a repertoire of cobbled dikes in the street. Laughing teams of women wove river reed into screens and canopies. We all used wobbly plank bridges and steps made from old crates.

And the necessities of the season also brought opportunities for entrepreneurs. There was a brisk back-street trade in scraps of canvas, collected and patched into crazy quilt tarps. The Ma'rhu carried treasures stolen from upstream, so a cadre of those willing to risk the covetous grasp of the current harvested the river daily. They combed the shoreline eddies or balanced on tethered rafts to snatch debris from the water that could be bartered and sold on shore.

For good or ill, the monsoon slows everything except the river. Heavy machinery could not move up the road, so the army retreated. Travel through the foothills became so treacherous the Khodataal kept to the highlands. It seems even terrorists and snipers stay home out of the drenching rain.

And it was a wet year. Several times, high water tore up the ferry dock, isolating Am'rha Bo for days. You can fight a thief or the government, the Rizha say, but against old age and the monsoon, there is nothing.

For my part, I confronted opium overdoses and a rise in tuber-culosis cases. To my surprise, neither an addict nor the disease killed me that summer. The monsoon gave me time to think, but I did not find any satisfying conclusions. The military was right, I conceded, to protect the border — ill-defined as it was — and attempt to bring the warring feudal clans under the banner of one comparatively modern government. But I argued the Khodataal also were right to defend their homes and to oppose the vicious injustices served on them. I suppose Tokmol was right to bring the force of law down hard on anyone whose actions might set off more savagery. Of course, the people of Am'rha Bo were right to swim with the tide, trying to please whomever was at the door in order to protect their families from the escalating violence. Kai was certainly right to put his heart into building a civil infrastructure as the best defense against unrest and despair. And I was right to heal the sick, one patient at a time, without passing judgment on their lives.

The monsoon also gave people time to talk and, that year, orga-nize. The merchant guild made an institution of itself. Membership in the guild magically transformed a cobbler into an impassioned politician. Petitions were signed. Committees formed. Nothing much actually changed, of course, but the freshly minted guild members swaggered and primped with newfound pride.

They carried their black, broken-ribbed, secondhand umbrellas like family banners, furled but prominent under cover or held high in public, whether it was raining at the moment or not. From the balcony of the Café Royale, I liked to watch them congregate on the plaza, then scatter, then rearrange in little clumps as new conversa-tions began, then burst apart, only to coalesce again as business and politics were conducted beneath their dubious shelter.

In that time, we had a community that sparkled out through the faceless crowds. I am thinking not just of my patients for whom I had softened or shortened a disease, though they embraced me as we passed in the market, spilling baskets, blocking the way, and drawing smiles all around us with their exuberance. Such memories I also have of the young mothers living far from the child-rear-ing wisdom of generations left behind in their villages. They also circled around me, not so much for my medical knowledge but for the sisterhood they found together through me. I think of the chil-dren who taught me songs, then required me to lead their chorus each time I met them, so I had music everywhere I went. And what became of my dark refugee friend, forced into the streets again, who came naturally to me in the morning? He came to receive my concern, though that was all I had to offer him. But it was my caring he needed, so he could bravely chide me for it, laughing at how things could be worse, after all, because we're not dead yet, he said.

And others from foreign lands surrounded me, as though I were the native, as though I belonged and they could, too, if they kept close to me. We shared many languages between us — English the least among them — and often spoke in the fluent universal grammar of smiles and shared bowls of rice. Yet I also had many who were raised there in the slums who took me as their own mysterious white woman, link to a larger world, doctor, storyteller, key to their own gritty lives somehow, and friend.

I do not know why so many orbited around me. I simply showed a genuine interest in their sorrows and joys. I took their concerns as my own. I healed and taught when I could. I shared grief and silence when all else failed. Just followed my heart I was richly rewarded.

DISCREET CORRESPONDENCE OPENED a dialog between Kai and Tet'shri. Then an invitation arrived, with an oblique mention of me, so it was understood that I was welcome, too. I wore my best Rizhmadi dress, repaired since the New Year's incident. Kai chose an austere family robe over a Western business suit. Though incongruous to my eyes, it was a common hybrid fashion in Am'rha Sa. It expressed a double message of modernity and tradition that Kai carried with grace.

We arrived during a break in the rain at the wall of camellias that shielded Autumn House. I cringed when two burly guards threw the gate open, then slammed it shut again behind us with a tactless clang. I stole a glance at Kai. He was frowning at the gardens. New gardeners had pruned a row of bloomed-out azaleas into a severe straight line. Gravel replaced the border of begonias along the walkway. The twin reflecting pools needed cleaning. We walked without speaking to the great front portico.

Tet'shri met us at the door with ritual greetings and deep bows. But, once past the formalities, he dispensed with the stiff customs. Draped in his customary burgundy and gold, he made a great effort to be effusive and cordial. He led us into the parlor, with apologies for having failed to match Clan Kyornin's taste in furnishings.

They served us tea in translucent porcelain cups with sterling silver spoons. At first, Kai would not sit down. I tried to compensate, responding warmly as Tet'shri tried to thaw the atmosphere between us. Finally he paused, looked us over, and drove straight into the subject at hand.

"I have pursued this very carefully, and I am very, very pleased with the response I have gotten from everyone of influence," Tet'shri said. "Naturally, I used your name to gain respect from many. I carried your idea around the capital and to some key supporters on the coast. Tonight, I will point out those of the Council I think will support us. I mean substantively," he said. He set down his teacup for effect. "And I made the proposal to the military."

"The army was responsive?" Kai asked carefully.

"Oh, they were short-sighted and wanted to throw a narrow, single lane across right away. One that would only last a few years."

Kai shook his head.

"I know," Tet'shri continued. "I told them so. And I told them, look at how the Kyornin builds things. If the bridge is built to last only a hundred years he won't be satisfied!"

"They have to understand there are just no shortcuts for such a long span," Kai frowned. "There's the weight ratio, and compression issues, and the rotational members needed to break the continuity of stresses, and … "

Tet'shri laughed lightly. "You know I am no engineer! It remains for you alone to explain these things to them. And to the Council. But here's the news! I have secured an agreement — pending contract negotiations, of course — for the government to underwrite design and construction."

"All of it?" I gasped.

"Nearly," Tet'shri grinned. He was flush with the success of his deal-making. "The city, through the Council, provides all the land necessary. And day-to-day management of the workforce and such." Tet'shri waved his hand. "The details."

"The river guild has jurisdiction over the shoreline already, doesn't it?"

"Yes, of course," he smiled. "However, it is all dependent on the Kyornin agreeing to supply certain other … requirements." He studied Kai's face.

"An easement. I know." Kai took a deep breath.

"A great gift to Takau."

"Necessary," Kai said. "The Rhu'pasham will share a similar burden on both shores?"

"Willingly," Tet'shri nodded.

My mind leapt forward into the practicalities I could see. I thought out loud.

"For something like this, you'll need a base of operations. And office space."

"And here is my proposal to you!" Tet'shri declared. He waved a sheaf of papers. "Renovation orders! I have already put my signature to them! The first step toward building our bridge will be the renovation of the old guild hall on the Am'rha Bo quay! There's work for your people," he smiled at me, "and a proper office for the head engineer! You know, it was abandoned in my father's last years. Turned to warehouses. Rats' nests. Something of a shame and embarrassment to the Rhu'pasham, I must tell you. But here is my first contribution! And my commitment to Am'rha Bo! If," he added slowly, "I am assured of your full participation?"

"Why, that's fantastic!" I exclaimed. "The guild hall will stand like an invitation to cross the bridge. And a good place for you to work, Kai. Tet'shri, we've been waiting for others to begin investing in the western shore again. I knew we could count on your leadership."

"I am following the Kyornin," Tet'shri said. "His vision. And his business genius," he added, winking.

Kai took a deep breath. "A commitment across the river will bring great rewards to the Rhu'pasham. You will not regret it."

I was annoyed that Kai kept his stiff demeanor. This was our breakthrough. This was a victory in hand!

"I am sure I will not regret it," Tet'shri replied. "And I am confident it will bring a high return on your investment, as well." Tet'shri gave me an apologetic look. "We are businessmen, after all."

"This will bring great honor to the Rhu'pasham," I said, trying to use the formal syntax.

Tet'shri tipped his head in appreciation. "And glory to Clan Kyornin," he added, extending his hand. They shook hands, then instinctively followed the gesture with a bow. I wanted to hug them both. I hugged myself. And now, I thought, we will finally make Takau embrace my Am'rha Bo.

THREE WEEKS LATER, September and the fog arrived. Walls steamed in the sunlight. Gentle breezes chased the dissolving clouds. People lingered in the streets again.

We came to dance in our plaza. At nightfall, the fog poured up the alleys from the river to swirl around the fountain, and we gathered with the musicians. Players tuned their yalas and flutes. They tapped and tightened drum heads and grunted approval of subtle tone changes. Few words were spoken; the conversation passed between instruments.

Men and women arrived like apparitions out of the fog. This was a cool, thick, shimmering fog that veiled the perimeter of the plaza. Clusters of wide-eyed children watched the adults. The children knew instinctively that magic was afoot.

Magra appeared. She held a blue vial of scented oil. She startled the musicians as she circled and anointed each one on the forehead. I heard her chanting under her breath as she approached. She reached up and anointed Kai, who was standing next to me.

"Ma'rhu keeps singing," she whispered.

"Forever and with love," Kai answered and bowed.

Magra touched my forehead. I smelled rosemary and cedar.

"Ma'rhu keeps singing," she whispered.

"Forever and with love," I said.

Her craggy face was radiant. I remembered the thousands of doorways Magra had silently blessed with a touch of her crooked hand as we left the homes of our patients. I heard her admonishing and teaching and scolding and soothing and mourning. I saw her carrying the heavy funeral basket across sooty Death's Door. I saw her with arms raised over the water. In the same heartbeat I pictured her bending over the cribs of newborns, giving each a secret name while she tucked a sachet of protective herbs under the blankets.

Magra touched my chest with a bony finger. Her glistening eyes became those of a girl at her first turning, when an old healer abruptly took her by the hands. I saw a young Magra bartering at the counter of a shadowy apothecary, and saw her following her mentor up a damp alley. Another stooped but agile woman ahead of them looked over her shoulder and laughed.

"My daughter," Magra said. "Dance!"

She turned and found herself a seat on the lip of the fountain with demons spitting behind her. And the drummers agreed on a rhythm.

Men answered the beat with syncopated stomping. A moment's fear shivered through my body. I hadn't realized there were hundreds of men on the plaza. They sounded like an army fallen upon us out of the dark. The deep heartbeat drum thundered a command. The men gathered in the east with an angry strength in their dance.

I joined the answer from the great flock of whistling and shouting women. We poured together in the west, feeling barefoot women's joy.

Everyone rose on tiptoe to the chorus of the middle drums that bound the fog music together. Then the high singing drums burst in exuberantly. The flutes met somewhere over our heads. The yalas filled the mist with rich harmonies.

The beat quickened. We women, snake-armed and swirling, rushed up behind the men. We hissed and moaned and let our hair fall free and fly. The men turned and charged. We howled and screamed and stamped. The men spread their arms and withdrew, drawing us magnetically into the south. We circled and feinted and surged. We lost them in the fog. We found them in the music. And in the center, wafting in and out of view, the fountain sang for us all, flowing through its endless cycle of seasons.

A delicious spasm coursed up through my belly and, irresistibly, with skin hot and tingling, I threw up my arms. I felt it in every woman around me. The men rushed in among us. A single frenzied, brilliant drum filled the plaza.

Then the flutes and the yalas found one harmonic chord. The heartbeat drum hit a solid earthen foundation. The drums flew into a driving ecstasy.

I knew it when Kai came up behind me. I spun about, and our hands — almost glowing, but not quite touching — mirrored outward circles between us. We danced together and the world turned lightly around us for a long time.

When the drums finally brought us back from the journey and the yalas sang a closing prayerful refrain, we became hundreds of dancers standing in a thinning fog again. The most restful and timeless music of all embraced us as we held hands around the fountain. Serenely, we faded into the holy dark together.

15

TET'SHRI KEPT HIS PROMISE to renovate the old river guild hall. He summarily evicted the vendors under the veranda, along with the pigeons and rodents. In short order, the river guild cleared rooms, refinished floors, repaired walls, stripped and polished woodwork, and installed new doors of oak and teak. Fresh paint perfumed the building. Outside, the boats that floated in the carved relief that ran around the balcony glistened again. The acid-washed marble stairs blinded the common crowds along the riverfront with a white glare so incongruously clean that no one dared step on them.

Kai led me up those steps and under the gilded boats. From the entry atrium, a large room opened to our left. Inside, three lanky porters and a uniformed chamberlain of the river guild argued furiously.

"Delivery of new furniture," Kai explained. "Drafting tables, I think. The assembly instructions are in English or German, so of no use. They've been fighting about it all morning."

"Maybe they need an engineer."

"They need a supervisor. Tet'shri ignores details. He's only interested in the big contracts and his new political influence."

"He should just hire some good managers."

"I've heard he may bring in an American firm. The military would like that."

A team of craftsmen lined a broad staircase. They had half of a hardwood banister built. We climbed around the carpenters to reach the second floor, where there was no railing at all, which gave me a dizzy feeling when I looked down into the atrium. Away from the open landing and past a ponderous line of large, ornate doors, we paused at the end of the upstairs corridor.

"My office," Kai announced.

"I approve," I smiled as I stepped into the room. A silvery Takau carpet softened the freshly polished hardwood floor. Kai smiled, too. My approval was of no consequence, but it pleased him anyway.

The office commanded the back corner of the building, farthest from the constant clattering of the quay. To my right, a setting of lustrous cushions and a tea table waited graciously for company. Before me, at an inviting angle, stood a broad desk with room to walk comfortably behind it. Light slanted in through a tall window. A vase bursting with fresh daffodils distracted my eye from Kai's familiar pens and papers.

"This," Kai said with a note of playful conspiracy in his voice, "is Tet'shri's father's former private office. You have no idea how unlikely it is that Clan Kyornin would be welcome here."

"Well, Kai, I think Tet'shri doesn't care about old family feuds. He wants to make a fortune on the commerce that will come over the bridge."

Kai lifted a long role of curiously shiny indigo-stained paper from his desk.

"That's fine. I hope so," he said. "I have to hope so." He rummaged through a desk drawer and pulled out a box of thumb tacks. "But now. The big moment!" He smiled again. "Will you help me put this up on the wall? I'll never get it up there nice and straight without you."

Together we unrolled the blueprint for the bridge and held it up across the wall. I remember feeling enchanted by the crisp paper with its odd smell and the artistry of detail laid out before me. Holding the edges, I aligned a corner with the high ceiling.

"Bring your corner down a bit. There. No, too much." Kai rolled his eyes. "There, okay."

I held down a bottom corner so it wouldn't curl up again. A

spider web of lines wafted over ponderous-looking foundations, all precisely labeled in the secret code of engineers. I leaned into the drawing to study it more closely.

"But this shows a tower sitting on your island," I said, pointing. "Right at the dock."

"That's right. That will be the easiest pier because we won't have to build a check dam and caissons. It would be impossibly expensive, and maybe just impossible, to make the span any other way. The island is solid rock."

I hesitated, but kept my nose in the blueprints. "So how do you feel about that?"

Kai pinned another corner. "I guess the Kyornin has given his permission, for the good of Takau."

The tone of his voice stopped me. I looked up to read his expression. Kai stared at the spider web spread before us. But we all have moments when we see and yet do not grasp what we are seeing; when consequence is written plainly across a companion's face, and though the mind captures the visage to be played back in years of haunted dark nights to come, we inexplicably, sometimes fatally, fail to recognize our chance to stumble over the right words, or any words, or offer a knowing touch or even a telling glance or any of ten thousand obvious, simple, momentarily redeeming answers.

Instead, I turned back to the design. "This looks wonderful!" I said. "So when does construction begin?"

"It already has. The river guild has laid its claim to property on both shores, to make room."

"Sounds more like America than Takau!"

"The government is backing it now and wants it done in a hurry."

"You will make them build it well."

"They have to admit I know more about the Ma'rhu than anyone else. I argued that if they don't build it well, after the first monsoon they'll have to build it again."

We finished tacking up the blueprint and stepped back to admire our work.

"It's beautiful, Kai. It is a work of art, and it will change lives, the way a real work of art always does."

"You always have the right words to say," Kai laughed softly. He sank into his desk chair. "We keep working, that's all."

"And speaking of work, I have a family in Rhu'mora with the flu.

179

I need to go stop another epidemic." I was only half joking. Kai knew it.

"Let me know what supplies you need," he said. "I have an open purchase order with the army now."

"Hey, that's great! I'll bring you a list."

"Within limits."

I stood in the doorway. "Of course. Always limits." I studied the blueprint once more. "Nice and straight," I noted.

"Tonight?" he asked.

"You have a guild meeting, remember?"

"Oh, yeah."

"They need you."

"I guess."

"We'll make plans to get away together. Soon, okay?"

He smiled. Our eyes met. I blew him a kiss and pulled myself away. I hurried down the stairs, through the atrium, and out to the job at hand. Curious that I remember that scene so clearly.

PREPARATIONS FOR THE NEW YEAR'S festival were subdued. We missed the invigorating anticipation of a great celebration. We made garlands, but only enough to line the plaza. We collected flowers, but only enough to cover three public altars. We did build a platform for the goddess Yasol'rhishá, and plenty of young apprentices still volunteered for the honor of carrying her around the plaza. However, Tokmol banned the bonfires on the spiral towers. Safety hazard, he said. No racing through the city. We hoped the goddess would understand.

There would be no stage in front of the fountain, of course, and no one expected any guests from Am'rha Sa. Nevertheless, Kai nudged the guild into making the event a citywide crafts fair. He calmed the merchants' fears and stoked their entrepreneurial defiance. For a carpet seller to join the merchant guild meant immediate excommunication from the powerful old weavers' guild, which had protected and dominated his clan for generations. But when a tool wears out, Kai reasoned, don't you fashion a new one that will do the job better? When bakers — organized by Kai for collective bargaining — complained they were suddenly charged higher prices for flour, Kai reminded them that when all the bakers join the guild, the millers will be eager to deal.

It was illegal to display the merchant guild's crest — Yasol'rhishá's crown of stars — outside of Am'rha Bo. The edict was a rude reminder of the older guilds' stranglehold on commerce. But Kai, true to character, insisted the ban was a great compliment. It revealed the old guilds' jealousy and respect, he said. Soon, the crest hung in every shop and stall in Am'rha Bo.

Wherever Kai turned his gentle hand, the old guilds' revenues and grip on authority began to dwindle. Naturally, they waged back-room wars to crush his efforts. But all this he never discussed with me. He knew I had no head for commerce anyway, and at that time I would have shouldered his battles as my own. He knew I approached every obstacle as a disease to be cured. Through the years, I have slowly found other approaches. But in the Rizha way, Kai accepted each challenge as the game at hand. Unlike the poor, he had grand dreams and plans. Unlike me, he was content to dwell in the midst of the work, where conclusions and outcomes hung immaterially in a cyclical future.

In love our roles reversed, however. True love lives out its span and dies; that finite lifetime must suffice for the eternity proclaimed by poets. I saw our relationship evolve and thought I could trace its natural history, at least in my heart. I felt no contradiction between our summer and winter, only the inevitability of changing seasons, the game at hand. But Kai held firmly to the sparkling ideal born of the garden in spring. Though I surely must have driven him to doubts, I believe he repeatedly beat down any hesitation in his love as unworthy of his chivalrous spirit. He assumed we would grow old together. But, by the time the bridge began to rise from the banks, I found my strength in momentum itself, and, I suppose, in the simple pride of keeping our world from unraveling.

THAT SUMMER, MUCH OF MY WORLD centered around Tlia's family compound. Magra never came for me there. Tlia and I told stories over pots of rice while the children, all of them healthy, played across the courtyard from the kitchen. Like a cloister, doorways surrounded the courtyard on all sides. The deep eaves hung like sleepy eyelids over the doorways, protecting the children running in perpetual circles. They used the rain as a gauze curtain to obscure their world from too-watchful adult eyes.

"That one is special, isn't she, dear?" asked Tlia, as we habitually checked on her granddaughter and the cousins.

"Jhamya? Yes. Gets teased by the others, though. Because she's so … intense about everything."

"And always bringing home baby animals and mixing potions! Goodness."

"Well," I grinned, "I'm partly to blame for that. She has been so fascinated by my medicines that I've been showing her how to make teas and such. She remembers everything exactly."

"We've planned her naming day for the next moon, you know. It's still a surprise. You will have to be here, of course, dear," Tlia said.

I drew her away from the door. "I knew it was coming," I said with a conspiratorial grin, and opened my field bag. "I hope it will be all right with her mother, but … I bought a little gift."

I made sure there were no children flitting about, then drew my surprise from the bag for Tlia to see. It was an oil lamp of the style Tlia's family used.

"Goodness! What a treasure! Such etching! Look at this, oh!" Tlia held it to the light. "Oh, dear! You shouldn't have!"

"Jhamya is the eldest daughter of your eldest daughter, right? She'll need a nice one."

"We'll have you help her take the flame at the turning."

"I would love that."

"Shall we show her parents?"

"Of course! Uh oh, look out!"

The cousins, all five of them, suddenly stampeded through the kitchen. Tlia stuffed the lamp into a sack of onions to keep it out of sight. Jhamya gave me a sly look as she shot through the room after the other children. There went a girl who could smell secrets, I thought.

"An old soul," Tlia whispered. "I wonder why she chose us?"

"No better place to learn the lessons of love," I answered, and squeezed Tlia's arm. We rescued the lamp and slipped it back in my field bag.

Jhamya already knew the names of all my tonic herbs. She knew about iodine and ether and aspirin. If I listed a set of symptoms she could name the disease. She knew English words like 'antiseptic.' She also whispered to her dolls in the old Rizha dialect, though no one in Tlia's family spoke it at home. Easily enraged by the childishness of her peers, Jhamya often played alone. Equally scornful of patronizing adults, she sought my company because I gave her serious answers to her probing questions. I loved her.

"I'm making her a new dress," Tlia said. "My daughter has alerted all of Jhamya's great aunts and uncles. I think everybody will come. We'll have to set up the altar out here in the courtyard if it's not raining too hard."

"Who chooses her new name?"

"The girl herself. Though her gramma has a say in it, of course," Tlia winked. "It's customary to take the name of a respected elder in the family, and that way names carry on in the clan."

"You'll have to teach me what to do during the ritual."

"You always know what to do, dear."

"But this is new for me, remember. You must teach me the right words."

Tlia laughed. "We'll sit you down with Jhamya's parents, who are very serious about the details of such things. They didn't learn that from me! The family comes together; that's all that matters."

"And stories to tell about it," I teased.

"Well, of course, dear. We don't understand anything until we've told stories about it."

KAI WORKED LATE, settling merchant disputes. I fought another cholera outbreak on the outskirts of the district. We met after dark at the fountain. As I listened to the splash of the water, Kai could not resist pulling off a valve cover to adjust the pressure. Annoyed, I talked to his back while he tweaked a valve a quarter turn, listened, then turned it back.

"I saw Tet'shri at the guild hall today."

"Touring the site with a pair of generals from the capital," Kai said.

"Smooth salesman."

"Oh, yes. Tet'shri is a master. The river guild was named general contractor, you know."

"And that means?"

Kai turned to face me. "It means Tet'shri gets a cut from every supplier. Every labor crew. And the management contract when it's finished."

"No wonder he's so cheerful."

"Greatest success the river guild has ever seen. The rest of the Council worships him."

"And the army buys him dinner. Or anything else, I bet."

"That's right," Kai said. He turned another valve. Demons sputtered.

"He's been good for his word on everything and supported you from the start over here."

"He has, yes."

"But you are still suspicious," I frowned.

"Well, at least cautious. Tet'shri has discarded a clan rivalry that reaches back for centuries. And he threw his support behind a high-risk business venture — I mean the road and water line — before the potential profits were apparent."

"He must be a bit of a visionary, like you."

"And that is why I am suspicious. Tet'shri is not like me. He has always been a cheerful, talkative, ambitious, and ruthless business-man."

"Like you said, your merchant guild will temper his reach. He may control the river, but not what moves up and down it any-more."

"Hmm. That's the plan. We'll see." Kai looked skeptical. "With the engineering design complete, I'm not consulted as often. I'm becoming something of an errand boy for him."

"Oh, they'd be lost without you, and they know it!"

Kai pushed the heavy valve cover back in place. He stood up and brushed himself off, then reached out to take my arm.

"You are a little biased on that point, I think, but thank you."

"It is just because over here you are still the Kyornin's engineer. I think you like it that way."

"Makes it easier to talk to the welders, that's for sure."

"Of course."

"Sooner or later, that little secret will get out."

"I still worry for you."

"You worry too much."

"I can't help it."

"Right now I'm worried about those soldiers over there," he said, pointing toward the café.

"Damn them all. The soldiers don't keep out the Khodataal, they just frighten everyone else in the city."

We hurried into the shadows. "It shows who controls the streets," Kai said. "I wish you didn't know so much about the Khodataal," he added.

We hesitated at my door. I did not want to have that conversation again and I needed some time alone. Kai could tell. When we kissed, I let go a little too soon.

"Good night," I whispered, and gently closed the door, though he was still trying to read my face in the dark.

TLIA AND I HAD FINISHED cleaning up from the evening meal and she had just left the kitchen when Jhamya appeared in the doorway. Her three eldest cousins fell into formation behind her. She had a bundled blanket in her arms. She held it, with practiced care, like a baby. They looked up at me with huge, innocent eyes and dour expressions. As this was entirely out of character for them, I was immediately suspicious. I studied their faces while the cousins waited for Jhamya to speak.

"What's the matter here? What is it?" I asked.

"Miss Kat'rhin, our dog is sick!" said Jhamya, their official delegate. "We found him up the hill. We fed him and got him a box to sleep in and everything. But now he won't eat and just lays there all the time. Can you help?"

"Well, first of all, you have him so wrapped up he can hardly breathe, poor thing," I said, and pulled back the blanket.

I screamed. The children squealed with evil delight. And their dog — nothing but a picked-clean dog skeleton — grinned up at me.

"You monsters!" I shouted as they bolted for a doorway across the courtyard. "There will be dog ghosts drooling at your feet when you go to bed tonight!"

They retreated into hidden recesses of the cluttered home. I turned back to the pots and pans, wondering that Death was so near at hand here even children could play with him. I hung up the giant iron skillet. Then I heard a small sound behind me in the doorway.

"They made me do it," Jhamya said.

I turned. She was trying to apologize, but still smiling, despite herself. She stood a little straighter when our eyes met.

"Don't pass blame," I answered, seeing a moment to teach. "They cannot make you do anything you don't want to do." I tried to look stern, thinking of Magra.

"I know," she said, but her gaze fell to the floor. She hesitated. I put my hand on her shoulder and moved to a sagging wicker chair in a sheltered corner of the courtyard. The rain swelled, dancing on the flagstones in front of us. The sound reminded me for a moment of Autumn House. Jhamya fidgeted around the chair.

"What's it like where you grew up?"

"Hmm. It gets very cold for part of the year. But houses are warm and pretty. All the children go to school. We have different holidays. Right now it's summer vacation, and hot. Lots of ice cream. You'd like that!" I laughed. There was no word for 'ice cream' in Rizhmadi.

Jhamya leaned her back against my chair, making the wicker squeak. "Do you think I could go to school and become a doctor like you?"

"If you want it with all your heart, then yes, you certainly can. You need to do very well in school here, then go to a university in Europe or America."

"I'd learn English and French and Latin!"

"Latin? How do you know about Latin?"

"You said your medicines were written in Latin." Jhamya turned and frowned at me accusingly.

"Ah, yes. Well, that's absolutely correct. It would be very useful to learn Latin, too. Start with English, though. That's the hardest."

"How do you do?" she said in English, with a curtsy.

I grinned. "Very well, thank you. And how do you do?"

"Very well, thank you," Jhamya mimicked my inflection exactly. She was suddenly at the end of her English vocabulary, so she switched back to her native tongue. "Do you really think I can?"

"Yes, I know you can. Keep your heart set on it, and you will always find teachers to help you. I won't be here forever, you know." I hadn't thought about it before that moment.

"I know," she answered quietly. Uncanny wisdom, heartbreaking small voice, I thought. But then, with a terrible clatter, the marauding cousins burst back into the courtyard. Jhamya and I watched them like scientists observing the strange behavior of an exotic species.

"Take that dog to the ravine," I insisted. Jhamya nodded. "And make them all wash their hands after handling that thing. You understand, doctor?"

Without another word, Jhamya marched off to take command. She paused on her way for a quick hug from her grandmother, who stood in the kitchen doorway. Tlia watched her go, then looked at me. We shared a tacit moment of womanhood and friendship, then we laughed.

THAT SWELTERING SUMMER, while America crumbled into the Great Depression, Takau edged timidly into the twentieth century. I knew no one read about Takau in the West. But the Rizha believed a bridge across the mighty Ma'rhu would show everyone that Takau was a modern, advanced country to be reckoned with on the world stage. No one complained, therefore, when the river guild razed warehouses, shops, and homes on both banks of the Ma'rhu. Hundreds of men and women waited in line for days to sign on for the menial labor ahead. Military attachés strutted about and pointed, looking official and accomplishing nothing. A steady stream of dignitaries, contractors, and swindlers poured through the river guild hall doors. Kai, as lead engineer, had to accept social calls from most of them, which prevented him from completing any meaningful work during much of the day. But he incorporated his advocacy of the new merchant guild into all his business, the way I snuck Western medicine into Magra's traditional treatments. There was no time left for the garden.

We managed to escape occasionally, however, at least to Am'rha Sa. And one day we took Jhamya with us.

"Keep a hand on that railing!" I called to her, sounding like my mother.

Jhamya ran ahead of us to the prow of the ferry.

Kai laughed. "She's so excited, she might just fly across."

"But I think this is the first time she has left your side since we three have been out together," I said.

"Jealous?"

"Yes," I smiled.

This trip was Kai's idea. Jhamya had never been across the river, and she did not know any children who had. No doubt our trip gave her an exalted status among her hillside peers. Except for her excursions around the district with me, Jhamya's world did not extend beyond the shadowy perimeters of the markets or the ravines and alleys around her home, bordered by the dangerous territory patrolled by the riverbank children.

"She worships you," I said.

"No. Maybe a little crush. You, she worships."

"She hangs on every word you say."

"And I worry about how she will remember it," Kai frowned. "How do you always say the right thing to a child?"

I laughed, and shook my head. "You can't. Every parent tries, and fails every day, they think. Relax."

"I look at her and see the hope and future of Takau," he whispered.

"She wants to be a doctor."

Kai looked from the girl to me, and back again. And he smiled softly, leaving me to wonder how much he understood and how far into the future he could see.

The ferry churned across the Ma'rhu and thumped against the dock of a new world for Jhamya. We took her to the Court Plaza, and Kai gave us a tour of the Council Hall. Jhamya was speechless for a long time. Next, we stopped at the American Café, where she heard swing music and tasted the strange food. We visited a few uptown shops, where Jhamya saw impossibly expensive clothes and shoes.

"Can I touch it?" she asked of an umbrella from Britain that cost more than her father earned in a year.

I put a sampler of perfume on Jhamya's wrist.

"I'm going to France!" she declared with wide eyes. We laughed together until we cried.

"Choose some of these for your cousins," I suggested as we stood in a shop bulging with baskets of wrapped candies. "It is good to bring back gifts for our loved ones, to show they were on our minds while we were away."

Jhamya nodded. "It will prove to them I was really over here," she reasoned.

By mid-afternoon, the perpetual drizzle swelled to waves of monsoon cloudbursts. With undampened spirits, we wound our way back toward the ferry dock.

"Here is where the bridge starts," Kai said. "On this side, it will sail right over these buildings and meet the highway along this ridge."

"What was here before?" I asked.

"An old market and some boarding houses. The Council simply condemned them."

"Will they let everybody cross it?" Jhamya asked.

"Everybody," I declared.

"Then I could come to school over here."

"Yes," answered Kai, "and perhaps you will."

We circled the mud-choked construction site and crossed the slick cobblestone street to the dock. On the ferry, we huddled together against the rain, whipped by the wind over the open water. Midstream, we strained to see the islands, but the monsoon obscured the whole world. We had to guess where the cathedral of cedars stood. Kai dutifully listened while Jhamya rehearsed the stories she would tell her grandmother about Am'rha Sa. I turned my imagination toward the future, picturing a brave steel highway sailing overhead.

THREE WEEKS LATER, Tlia's courtyard sang with ritual and party preparations. Jhamya's naming day had arrived, and so had all her aunts and uncles and their families from around Am'rha Bo and beyond. In this house, the commotion was native and familiar. The rain had taken a holiday, too, so a jumble of stools and benches congregated in the middle of the courtyard, facing the altar. Bursting with fresh flowers and paper chains, the altar filled the south corner. Tlia added a low table in front of the usual family shrine to hold all the extra candles, statues, and brass trays of offerings and sweets. The centerpiece was, as always, the family oil lamp. It flared with anticipation on a bed of rose petals.

Jhamya was supposed to be closeted out of sight like a bride. Instead, she insisted on greeting all her guests and acting as hostess. She looked quite the grown lady in her new dress, but she momentarily lost her cool demeanor when Kai appeared at the door. He quickened my heartbeat, too, because he was wearing his best European suit and looked like a movie star. Jhamya ushered Kai to the front bench where she wanted him to sit. Since there would be an hour of tea and chatter before the ritual began, Tlia and I rescued him, with much laughter, and introduced him to the extended family. Then he and I found a moment to ourselves.

"You look marvelous," I whispered to him.

"Western threads to impress the neighbors. And since she talks about going to school in America … "

"And because she adores you."

He pulled an envelope from his breast pocket. "I have a little gift for her, besides the book I told you about. I thought I could give it to her mother on the side, you know, quietly. What do you think?"

I scanned the letter and took a deep breath. "Oh, you dreamer, that's perfect! A bank account in her name?"

He nodded. "To help her through boarding school and a reserve held for college. Hard for a young woman to get scholarships, you know."

"Oh, I know," I said with the voice of bitter experience.

"Not too much that it offends them, I hope."

"It's perfect," I repeated. "Best to wait until after the naming, though."

"Of course."

With her mother beside her, Jhamya stepped to the altar and the naming began. Led by Tlia, a line of women came forward, singing. Tlia carried a platter of flowers and spices and rice. Their song and the incense sweetened the air of the courtyard while Jhamya's mother consecrated a jar of new lamp oil. The women stepped aside, an expectant hush fell, and Jhamya's mother knelt at the altar with the jar in her hands.

Jhamya's father stepped forward. He was a slender, quiet man, and clearly the source of Jhamya's austere demeanor. Every move he made during the ritual fairly hummed with energy.

"He would have joined the ascetic monks if he hadn't met my daughter," Tlia whispered to me with a twinkle in her eye.

The men took up a chant in support while he prayed and blessed objects on the altar. He raised a wildly ornamented dagger. With pride in his eyes, he dipped the blade of this family heirloom in the jar of oil. Then he brandished the knife aloft as he took a step back. His wife rose to her feet in the same heartbeat, and the women joined the chant. She turned and nodded to me. I thrilled at the beauty of it as I moved to the altar with the new lamp in my hands. A drum joined the chant and the tempo quickened. I held the lamp as she carefully poured in a bit of the consecrated oil. This done, Jhamya's father took the jar and stepped aside, while her mother picked up the burnished family lamp from the altar for all to see.

The scene grew a bit misty for me as I presented the girl with her lamp, and, it seemed, her future. She accepted it with great poise. Facing her raucously chanting family, she held it up with both hands as an offering and tipped her head. When her father shouted the clan name, the courtyard fell instantly silent. Then her mother, hands unsteady with emotion, touched the wicks together. The light doubled. We burst into cheers. Jhamya lifted her head and held the moment for us all, focused on the new flame.

Only when her mother turned and replaced the family lamp on the altar did the shouting and throwing of flower petals subside. Then it was my role to introduce this new person to the family. I leaned close and, as I had so many times while teaching her, fell momentarily entranced by her dark but piercing eyes with golden flame reflected in them.

"Ma'rhu's child, you are the joy of your parents, the fruit and flower of the clan, and the hope of Takau. What is your name?" I said, using the ritual phrases I had practiced so carefully.

With a hint of that sly smile, Jhamya told me the name she had chosen. I gasped, and looked at her mother. I pointed to myself and she nodded her assurance. I looked at Tlia, who laughed with delight. I noticed Kai tip his head, curiously reading my expressions. I looked at the girl again, who was watching me with an intensity quite unbearable. I took a deep breath, stood tall, and put my arm around her.

"I present to you Jhamya Kat'rhin! She is a bright flame in your family and in the world."

We closed the ritual with a fast and happy call and response song which collapsed into laughter. For a few minutes, the adults basked in the glow of ceremonial mood. The children, however, instinctively feeling the weight of ritual time lifted, exploded from their places, best new clothes forgotten, and raced around the courtyard. And because this was Tlia's house, where food and love were inseparable, the feast began immediately.

Jhamya stayed by my side until the time came to receive her presents. Then she took the stage again. First, she theatrically displayed a bolt of cloth that would become school dresses. Then, without too much impatience, she received the carefully scrawled scriptures attached to paper flowers from her younger cousins. Next, she modeled a tortoiseshell hair comb purchased collectively by her siblings.

She made a great and well-deserved fuss over a small yala. It was an extravagant gift from an eccentric uncle who was a successful merchant visiting from the coast. Finally, Jhamya accepted a package from Kai. She gingerly removed the colored tissue paper from Am'rha Sa, itself a treasure to be used again later. That wonderful young hunger for knowledge lit her face when she saw the book's cover. Kai had found a tattered beginning English primer. In the weeks ahead, Jhamya and I poured over every page a hundred times.

Just before we left, Kai took Tlia and Jhamya's parents aside. He handed them the envelope and explained how the account would be held in trust for the girl. Of course it was a bewildering sum of money to them, but I explained it was in no way enough for full tuition and Jhamya would still have to earn scholarships and work. Tlia, who by then knew and kept all our secrets, including Kai's true social status, said it was the greatest honor her clan had ever received. The day felt as full of promise as a wedding. And, as time revealed, it did indeed set Jhamya on a path that gladdens my heart today.

BY THAT FALL, a checkerboard of pits and ramps scarred the construction area where the Am'rha Bo tower would rise to anchor the heroic span. Crews dug to bedrock and bore holes for pylons. An endless line of men and women followed a trail of planks, excavating the clay and gravel one squeaking wheelbarrow at a time. The outermost pit was protected from the river by a weir that was constantly shored up and reinforced. Sump pumps throbbed as picks swung lower and lower below the river's surface. Gravel and clay left the pits in buckets to make room for multiton cornerstones. Lowered into place like coffins, they became a foundation not even the Ma'rhu could shoulder aside.

The work got done only with much cursing and bullying. But when someone complained that the cross-braced wall of the weir at twelve feet below the water line was bulging, the crew refused to climb back down, and the supervisor lost a fist fight trying to enforce his orders. So Kai, with Baan, his secretary and constant on-site companion, and the pit foreman backed down the long bamboo ladder into the ankle-deep mud to inspect the heavy check dam wall.

Bracing was engineered to Kai's specifications. Seepage was inevitable but not excessive. The weir was built according to design and looked secure as they walked along the upstream end.

But Kai remembered saying, "Hey, this support looks like it's been sheared off. It ... " and he put one hand on the wall. "Everybody out!" he cried. "Now! Out!"

16

THE MEN FLAILED through the mud to the ladder. Kai shoved his assistant ahead. The foreman flew up the ladder ahead of them and reached the planks above. A beam cracked. When the wall burst, the clay-red water blew into the pit sideways with the weight of the Ma'rhu behind it. The jet shattered the ladder one wrung beneath Kai's feet. He and Baan tumbled into the churning flood.

A slab of the wall gave way altogether and the pit became a whirlpool. Men overhead clawed their way up heaps of gravel in panic, as if the river could reach far out of her bed and pull them under.

The rest of the check dam held. The Ma'rhu could not tear tons of mud and stone away with one swipe. So the water in the pit swirled into a foamy dark eddy. The frantic shouting subsided. Five sturdy men rushed back to the lip of the pit. The silty water bubbled and gurgled. Fragments of boards, half a ladder, and an empty crate floated in a slowing orbit eight feet below them. A hush fell.

The next moment, Kai burst out of the gray foam with a gasp. He thrashed through the debris. He found Baan and pulled his head out of the water.

Men brought ropes and secured them from above. They scrambled down the muddy edge and pulled Baan, unconscious, up the slick pit wall. Kai climbed hand over hand up a rope until his feet slipped out from under him and he fell face first against the muddy slope. They hauled him out. He said later that when the water hit him he tucked himself into a ball and tried to protect his head. He knew if he didn't get pinned under the debris, he would pop to the surface eventually. He was more concerned for his assistant.

Kai wondered why someone would sabotage the reinforcements on the check dam, just before an inspection, putting so many men at risk. It made no sense, Kai complained. The construction schedule was set back ten days.

BUT A BRIDGE IS DEFIANCE. Ingenuity and muscle stand against a flood rolling to the sea. That is what we were doing in those days.

A year passed while crews on opposite shores raced to complete the foundations for the towers. Jutting as far into the watercourse as they could, the tower bases looked like fortresses under siege. They were surrounded by scaffolding and moored barges. It sounded like a war, too, with syncopated hammering and the shouts and curses of working men. And the army was, in fact, on hand, with heavy machinery and heavy-handed discipline.

A mountain of dirt and stone slowly took the shape of a burly ramp on the Am'rha Bo shore. The road would rise to meet the western tower, leap across the water to the garden island, then sweep over to the far bank. Most of the Rizha did not believe it possible. But an unquenchable curiosity overtook the population of Am'rha Bo as the dull gray frame of the bridge began to climb into the sky. The bridge skeleton cantilevered over the restive Ma'rhu. The river murmured to itself, perhaps planning its attack, knowing the monsoon approached again. But the people watched with fascination. I did, too. Soon we could see the towers from almost anywhere in Am'rha Bo. They rose out of all proportion to everything in the landscape, promising greatness.

The ferries maneuvered through the construction site along the shore. Except for the ferrymen themselves, who knew full well the monster overhead would soon devour their livelihoods, everyone on the ferries stared up at the steel grid slowly growing out from the towers. When they saw passengers watching the construction spectacle above them, the ferrymen slammed their crafts against the dock, throwing the inattentive to the deck.

Once, a supporting line snapped and a twenty-ton truss fell into the river, killing eleven men. The Ma'rhu swallowed them. I was often called to the site to set broken bones. I saved a howling Greek welder from bleeding to death after a cable slipped and severed his left thumb. Injuries were so common the army detached a medical unit to the site. They worked from the modern, convenient side, of course, leaving me responsible for everything that happened on the Am'rha Bo shore.

I heard the helpless protests. I shared new reasons to grieve. The Rhu'pasham razed a long line of waterfront shanties to make room for a fallen forest of steel girders and beams. No matter that families had lived in those shanties on the shoulder of the river for genera-tions. The supply yard grew from week to week with spools of cable thicker than my arm, innumerable wooden crates, oily steel drums stacked in shaky towers, and lines of pallets heaped with canvas bags and iron pipes.

I met Kai one afternoon in the shadow of the growing tower.

"Why must someone always get pushed out of the way?" I asked.

"Where would you put the girders? We're cramped over here as it is."

"I don't know. Not in somebody's living room," I fumed.

"You know they cleared the Am'rha Sa riverbank the same way."

"I know."

"Kath, I can't fix everything."

"I know," I nodded, and looked out over the water. He didn't have to remind me again that I had set all this in motion. I felt like I had swallowed a box of Kai's monstrous steel bolts.

"Why are we always betrayed by necessity?" I asked. If Kai heard me, he chose not to respond.

THE KHODATAAL SHOT down the only airplane in Takau as it flew over the foothills on a surveillance mission. They dumped the propeller and the pilot's burnt helmet on the steps of the Council Hall in Am'rha Sa. This intrusion across the river infuriated and terrified the prosperous citizenry, so the government declared mar-tial law in Am'rha Bo. The military enforced a curfew from dusk to dawn and arrested people without provocation, sometimes just for practice. Men faced immediate conscription for border duty. Women often disappeared.

Many times I snuck back to my apartment long after dark, though the risk to a foreign woman was severe. I frightened rats in the garbage heaps as I jumped into corners out of the way of shiny-faced young soldiers double-timing down alleys with bayonets on their rifles.

It was a long year.

A DOZEN CANDLES floated in a pool. They flickered when I touched my toe to the water. Six weeks into the monsoon again, and the waning moon slid behind clouds. A bird no one ever saw called from high in the cedar behind us. I told Kai it sounded like the bird was saying, "Hey, you there!"

"That's about right," Kai said. He poured some tea. I herded the floating candles into shapes.

"It is nice just to feel safe," I sighed. "No one calling for the doctor. No angry people standing in the shadows."

"I think we get fragile when we're tired," said Kai.

"Yes."

"What can I do to help?"

"I don't know."

I nudged the candles into the shape of a 'K.' I let them drift apart again. When I needed him to listen, Kai sat, poised, patiently agreeing.

"It is wrong of you to always agree with me, I think."

"You are almost always right," he said with a smile. "That makes it very difficult for the rest of us, you know."

"I do stupid things," I said.

"But you always do them for the right reasons."

I fluttered my foot in the pool. The candles bobbed, making the water glitter. We heard the bird in the dark tree call again.

"It doesn't migrate. That bird, I mean."

"Always here. Always has been, I'm told."

"Didn't you try to see what it looked like when you were a child?"

"Of course! Once I sat in what seemed its favorite tree for hours, trying not to move." Kai sipped his tea. "Finally decided it can't be a real bird. Must be a spirit."

"Now you're just telling stories!"

"No. Maybe it's the spirit of what we never see."

"It's just a nocturnal bird."

"If you like," Kai said, almost whispering. We waited for the bird's call again. It only said, "Hey."

"What do we never see?" I asked.

"We never see around the next corner. I think we often don't see what is closest to us. What do you think?"

"We can never see all the possible results of our actions."

"But we must take action anyway."

"Yes."

A sultry gust of air rolled through the garden. Clouds shrouded the old crescent overhead.

"Where I come from," I frowned, "a thunderstorm arrives, puts on a good show, cools everything off, then politely goes on its way." The first fat raindrops plopped on the pool. The candles flickered. "I hate the monsoon."

"But it brings life with it, too. Sometimes more than we know how to handle."

"It's like the rest of Takau. Everything taken to the extreme."

"Sorry."

"It's not you."

"Come inside," Kai said softly. He took my arm. We stood up.

"Hey, you there!" said the bird. I automatically looked back toward the cedar, darker against the night sky.

"Never see him," said Kai.

"Last star," I replied. "Over there." I pointed, but the dot of light winked out. The sky rumbled. The rain returned in earnest before we reached the fern bank, and we ran for cover.

Upstairs, we shed our damp clothes and made ourselves comfortable for the night. I liked the golden light from a single lamp trimmed low. Kai's familiar body brushed past mine. It was easy to be naked together. I watched him close the lattice shutters to keep the rain from splashing the furniture. He tossed aside some pillows. I blew out the lamp and crossed the room. His feathery touch guided me onto the bed.

THEY SAID A CHAIN SLIPPED. The girder swung free, pivoting like the yardarm of a sailboat. But by chance, Kai was out there on the open deck of the bridge. The steel skeleton extended eighty feet over the water, with riveters crawling on it like ants on ripe fruit. Kai had heard a rumor that a foreman was skimping on bolts and using lower-grade plates and supports to siphon off some profits. Kai liked climbing out on the site with the crew, so he readily volunteered to inspect the work.

The girder picked up momentum as it swung. Kai said he saw it out of the corner of his eye. He spun himself around an upright beam. The girder, packing two tons of steel, put a deep crease in the beam, level with Kai's nose. There was much cursing and scrambling of angry men. No witnesses saw anyone near the girder when it slipped free. Kai lectured the steelworkers about putting safety first. The incident was dismissed. Work continued. Kai duly reported that all materials and construction matched the design specifications.

I NOTICED FOREIGN MEN dashing in and out of the river guild hall. They wore shirts as white as the marble steps. They carried reams of paper and fat briefcases. They moved too quickly to survive long in Takau, I thought. It was only March, but sweat drenched their stiff collars. They were fair-haired and had milky skin. They squinted at everything, as if that might help them see less of the crudely engineered world around them. I found them amusing.

"Like lizards over hot rocks," I said to Tor, using one of his aphorisms.

Tor nodded. "You used to run into the sun like that."

I laughed. And only then realized these exotic strangers were, in fact, my countrymen. I stared. These were the first Americans I had seen since coming to Takau.

I had long ago forgotten how to feel homesick, but the sight of the tall, brash, strange Americans made me thirsty for news. I decided to intercept the lanky young man coming down the glaring steps.

"Hey, Yankee! What's the news from home?"

He stumbled on the step. He stared at me wide-eyed, as if I had two heads.

"You speak English!" he blurted.

"You'd prefer Eskimo?"

"You're American!" he cried, even more amazed.

I held out my hand. "Katherine. I'm a doctor. Been here a while." English sounded foreign to my ear.

He shook my hand automatically, but he was still stunned. He looked from me to Tor, who was standing behind me at his enigmatic best.

"Really, you are too fair-skinned to go out without your hat in this climate," I said, teasing him mercilessly. He flushed and almost dropped his briefcase. He touched his head to confirm that he wasn't wearing his hat. He looked apologetic.

"Well, I ... " Then he caught himself and looked me over again. "It's just that you ... well, gosh! You look so ... native! Beggin' your pardon, ma'am."

"*My* apologies," I grinned. "You're no Yankee at all, are you?"

"Savannah, Georgia, ma'am. Halifax Dumont. Call me Hal. Pleasure, ma'am." He felt he had to shake my hand again to get it right.

"What is the word from the States? We don't get much world news here. You've probably noticed."

"Yes, ma'am. Feels like another planet to me. Well, did you hear? The Lindbergh baby was kidnapped."

"No!"

"Right out the upstairs window. Ransom note for fifty thousand dollars. The whole country is praying for them."

I shook my head with disgust, outraged by the crime, but also imagining how the world would dwell on the fate of this one privileged child.

"And I guess Hoover is on his way out," Hal continued. "Reckon things can't get much worse, with all the banks closing and good folks out on the streets. We wonder if there will be any jobs when we get on back."

"What brought you here?"

"Engineering school, ma'am. Chance to build a bridge. And let me tell you, this one is going to be a ... a challenge, to be polite about it."

"Why's that?"

"All of this!" he said, sweeping his arm across the riverfront. "And just getting decent building materials out here. And the monsoon floods they've told us about. And, well, you know ... the local folks."

"They are a challenge, all right," I smiled. "Oh, by the way, this is Tor, my assistant."

Hal grinned nervously and offered his hand to Tor, who gave him a firm handshake and a glancing bow, but didn't say a word. Tor never revealed how well he understood English. Hal was off balance again.

"Gosh," he said to me, deciding to pretend Tor wasn't there. "How can you stand it? I mean, beggin' your pardon, ma'am, this is harsh. It's like a war zone."

"Some of it, yes. But the people are warm and wonderful, Hal, if you give them a chance."

"I reckon that's true anyplace you go. But if you don't speak the language, and the food … well … you're a doctor, you say?"

"That's right. Try to boil the water all the time."

Hal nodded seriously. He needed more advice. I suppressed a chuckle and put on my medical demeanor.

"Avoid the spicy foods for a while if you're having trouble. Don't eat fruit that's been peeled. Avoid dairy foods, but the yogurt is always good." I gave him my most reassuring smile. "And I've never known anyone who got sick eating those honeysticks they sell across the way."

Hal was embracing every word I said. I considered what advice would be most helpful in his case.

"I'm sure you know the mosquitos bite between dusk and dawn, so sleep with a cover of some sort, even when it's hot," I said. "And Hal, keep in mind that the, um, available women along the Am'rha Sa quay tend to carry syphilis."

Hal looked embarrassed again. I had to cover my mouth to hide my smile.

"So, the river guild brought in American engineers?" I asked, to rescue him from the awkward pause. "I thought they had an engineer from Takau managing the project."

"Oh, we have one," Hal answered. "He's sharp, too. Knows more about stress and loading than my supervisor, truth be told, ma'am. And knows this crazy river, how it floods and all."

"But he's not in charge?"

"Well, the top dogs here were afraid the Takau army people wouldn't trust a local engineer to run the show. I see their point," Hal shrugged. "So they brought in my firm to do it right. Fact is, they gave me his office."

"His office! To you?" I blurted. I caught myself and lowered my voice. "I'm sure your company is well respected," I said, wondering why Kai hadn't told me about this.

"We're known for getting the job done on budget and ahead of schedule, ma'am," Hal said with pride. He smiled sheepishly again. "Don't suppose this job will help our reputation in that respect. Damned near impossible to get things done on time here."

"Takau has a different notion of time," I agreed.

"Beggin' your pardon, ma'am, but speaking of time, I need to catch the next ferry. Big meeting across the river today." Hal leaned forward, suspecting that Tor might be understanding our conversation after all. "It's like a Hollywood movie, with their robes and bangles and all," he laughed.

"You can still make it," I said. "They sound a horn before the ferry shoves off. How long do you think you will be here in Takau?"

"They told me six months. I'm new with the firm, so I just nod my head and go where they send me. You know how it is. But I'm doing my job and getting out of here, believe me!"

"Well, you'll have great stories to tell back home," I said. "If you survive it," I added brightly, just for fun.

Hal blanched. I grinned.

"Ah! There's the horn! I better run, ma'am. Thank you for the advice! Been a pleasure!"

"Bye now."

He hugged his briefcase to his white jacket and ran toward the ferry mooring. It wouldn't pull away for another ten minutes, I knew. I watched him bump and totter through the riverfront crowd. Then I turned and stormed up the glaring marble stairs. The guard at the guild hall door stepped forward to challenge me, then thought better of it when he saw the look on my face. He let me pass. Tor followed, ever patient with my ferocity.

I flew past the large salon on the left with its double doors swung open and rows of draftsmen inside. They looked like sallow characters in a Dickensian factory. I took the stairs two at a time. But at the top I braked myself on the balustrade and took a deep breath. I paced my stride to the end of the corridor. The door to the former guildmaster's office was ajar. I opened it slowly.

"Huh? Ya need somethin' here?"

I had interrupted a balding man with sweat stains under his arms and suspenders askew. His Brooklyn accent had a permanently annoyed edge. He sat at Kai's spacious desk, which now faced away from the window. It was heaped with manilla folders. An arsenal of clipboards hung on raw nails on the wall in front of him.

"Excuse me," I said. "I had heard this was Hal's office."

"Dumont?" he snapped. "Desk in the corner there, if you wanna leave him a note. He's across the river. Or supposed to be."

Three drab metal desks lined up like soldiers in a row. They had identical lamps and straight-backed wooden chairs. The Takau carpet slouched in a corner, rolled up and ignored. The cushions and tea table were gone. Kai's artful blueprint still hung on the wall, but it was pocked with thumbtacks. Notes and numbers spattered the vellum like graffiti on a church.

"Thank you," I said. "Perhaps I'll just stop by some other time."

"Uh huh," he replied. He kept scowling at papers in front of him. He didn't look up as I turned away.

"Close the door," he called out behind me. "The door," he repeated as an irritated command.

I left his door wide open and walked back down the stairs. Tor, who had discreetly held back a few steps into the hall, quietly followed me again. I walked into the salon cramped with the standard-issue desks and drafting tables. Partly screened by a tall bookshelf, a bouquet of irises and fern graced one desk. A pad of paper with a list written in Kai's exacting script lay beside the flowers.

I dropped into the chair and picked up a pen. I tore out a clean sheet of paper and started to write Kai a note. Tor stood placidly beside me, though all the draftsmen were staring at us. Their pens stalled, and ink spread like bloodstains on their pages.

I stopped in mid-sentence. Kai would surely be embarrassed by this dishonor, I thought. He had not told me about it because he must be ashamed. I wadded up the paper and stuffed it in my satchel. I carefully replaced the pen. I looked at Tor, who muted my acquiescence with a slight, soft nod. He left the room. Without looking up at the frozen draftsmen, I followed him.

Looking back at this scene, I recognize now that Kai had no doubt just wished to avoid enduring my indignation on his behalf. We never spoke of it.

COCKROACH SEASON RETURNED. Springtime, when insects and microbes rejoiced in their fecund abundance. Roaches poured like waves down a narrow alley as I hurried to meet Magra at the riverfront. Another construction accident called us away from our rounds.

A gruff-looking foreman tipped his head to us as we entered the chief mason's office, just a sagging warehouse on the water near the supply yards. Magra and I approached a big man laying on a bench against the wall. Despite the chalky dust on the man's face, I could see he was pale with pain.

"Fell through the scaffolding. Out on the island," said the foreman. "His skull is too thick," he added, smiling at the mason, "so I think it's just his arm."

The mason growled at his boss. He can take a joke, so he's lucid, I noted. I studied him: equal dilation of the eyes, bruises, but no broken bones. The muscles of a champion. Deep laceration, right forearm, wrapped in a blood-soaked rag. He could move his fingers.

He didn't trust a foreigner, much less a woman, so it took longer than it should have, but I removed some splinters and stitched him up. He howled with great bravado, but whimpered like a child when it was done. Magra offered him a fresh bundle of our best pain-relieving herbs, but the man was from the coast and suspicious of her unfamiliar medicines. Magra shook her head and stood aside. I felt the terrible weight of the old healer's indignation, but the mason was blissfully numb to it. Magra had never needed to master the art of ignoring ingratitude like I had.

The waterfront faded into deep shadows as we left the office. Magra shuffled beside me between the crates and pipes, past coils of cable and steel beams.

"We need to beat the curfew," I said.

"Paagh."

I wanted to explain that while the soldiers might ignore her, I still needed to be careful. But Magra could not imagine being ignored, either. I decided to avoid an argument and just quickened my pace.

We were deep in a canyon of pallets and barrels when we heard a clattering of metal around the corner ahead of us. We heard the unmistakable scream of a man mortally wounded. Magra and I ran straight toward the sound without thought for ourselves.

A knot of men fought in the cluttered supply yard. They crouched and lunged. There was no shouting now, only fatal intensity. Though the scene was momentary, the backlit tableau is indelible in my memory.

Magra did not hesitate. She charged forward.

"Stop!" she commanded. "Away now!" Her voice hit the men like an explosion. Angry shouts rose between them. One snatched up a knife from the ground. Five men ran off together, with one, slumping, supported by the others. Three were left. One, with a short length of pipe in his hand, ran three steps after the assailants, then stopped, still primed to fight. The second dropped to his knees by the third, who had fallen, clutching his chest.

17

MAGRA AND I RUSHED over a jumble of iron pipes and a torn bur-
lap sack of joints and fittings scattered across the yard. I gasped
when Kai looked up at me. He held the fallen man in his arms.

When he saw me, Kai looked back over his shoulder to be sure
the assailants were gone, then looked from me to the man whose
head he cradled. I knelt down. It was Baan, Kai's assistant, stabbed
in the chest, just off the sternum. Baan choked, convulsed horribly,
and coughed up dark blood. He died with fight still in his eyes.

"Ha! Cracked his skull!" said the man with the pipe triumphantly.
"Did you see that? He won't be jumping us again! They won't … "

He stared in disbelief at Baan. Slowly, he took a step back, shaking his head, then looked wildly around in blind rage. He spun
about with a scream and flung the pipe across the deserted yard.
We heard the dull thud as the pipe hit bare dirt.

He turned again, tears streaming down his face, and crumpled
beside us. He took the dead man in his arms, sobbing, "Baan,
Baan!"

Kai stood aside. "They are brothers," he said quietly.

I stood up and stepped away while Magra knelt, reciting a prayer
of comfort for the dead in the old dialect. She could always keep
others from dying of grief.

My hands reached for Kai. "Are you ... did they ... ?"

"No. I don't think so," he said. He looked himself over, a little surprised. "No, they missed me."

"What the hell was this about?"

"Salvage thieves. We stumbled right into them." Kai pointed vaguely at the supply yard around us. "Easy target."

"Doesn't the guild have guards posted here all the time?" I asked.

"Supposed to. Inside job, I guess. No guards around when we got here to take inventory." Kai frowned at the debris at our feet. "We do inventory at the end of every week like this."

"So they must have known."

"Gates unlocked. Guards paid off. And we were just three men armed with ledgers."

I glanced back at Magra, rocking slowly with the grieving brother. "Kai, it could have been you."

He touched my shoulder. "But it wasn't," he said.

I caught his hand. He was shaking. I looked at Baan's blood spattered on his chest.

"Kai, it was supposed to be you. All these accidents ... someone is trying to kill you!"

"That's ridiculous," Kai said, without much conviction in his voice.

"This is all out of control, isn't it?" I whispered, clutching his shoulders. "Kai, I'm frightened."

I had never admitted it before.

OF COURSE, DELAYS plagued the bridge construction. For lack of a particular size bolt, essential cross-braces could not be mounted. Without the braces, major cables could not be installed. And without these cables, the entire skeleton groaned precariously in the slightest breeze. When the shipment of bolts finally arrived, already a month late, a third of the order was missing. The army howled. The American engineers cried at their desks. My Rizha friends smiled, wondering why anyone would get so upset about something so inevitable as insufficient resources.

Nevertheless, the bridge grew like a child. That is, from day to day, we could not notice the change, but one morning we looked up and saw the great towers linked, as if holding hands, across the water. Weeks later, surprised again, we noticed the broad deck, which would become the roadway, laid in place from shore to shore.

The monsoon arrived to blur time into a cycle of sunless days. It was a wet year, inspiring Ma'rhu to overflow her banks. She made a formidable effort to sweep away the bridge foundations, but it was too late. Instead, she lapped at the marble steps in front of the river guild hall. She stole riverbank warehouses in the night, leaving only jagged posts pointing toward the sea. Then she settled back into her bed and the fog-dance dissolved into a pensive winter.

One bright day in January, I walked along the riverfront with Tor. I squinted up at the bridge.

"You know, they will actually finish that thing this year."

"Eventually," Tor agreed, in his oblique way.

"I wonder if it will work," I said. I could feel Tor looking at me. He had learned that whenever I said something incomprehensibly foolish, it was best to wait quietly for my explanation. I laughed. "Oh, it will hold up under trucks and wagons! But will it bring prosperity across the river? Will it unite the people on both sides so we can catch up with the twentieth century around here? Will it tie Am'rha Bo to the world?"

"Big ideas can cross that bridge," said Tor. "Even the way men think outside Takau might cross that bridge."

"Hmm. And that's a heavy load. The rest of the world is changing so quickly, I wonder if Takau will ever catch up." We walked into the long shadow of the spars. "If it just makes people think about changing, that's a start."

"Something always dies to make room for change," Tor noted.

I shivered and instinctively turned my attention to a list of patients I needed to visit before dark.

IN MARCH, TASH'ANGHANI grew bold. He had acquired new weapons from somewhere. He struck hard at the army camp at the Bishtafi ruins. The fighting damaged the pipeline, cutting off our fresh water supply. Kai's fountain fell silent.

I immediately saw a rise in dysentery cases. I went to Tokmol. He said the water line was far beyond his district. He said he had urged the commander at Bishtafi to restore and protect the road. The commander said the Khodataal made it too dangerous to make repairs, that soldiers holding shovels instead of rifles were at too great a risk from snipers. Three soldiers had been killed, five wounded.

One week without fresh water to the district stretched painfully into two. I predicted a cholera outbreak as our sanitation system failed. Tokmol said the Khodataal were holding the city hostage just to take some easy shots at the army. He wondered why the rebels did not realize or did not care that their own friends in Am'rha Bo were suffering from it. He thought it very poor strategy. For once, I agreed with him.

An eight-year-old girl, weakened by dehydration from diarrhea, abruptly died in my arms. The girl used to sing for me in her doorway.

I was so angry that I walked out that afternoon and hiked up the hill without telling anyone where I was going. I stormed across the little bridge over the funeral road and marched up the highway toward Bishtafi. Before I reached the army checkpoint, I left the road where a faint trail snaked into the hills and followed it up a deeply wooded canyon.

I assumed I was being watched from the ridge line. Two miles up the trail I came across a sullen group of men and women encamped in a small clearing. They did not appear surprised to see a foreigner turn up, which proved without doubt I was being tracked. I approached the matriarch, who looked me over first to decide if I had anything worth stealing.

"Hello, I am the doctor from Am'rha Bo."

She made no response, as if I weren't speaking her language, though of course I was. It occurred to me they might kill me just for something to do. Too late now, I thought. Might as well keep moving.

"I have to see Tash'anghani."

The woman's eyes grew wide, then relaxed back to squinty suspicion. One man in the shadows slowly stood up. He slouched against a tree and rolled a cigarette.

"Where will I find him?"

No response.

"He knows me. We have to talk about water."

They stared at me with lazy defiance.

"Very well." I looked straight at the man standing by the tree. He was the only one wearing boots, so I figured he was my shadow. "Tell Tash'anghani I must speak with him. Tonight, since I have no place to sleep. Thank you."

They kept staring. I gave them one obvious glance toward the wineskin they had not offered me, then turned back onto the trail.

Another mile up the canyon, the trail suddenly ended at a wall of brambles. I stood beside an old fire ring. There was trash strewn around and the smell of human excrement, but I dismissed these common unpleasantries and focused on my dwindling options.

The last of the sunlight slid off the ridge overhead on my right. At this time of year in the canyons it could get cold. I had no blanket or cover. I listened for a long minute to the sounds above and behind me. Small animal noises. Birds in the brambles. Scuffling that could have been boots over rock.

They will either ignore me or come for me, I thought. Either way, there was nothing to do but wait. I studied the fire ring at my feet. I was still angry enough to hold my ground.

I had matches with me. So, using dead twigs and branches from the undergrowth, and with considerable trouble and smoke in my eyes, I got an adequate fire burning. It might keep animals away. The smoke would also telegraph my presence to humans, I knew.

I waited. It was a star-filled, quarter-moon night. The unfamiliar constellations marched overhead. I shivered, added some sticks to the fire, and hunkered a little closer. My ears ached from listening so intently to the night noises around me. I had tried to treat invariably fatal snake bites from a viper that preferred these moist canyons. I had heard reports that a rare species of lion still ranged through the foothills. I gasped when a swarm of tiny bats fluttered by my head. I forcibly muted my imagination.

Just when I had about convinced myself the only serious danger was sure to be a pack of drunken thieves up here in hiding, I thought I heard something moving softly and evenly up from the creek bed. I crouched and shaded my eyes from the fire glow. Silence surrounded me, except for the crackling embers. I held my breath. Only suggestive shadows from the little flame broke the darkness. Then, real or imagined, I saw a pair of eyes looking back at me.

They were large, orange, feline eyes, broadly spaced and perhaps at waist-height, as best I could guess on the rough ground. I squinted, wanting them to be reflections from the fire. Then the eyes blinked, slowly and distinctly.

I chose not to move. The next moment, it stood up. That is, the eyes rose through the blackness and became less catlike, giving the impression there was now a small person standing there observing me. I took a sharp breath. I saw what seemed a woman's face in a flicker of the fire. Carefully, I rose to meet her eye to eye. A slight breeze passed between us. My little fire flared. Shadows wavered.

A sharp snap came from down the canyon. We both looked toward the noise. I heard obvious footsteps on the trail. I looked back, caught a quick rustling in the brush, and I was alone again.

The footsteps approached, so I backed away from the lowering fire to put myself in the shadows. Three men in mountain cloaks walked straight to the fire ring. They grunted a little at a private joke, scratched themselves, and sniffed loudly. One squatted and stirred the coals with a stick. One cleared his throat.

"Magra'shietá, you will come with us," he said.

So they knew me as the daughter or student of Magra, and that suggested I would be respected. I nodded to myself in the dark, pleased.

"Where?" I asked.

They grunted again.

"North."

The third man thought this answer was very funny. He had a low, breathy chuckle. With a few kicks they extinguished my fire. The chuckler stepped up and pissed on it. The embers hissed loudly.

I fell in line with one man ahead and two behind me. They led me under a screen of branches and around a fallen tree, where the hidden trail picked up with switchbacks toward the ridge.

The men knew the trail like I knew the alleys around the plaza. The trail dropped sharply over the ridge and ran along the mountain's shoulder. Three ravines and ridges followed. The quarter moon dropped to the horizon. It was so dark, all I could do was follow the feet of my guide. Unseen brush caught me in the face. I slipped on eroded ledges. I turned my ankle on a loose rock.

The ground turned to slippery shale and the undergrowth gave way to pine forest. Our route grew ever steeper. I worked to keep up with their tireless, loping gait. Two long hours later, we came to a glade among the trees tucked under a cliff. I could see a black wall towering overhead. The men exchanged a few guttural words. The chuckler vanished into the night.

"You will wait here, Magra'shietá," said my guide.

From behind a jumble of rocks, they produced a leather bag full of nuts and a large bladder of fresh water. I was in no position to refuse their brand of hospitality.

They offered no explanation for why we stopped at this spot, nor any hint as to how long we would wait. And it was clear that I'd not get an answer if I asked. So I nibbled on a handful of nuts, considered the odds of this mountain water introducing a new strain of bacterium to my intestinal tract, and practiced my imitation of old Magra's appearance of regal impatience.

A cold draft poured down the mountain. They handed me a heavy mountain cloak. It was scratchy and coarse, but admirably warm. I pulled the cloak tight and made myself as indistinct in the dark as possible before dozing off.

When I woke, a half dozen new figures stood nearby. They had built a small fire. One arranged an iron kettle to boil water. When she tossed back her hood and pulled an errant lock of hair behind her ear, I could make out her strong cheek bones. The men sat beside their packs and rifles.

I stood up, and their sparse conversation stopped. I stepped up to the little fire and squatted to warm my hands. The woman met my gaze and betrayed a smile of sisterhood in her bright eyes. I immediately felt more at ease.

Across from me, she laid out a small carpet and arranged a tea set beside the fire. She lit a lantern that hung from a tree branch. I watched her carefully lay out a cloth with fruit and strips of jerky on tiny trays as if preparing an altar.

"What spirit is it that has cat's eyes but then takes human form? Is she light or shadow?" I asked, using the Rizha distinction for friendly and malevolent spirits. "Light, I think. She came to me tonight."

The woman looked frightened, but I tipped my head and smiled at her, the way women share secrets in front of men. She handed me a scalding hot cup of tea.

"Light, with shadow power," answered a tall, bearded man who stood nearest the fire. I liked his steady voice. I guessed he was the captain of the band that had just arrived. "That's why she has a woman's face," he said thoughtfully.

"Wath'wahao," whispered the woman. "A foothill guardian."

"Men who travel alone in the foothills always leave her an offering of a bit of meat marked with a feather," the captain explained.

"Set upright, like so," said the woman. She produced a small gray feather from a pocket in her robes and set the point in the ground by the fringe of her little carpet, right by the trays she had laid out.

"To the south," the captain added. The detail was important to him.

"She can keep wild animals away. And bad men."

"But if you forget her," the captain said, "sometimes they only find your boots."

"Men never see her, I think. Women, sometimes."

"You saw her?" asked the captain.

"Yes. Tonight." I left it at that. They nodded solemnly. The woman finished setting out the meal and looked up at the captain. He gave her the quick Rizha hand sign of approval: a turn of the wrist with two fingers extended. He took a step back with a slight bow to me before walking away from the fire. The woman smiled at me again.

I enjoyed a few sips of sweet tea. Then, by some signal I missed, the others knew we had company arriving from above. Everyone stood up.

"Tash'anghani Kor'pasham," the woman assured me.

A rugged troop of about two dozen men poured out of the trees. They quickly posted sentries behind us. They slapped each other on the shoulders and shared business-as-usual greetings with those who had been waiting with me.

I recognized the man who exchanged a few stiff words with the captain then posted himself beside the fire, just to the right of the carpet. It was the man with the long scar across his face who had alerted Tash'anghani to the raid on the merchant guild meeting. He glowered at me. I ignored him.

Tash'anghani walked straight to the fire and lowered himself stiffly onto the carpet. Cloaked for the mountain night, he appeared even more stout and imposing than before. He swept off his fur hat with one large hand. He did not look at me. First, he busied himself with a Chinese orange, and he gnawed on a leathery strip of meat. He slurped his tea.

"Next time, send a message and I will have someone meet you in Am'rha Bo," Tash'anghani began. "I can't endanger my people to protect you."

Uninvited, I sat down.

"I don't need your protection. I need to discuss your attacks on the city."

He looked up momentarily. "You do need my protection," he sniffed. "And I don't attack the city. Nonsense."

"By your deeds, if not your guns," I insisted, "you are at war with everyone, including the poorest Rizha in the city."

The deputy put his fists on his hips. "You will speak to the Kor'pasham with proper words," he commanded, meaning I should have been using the formal grammar reserved for speaking to revered elders. I ignored him still.

"I am here as the voice of Am'rha Bo."

Tash'anghani folded his arms and gave me a patronizing look. "So. Now a foreigner is the voice of Am'rha Bo? Ha. Well, tell me, there is something more the city wants from me?"

"Yes," I scowled. "Water."

"When the army pulls their camp from Bishtafi, boom! No water problem. Tell them that."

"Do I look like an army commander?" I snapped back. "The army ignores us. But they listen to you."

Tash'anghani eyed me, uncertain. I was ready for his insolence and ego.

"Oh, yes!" I sneered. "They listen, because you make them laugh!"

He unfolded his arms off his broad chest. His deputy fingered the hilt of his long dagger. I didn't stop.

"You kill children in Am'rha Bo. The Rizha clans curse you. The few allies you have in the city break their alliance. Soon, the Khodataal hide like mice in the hills. So, the army sees all this and laughs. At you."

The deputy took a step toward me. Tash'anghani stopped him with a small wave of his hand. But the Kor'pasham's voice lowered to a threatening rumble.

"They die. They lose more every night. They don't laugh."

"What good do your attacks do? The army uses the road anyway."

"At a price. As high a price as possible."

"But the army has water."

"So?"

"You lose nothing by leaving the pipeline alone."

"I gain nothing. Their loss is always my gain."

"Twisted logic, Tash'anghani. You don't risk your men just to annoy your enemy. And you would gain good will in Am'rha Bo. That could be a treasure of great value to you!"

"Only children and doctors depend on good will."

That was more callous than I could stomach, and it made me hesitate. As he measured its effect on me, I replied in a slow, steady voice.

"The enemy of my enemy is my friend, you said."

"Yes, and friends come calling with more than rude words," he growled.

"And you are driving your friends into the arms of your enemy!" I countered.

"If the military does not control the water line, that is one more thing I control."

"But you don't control the water line by wrecking it. You only control outbreaks of disease among the refugees in the streets of the Rhu'ta. Some prize!" I tossed down my teacup and folded my arms.

This performance was more than his deputy could stand. Faster than a flicker of the fire he drew his dagger and thrust it at me.

"You will speak with respect!" he commanded in a hoarse voice.

I leapt to my feet and met him eye to eye so close he had to pull the knife aside or run me through.

"I came here alone and unarmed to plead for the lives of Ri-zha children. You would lecture me on respect?" And I stared him down.

"Sit, sit!" Tash'anghani said. He waved a second orange in the air dismissively. "Come now, Magra'shietá. You are known to us. Sit, please."

He slouched a bit and picked his teeth with a twig. "I have a blanket you want. You have a chicken I want. We'll come to an agreement here."

I let the silence fall. I sat down slowly. With a quivering hand, the woman handed me a fresh hot cup. I nodded to her. Tash'anghani kept eating. I sipped the tea slowly.

"Name your chicken, then," I said.

Tash'anghani laughed without ire for once, despite himself. Then he leaned forward like a carpet seller closing a deal.

"Medical supplies," he stated with a serious tone. "And a doctor for our wounded."

I shook my head. "I can't get enough basic supplies myself."

"You have a benefactor. You get what you need. Nothing is hidden from us."

"I can't be marching into the foothills all the time."

"We can arrange a place. Several places near Am'rha Bo, and safe."

This was what I had expected, of course. I sat back. It was time to name my price.

"You will send notice to the military that you will stop your attacks along the water line so that it can be repaired and maintained. And you will keep your word."

"With our friends, always. With our enemies … while we profit by it."

His entourage grunted and chuckled around us.

"No," I declared. "The water stops, and you go without medicine."

"From you. Perhaps I have other sources."

"I know better. And you will have no Western doctor."

"If we make this arrangement, you have my word. Then, if the water stops, it will not be by our hands. Maybe the goats in uniform still want your friends to go thirsty."

"The Commissioner wants the water flowing, too. Makes his job easier. So if you let them do it, the pipe will be repaired."

"Oh, of course we are eager to please the Commissioner," Tash'anghani said, his words dripping with sarcasm. But then he closed the deal by smacking the back of his hand. "You will be doctor to my people once every week."

"But I'll treat none who are wounded in one of your reckless attacks."

"Ha! And you will be the judge of what missions are reckless?"

"Maybe it will make you consider your orders more carefully," I said, pushing my luck.

"Enough," he snapped. "You come when we need your services. We arrange for delivery of medicines. I pull my men off the road. You get water. The army gets nothing. A good deal!"

"I will come when I can. And when it is safe."

"We can make it safe, Magra'shietá. Even for a foreign woman." He shook a piece of cheese at me. "The city will soon be ours anyway."

"How soon will that be, Tash'anghani?"

He scowled. He realized his boast revealed secret plans. He set down the cheese and reached for his tea. He glanced at the sky and checked the time by the position of the constellations against the jagged silhouette of the ridge.

"Can you find your way back to this place?" he asked.

"Of course not."

"Good. Trust is a luxury we cannot afford."

"Yes. It is priceless."

He replied with his derisive little snort. "You have a few hours before dawn. Get some sleep. At first light, we will take you back to the city."

Tash'anghani busied himself with his food and made it clear our conversation was over. When I stood up again, I faced the deputy and turned up my nose at him. I muttered an excellent curse I had heard Magra use on rats. He did not even manage a response as I pushed past him. Take the sweet small victories wherever you can, I thought.

The woman led me to a flat patch of ground at the base of a gnarled tree. She offered me an extra blanket and a woolen roll for a pillow. I thanked her. She hesitated, then also handed me a small feather and a fragment of dried meat. I accepted the gift and raised my hands in blessing. Her eyes sparkled then, and she backed away.

I arranged a tiny altar for Wath'wahao, with the feather stuck upright to the south of where I was about to curl into a ball on the rocky ground. I tucked a blanket around me. I listened for a minute to the hum of insects and the sounds of the stealthy encampment settling down around me.

My head shot up with a start. A dark figure stood close to me, then knelt down. I was up on one elbow when I felt a knife at my throat.

"Silence, foreign bitch!"

It was Tash'anghani's deputy. I froze, watching the hand that held the long blade.

"The Kor'pasham is soft with you. But I won't allow any more insults, you hear? You will learn respect for the clan elders, you shit-mouthed whore!"

"Tash'anghani wants what only I can provide," I said, carefully adjusting my weight. "You … "

"Shut up! Don't move! You just listen for once, bitch. You see this knife? You see it? I'll slice you so no man will ever look at you again, you hear me? I'll see to it that … that … "

The blade, close under my jaw, wavered. He reached down for balance and fell back. I looked up from the knife to his face. In the forest dark I barely made out the long scar, but I saw sudden terror in his eyes. He stood and shuffled back, hunched like an animal retreating, looking for an escape.

I leapt to my feet. He pointed at something behind me. I moved slightly to my left, but did not turn around. He opened his mouth to cry out, but no sound came. He stumbled backward.

"Go," I said, in Magra's dialect. "And remember."

He turned and scrambled away from me. I heard him shouting like a lunatic as he reached the campfire. I waited. I cannot explain it, but I could feel her very clearly, right behind me.

"Wath'wahao, thank you."

Then I slowly turned. She was already receding into the trees.

"Thank you," I repeated, and raised my hands in blessing. The orange eyes blinked. I heard a faint rustling of leaves. The insects started singing again.

I curled up in my blanket again and quickly fell asleep.

I WAS AWAKENED by the sound of hooves on the escarpment above me. It was barely dawn. The captain with the kind voice led two horses into camp and motioned that I was to mount. I folded the blankets and put the feather in my pocket. I was about to haul myself into the saddle when Tash'anghani lumbered up to me. Leaving us alone, the captain rode across the camp to collect water and food from the cook.

"So. You have made an impression on my men," Tash'anghani said. He stood so close I could smell his breath.

"They seem to be superstitious," I answered.

"And you bargain well, for a foreign woman."

"Thank you," I replied coolly.

"But of course there is more." He looked around to be sure he would not be overheard. "You were careful, with my people listening. That's good. But we have a wider range of commodities to discuss privately, as you know."

"What do you mean? You will have to be more direct with me, I think."

"Good. You will carry a message for me," he said, reverting to his customary tone of command.

I folded my arms. "Message?"

"You can tell our benefactor the new radio is excellent. And the ammunition will be distributed through our network, so one drop point is fine."

"I don't know what you are talking about."

Tash'anghani paused. "Suit yourself. But tell him we were hoping for more dry powder. You could suggest they add some in the next delivery."

"Whatever you mean, I know nothing about it."

"Suit yourself. We think the German bullets are best."

"Please stop. I will have nothing to do with your damn weapons."

Tash'anghani laughed at me one last time. "Tell him. And we will send a new list in two weeks."

He tightened a strap on the saddle and gave the horse a word of blessing before he walked away.

I turned his words over and over for secret meanings. Then, annoyed, I dismissed him from my mind altogether. I got on the horse and signaled the captain that I was ready.

"You will have to wear this blindfold," the captain said. He leaned forward and whispered, "Just for the first hour, I think."

I nodded with resignation. He tied the dark cloth around my head. It smelled like sweat and smoke. He caught a lock of my hair in the knot and made me flinch.

"Too tight?"

"Let's go," I said, and blindly handed him the reins of my horse.

We rode side by side down the mountain. I slouched on the horse like a sack of flour. The route was steep and the horse slipped and shied across the shale. But the captain guided us through the trees I could not see and warned me before we dropped off a creek bank and lunged up the other side.

"This should be far enough," he declared finally. "Take it off.

This canyon branches many times above us now. And I will tell them, 'If Magra'shietá can still find our camp, then she has other eyes helping her.' Please accept my apologies."

I pulled off the blindfold and handed it to him as he gave me the reins. I accepted his apology with a smile and squinted in the morning light. The landscape around us took my breath away. We stood on the edge of a meadow that meandered around groves of birch. The spring leaves shimmered. Purple flowers wafting in a breeze carpeted the field. Iridescent-winged butterflies made the air sparkle. Near the creek that sang to us from across the meadow, swallows did pirouettes over a bank of lavender rhododendrons.

The captain was very pleased by my reaction. "I must not tell you the name of this place, but I wanted you to see it. This is what I am fighting for. The government wants to mine for metals in this valley. The army has orders to take it by force and build a depot here. They cannot. My people have come here to die since the beginning of time. I just wanted you to see it," he concluded.

"Thank you. I will keep your secrets. This place is … it is beautiful beyond words. I hope you can protect it without shedding blood."

"We must hope," the captain replied. "But we must also fight."

After a reverent pause to drink in the scene to the fullest, we kicked our horses and galloped into the flowers.

The canyon narrowed, and we rode hard for several hours. Brambles with wicked thorns choked the creek bed, and we kept to the southern slope where we skirted around rockslides and bent under canopies of snarled vines. Twice the captain stopped and dismounted to encourage vipers out of our path.

"Do they drop out of these vines?"

"Yes. But the spiders are more common. Watch out for the ones with the yellow spots."

"How much farther, do you think?"

"Not far. But soon we must leave the horses."

Within the hour the captain detoured up a side canyon. We rode into a small valley where the bleating of goats surrounded us.

"We leave the horses here. We'll have to walk down to the city."

I was more than ready to be off the poor beast's back anyway. An old man disfigured by skin lesions hobbled out of the rocks. The captain exchanged a few words and the goatherd led the horses away. We climbed to the scrubby ridge and picked up a trail that led openly into the familiar foothill country above Am'rha Bo. We came out on a washed-out road on the back side of Death's Door. The captain scanned the hillside, measuring escape routes, I imagined. As we approached the first dwellings, he abruptly turned to me.

"Magra'shietá, can you make your way from here?"

"Of course," I said. "Thank you for escorting me. Please remind Tash'anghani that lives will be lost every day until the water line is repaired."

"The Kor'pasham keeps all his promises. And makes good on all his threats."

"Ma'rhu ta yalathé," I said, and smiled. The captain, clearly relieved, bowed, turned, and broke into a quick jog back the way we had come. I stood there alone, with the smoke of the funerary pyres graying the sunlight. More threats than promises, I thought. More burdens than blessings. I tried to engrave the memory of the flower-filled meadows in my mind, then I walked slowly back into my familiar ragged streets.

"WHAT IS IT, TOR?"

"Tlia."

"Haven't seen her since I came back from the foothills. Is something wrong?"

"Her family asks you to come."

I straightened my back. I had only been back for two days. "What's happened?"

Tor looked me in the eye. "Didn't say."

I hefted my field bag, slid past a line of waiting patients, and ran to Tlia's house.

"I did like you said with the water, dear, but I had to stay with my granddaughters. You know."

"Quiet now. I shouldn't have sent you around, visiting patients while the sewer system was down."

"Now don't be blaming yourself," Tlia said with her bravest smile. "I was happy to help."

"And you'll be back at it in no time. You're going to be uncomfortable for a few days. You've seen it," I said. Tlia nodded. "But then we'll get you right back into your kitchen."

Tlia sighed. My heart was pounding. I stroked her cheek. After a few minutes she drifted off to fitful sleep again.

I gave her family elaborate instructions. I drank another cup of tea with them. I gave Jhamya an extra English lesson. I lingered. Tlia slipped into the fever. All we could do was keep her comfortable. She is a strong woman, I told everyone, trying to convince myself. Not strong enough to endure the cholera, I feared.

I RETURNED AT DAWN. Tlia's eldest met me at the door.

"No, damn it! No!"

I fumbled with my stethoscope through my tears. Without even telling me another story, Tlia died.

I refused to believe it, until Magra arrived. She always knew. Though my back was to the door, I could tell when she walked in. Everyone looked up and took a sudden step back, pressing against the walls. But this time Magra deferred to me, and helped me recite the prayers. She comforted the family members the way I usually did, and let me mourn with them.

I don't remember much of that day. Arrangements were made. The sooty, one-eyed outcast from the hill arrived with a wagon. All I could hear was a roaring in my ears. Someone — maybe Kai — led me home that night.

I STOOD AT DEATH'S DOOR in a robe of sky blue. The ash and smoke surrounded and comforted me in their shadowed familiarity. Tlia's clan, heavily reinforced with friends, crowded the hill between me and the cremation fires. I tied a sash of dusty orange, Tlia's favorite color, around my waist. We passed out bright strips of orange cloth for all to wear.

They set the funeral basket at my feet. It was frayed and stretched with use, but still brave with blue ribbons and stout leather handles. Magra nodded to me. Jhamya stood poised beside me with her yala in hand. Scarves and flags fluttered.

"She is ready," I said, and lifted the lid off the giant basket. I pulled out a hoop drum. The three wooden flutes. Out came tambourines and rattles and bells and the bug-eyed demon mask. I found the Mardi Gras whistle and put it to my lips.

Tlia's eldest sister raised a small urn over her head. We all greeted Tlia's ashes with a terrific commotion. We shared a song that Tlia had loved, then the clan started down the ravine toward the river. I trailed, blowing my whistle at each dusty orange ribbon tied to the spirit poles. My heart was full and breaking. The daughters and sons called out their names, with a chorus of grandchildren behind them. Cousins, uncles, friends, and neighbors called out together, not to be forgotten.

"Tlia fed all of Am'rha Bo after the quake!" I shouted. Everyone cheered. The litany of memories cascaded through the procession and echoed off the walls.

It was a long walk. I glanced up to see a group of soldiers leaning over the bridge, watching us like tourists in a church gallery.

I blew the whistle again. "The stories!" I shouted, my voice catching against my will. "Tlia's endless, wonderful stories!"

"Tell us a story, Tlia!" everyone laughed. "The stories!" Tears poured down the ravine.

The road opened onto the rocky shoreline, and the Ma'rhu glistened between the cracks of the pier. We walked slowly out to the raw edge where the deep river swept by. I raised the funeral urn heavenward and prayed. Then I turned to face the family. The sun went down behind us. Death's Door and Am'rha Bo fell into darkness against a dusty orange sky.

"Tlia! Welcome home!" I cried, and tipped the ashes into the water.

18

THAT YEAR, THE MONSOON came late. In the countryside, crops failed. In the city, nothing dared move in the streets. Am'rha Sa closed down like a fortress under siege. Am'rha Bo cowered against her hillsides. The air we had to breathe was the enemy. We feared to speak of it. We sat helplessly in precious shade, praying for a breeze. I squinted at the cruel, cloudless sky and recognized the blue of death in Takau.

We waited on reports from the south. The monsoon was stalled off the coast. The monsoon hung within sight of the harbor. The monsoon, said the reports, might dissipate before it reaches Da'rha Ghand. We fought despair.

The great bridge across the Ma'rhu was almost complete. Crews worked at dawn, then huddled along the banks until dusk, when they climbed out over the water again. Very little progress was made.

"And when the monsoon arrives," Kai frowned, "it will be too dangerous to work high on the towers. My men will be washed away. Maybe we'll never finish it."

"You always finish what you've started," I reminded him.

"We're so close. Seems it's always so close."

"I heard another man fell yesterday."

224

"They say he burned himself on the steel, then slipped." Kai wiped his brow. "Sometimes they survive the fall, but then they drown before we can reach them. I even had a boat posted on the island. But the rescue crew was asleep."

I sighed. "How is the garden?"

"I was out on the deck of the bridge yesterday. You can see over the walls to the garden from up there. My riveters pointed and told jokes about what they'd do under the trees."

"The view alone will cool them off," I smiled.

"You have not been out there for a long time."

"I dream of it."

"And I dream of you."

"Thank you." I touched his arm.

"I will send for the boat tonight. Will you come?"

"Yes. Yes, I will come."

I BOARDED THE FAMILIAR black boat. The crew bowed to me and set off. Kai was not there. I assumed he would be waiting for me at the garden gate.

The boat slipped close past the beacon at the head of the island. We came within yards of hitting the jagged rocks, but I watched the lights of Am'rha Sa on the water. There was a moment of laughter among the crew when a rock scraped the keel just as we caught the current. They were amused by the close call. I laughed with them. The boat swept with a lurch into the grip of the Ma'rhu.

The crew methodically worked the boat around the island. We docked precariously against the rough base of the enormous tower that supported the bridge overhead. The stone blurred into angular steel outlines against the cloudless night sky. We had to step onto a narrow plank at the base of an iron staircase that spiraled down the foundation from the bridge deck. Though I could not make out the details in the dark, I could see well enough that the tower had overwhelmed the handsome, vine-covered bridge that used to lead to the main gate. Now a sterile flagstone platform lay before the entryway.

By the time I stepped through the gate and it whispered shut behind me, the servants were gone. There was nothing unusual in that. A few oil lanterns flickered for me. I waited, but Kai did not appear.

The private chambers were locked. I crossed the lawn and opened the massive door of the Great Hall. It was dark and cool. I stood for a long time at the threshold and enjoyed the soft air that brushed my cheek. I filled my lungs. The hall smelled of cold tile and old furniture, like a church basement in my childhood.

I walked into the garden. The fountains were mute. The water had been turned off for maintenance, I guessed. I realized how boisterous the garden had been, and I felt grateful for the tranquility. The water in the pools lay exceptionally still, relieved of its perpetual mandate to swell and fall.

I wandered into the blue pavilion and sat down. I don't think I fell asleep. But then, without warning, a Takau demon leapt through the curtains.

"Oh, dreams usually come unannounced in sleep," the demon whispered to me, "but this one arrives at your door, bearing gifts! No good having a gift without its story ... "

The wild-eyed mask waggled on his face like laughter. In his black robes he faded in and out of the shadows. But his hands kept dancing around me.

"Who are we, she asks? What is this?" The demon vanished again. "We are that which dwells in those corners," came the hoarse whisper behind me. A hand pointed over my shoulder. "There and there, where your eyes cannot penetrate."

I turned. The demon was gone. I stood up, folded my arms, and waited.

"And we are paradox," he said from the doorway again. "So where does this woman go? This old soul, where does she go? We watch, we know. She gives and gives and gives of her love, her self. She heals. She turns back death."

As he spoke, the demon threw small coins all around the pavilion. Then he squatted at my feet and looked up. His eyes glistened. I didn't move.

"She works near Death's Door. She walks the road. Now sometimes she does not come all the way back!" He launched backward, crouching again in the archway, clinging to his bag of coins. "All the people come to her. And she keeps giving and giving of her self, and her love." More coins glittered and sank into the cushions around me. "But she never comes all the way back now, not out of the shadows."

The demon rose, seeming to grow larger.

"The time had to come. We watch. We see. Others know. Nothing more to give, to love. She walks in darkness." He turned his back to me then. There were eyes embroidered on his robe; this demon watched me from wherever he stood.

"She feels she is first on this path," he said quietly, still turned out to the night. Then he spun about, pointing at the floor. "But look now! Footprints everywhere; old ones, recent ones. Why did she not see them before? Because it is dark, of course!"

With his body swaying, the demon lapsed into chants in ancient Rizhmadi. He broke off. "Does the woman know this story? She is in it, here, now, forever."

He returned to chanting. Then, suddenly wrapped around a pillar, he pointed at me. "We all abide by certain laws. You cannot know them all!"

I nodded. He disappeared.

"Nothing left to give," the demon shrugged, standing beside me. "She finally does something for herself. She cuts the cords. She cuts and cuts and cuts until she even cuts the fine gold band around her beating heart. And she empties herself."

He turned his coin purse over, and a tiny black pouch fell at my feet.

"But look! Here she is left with darkness. It is heavy! Seductive! Restful, like ashes floating down the river."

The mask slipped a little as he bent to pick up the pouch. His hair was matted with sweat. Gently, he offered me the black pouch. I took it gingerly into my cupped hands.

"See how readily she takes it now! She will curl warm and naked in the folds of Yasol'rhishá's robes. And find the secret." He stood tall in front of me. "But, please, there is more to the story. This part is the dream! She knows she cannot remain all darkness. She is a healer called to life, not death. So she holds the darkness close to her heart. Makes it part of herself," he said, holding my hands, with the pouch close to my chest. Carefully, he drew a silver ribbon from the mouth of the pouch. He tied it around the neck of the black bag as I held it for him. His hands were shaking. "She draws a line around it with light," he whispered. "She needs the lessons of lightness through the lessons of darkness."

The demon backed away. "She needs the garden," he said, with arms outstretched. "And one who harbors a madness to match her own and a love to endure the journey!"

The vision blurred through my tears.

"She must risk everything," he said, "while he must give everything."

I closed my eyes and took a deep breath. When I looked up, the demon had vanished. "I don't know," I answered, too quietly for the shadows to hear. "I'm sorry."

BEFORE LONG, I WALKED back up the row of rosebush shadows. I climbed the stairs where my footsteps fell much louder than the hesitant drip of water out of the still pool. I found Kai sitting on the lawn near the gate, under a stone dragon. He was wearing his usual loose Rizha trousers and green shirt. He studied the grass by starlight as I approached.

"Quiet tonight," I said. "Mostly."

"And not as hot," he replied. "There is almost a breeze in the trees."

"Yes."

"How are you?" Kai asked.

"Feeling more peaceful, I think."

"That's good."

"I had no idea the bridge had to swallow the whole island out there."

"Yes," Kai nodded.

"And that staircase?"

"Tet'shri insisted. He had it built without asking me. He called it a gift to the Kyornin."

"You hate it."

Kai did not answer. I looked back into the shadowy garden. "The water's not running," I said.

"I sent the gardeners away."

I leaned against the dragon. I ran my fingers through my hair. "Maybe you heard," I said slowly. "I need to go to the north again."

"During the monsoon? That's crazy!" Kai twisted around to look at me. I shrugged in the dark. He turned back to pluck a blade of grass. "Not enough for you here?" he asked.

"Enough what?"

We were silent a long time. Suddenly he stood and faced me. "It's not too late! We could start again. We could go away. Anywhere you like. We could … " Looking into my eyes, he saw that he could not reach me.

We slept that night in the pavilion under the willows. I kept my back to him. I was afraid to move. Before dawn, the boat took me back to Am'rha Bo.

I BLINKED SWEAT out of my eyes as I read the reports in the paper. The monsoon hit the coast yesterday morning. Lower than average precipitation. Moving inland slowly. But a sidebar said the incoming storm threw a cargo ship into the portmaster general's headquarters. A good sign. Officials expected the monsoon to reach the capital by midweek. Drought was blamed for the deaths of eighteen children in the farm community of Dobé.

Reports announced that Ashka'rhuna reached the capital during the night. Main thoroughfares flooded, despite the government's annual preparations. The monsoon finally picked up speed over land. Officials in Am'rha Sa predicted first rains before dusk.

And I stood with Magra down in Rhu'mora with a destitute family who had lost their patriarch that morning. I felt a crackling in the air around me. Clouds had been boiling overhead all day like expectation condensing in our dreams. But now I looked up. Magra was watching me. She nodded sharply, just once, with a glint in her eye. We rushed into the narrow street.

I was startled to find the alley jammed with people, most of them familiar to me. A teasing drizzle evaporated on the cobbles at our feet. I heard a roar. Ashka'rhuna was rushing up the river. But this crowd kept their attention not on the sky, but on Magra. No, they were watching me. I turned to Magra, with my back to the approaching deluge.

"What?"

The old witch held up her worn little Takau bowl, but instead of raising her arms to catch the rain, she handed the bowl to me.

"Why?"

Magra raised her empty hands. "Now!" she commanded, and pointed behind me.

I spun around and caught my breath. I raised the bowl high. Quickly, I saluted the cardinal compass points. Everyone mirrored my actions. That strange Takau whistle rose from the crowd and drew more people outside. I aligned myself instinctively with the blast. And the rain slapped me full in the face.

More like a waterfall than like rain, the water drenched us with such delightful ferocity little of it stayed in my bowl to drink. But I put it to my lips and the crowd shouted and whistled.

Amidst the downpour thundering around us, dozens of former patients, shopkeepers, aids, friends, and acquaintances — the soul of my Am'rha Bo, now dripping and laughing — bowed to me and offered their congratulations. I stood smiling and confused in the middle of the street, staggering against this double onslaught. Finally, I turned to ask Magra what on earth was going on. Magra was gone.

19

THERE SHOULD HAVE BEEN fog music. And dancing on the plaza, like before. Maybe someone danced, but I didn't hear any drums. The monsoon lingered through its usual season, first a blessing, then a curse, as always. But there was no clean conclusion to it. Like everything else that year. Just halfhearted, random cloudbursts between annoying drizzle. So we didn't know when to dance.

They finished the bridge. Except for safety railings on the approach ramps. Except for signs. Except for paint on the toll booths. Except for an opening ceremony.

"We've planned a ribbon-cutting and a procession from Am'rha Sa," said Kai.

"We need to cross from Am'rha Bo, too," I insisted.

"Not at the same time, anyway."

"First then."

We pushed through the morning fruit market. I made a mental note that the flies were getting worse again. They came in waves.

Kai looked down. "Please don't make it a protest march."

"Of course it's a protest march. Everyone in Am'rha Bo has something to protest."

"Can't we just dedicate the bridge? A grand opening. Like a department store in New York."

"More like welcoming a new baby in the back streets."

"Okay, like a baby. That's not a protest."

"You've never attended a birth."

A man with no front teeth stepped too close and offered us a freshly plucked chicken. We both waved him off.

"Well then," Kai tried again. "Have you asked Tokmol for permission?"

"Why should we have to ask permission?" The thought made me angry.

"Because his job is to keep the peace."

"Crowd control."

"Because it is safer for everyone if we work with him. And because it is polite."

"Because they have guns."

Kai stopped. "Why are you letting yourself get into this? Who are you doing this for?"

I stopped too, but spoke toward a burnt-out building across the street. "The people who are starving while the army drives by with tons of rice," I answered wearily. "The people whose children have dysentery and I can't help, because the vaccine is carried right past their doors."

"I know, Kath, but … "

"I'm doing it for the families up in Nes'fhan who were driven out of their village last week!"

"You mean the Khodataal who have been gathering here all season."

"They're in the foothills. They have nowhere to go."

"You mean them," Kai said, pointing to four men wrapped in mountain cloaks who slouched in a corner, watching us.

"Look, I have work to do."

"Kath. You can't give yourself away to everyone. You've got to protect yourself."

I felt my chest about to burst. "I know. Really, I know. But I can't stop."

"You'll have to."

"I know."

"Kath … "

"Kai. There's a journey I have to make. No one can make it for me."

"What does that mean?"

"I feel like I have to go alone."

"The whole city is with you."

"I mean us," I said.

"You've cut yourself off from everyone who loves you."

"You don't understand."

"You won't let me."

"Maybe no one can."

"You are not giving me a chance!"

"I don't think you can understand," I said in a whisper. I wiped a tear off my cheek. No, I can't make him understand, I decided. I didn't have words for it. I straightened my shoulders. Kai saw the gesture, and his face softened.

"Can we talk again? Soon?" he asked with resignation.

"Oh, always. I appreciate you so," I offered. "And thank you," I added. "I'm sorry. I can't explain it to myself yet."

"We have time."

"I hope so," I said softly. He can't hear me, I thought. I hurried away across the plaza.

I FOUND MYSELF at the head of the crowd on the graveled ramp that led onto the bridge. I shook a rock out of my sandal and looked around. The crowd swelled to cover the riverfront and pressed around the guild hall. Behind me, huddled around the unfinished wooden toll booths, a detachment of Tokmol's officers watched and spoke nervously among themselves. Out of the corner of my eye I saw one officer leap onto a bicycle and race off across the bridge. The lone messenger had the causeway to himself.

Construction workers stood nearby in loose circles, proud and awkward like boys waiting for a compliment. A team of teenage girls rushed around them, distributing flower necklaces. The steel-workers looked ridiculous wearing flowers, of course, but they grinned happily just the same. I remember the sudden perfume when the girls dropped a necklace on my shoulders. I laughed in spite of myself, for where but in Takau would my fears be answered with flowers?

Kavita and her gang appeared, aloof in their cosmopolitan youthfulness. I marveled at her ability to be excited and irreverent at the same time. She sidled up behind the cluster of self-absorbed merchant guild representatives and mimicked their primping and posing. Her performance was vicious and perfect. Her friends fell on each other in spasms of laughter. A guild member looked over his shoulder, and Kavita, instantly transformed, offered him a somber, respectful bow. Her friends turned away, holding their sides. Then Kavita caught me watching her, and to me she gave an unabashed, shining smile. More fears answered with flowers.

Tor pushed through the crowd to me. He thrust a small, dark basket at me, as if it were a poison he did not care to handle.

"Twenty-eight ribbons," he said.

"I thought it was twenty-six," I frowned.

"Counting the two who drowned last June."

"Oh. Sure." I set the basket at my feet. "Do you think they will all stay in line?"

"Afraid over the water," Tor declared. He always carried a quiet disdain for anyone who feared anything. "They will walk like sheep," he said, with his hands pressed together.

"They're not sheep," I snapped. Tor shrugged, a gesture he must have learned from me. I scanned the crowd again. "Have you seen Kai?"

"No."

"In the West we'd have long, dull speeches first," I said. Tor looked at me blankly. "Guess we'll just get started," I sighed. "Tell them it is time."

Tor walked over to a cluster of five wizened women standing out of the midday sun. He bowed and exchanged a few words. The clan matriarchs of Am'rha Bo looked at me. I raised my hands in the traditional blessing. They pulled themselves together for the long walk. What if one of them can't make it, I worried. What if they move so slowly the crowd gets impatient? I thought with the matriarchs in the lead, the procession would stay calm. But tensions were high already. The old women hobbled toward us.

"Maybe this was not such a good idea," I said, when Tor returned to my side.

"Safer," he assured me.

"Thank you."

The flower-decked construction crew fell into formation behind the honored grandmothers. The merchant guild jostled for position. Soon, the determined and the curious coalesced behind them. I picked up the basket of ribbons. As I turned toward the bridge, flutes whistled and drums took up a marching beat. My heart pounded in my throat when I realized they had all been watching me for their cue. I had come to the point where just by turning around I set events beyond my control in motion.

The officer on the bicycle returned with a message for his compatriots. They looked greatly relieved. The word was to let us pass, of course. They had no choice anyway. I walked up the ramp with as steady a stride as I could muster. The toll booth arm tipped up like a salute. In a commendable show of discipline, the six men fell into formation and marched ahead of me onto the bridge.

I could see down the length of a tunnel of steel. The stately procession of the Council, flanked by the Commissioner and his men, fluttered at the far end. No, they were perhaps a third of the way across already. At that distance I could just make out their swirling robes and crisp banners snapping in the breeze. The river carried away the sound of their drums and music.

We walked slowly out over the water. Nineteen, twenty. I tied the ribbons along the steel railing for those who had died during construction of the bridge. Twenty-one, twenty-two. The matriarchs followed with a prayer and flower petals scattered into the river for each one. Twenty-three, twenty-four. The excited throng surged forward. The steelworkers linked arms to keep the procession from overrunning the old women. I signaled Tor.

"Can we get them to change the music?"

He shook his head. The musicians had fallen into a boisterous reverie. The drums pounded out a warlike march, not a dance. But soon the magic of walking over the river hypnotized the crowd. Except for the construction workers, who felt right at home, the parade slowly squeezed toward the center of the roadway. People fell silent one by one as the height over the water took their breath away.

"This high off the water, the air feels different," I said lightly to Kavita, who had come to my side, looking entranced.

"Damn," she replied.

Twenty-seven, and twenty-eight. Glancing behind me, I saw dozens of people pointing upstream. They pointed over the walls of the palace to the green blur of garden within. They could see over the Great Hall to the terrace with the double colonnade and the fountain in the center. They had a clear view past the private quarters to the rose garden. They looked down on the willow trees, though only I knew what lay along those secret paths. The cedar grove stood between the spectators and the silver pavilion, but I felt obscenely exposed. I looked down and discovered that I stood at a break in the bridge railing, the very spot where the staircase spiraled down the tower to splay onto the stone walkway in front of the palace gate below.

The music fell into the water, suddenly soggy, then silent. Movement stopped in a wave running back to the hazy Rhu'ta district. The grandmothers waited. They made little accusatory clucks at me. I blushed in the bright sunlight. What did they know? What were the old hags saying? Why did I have to stand in front of all these people this way? I threw the empty basket off the bridge in a rage and faced Am'rha Bo. Everyone stood still. Then Tor leaned forward, and quietly pointed to something behind me. I glared at him a moment before I turned around again.

Tokmol's grim-faced deputies stood in a sharp line across the causeway, just twenty feet in front of us. The six from the toll booth had fallen in with the Commissioner's guard. All had rifles tipped with bayonets. Behind them, the Council fluttered, hastily completing a dedication ceremony. I recognized their nervous faces as they furtively glanced our way.

Tokmol stood at parade rest near the upstream railing. When I looked his way, he tucked his baton under his arm and took a few steps into the immensely empty roadway between us. Many around me took a step back. It was an impressive display of power for such a little man.

"Oh, you're awfully good at that," I thought out loud. Alone, I walked forward.

I do not know what Tokmol might have done. I certainly didn't know what I was going to say. But we were both spared. Two startled officers on the front line turned aside, and a member of the Council stepped out to intercept us. The sunlight gave the green silk of the Kyornin's finest formal robes a silvery shimmer. His expression was calm. There again was that dancing lightness in his step. We drew near, oddly like three old friends meeting by surprise in the middle of the street.

"We have not yet cut the ribbon," Kai said simply. Tokmol and

I looked at him. He kept his voice low. "What I suggest is that we ask the Council to complete the dedication and opening, with, say, these matrons and the merchant guild from Am'rha Bo helping. Your men step aside and serve as an honor guard," he said to Tokmol, "and you," he squinted at me, "help ensure the parade turns here at the ribbon and heads back to shore."

"But these people want to cross the whole bridge. And they have the right."

"Yes," said Tokmol quietly. "But not now. Whatever happens here where we stand, I have been ordered to prevent this ... assembly ... from entering Am'rha Sa. You understand my position here."

"But ... "

"Just not all at once, Kath. And not with drums."

"You can't stop us," I declared.

"He has trucks on the east bank," said Kai. Tokmol merely shifted his weight. "Look at them, Kath. They're ready to get back on solid ground."

The matriarchs leaned on their canes in a tight knot, watching us with nearsighted intensity. My trained eye saw their fatigue. The merchant guild contingent inched forward, wanting to exert their new authority, but they were just frightened shopkeepers under their ritual finery. The construction crew pretended to study the rigging overhead: Some of them held the flower necklaces in their hands like men stuck holding women's handbags. Behind them, the line of people shifted uneasily in shivers that ran like a chill down the spine of the bridge.

"Don't make it look like we've been turned back," I said.

"You have not been turned back," Tokmol answered. "Not yet."

"Good," said Kai, to close the deal. "I will explain our plan to the Council."

Tokmol nodded.

"I'll ask the matriarchs for a prayer. A short one," I added.

Kai smiled with relief. "And I'll talk to the merchant guild."

"My compliments, sir. I hope this works." Tokmol turned on his heel and left us alone.

"Kai, now everyone in Am'rha Bo knows who you are."

"And what better time? How do you like the view of the garden from here?"

"It's beautiful. Like the birds see it. But I feel so ... exposed."

"Old Takau saying: Memories are like fine robes. They may keep you warm, but you are still naked inside them."

"What about you, Kai? Now you're alone in the middle of everything."

He nodded, as though unconcerned. "Hmm. Your culture has a name for that place."

"Purgatory. But that's between heaven and hell."

"So. Then I'm just in the middle with everyone else. That's where I belong."

"But the garden, Kai. I didn't know."

"I guess now I can share it with everyone."

Suddenly there was nothing more to say.

"Ma'rhu keeps singing," I said softly, and hated myself for it. But Kai laughed. I looked out over the river. The breeze stopped. I heard the water complaining about the bridge footings beneath us. We were out of time.

"Kath, there may be trouble yet tonight."

"I've heard."

He nodded. "I will come over to be with you."

"Be careful."

"Such advice, coming from you!" Kai said. "Okay, let's do this right." Our hands touched for a moment, but it was that touch reserved in all the world for old friends parting, perhaps for the last time.

Waving off their questions, Kai instructed his merchant guild disciples. He gave them directions, making spinning motions with his hand. I told my wobbling matriarchs we needed a final prayer, as their chance to get the last word in, after the Council. They liked that notion, and consulted sharply with one another about the best words for the occasion. Kai slipped back behind the soldiers to where the Council waited.

Tokmol flashed commands to his men. They pealed away. The ceremonial red ribbon strung across the causeway fluttered nervously. Tet'shri and the rest of the Council clustered behind it. The Kyornin stood among them. My old women used the last of their flower petals while invoking a kind of spell, running on rather too long after all. Before they were quite finished, I signaled Tor. He set the parade back in motion. First the proud merchant guild representatives strutted by, giving the tense guildmasters across the ribbon hard looks. The construction crews marched up and made their about-face. The long, long line of Am'rha Bo peasantry followed, and I took my pleasure in seeing the whole Council forced to stand there confronted by the stream of people; not a mob, but so many distinct faces, each individual.

We were lucky. Everyone accepted that thin red ribbon as a legitimate line and a good place to turn. Kavita, who had not seen our conversation with Tokmol through the crowd, stepped closer than anyone else to the ribbon. I dreaded what she might do. But then she saw Kai, and recognized him, and her jaw dropped. Kai held up his hands in blessing. The press of people making the turn pushed her on, and she regained her composure quickly enough to give Tokmol, watching from the side again, a haughty flick of her long hair. He took one step forward, but realized even as he moved that he could not detain anyone without disastrous consequences. She knew it, too.

As chance and the narrow causeway dictated, I ended up standing next to Tokmol throughout the parade. We both watched the crowd swing past us. We stood elbow to elbow and did not look at one another.

"Your men show great discipline under pressure, Tokmol."

"Thank you. Restraint is the most important martial art." After a pause, he added, "And you have a great gift with people."

"Thank you."

"I wish you could heal these old divisions, as well as you heal disease," he said.

I risked a glance at him. He was still building a catalog of faces as people marched by. "At least we've brought everyone this close," I said.

"Yes," he replied, without turning his head.

We continued to stand like royalty reviewing the procession. I nodded to many who, familiar to me from sickbeds or market stalls, recognized me as they passed. Tokmol betrayed no emotion.

"I have a witness who claims you have been treating wounded rebels," he said in a low voice so only I could hear. "And evidence the Kyornin has been shipping weapons and supplies to a Khodataal faction."

I faced him. "That's ridiculous! Kai ... the Kyornin hates the Khodataal! Look at all your evidence: all he's built, all he has given the city. He gives people jobs and hope, not weapons!" I suddenly remembered Tash'anghani talking about ammunition from a 'benefactor.' I scowled. "Listen, Tokmol, the Kyornin is being framed! He doesn't know anything about shipments of weapons! Don't you see? Someone is using his name."

Tokmol, who never missed a clue or innuendo, studied me. "That was my suspicion, yes," he nodded.

"And those accidents! Are you aware that someone has been trying to kill him?"

"I opened an investigation. The Kyornin asked me to keep it quiet."

I groaned in exasperation and turned back to smile at a familiar clan of weavers as they passed.

"And you?" Tokmol asked.

"I treat anyone who comes to me. I don't ask questions. Arrest me for being a doctor if you like."

The parade began to thin out. But then Tlia's family appeared. They made a fuss as though I were a long-lost relative. Jhamya wanted to stand at my side.

"You need to lead your family back into Am'rha Bo," I told her, and nudged her into her father's arms. I got the clan turned toward shore only after many hugs and blessings.

"Gifts can become burdens, can't they?" Tokmol said.

"Some gladly carried."

The last of Am'rha Bo eddied past the red ribbon. A dozen curious young women with tired children slung on hips followed a pack of wide-eyed boys out on a dare. The rest of the stragglers swung back toward shore without approaching the ribbon at all. Finally, Tokmol turned to me.

"I had hoped the Kyornin would succeed," he said, "but his adversaries are outmaneuvering him."

"What do you mean? What are you saying, Tokmol?"

"And the army will ruin us all, unless we stand aside and wait. The Khodataal have also forgotten how to wait."

"What can we do?" I asked.

"Our duty, as always. Sacrifice, as necessary."

"Of course, but … "

"Try to warn the Kyornin," Tokmol said, then stepped forward. The chairman of the Council jiggled up to the red ribbon. Tet'shri handed him a jeweled knife. The ribbon, once cut, fluttered to their feet.

The Council congratulated itself. Kai moved among them quietly. He did not look back at me. Tokmol nodded a command; his men snapped into formation across the causeway. He took up his place behind them.

As if on cue, the fog lilted down on us. The mist rolled in, hiding both shores. The late sun became a white disk. And the sky closed down on the bridge towers. The Council started back to Am'rha Sa. No drums. I looked at the ribbon. Such a frail line, lying severed and limp. Keep moving now, I thought. Tor had waited for me, of course. We started back toward the old city, and soon overtook the last of the crowd, so we did not have to pierce the fog alone. I wrestled with what Tokmol had said. And the Ma'rhu rolled under us, apparently unconcerned.

20

WELL AFTER DARK, a long convoy led by two military motortrucks rattled through the fog and across the bridge from Am'rha Sa onto the Am'rha Bo dock yard in front of the river guild hall. I stood with Tor on the edge of the old ferry landing and tallied the inventory as it rolled past. Under the trucks' canvas covers, soldiers straddled cases of ammunition and drums of oil. Nervous mules pulled the wagons that followed close behind. They hauled lumber, wire crates full of chickens, boxes of nails, sacks of lime, cable and rope, bolts of canvas, and bushels of rice.

It was no secret the army had stockpiled supplies across the river, awaiting the opening of the bridge. The military took advantage of its investments immediately. But it was also a poorly kept secret that the convoy was targeted for a protest. Tor and I exchanged a glance.

Predictably, before the last wagon in the line left the bridge, the convoy ground to a halt in front of the guild hall. A donkey cart blocked the corner where the road turned up the hill. A determined group of men and women stood in front of the cart. The shouting began and the police converged from all directions, followed by a wary crowd attracted by the noise and premonitions of bloodshed.

The police, with batons poised, already had the protesters surrounded when Tokmol climbed out of the first truck. He signaled his officers to wait and stepped to the front of the convoy. I saw Kavita rush up to him. I forced my way closer.

"Am'rha Bo needs these things," she declared. "We will buy them, full price. Don't take them north."

"These are military supplies. They are not for sale. Obstructing the roadway in this manner is a serious offense. Move aside. Now," Tokmol ordered.

"Nothing that crosses the river stays in Am'rha Bo. It has to stop," said Kavita. I gasped to hear my own words repeated.

"Young lady," Tokmol said, "listen to me. You are being used." There was no mistaking Tokmol's tone of voice. "I am warning you once more to move aside."

"You shit-brained, goat-humping bastards don't get it, do you? The people of Takau need these things right here!"

Tokmol slowly lowered his hand to the hilt of his sidearm. He shook his head slightly and pursed his lips. Then he gave his men a sign.

Six officers rushed at the protesters around the cart. Two grabbed Kavita. Seven more, shoving with their batons, tried to force the crowd back. Kavita wriggled free, cursing. Then I saw the arc of the baton over her head. I was close enough to hear her skull crack.

"No!"

I jumped in and grappled with the man trying to drag her aside by one arm. I fell with Kavita clutched to my chest.

"Keep back!" commanded a voice over me. It was Kai. "Give her room!"

I looked into Kavita's eyes. She was blacking out. I held her cold hand. Then I heard screams and the road cleared behind me. I wiped my face and looked up. Soldiers, rifles leveled, fell into formation in front of the truck.

"Get out of the road!" Tokmol pleaded.

Kai stepped between us. "You mustn't ... "

Tokmol leaned close. "We have no time. Move away!"

"But ... "

"You are not protected here!"

"But ... "

Tokmol glanced frantically around us. "Ambush," he hissed. "Move, now!"

"Not until ... "

Tokmol drew his pistol. But when Tor saw the gun, he leapt forward. With one blow, Tokmol flew backward and splattered at the soldiers' feet.

Tor looked up. I saw him square his shoulders. The report of the rifles echoed off the guild hall walls. Tor fell just beyond my outstretched arms.

Everyone stared at him for a shocked, horrid, fleeting moment. There lay all the tenacious loyalty to the dream that sustained us. I crouched, with my aching soul suspended for a heartbeat, unable to breathe.

Then I heard a Khodataal battle cry. Other shots rang out. A soldier screamed and fell. Two others crumpled. The crowd panicked and ran, madly trampling people on the marble guild hall steps. Engines roared as the trucks reversed and rolled over bodies to turn around. Soldiers fired directly into the crowd. Tokmol's men condensed into a tight wedge, scooped him up, and retreated with the trucks. I scrambled out of the street on my hands and knees while bullets crackled overhead. I fell against a wall and clawed the stone to steady myself. I felt Kai behind me. Panting, with my cheek pressed against the cold surface, I looked back. A swarm of men in mountain cloaks charged the convoy.

The soldiers abandoned the wagons and ran toward the bridge, firing all the while. Bullets ricocheted off the steel. The second truck swerved wildly, missed the ramp, and overturned. A moment later, it exploded with a ball of fire that threw corpses across the docks. Black smoke overwhelmed the ghostly fog. Shrouded in the river mist, the soldiers briefly held the causeway. But without cover, they had to retreat, and the Khodataal drove them out over the water.

Behind the battle line, the mob turned again and pounced on the undefended convoy. Men gone mad pulled a driver off a wagon and beat him to death before my eyes. Wagons overturned, and the mules broke their harnesses to gallop in terror down the riverfront.

The mob ransacked the wagons in a moment, but soon the looters began fighting among themselves for gashed bags of rice or cans of cooking oil. As people ran into the alleys with their arms full, others swarming down for their share jumped them. The guild hall burst into flames. Soon the mob began to tear at doors and shatter nearby shop windows. Goaded by the Khodataal, Am'rha Bo turned to devour itself.

Kai and I ran for our lives. Struggling uphill against the tide, we held each other up as the riot flooded over us. The mob knocked an old shopkeeper to the ground and looted his little shop even as we stumbled past. We threw ourselves into a doorway as a howling line of Khodataal charged down the street with sabers drawn. As soon as they passed, we ran on.

The fog darkened into drizzle when we paused under a spiral tower. Keep moving or break, I thought. Won't break. Move. I wiped my hair out of my eyes.

"Are you hurt?"

Kai looked dazed. "Hurt? No, but ... " He gasped for breath.

I looked him over. "You're not wounded, Kai. We've got to keep moving now. I need my field bag."

Kai accepted the habitual pull of my pragmatic will. A broad-hipped woman, carrying a coil of rope and a live chicken, over-took us. We ran up the road, past my old clinic, still in ruins. We reached the plaza. It was eerily empty, and too dark to see across to the stalls of the bazaar. I mistrusted the deep shadows around us. Then an enormous explosion lit the sky. We turned in time to see the flash fade into a billowing cloud of smoke on the hill, in line with the highway.

"The road," Kai said, with a flat voice. "They've blown up our little bridge over the funeral road."

I continued the thought. "Cut off the army from the north."

"They can hold the old road around Death's Door for some time."

"And they've driven the army across the river, too."

"Your Khodataal have Am'rha Bo in hand, with a riot for easy cover."

"I didn't know," I said, but suddenly felt no need to defend myself again. Keep moving or break.

"I know you didn't," said Kai.

I did not want to be forgiven, either. We reached my apartment, and I rushed upstairs to my room. I found a candle stub and dared light it. I threw my leather satchel over my shoulder, grabbed my field bag, then stood still in the middle of the little room for an-other breathless moment. I memorized the soft lines of my sleeping mat and the exact layout of my little altar. A faint glow outlined the east-facing window from light reflected off the Ma'rhu from Am'rha Sa, even through the fog. I wondered absently if I could see the silhouette of the island.

My thoughts sharpened. The island. "Kai! How did you get across the river tonight?"

"The boat, of course. No secret now, but couldn't use the bridge yet."

"So it's waiting for you?"

Kai touched my arm. "The crew! We've got to get down there!"

We ran back into the dark, drenched streets, keeping to the steep alleys that wound down toward the docks, passing unseen by all the doors locked with rusty bolts and fear. The sounds of raw anarchy thudded off the sagging walls around us. Without warning, a dozen looters rounded the corner. A wild-eyed man waved a jagged knife in my face. A woman cackled and ran by with an armload of sandals.

"Hey!" I yelled, anger replacing fear.

They threw me against a wall. They knocked Kai headlong into the street. But we were merely in their way. They ran laughing up the alley.

Keep moving or break, I thought. I saw Kai struggle to his feet.

"Come on," I said. "We've been lucky so far."

"This is lucky?"

"We're not dead yet."

When we reached the riverbank corridor, we turned left, running hard. Behind us, the riot raced up the docks like a prairie fire. We ran past deserted and doomed warehouses. But when we reached the boat, I hesitated.

"Get in!"

"People are hurt … "

"And you'll be killed! What good is that? Help them in the morning!"

He grabbed my arm. Gunshots close behind us changed my mind. Kai's anxious crew pushed off as we jumped aboard. The black boat slid quickly into the hiss of dark water, and the fog surrounded us.

With their sure instinct, the crew got us to the island through the mist. But as we tied to the mooring against the foot of the bridge tower, the fog lifted like an invitation. The causeway overhead reappeared, and the steel skeleton glistened. The bright gas lights of Am'rha Sa glittered like jewels within an arm's reach. We sprinted across the stone platform and through the great gate. Pao, the senior servant, slid the double bolts across the bronzed doors behind us.

"No lights tonight," Kai instructed. Pao tipped his head. "Food?"

"Enough for us," Pao said. "Perhaps for a week, if necessary. It has been difficult, since the bridge."

"I know. That's fine. Those with families on shore should leave now."

Pao glanced at the other servants standing beside us. "This is our family," he said. Kai, words failing, bowed deeply to them.

A sound, at first like a distant train, then more like animals howling, reached my ears from over the palace walls. The instinct to keep moving welled up inside me again. I ran up the steep steps that led to the roof of the palace and the parapet of the outer wall. Kai followed me.

On my left lay Am'rha Sa, raw in its own light refracted in the dissolving clouds. On my right, the slums burned. Before me, a flood of people poured across the bridge. They carried flaring torches and lanterns over the water with them.

"Look!" said Kai, behind me. "The towers."

Bursting through the night in sequence, the spiral towers lit up as a call to arms. The first one flared far downstream, then each tower extended the yellow scar across the face of Am'rha Bo. I remembered running that course. I knew those streets.

"So the Khodataal have control of the whole city," I said.

"For now."

In counterpoint to the towers, riot fires consumed the warehouses along the docks. In the moon-starved night, the shoreline was blurred, so it looked like the river was burning, too. And the torch-carrying mob poured over the bridge in front of us. These were the people from the streets of my Am'rha Bo. The Khodataal drove them onto the bridge, I thought. Their own homes were burning, so the narrow path over the river was their only outlet for a vague revenge. I held my breath as the bobbing torches reached the tower where the iron stairs led down to the island, but we were just a shadow on the water, and the lights of Am'rha Sa sparkled. The mob ran straight on along the causeway. They were, after all, only responding to the same instinct I was feeling: to keep moving or break. I wanted to run out and somehow turn them back. Yet I wanted to charge at the head of the attack into the arrogant little gas lights. I could only bite my lip and stare.

The army waited with barricades. I was glad it was dark and distant so I could not see too clearly. Guns flared. Round after round. Torches fell. Some tumbled off the bridge. I could imagine those who, losing heart at the barrage in front of them, turned back, only to be pressed forward by the charging wall of rioters behind them. Then, these same, without options, charged the soldiers with blind rage at their own desperation, only to be cut down by the next fierce volley of bullets.

The horrible impasse lasted only a few minutes, however, because the mob never paused. The torches overwhelmed the line of rifles and broke through the barricade. I watched in dreaded fascination as the mob hit the streets of Am'rha Sa. As riverfront buildings burst into flame, more gunfire crackled over the water. Then, as if a monstrous breath had snuffed them out together, the street lamps throughout the city sputtered out.

"They shut off the gas," whispered Kai. "Smart."

We stood on the parapet for hours, watching the flames and guessing at the carnage as the army hammered back at the rioting swarm. It soon turned to dirty street fighting as the soldiers swept across the Great Plaza from the east, driving peasants back down the hill. Stragglers fell dead in front of the fortified guild halls.

The thud of cannon fire turned our heads back to the old city. First a flash, then the dull thump of the cannon from Death's Door. The army, briefly cut off from the north by the Khodataal, had already retaken the hill. The artillery fired down on the slums.

"God, no," I breathed.

"They'll only use the cannons until they retake the riverfront," said Kai. "I hope," he added.

I knew the contours of Am'rha Bo well enough that I could follow a convoy by the sweep of its headlights and the gunfire sparking out from it as the trucks from Bishtafi moved across our plaza. The convoy paused three times on its way down the road through the Rhu'ta district until each gunfight subsided. Much was lost to my sight in smoke.

At the same time, we began to see dark figures running back across the long causeway from Am'rha Sa. Singly, then in clusters. All running. They could not know what was happening across the river.

"Trapped," I said simply.

Kai did not answer. We stood, utterly alone together, looking from side to side as the army squeezed down both banks toward the river. The rioters sprinted onto the bridge from the east bank. The convoy through Am'rha Bo hit the riverfront. There, the rebels put up a fierce defense. But a set of headlights lit the bridge platform from the Am'rha Bo shore. The Khodataal lost their hold. They would scatter into the alleys now, I knew, and retreat into their foothills. I wondered if they had expected more, after all. In Takau, a revolt was really a battle against the cascade of time. Time wins.

All those who had hoped to retreat from the aborted ravaging of Am'rha Sa were back on the bridge. Only a few sharpshooters were required to cut off the ramp to the causeway.

The headlights and a rifle shot from the Am'rha Bo shoreline announced the rioters' brutal plight. The army inched onto the bridge from both banks, firing as they came. The soldiers were slowed by an armed rebel band that had been caught up with the crowd on the bridge. The Khodataal made a stand, using the dead and wounded for cover. The rioters had reverted to terrified peasants. Then they discovered the staircase off the bridge that led down to the island.

"Get down!" said Kai.

I crouched against the rampart but kept watching in horror. Dozens rushed down the narrow stairs. At the base of the tower, they discovered the Kyornin's boat. Momentarily safe from the gunfire overhead, people fought among themselves for a place on board. Our sleek boat pulled away from its mooring. The Ma'rhu grabbed those thrown overboard and pulled them into the deep current. Overloaded and rocking, the boat listed hard and swamped. Many who fought to get aboard now splashed their way back onto the rocks. Our boat rotated about its sunken keel and sailed away like driftwood, with only a few men clinging to the fine lacquered prow above the waterline.

I went numb to my own fear. This close, I could see the wounded stumbling off the bridge. The smell of gunpowder burned the back of my throat. I could not bear to just hide inside the walls. Had to keep moving. In an animal crouch, I leapt down the parapet stairs. Kai came down behind me. He caught me beside the entry fountain.

"Can't just watch," I said. "I have to go help."

"After the shooting stops. Plenty to do then."

"They're dying out there!"

"Yes! So will you!"

"I've no choice."

He held my arm. "Kath. You go out there and you'll never come back. No matter what."

Suddenly I felt a great calm. I stood very still. Kai let go of me. He took a deep breath to steady himself.

"I left a long time ago," I said.

He bowed his head. "I know."

So he did not stop me as I went to the gate and threw the massive bolts. I listened for another moment to the sporadic gunfire outside, then inched the door open.

A stick shot through the opening, almost at my forehead. Fingers grabbed the door.

"No!" I cried. I couldn't slam it shut again. We had not seen a crowd in the shadows at our feet around the base of the palace walls, huddled to avoid the rain of bullets. They heard me slide the bolts and were ready. The first swarthy man slid through, waving a pistol. More followed. A few carried guns; most had only sticks and knives. Even as they swept in at me, I read both hardness and fear in their peasant faces. No doubt they expected armed guards or sword-wielding ghosts as they flew into the mysterious palace at last. Instead, they rushed against only Kai and an American woman. They swept us aside.

"Hold them!" someone commanded. Two young men flanked us. Their faces shone with sweat. They threw aside my field bag and pushed us across the lawn, away from the gate, to the edge of the garden. They threatened us with butcher knives, but they stood with the familiar baseless swagger of boys parading on the plaza. I had to remind myself these boys likely had become murderers just hours earlier in Am'rha Sa.

It had happened so fast. In that moment, the garden was not ours anymore. It dissolved by one small action of my hand. It was my quiet decision, irretrievable, and though I feared for my life, a dispassionate part of my mind watched and recorded these memories with simple, mild curiosity. Unable to take a firm hold of any defining emotion in myself, I looked at Kai, supposing he was seething with resentment or raging inwardly about betrayal. But as the first men through the gate threw the huge doors open, Kai tipped his head my way.

"My servants," Kai whispered in English. "We've got to get them out."

"Where are they?"

"Probably in the kitchen. Service corridors under the halls from there. Best escape routes."

Everyone, including our young guards, watched the portal yawn open, admitting dozens of rioters turned to refugees. None of them seemed sure whether they were storming the palace or retreating from the bridge. Each was brought up short by the sudden splendor and the dangerous-looking shadows. My attention was diverted, too, as the wounded were pulled or dragged across the threshold. Head wounds, bullet wounds — I automatically categorized battlefield injuries — and fretted that my field bag was sitting almost within reach.

Even now, you cannot stop, chided the dispassionate voice inside me. Too late now, so keep moving. All the wounded dropped on the grass right in front of me. I forced my gaze over their heads.

Shots rang out from the bridge. Bullets pinged off the door. A handful of men with stolen rifles kept the soldiers from starting down the stairs off the bridge, but there was a frenzied stampede among the last rioters through the gate.

"Here's our chance," Kai hissed. Move, I thought. We took a step backward. Kai pointed the direction. We cut behind a tree and in a moment I was following him along a wall shielded with camellias.

With a shout, the boys with the butcher knives plunged into the bushes behind us. But I followed Kai's smooth weaving under branches and around mossy walls. The boys' cursing and crashing fell behind.

We paused to catch our breath. We heard our pursuers below us by the reflecting pool.

"Always came this way as a child," Kai whispered. "Through here now."

Down a flight of tiny and slippery stairs, we came to a low archway. I calculated that the dance hall was overhead, so the main kitchen must be in front of us through this unlit tunnel. Without hesitation, Kai plunged into the thick blackness. I followed blindly.

"Keep one hand on the wall," he said. "It turns here." Twenty paces on, he stopped, and I plowed into his back. He reached out to steady me.

"Watch your head. I remember all this so much bigger."

"You were smaller," I said.

"Oh. Of course." We took another step. "Now there should be three steps up, then a door just past that. I hope it's not locked."

"Me, too."

We shuffled forward. "Ah. The steps." I heard a wooden thump. The rattle of an iron latch. Then I squinted at Kai's silhouette in a Gothic archway against a searing light pouring out at me. He took my hand and pulled me through the door.

As my eyes adjusted, the terrible glare became one dim lantern set on a table. The rest of the cavernous kitchen flickered in deep shadow. The servants, obviously interrupted amidst a desperate debate, stared at us in astonishment.

Kai lifted his hands in the traditional greeting. "Dear friends. No time to lose. You've blocked the doors?" They bowed in unison, still stunned. "But the service corridor to the private chambers, it's still open?" They bowed again. "Good. Pao, is everyone here?"

"Yes, sir."

"We've got to get you out of here. Let's go." Kai snatched up the lantern and led us without hesitation into the servants' narrow passageways under the palace.

I stopped and looked up at the ceiling, instinctively cringing from what sounded like an avalanche. The rioters had poured into the Great Hall.

"It sounded just like rain when there were dances up there," said Pao from behind me. We hurried on.

Above us, the intruders had the gate secured. A few stranded Khodataal on the parapet kept the army at a small but cautious distance. Now the rioters turned to seek out manageable enemies within. They fanned out to search through the rooms of the palace and down the aisles of the garden. We were hunted.

The corridor constricted. It felt like a mine shaft, but thousands of passes by shuffling servants' slippers had polished the floor as they hurried with hot meals under the lawns and entry fountain to the private quarters. When the tunnel opened into a laundry storage room, Kai led us quickly left and right through a labyrinth of chambers.

"How can the Kyornin know his way so well down here?" asked one of the servants.

I heard Pao chuckle, despite the circumstance. "The Kyornin was a sly child," he said kindly. "I often had to chase him out of here."

"You remember that?" Kai laughed.

"I remember everything," Pao replied.

"Shhh! Voices!"

"The library," Kai whispered. The servants groaned, guessing by the painful sounds what priceless treasures were hitting the floor. We hurried on.

"SIR, THERE'S NO EXIT THAT WAY."

"But that route past the cistern … " said Kai.

"Been blocked off for years," Pao answered. "The floor gave out."

"You should have told me."

"That was in your father's time."

We all stood motionless in the gloom. "Then how about the grotto, through the jade room?" Kai asked.

"We would have to come out into the salon and go down the hall."

"Our best chance, anyway. Hurry!" Kai led us along the damp tunnel.

We climbed a flight of stairs. Kai snuffed out the lantern and left it behind when we came out the back side of a hidden doorway that opened into the salon. I knew the room. It was the most European room in Takau. It was crowded with imported Victorian furniture and accessories intended to make British visitors feel at ease. High tea was served on a little walnut table with fluted legs. There was even a painting of riders in red hunting jackets pursuing a pack of hounds over a rail fence. Yet the room had always been slightly askew, in that indefinable way everything European was arranged in Takau. I had once studied the room, trying to determine what caused the effect. Somehow, the angle at which the chairs faced each other could not have occurred in London. Or perhaps it was the way a leather couch stood across the room directly in line with the door? I never figured out just what was wrong, but I always stubbed my toe on end tables in this room.

The servants filed silently through the doorway and around me. I felt large and clumsy, sensing how they slid with practiced invisibility in or out of these rooms where they had always been expected to work without being seen.

There was just enough texture between ash and pitch for me to move across the room without knocking a porcelain figurine off a pedestal. We stood at the hallway door. Kai peeked out. We listened, as small animals listen, with our whole bodies. Kai gave us a signal.

This was the worst because we were in full view down the long corridor. The tapestry with the Kyornin's barges floating in festive grandeur down the river was no comfort now. The ebony dragon with the sapphire eye was not about to help either. We ran, with my hand lightly on Pao's shoulder. I needed him to pull me on.

"Out of the hall, quick!" Kai whispered. He closed the door behind me. We stood, listening again. No shout like the bay of dogs on the scent. We heard doors thrown open, but still back near the library.

So. This room. It felt smaller, like a childhood classroom revisited. But the right smells. Of silk. Of old teak. Of Kai, next to me.

It was always dusky like this in the jade room, a favorite. We had slept here often. Like dreaming, but little sleep. The room remembered. I felt heat embedded in the walls. No smoke. Pure, clear heat. Yet memory is impoverished. The press and tangle and whisper of skin can never be reclaimed. We cannot wholly recall touch so charged by mind and heart. But it was real at the time. I think it was. Like music, which always exists only in the moment.

Nostalgia is crippling, I thought. Keep moving. But the silhouette of the bed burned darkly. I smelled the faint hint of incense, like old prayers. He had cooled me with rose water. I, languid. Then tensing, wanting. Feeling my wet thighs. A soft, soulful moan — my voice, a foreigner to such aching bliss — echoed off that burnished ceiling. Yes, it was real at the time.

And the easy certainty. And my eagerness to tell him and show him. And leaving secret tokens. And feeling lighter when he walked in. And sneaking away into safe shadows. And delighting in how he poured my mint tea. And precious silence together. And plans. And poetry. And the dancing. Reason for dancing!

"Yes," whispered Kai. He was watching me. "And you will have all that again. I pray you will."

"And you, too," I said gently.

"Thank you. Yes."

Pao unlatched the glass-paned door that led to a private grotto. We filed out into the faint, waning moonlight and her shadows. The grotto had a little waterfall, mute now along with the rest of the fountains, and a bench for two with azaleas nestled around its feet. Clematis vines richly draped the walls. A gargoyle over the gate smiled foolishly at us. The old iron complained loudly when Kai forced the gate and ushered us out into the open landscape.

We ran in line through the blue-black jungle, ducking philodendron leaves. I fell once, into a bank of ferns. Arms in black with gold braid lifted me. Then between palm trees. Down the edge of the rose garden. Behind the silver pavilion.

Ferocious shouting came from the upper terraces. Glass shattered behind us in the palace. The cacophony of an unleashed rampage replaced the music of the mute fountains. And the hateful racket was closing in on us.

With the rattle of greased chains, the antique boat touched down on the water as I came through the boathouse door. Kai grabbed the old lance from its place against the wall and used it to pull the boat against the planks. He turned to Pao.

"Hurry. Get in."

None of the servants moved. We heard shouting from the rose garden.

"You first, sir," said Pao.

"Get aboard," Kai commanded. Reluctantly, the servants climbed into the low-slung boat. Kai nodded to me. I folded my arms. He sighed and poised himself to shove the boat out into the pond.

"Sir!" the servants cried in alarm.

"Don't you see?" Kai said with affection. "My forefathers put this here for you, not for the Kyornin. Now go!" He leaned on the lance with all his weight and pushed the boat through the portal. Still protesting, the servants scrambled for the oars. "Hurry!" Kai urged. They brought the boat about, then stopped again, looking as though they might pull us over the water by wishing it so. Kai pointed angrily across the pond. Pao barked once. Black sleeves and gold braids rowed straight for the outer wall.

We heard shouts from the rose garden. With a grin, I pointed to the cabinet that held the antique swords. Kai laughed and set the lance back against the wall. We stepped outside to see what would happen next.

21

"THEY'VE SEEN US," I said, stiffening.

We waited. Five men charged down the path toward us. One ran with a rifle pointed our way. The others carried clubs. We stood our ground. They closed in, then surrounded us.

Up close in the soft light, I saw they were not big men. In fact, they were not especially fierce, either. The one with the rifle was overweight and sweating profusely. The others were as thin as their clubs. And they stopped, weapons dropped at their sides, staring.

"Kai?" asked the tallest one.

"Doctor?" rasped the fat one.

"Good evening, gentlemen," Kai answered, recovering more quickly than I could. "Welcome to my garden. I had been planning to invite the merchant guild out here for a conference soon, but I'm afraid events have overtaken us."

These Am'rha Bo shopkeepers who had been swept along in the madness of the riot now stumbled through this dreamlike landscape in shock and amazement. Instinctively, they ran as far from the army's line of fire as possible. They had not seen us captured at the gate. Here, they kept staring at us. They must have thought me mad when I started laughing with relief.

"Kai, the Khodataal trapped in here will kill you," the tall one realized.

"Useless as a hostage," Kai agreed, "because the army probably wants my head, too."

"Do you have a place to hide?"

I laughed again. "In here, he can become a ghost, walking through walls!"

They squinted at me, even more certain I'd lost my mind. Kai just nodded. He turned to me.

"You will go help the wounded, I suppose?" he said.

"Of course."

"What will you say when they ask about me?"

I thought a moment. "These, um, angry men will drag me back to the Great Hall, saying they caught me, but the Kyornin got away."

"And why were you out here in the first place?"

"I came out to help the wounded and got trapped in the fight. True enough. They'll see my field bag. Anyway, the Khodataal know me and will let me work."

The merchants confidently assured us my reputation would protect me. Kai took a deep breath. He turned back to his friends.

"Kindly don't destroy anything else here. Clan Kyornin has been good to you."

They hung their heads. I started worrying about the heavy-set merchant, who did not seem too familiar with how to handle the rifle he was holding.

"And try to stay away from the front gate," Kai added.

We heard others coming toward us.

"Go, Kai. It can't last too long," I whispered.

He hesitated.

"Sometimes you lose what you love most in the world," he whispered, "and for no good reason."

"I'm sorry about all this," I said, gesturing into the dark.

"Oh, I don't mean the garden." He touched my cheek, smiled, and turned away. In a twinkling, he vanished into the landscape. The merchants looked around us, slack-jawed.

"See?" I said. "He's a ghost. Now, take me back to the gate. People are dying." They did not move. "Now!" I commanded, using Magra's old dialect. At once, the men pulled themselves together and we hurried back through the roses.

Somewhere behind us, a rusted grate fell away and the servants slipped under the wall. Black uniforms and the small black boat shot into the obliging Ma'rhu. They floated unseen under the bridge and downstream to safety.

My merchant captors escorted me back to the Great Hall. I retrieved my field bag. A dozen men from the north had assumed control within the walls by virtue of their weapons and the gruff authority of the two clan chiefs among them.

As expected, when they learned I was the doctor from Am'rha Bo who had treated Tash'anghani's people, they ordered me not to leave the Great Hall and to help the wounded men of the mountain clan first. Then they forgot about me.

The Kyornin, they declared, would be captured and questioned. Some thought he was an ally who had supplied weapons to the Khodataal. Others thought he was just another aristocrat who should be hung from the palace wall in view of the government soldiers. The clan chiefs organized a search of the palace grounds.

Outside, the army laid siege to the island. They had only to wait. The bridge bristled with soldiers and weapons. The army told us to come out unarmed and we could avoid bloodshed. A few Khodataal responded with gunshots from the parapets.

I stabilized the wounded. Those first hours, the hall was awash in blood. Half a dozen died. I used the last of my iodine while removing a bullet from a young man's shattered shoulder. I said Magra's words without her herbs.

There were some women within the walls who had been caught up in the charge across the river. Their faces were gaunt, and it was clear the righteous rage or visions of looted prosperity had evaporated long ago, and now they recognized their lives were nearly forfeit here among desperate men.

I instructed these women on how to dress wounds. I tried to keep them busy. We made bandages from the Kyornin's fine sheets.

We could not send a message to the shore. Nevertheless, a group of the mountain warriors among us feverishly argued the Khodataal would still sweep through town and over the bridge to rescue us that night. But I knew Tash'anghani and his band were already running for their lives back toward the northern border. All the other men in Am'rha Bo were shaking with fear behind locked doors, hoping their families would not be dragged into the streets and executed. Of course, many were.

About an hour before dawn, I decided I had done all I could. Without being followed, I slipped out of the Great Hall through a servant's door. I climbed a long set of steep stairs to a tiny balcony Kai had shown me one clear winter's night. It hung over the deep-river side of the palace wall. I reached it through a hidden portal at the back of a small room. It must have been the secret refuge of some young princess centuries ago. I snatched up a blanket and a pillow on my way.

My dreams were brief. The morning sun sparkled on the river. There is little comfort in a lovely view from a prison window, I learned.

I could see the bridge from my little aerie. Troop movement was leisurely and continuous. I stopped watching.

Before I was missed, I shuffled back down to the Great Hall. I made my rounds. Then I stepped outside to the gate. No one paid me the slightest attention, so I climbed to the parapet for a view of Am'rha Bo. The slums smoldered. But smoke rose from Death's Door again. And cannons were positioned on the bridge, aimed at me.

IN OUR FAVOR, we had an ample supply of water filtered from the silent fountain pools. But with so many trapped inside, our small store of food was already gone. One or two days without food was nothing unusual to most of these people, of course. They knew not to move unless necessary. But it was empty stomachs that had driven many of them into the streets. That was the point. They were re-signed to hunger, but not immune, and everyone slowly grew listless. Here, however, I expected to see spirits starve before bodies failed.

There was little gunfire during the day. A handful of sharpshoot-ers on the bridge kept the Khodataal pinned down.

We received a message. They told us to come out unarmed and we could avoid bloodshed. No one moved.

The women worked closely at my side. We carried water. We listened, without looking up, to the debates among the men, who squatted in the shade just as they did on market day on the plaza. Talk ran in circles. It had nowhere else to go.

Some resolved to stand their ground until they collapsed. Bet-ter to starve to death than surrender, they argued. Some wanted

G.L. KAY

to storm back out onto the bridge. Better to commit suicide than starve to death. Some thought they could swim away under cover of darkness. Wait for the new moon in two nights. Better to risk drowning than commit suicide.

The men in mountain cloaks stood apart from the rest and argued among themselves. An easy solution, I thought: They will get so angry in their impotence they will simply kill each other and save the army outside the trouble.

The men tried to catch Kai. Some thought he might still be a useful hostage. So they organized hunting parties. They combed the garden. They scoured the private quarters. They broke open every room and closet. They found the servants' corridors and rummaged through the cellars. Like trying to catch a ghost with a fishing net, they grumbled.

Kai listened to their plans. Wearing his ceremonial robes, he watched them from a window but was gone when they rushed into the room to trap him. A flutter of green silk sent men howling down a dark-paneled hallway into the empty library. They saw him near the blue pavilion after dusk and chased him back to the boathouse. They found the antique swords, but no trace of Kai.

I watched from the terrace of the Great Hall as the enraged hunters closed in on him near the reflecting pool. He looked up and waved at me, an amused salute. I raised my hands in blessing. The hunters came at him from two sides. Kai stood there in plain view. I laughed with him. And just before they grabbed him, he leapt through a veil of ivy into the maze.

They fell for it, of course. The entire search party followed him into the maze. From my vantage point I saw Kai quickly reach the grassy circle in the center. His pursuers fanned out and were soon hunting each other. They began shouting for one another in frustration and fear. Long after Kai had slipped through the secret door and sauntered away to a secluded spot behind the willow pavilion, his would-be captors still struggled to find their way through the leafy labyrinth corridors. An hour after dark had fallen on the garden, the last men finally shuffled through one of the exits. Shamed and furious, they seemed to forget their desperate situation while they debated strategies for capturing Kai. A comic metaphor, I thought, for how most people spend their lives. I complained only when they threatened to burn the palace down to

260

flush him out. Let the army do that, I said, to remind them who their real enemy was.

WHEN I GOT to my little balcony the second night, I found a fresh bouquet of roses waiting for me. I wished I could imagine an adequate reply to him. I thought of the men using the bank of camellias for a latrine. I thought of the cannons. And I searched my heart for choices to make. No shadows hinting of light. Even the last sliver of moon was waning. Yet the desperate darkness gave me comfort, or at least relief. After all, this was the first time I did not have to make any difficult decisions. The work was done.

I listened to the sniper fire from the parapets, wondering why they wasted their meager supply of ammunition. I waited, weakening, for a conclusion of some kind.

I dreamed of dancers circling a fountain taller than the foothills. I heard songs of worship. But an eerie glow from the river woke me. I sat up and struggled to remember where I was. The gas lamps of Am'rha Sa had been re-lit. The city glowed again with modern promise. I turned my back.

I WAS NOT SURPRISED to find two more had died in the night, both from internal bleeding. There would be no funeral pyre. Even the dead had to wait. We stashed the bodies in a back room.

Kai became a frequent apparition with a keen ability to catch the distraught refugees unaware and unable to respond with more than choked cries and leaden feet.

He found a large bag of flour somewhere deep in a kitchen storeroom and brought it to me. He walked right into the Great Hall and handed me the bag with a deceptively calm expression on his haggard face. With a soft click from a terrace door, he was gone before anyone could react.

Twenty-five angry men with nothing else to do searched the entire palace again. The hunt was called off only when the sentries on the parapet issued a warning that the army was moving. Anyway he's mad, the hunters muttered.

The army merely changed the watch, while more troops arrived from Da'rha Ghand. A large force moved across the bridge into Am'rha Bo. Boats patrolled the waters around the palace walls.

Three women, returning from the garden with buckets of fresh water, reported to me how Kai had appeared to them and had given them words of encouragement. But he looked through them like a mystic with one foot in another realm, they said. Then he vanished into the landscape. I could guess where he had slipped behind the cedars and over to the grotto near the fern bed, but I just nodded solemnly as they told their story.

I fed the last of the fry bread, made from Kai's sack of flour, to the wounded who were still fighting for life. Outside, the men sat on the grass as still as the statues. They had stopped fighting. They merely waited. Those who had held out hope of a rescue finally cast it aside.

I climbed up to my balcony retreat with hunger distracting me from scattered waves of foreboding. Strange sounds off the river interrupted my dreams of gently singing voices.

WE RECEIVED A MESSAGE. The army told us to come out unarmed and we could avoid bloodshed. Men lowered their eyes.

We knew from the taste in the air at dawn that the day would be unseasonably hot. Shadows inched across the palace grounds. We wavered between exhaustion and aching restlessness.

Near noon, I stepped out for no reason and stood near the dragon statue. I watched a few men and women shuffle into the garden. They were taking this one chance to wander through paradise with hell waiting for them outside. Idly, I followed them, but soon turned off onto familiar narrow paths.

At the base of the central terrace, I came upon a ferocious Takau monster that was supposed to be spitting at a phalanx of armored heroes. The river was supposed to be churning around their feet. Suddenly, my heart ached for the sound of the water. What the hell, I thought. So I made my way to the waterhouse. It was undamaged, indeed undiscovered. It smelled of algae and rotten wood. I stood for a moment listening to the cool drip, drip. Then I began to turn valves. Here was my answer to Kai.

Outside, the garden burst to life. My laughter echoed among the rusty pipes when I imagined what effect I was having on everyone. I forced open the floodgates.

Only one man knew where to run when the fountains bubbled to life. Kai burst into the waterhouse and I laughed again with what must have been my old fearless laugh. He gave me that sly, sidelong glance once more. Then he set about with me, turning on all the waterworks for their full gushing effect.

With the fountains reborn, we latched the waterhouse door behind us. Not a word was spoken. Kai disappeared again into the dappled light. I strolled past the spitting monster and enjoyed the wonderment and delight of my fellow captives.

At first frightened by the noise of the waterfalls as they began to roar, the refugees were soon entranced, briefly distracted again from their plight. Playfully, a young Khodataal threw flower petals into the upper pool and chased them downstream over waterfalls and around demons just to see where they went. The walking wounded reached out to let the water splash their arms and faces. My friends from the merchant guild built an altar on a bench beside the tallest fountain. And that led to an afternoon spent singing prayers and invoking Yasol'rhishá. I recognized the songs in my dream.

THAT NIGHT, UNDER the dark moon, the army made its move. Without warning, the cannons fired point blank at the gate. I was working in the Great Hall. Around me, the weak and wounded alike leapt to their feet. I ran to the doorway. The gate rebuffed the first round with a shudder, and smoke shot along the marble floor. The second round followed immediately, and shards of the stone towers fell in a shower of dust around the entry fountain, still burbling all alone. In the awful pause before the next blast, the Khodataal and refugees massed together on the grass, as though they were only spectators. They were Rizhmadi, so they wanted to die on a green lawn.

A shot from the bridge whistled over the wall. It hit the table where Kai had first served me dinner. The fluted colonnade blew into rubble and rained into the reflecting pool below. Succumbing to instinct, everyone ran for cover.

The next cannon round hit the towers again, with a force that made the ground under our feet heave. I thought of the earthquake.

But then Kai appeared, still dressed in his dusty robes. He charged the gate and tore at the locks. Two men tried to pull him away. He knocked them aside. A single shell hit the gate squarely. The shock wave threw Kai onto the marble tiles, almost into the fountain, but still the gate stood firm. Kai got back on his feet. We watched now, transfixed.

"No more! There is no more to lose!" he screamed, slamming back the bolts on the gate. Before another cannon shot went off, Kai threw his weight against the bronzed doors and they swung wide open with a double clang. He ran through the threshold, robes fluttering, and stood alone on the glassy entryway. "Stop it! No more!"

It was an absolute miracle that among all the soldiers massed on the stairway and across the bridge, no one pulled a trigger. For a moment, it was so still we could all hear the river rippling around the rocks.

"Hold your fire." A clear command from a familiar voice. Tokmol stepped from among the bristling rifles and walked without hesitation up to Kai. I wonder what words they exchanged. But in a moment, at some slight gesture from Tokmol, the host of infantry charged in at us through the gate.

A man next to me raised a rifle.

"God, no!" I cried, and grabbed the barrel. It was the most fragile, luckiest moment I have ever known. Perhaps my voice stayed his hand. The shot did not go off.

I looked up at the front line of troops at the gate with their weapons leveled at us. The same moment, soldiers appeared around us on the lawn. Kai must have known. They had scaled the northern wall during the cannon attack and poured into the garden unchallenged. It was funny how the patter of boots running over tiled walkways sounded just like splashing fountains.

22

"HAVE THEM DROP their weapons," Tokmol called out calmly as he approached through the portal. The refugees looked at me. I drew myself up and glared at Tokmol. Then I made a small motion with my hand, palm down. Our few guns and all the sticks and pipes and knives set down silently on the grass. Now, so suddenly, it was over.

Soldiers quickly herded the Khodataal together. Those rebels who survived the interrogations would be hauled off to prisons and work camps. The merchants and others from Am'rha Bo would not fare much better. For the moment, the Great Hall became a prison block.

I stood beside Kai. We held onto our silence, the only thing we had left. An hour later, Tokmol singled us out and escorted us with armed guards into the library. The room had been ransacked. My Dickens reading chair lay on its back. Books were swept off shelves and kicked around the floor. Maps lay crumpled and heaped as if in preparation for a bonfire. Kai moaned softly when we walked in. I suppose I did, too.

"You will be held here until we have the island secured," Tokmol said. He posted his men in the hallway. He looked around the room and shook his head. "Unfortunate," he said. He rubbed his forehead wearily and looked at us. "Listen," he frowned, "the military is going to take your case. You understand it is out of my control."

We nodded. Tokmol picked up a jade paperweight from the floor and set it on the table. I did not expect or want any mercy or special treatment from him. Yet, I was surprised by what looked like concern on his face.

"High prices paid, by all of us. I understand that you … "

Kai held up his hand. Tokmol stopped.

"Yes. Very well." He straightened his shoulders. "By the way, sir, the Rhu'pasham is on his way from Am'rha Sa even now. I have made an … arrangement," he added softly and touched his ear. Kai tipped his head. Then, with his customary about-face, Tokmol left the room and closed the door, without sending his guards in to watch us. We stood, with priceless books strewn at our feet, in the absurd silence.

I bent down and smoothed a page in an enormous book of botanical illustrations. I closed the leather cover and set the book back on a shelf. Kai laid out a crinkled map of the Ma'rhu and gently rolled it up. I righted the Dickens chair. He straightened a random shelf. I sat down. He leaned against the great map table. We waited.

We both jumped to our feet when the library door flew open and four men dressed in burgundy and gold burst in on us. Tet'shri planted himself in the middle of the library and surveyed the room with ravenous eyes. His three attendants crossed their arms in smug anticipation. When his gaze fell on Kai, he laughed. A cruel, contemptuous laugh.

"The Rhu'pasham wishes to thank Clan Kyornin for finally returning the island to us," he sneered. "We appreciate the care you've given the palace all these generations, but we are quite pleased to reclaim our rightful property."

He paused for a spiteful chuckle. Kai moved slowly around the table. He faced Tet'shri as if ready for a fight. My mind raced. I couldn't move. Tet'shri stood, gloating, drunk with his victory, with the open doorway behind him. His attendants kept their attention on Kai, wary that any moment the tattered madman might attack.

"Really, boy, you've been so very accommodating. And you, too," he said to me.

I recognized him at that moment: the hand of Fate caught holding a knife, and the obvious outcome love never sees. Shaking, I found my voice.

"This was your goal all along, wasn't it?" I took one step forward and stopped again.

Tet'shri regarded me with ugly disdain.

"So exquisitely naive! So pliable. You Americans will all be stabbed in the back by the little countries of the world, eventually."

Then he was through with me. He focused on Kai and his ancestral revenge.

"Oh, how pleased I was to let the Kyornin squander his clan's fortune in the slums," he crooned. "So noble! Naturally, I threw my heartfelt support behind him. Delighted to let him open the trade route for us, too. You asked too much for Autumn House, by the way, but as it was going to such a worthy cause, and would make my ... consolidation ... so complete, of course I just had to accept your offer. A delicious touch! And when your foreign lover came to me with the bridge idea, ah, then I knew the island was mine."

"You knew about us?"

He scoffed at me. "I'd had you followed for weeks. With your little black boat waiting every night. Secret lovers' trysts. You never noticed? Ha! I was concerned when you stopped sneaking out together so often, because I needed you as a tool to manipulate him."

I glanced at the open doorway, then took three careful steps forward to stand beside Kai.

"The river guild would control the bridge," Tet'shri continued. "The bridge had to be anchored on the island. Then, if an unfortunate accident befell the last and unmarried young Kyornin, someone would have to take custody of the island, of course. Properly and inevitably, the Rhu'pasham! You know," he added viciously, "my clan will honor me for generations to come for regaining the island from the damn Kyornin. Having you engineer the bridge adds a sweet irony, don't you think? Of course, after that you were just a nuisance, a political threat."

"So you tried to have him killed," I said slowly. "All those accidents ... "

Tet'shri was watching his effect on Kai. And Kai remained coiled in his dusty robes as if about to strike, keeping his eyes, unwavering, on Tet'shri.

"You proved too difficult to eliminate ... quietly. Frustrating, really. After the setup at the supply yard failed, the Commissioner's men got suspicious. Then it became more convenient to play you as a Khodataal sympathizer. They so appreciated your donations!"

"Tash'anghani," I said. My voice was hoarse.

"You supplied him, in my name," Kai added.

"And wasn't he grateful?" Tet'shri cackled. "Though I hear they burned down my guild hall over there, the bastards. They'll pay, in time."

Kai kept his eyes steady. "So now you have us out of the way, and you will just pay off the Commissioner's men and threaten the rest of the Council into giving you control of the island."

"There," Tet'shri smiled. "The young Kyornin is finally learning how the game is played. But too late: What a pity! Your father was the same kind of fool."

If Kai could be goaded into attacking, Tet'shri's attendants would stop him, the guards would be called, and Kai would be hauled off to rot in an asylum. But Kai only shifted his weight.

"But what's-his-name, the new Commissioner," Kai said, in a thoughtful tone. "He is too ambitious, don't you think? He'll give you trouble."

Tet'shri waved his hand. "Another noble servant of law and order. He'll be removed. I'll put someone convenient in that seat."

"And what of the army?"

"Officers can be bought," Tet'shri shrugged.

"We have heard enough," Tokmol declared from the doorway, where he had been listening. The battalion commander stood beside him as a witness.

Tet'shri and his attendants spun about. In that moment, Kai might have leapt forward and killed Tet'shri before anyone could react. But Kai, who had seen Tokmol at the door throughout the conversation, relaxed into his dancer's casual balance and folded his arms. I touched his hand. The hint of a smile softened his mouth.

Tokmol's guards poured into the room. He pointed at Tet'shri.

"You are under arrest for attempted murder of a Council member and clan elder and for treason in support of rebel forces, among other things." Tokmol signaled his men. "His attendants, too."

The guards hauled Tet'shri and his attendants out of the library. Tet'shri sputtered and cursed and flailed. We waited while the noise receded down the hall.

"A full confession. How sweet," Tokmol smiled. "Better than I'd hoped when we let him in!"

"I am indebted to you."

"Not at all. The Rhu'pash has had every petty gangster on the docks in his pocket for years. He has threatened and attempted to bribe most of my senior officers. We have investigations open on him on behalf of several other clans. Two guildmasters fear for their lives because of him. And I have no intention of being replaced by someone 'convenient,' either."

"The merchant guild will be pleased to turn over their collected evidence of his intimidation and racketeering to your office as well, of course."

"Very good. We may glean a bit of justice out of this catastrophe after all."

"And will you see to it that the island is at least protected?"

"Yes sir, within my power, I will."

Kai bowed in acknowledgment. Tokmol snapped to attention and nodded, then returned to parade rest. He spared me any further reproach. We held onto the empty moment.

As more soldiers poured into the room, the commander stepped forward. He did not care about moments of poetic justice or philosophical reflections.

"I will bear witness to what we have just heard," he said. "But I am still required to place you both under arrest. You will be tried on charges of conspiracy and sedition against the state. You will come with me. Now."

Tokmol stepped aside, but raised a hand, then, hesitating, dropped it again. "Ma'rhu keeps singing," he offered. The soldiers led us away.

I was transported to the south and detained in a rat-infested jail near Da'rha Ghand. After a few miserable weeks, the American consulate got me out. I was escorted briskly onto a British ocean liner, with only my satchel for luggage.

There were no farewells, no parting rituals, and there was no storybook sense of closure. No one noticed me leaning on the starboard railing. As the ship pulled out of the harbor, I felt no movement. The land receded from the ship. Takau just faded away until it vanished into light.

From London, I heard that the Takau tribunal failed to convict the Kyornin of any crime, but, due to its highly strategic position, the military refused to relinquish the island. Not surprisingly, the government still retains custody, calling the palace a national treasure. Today, tourists follow perky young women in red jackets on tours through the Great Hall, and scholars write expensive books about the symbolism and mythology expressed in the fountains.

The army clamped down on the northern province, though concessions were made for ancestral clan territories. The Rizha continue their dance. Yasol'rhishá returns to bless the crops and comfort the weary.

I never returned. The rise of fascist regimes in the West eclipsed our little revolution. My work took me through Europe during the war and to Jerusalem, where I found new love among a people struggling to create a homeland.

Of all the suddenly severed ties from that season of my life, one unrequited relationship haunted me; the glistening eyes of a studious young Rizha girl watched me in my dreams. So it is with inexpressible joy all these many years later that my memories flood back, vivid and alive, resurrected by this extraordinary letter I just received:

Dear Katherine,

I was searching through a registry of medical professionals with experience in "foreign" countries (I am applying for grants — of course — and need sponsors) when I found your name listed with the years you spent in Takau. Confident there was only one Western doctor named Katherine in my home country at that time, it is with great hope — and a little trepidation — that I write this letter. Do you remember me? I followed you around Am'rha Bo relentlessly. You attended my naming day (Yes, I still use the altar lamp!) and my grandmother's funeral. You let me mix herbs and carry your big leather satchel. (It was big to me then, anyway!) Katherine, I remember the first time I held a stethoscope: It was yours, and you let me listen to your heart. You showed me how Western medicine works. More importantly, you taught me how to learn and how to teach myself.

A letter of sponsorship from the Kyornin got me into a good boarding school in Am'rha Sa. At that time, a girl from Takau had a chance of entry into universities in France. By some miracle, I was accepted, and off I sailed to Europe. I didn't see my family for four years. When I did come home, I was shocked by the contrast between my worlds. Before the next monsoon, I booked passage to New York, armed with transcripts from a French university and a scholarship from the Takau merchant guild. I made it into medical school, where I met Don Sudduth in a pediatrics class. A year later we interned at the same hospital, and he told me about his dream to build community health programs in poor countries. We got married between shifts. After two years of grueling residencies, we moved to Takau and built a hospital within a mile of my family's compound. We are still a small operation, with only nine full-time staff members. (I can't imagine how you did it in those days!) But we hope to open a new wing in time for the New Year's celebration.

Because he was my patron, I felt obligated to keep the Kyornin informed of my progress. Because it was Kai, he sweetly answered my letters with encouragement. Clan Kyornin continues to support our work. You may be interested to know that Kai lost much of his personal wealth in the Khodataal uprising but he quietly built the merchant guild into a powerful trade union. He built a road to the coast that is still the main highway today. He also brokered Takau's first international commerce treaty. Kai still travels widely and promotes science and art throughout the country. I think he built for himself a rich life of service and passion.

I am certain that service and passion define your life, too. I trust this finds you in good health and happy. I would treasure a brief reply from you.

With warmest regards,

Jhamya Kat'rhin Sudduth, M.D.
Rhu'ta Medical Clinic
Am'rha Bo, Takau

Of Am'rha Bo, I remember best that which was never seen or touched. I hear the cry of a newborn down a narrow alley. I hear gunfire. I hear Magra's voice, always commanding, and I hear the soft tones of a yala, always just around a corner, always beckoning.

A caress of fog on my skin brings back the soft breezes off the Ma'rhu in the autumn, where our dreams were born. I also recall the crippling heat and then the first splash of the monsoon deluge in an old ritual bowl.

Takau taught me that love and beauty live in the perilous balance between our emotions and our obligations, between devotion and destruction.

I left when the songs no longer made me laugh or cry. Yet, when I glance at my old leather satchel that holds all these memories, I recall the music of the fountains and the scent of rain and roses in the garden. Ma'rhu keeps singing.

GLOSSARY

Am'rha Bo an old city on the western bank of the Ma'rhu River in Takau

Am'rha Sa a modernized sister city of Am'rha Bo on the eastern bank of the Ma'rhu

Am'rha Boae'Sa the formal name for the urban area that includes Am'rha Sa and Am'rha Bo. Also the province that encompasses the cities on both banks of the upper Ma'rhu

Ashka'rhuna a crone goddess blamed for the excesses of the monsoon

Bishtafi an ancient town in ruins located in the foothills of Takau's northern province

Esh'rhu a small river that flows out of the border region to join the Ma'rhu about four miles north of Am'rha Bo

Fa'rhouzi a comic character known for his red costume and mischievous pranks who brings gifts to children during the New Year celebration

Khoda a fiercely independent mountain clan known for its sister-hood of warriors

Khodataal a coalition of militant clans in the foothills of the north-ern province of Takau united to oppose the military occupation of the region

Kor'pasham roughly translates 'master of the forest,' an honor-ary title used by the clan elders in the northern province

Kyornin an ancestral clan of Takau, known for its public works projects and for its palace on a set of islands in the Ma'rhu River. Also the title of the clan elder

Makli panjira 'new mother's soup,' a potato soup served to mid-wives and family women attending a birth

Ma'rhu the primary river of Takau. Also the goddess of the river and the central deity of the Rizha pantheon

Ma'rhu ta yalathé vernacular farewell expression meaning 'Ma'rhu keeps singing'

Mortash'rhondí a fearsome god of death always pestered by demons and blamed for natural disasters

Nes'fhan a mountain village at the headwaters of the Esh'rhu

Nisché spirit guides said to take the form of small animals

Rhu'mora a poverty-stricken district of Am'rha Bo squeezed be-tween the river and a low, cave-pocked cliff

Rhu'pash the ancestral clan that controls trade on the Ma'rhu. The patriarch of the river guild is called the Rhu'pasham.

Rhu'ta the central district of Am'rha Bo

Rizha the native people of Takau

Rizhmadi the official language of Takau, noted for its many dia-lects and required use of variable syntax depending on the social status of the speakers

Shen'te a term of endearment acknowledging an honorary member of a family or community

Sybalo a god who is forever on a quest to find his lover, forming the foundation of an elaborate mythic story cycle

Syftarhó Ruling clan of the textile guild

Tash'anghani patriarch of a mountain clan and commander of the Khodataal

Wath'wahao a nature spirit believed to protect respectful travelers in the mountains of Takau

Yala an eight-stringed instrument similar to a small sitar but carried like a guitar. Used for folk music and ritual throughout Takau, the yala's complex harmonies and plaintive tone give Rizha music its distinctive wailing sound.

Yasol'rhishá goddess of the New Year, who comforts the recently dead and brings fertility to the land

The Island Gardens of Takau

by G.L. Kay

READING GROUP GUIDE

Questions for Discussion

1. The author contrasts the Rizha culture's patriarchal veneer with the fundamental matriarchy that holds it together. Coming from the West, Katherine struggles to find her place in the society. Does she succeed? How are the Rizha attitudes toward family and authority different from cultural structures in the West during the 1920s? Today?

2. The myths and legends of Takau illuminate the culture. On several occasions, Katherine experiences the magic directly. How do these myths intersect with events in the story?

3. The novel skirts the issues of colonialism and Westernization. Takau was never part of the British Empire. Katherine arrives to bring modern medicine to the slums, and Kai sees industrial-era development as a blessing, yet only Takau's isolation has protected the culture they value. Discuss the paradox of modernization versus preservation of culture and national identity. How does Takau compare to Cuba or Burma?

4. Katherine passes judgment on Tokmol as a corrupt 'petty dictator.' Interactions with him throughout the story, however, reveal a more complex character trying to balance conflicting

responsibilities. Do his means justify the ends? Is he an enemy or ally? Does he understand Katherine better than she understands him?

5. A central theme of the book is the price paid for unyielding idealism. When does idealism cross the line to fanaticism? Which characters cross that line? What happens when devotion to a cause takes on a momentum that runs out of control?

6. *The Island Gardens of Takau* can be read as an allegory of a relationship born in a struggle for a noble cause. Throughout the book, story elements and characters are identified, literally, as what they represent:

> "Tor distilled the loyalty of the passionate people who surrounded me."
> "In Magra, I met the uncompromising ideal of service and devotion; though she may eventually save the world, she consumes your soul."

What do some of the other characters and elements in the story represent? Does the allegory hold together as a symbolic representation of a relationship that runs its course?

7. "But a bridge is defiance … That is what we were doing in those days," the narrator declares. The bridge across the Ma'rhu is both the culmination of Katherine's efforts to improve life in Am'rha Bo and the road to ruin for all she's loved. Is the bridge a mistake? Inevitable?

8. The narrator is the central character reflecting on the events of the story from the perspective of many years gone by. However, the author lets the narrator reveal her opinions and judgments along the way. How does this device color the story for the reader? Does the narrator come to a clearer understanding of herself in the course of telling the story? Does the reader come to a different conclusion?

About the Author

THE SETTINGS AND CULTURES that evolve in G.L. Kay's writing are strongly influenced by his travels around the world. Kay lives in southern Oregon, though he would like to spend part of the year in Italy. He holds degrees in comparative literature, environmental studies, and science communication. Given more time, he would study C.G. Jung, entomology, and Sanskrit. He would like to see democracy in Burma and a global ban on landmines.

OTHER FICTION TITLES FROM RIVERWOOD BOOKS

The Franciscan Conspiracy
by John Sack

700 years ago Church officials
hid the body of St. Francis
from the world.

What secret went with Francis
of Assissi to his grave?

Historical Fiction • Cloth $24.95 • ISBN: 1-883991-91-9

Stolen from Gypsies
A Novel
by Noble Smith

"Noble Smith's wit and inventiveness, and the astonish-
ing range of his learning, recreates the picaresque novel
almost single-handedly, then promptly stands it on its
head, all the while reminding us of what real storytelling
always was, and still can be. The book is a pure delight."
—Peter S. Beagle, author of *The Last Unicorn* and *Tamsin*

Fiction / Fantasy • Paperback: $15.95 • ISBN: 1-883991-82-X

Tara's Secret
A Novel
by William Garlington

IN 19TH-CENTURY INDIA, a young man has conflicting
religious experiences that guide him to become a priest
at the temple of the goddess Ma Tara in Benares. He
becomes the symbolic head of a national revivalist movement, but as Shri Jayananda, he often finds his own visions of enlightenment at odds with orthodox ideology.
It is only with Jayananda's death that the question of Ma
Tara's secret is resolved.

Fiction / Eastern Spirituality • Paperback $13.95 • ISBN: 1-883991-50-1

DATE DUE
